SOLVING CADENCE

A NOVEL

MOORE

GREGORY STERNER

Book designed by Stephen Wagner.
Cover photo by James Zwadlo.

This book is dedicated to William and Allison Sterner, who raised me to believe that my goals were possible, and also to Abby, Jordan, Austin, Alexis, and Jack, who inspire me day to day. This book would also never have reached completion without the friendship and encouragement of Meghan Cocuzza and the opportunity and assistance provided by Aperture Press.

As I sit and breathe here in this room, it is twenty minutes to 2:00 a.m. on this fine Friday night; well, I guess we're talking about a fine Saturday morning now. Anyway, it makes no difference. I will cherish this time in my life for as long as I live. It has allowed me to do things I never dreamed and if my career is over, which it surely is at this point, I can at least say Charlie Marx went out with a roar and not a whimper. But there comes a time when we must face facts, my friends. Bill Mattingly isn't coming. I've already admitted to you all that I'm a liar. Now… I am forced to tell you… I'm also a failure. God, I'm so sorry. It would have been so much different than this. I wanted it so badly. I wanted to solve Cadence and bring her justice, more than I've ever wanted anything in my godforsaken life. It should have been… I'm sorry… I'm so sorry.

1

The Pitch

Charlie Marx sat with his arms crossed, refusing to visually sell his reaction to the sales pitch he was getting. As a successful conspiracy radio show host, Charlie had learned to trust nothing but consider everything, qualities which had made him very effective throughout his career.

His boss (as well as his mentor and friend), Tyler Reubens, had been in the public radio game for fifteen years, becoming a national celebrity by hosting a hugely successful syndicated show covering everything from intimate personal stories to murder mysteries called *United Way of Life*. Tyler, while still sitting at the helm of *United Way of Life*, was also now a big player at the executive level as a senior producer for WHHW (his home station) and programming liaison to UPR (the public radio juggernaut of which WHHW was an affiliate).

Tyler's superiors were looking for on-demand content for various multimedia outlets (a trend the entire entertainment world had already been moving strongly toward for five years and public radio had been one of the first to plant a flag in podcast land, but had never had a smash hit). Tyler was reaching out to the one person who in his mind had the one show he was almost positive would connect with a large audience for the podcast mini-series UPR was prepared to push to the moon (or so went Tyler's initial sales pitch).

The one man with the one show also happened to be a personal protégé of Tyler Reubens himself, Charlie Marx. Charlie was a former college DJ and conspiracy newsletter writer. Tyler had plucked him from obscurity and offered him an assistant producer job for *United Way of Life*, simply because he liked his work and was impressed by the buzz Charlie had managed to drum up for his conspiracy rag. Charlie produced a few conspiracy oriented segments for *United Way of Life* during anniversary years of the Kennedy Assassination and the Apollo Moon Landing. These segments had garnered such positive reviews that Tyler lobbied for Marx to be granted his own time slot on WHHW with a conspiracy-themed show called *Underground Broadcast*. *Underground Broadcast* eventually became one of the most popular programs on WHHW and had been considered at least on two occasions for national syndication over UPR stations, although that had never actually come to fruition.

All of that had taken place three years before and now Tyler wanted Charlie to captain a new vessel, one which would sail into the on-demand islands and, if all went as planned, land Tyler a fat new contract when his re-up period went into effect a few months later.

Tyler knew Charlie wouldn't argue with him or refuse the offer. But at the same time, he'd been around a long time and he knew how to get what he wanted. You could force a man to walk the plank at the point of a sword or you could gently take his hand and lead him there. You could train a soldier to take orders or you could gain his respect and have him willing to die for you on the battlefield out of loyalty alone. Tyler knew good sales pitches needed emotional buy in. He had to sell the concept, sell the logic of the concept, and sell the benefit of the concept.

Tyler was very good at this approach and he knew Charlie was stone facing him across the desk, trying not to show any cards at all. Tyler liked that. He'd trained this man well. But just because he taught Charlie everything Charlie knew, that didn't mean he'd taught him everything Tyler Reubens knew.

Tyler looked straight ahead and leaned forward, his smile never wavering. He said, "Charlie, this is an opportunity. Now before you say anything else, rest assured… I read your email. I understand you think this case is a bottomless pit. But listen buddy, your credibility and your show's credibility is not at risk here. It's all in how we play it. I've been doing this a lot longer than you my friend and the story is what it's all about. If the story is there, the ending is inconsequential… if not completely, then at least secondary to the journey. Even if this thing is the ultimate cold case… even if we're barking up a dying tree, if we carve out the right story we *will* succeed. We will accomplish what I've promised my bosses we *can* accomplish.

"I stuck my neck *way* out for you guys. For me too… I'm not trying to bullshit you. But I did that because I believe in you and I think your show is going to be the one that breaks through. They could have had Artie Rothstein do a podcast, they could have had Barry Shearing do a podcast, hell… half of the national guys already have podcasts, but this isn't just a podcast Charlie… it's a series and it's a live radio special to conclude it. UPR's never done anything like this before.

"The big bosses aren't sold on it either, you can bet your last long dollar on that one. I've had to tread very lightly every time I've pushed an angle on it. At this point, every UPR show which also airs as a podcast has been barely a mild success as far as downloads go. The bigwigs have no reason to think a special is going to be any different. But these guys are fossils Marx. They haven't seen the trend that's been creeping up on their asses for half a decade now. But *I* see it. I know *you* see it, too. You've been water coolering the podcast angle for at least a year… I hear everything my friend."

Charlie continued to sit with a stoic expression on his face, nodding every few moments and sitting slightly forward to express that he was paying attention. But he did not facially sell a single word of this. Not yet. He loved the idea, he loved the potential, but he hated the case. He'd personally been obsessed with Cadence Moore for years but he didn't think there was anything he could do with it that hadn't already been done and he feared this program would be a disaster and a letdown if they went in the Cadence direction.

Tyler kept rolling, "So, of course you know the reason none of them have been runaway hits as podcasts is because ninety percent of the fucking audience listens on the radio. Listeners are creatures of habit, we all know that. They might tune into a podcast here and there if they're at the gym or they miss a week but usually when they discover something on the radio, they're likely to keep listening on the radio. But if we sell it as something new… something different… c'mon Charles, you see where I'm going here.

"And besides all that, the reason I know *you* and *your* show are the way to go with this thing is because Rothstein and Shearing… just to name two, their formats won't work to generate a mass audience of new listeners… I'm confident about that. Shearing's a commentator… a satirist. Rothstein's a writer, a sketch guy… a brilliant one sure, I mean they're both great at what they do, but their shows don't lend themselves to breaking new ground.

"In your case, I'm confident that your format is exactly what the doctor ordered for this particular story, and I also truly believe people will like the idea of a local radio guy, someone who's not a national name, breaking into the mainstream with a special about an unsolved case which just recently became hot news again. I'm not talking out my ass here pal, I have good instincts and I know there is a right and wrong way to do this thing. The big bosses aren't sold, but I guarantee you, once I'm through with them, I can get spots, I can get the air time… we will push this to the moon!"

- 2 -

Tyler noticed the very subtle grin that had permeated Charlie's face. Charlie hadn't intended it to be visible but his facial muscles betrayed him. Tyler drove in a little harder, "I'm not fucking around here man, I believe in it! And… I appreciate you guys, I really do Charlie. You've brought a damn big audience to WHHW. You guys aren't a *huge* deal yet but you're a *big* deal. I think this is exactly what is needed to make you bigger… to make you national names. If this works out the way I envision it working out, it could make your career and hammer out a giant hit for us.

"The Cadence case is truly one of the classics… never been solved! It's a favorite of yours, that's no secret… and I agree with almost everything I've ever heard you say about it. This is one of those deals where once you get into it, you can't get out. How many of these things, these legendary cases, are actually still floating around without a conclusion?

"Cadence Moore has hooked people from the start and she will hook them again, Charlie. The *Moore to the Story* film got the public ramped up about wanting to know what happened to that girl. Jesus, half the people who saw the film didn't agree with the answer those guys came up with. They still want closure and they've never gotten it. *Those* people are the ones I'm counting on to be the new listening audience once we start popping out the podcasts.

"I think, if nothing else, you guys can do a better job than those dicks Barnes and Angstat did with the movie and if you can't solve anything, you can at least offer something fresh. Your mission, your crew's mission, is to get this as close to solved as possible so when the finale airs people believe the answer is coming. *Close* is the operative word here Charlie. You have to run a completely different angle than the film ran. And if the real answer doesn't come, which, let's be honest, we both know it won't... people need to feel like they got *something*... something better than they got with that shitty movie."

Charlie Marx knew where his bread was buttered and he respected Tyler Reubens more than he respected just about any man in the world. This man was his boss but also the person who'd given him his one and only break in professional life, but Charlie was diametrically opposed to Tyler's take on this particular program.

He felt if they tackled Cadence, they'd wind up with nothing. There were reasons a case stayed cold for a decade. They'd hit brick walls and the whole thing would be considered a grand failure that would damage Charlie's credibility and cost him a good portion of his dedicated listeners (If only he knew the position he'd be in in a few weeks, losing a few listeners would have seemed like a pleasant dream). Charlie had things to say but dutifully waited until he knew it was his turn to talk. Once he was sure Tyler was finished, he began his own pitch.

He responded honestly, "So, if I understand correctly, you're telling me Tyler... even if we don't solve it... which as you said, we won't... this thing will be produced like one of your *United Way of Life* stories... no matter what the ending, the audience will stick with us if they think *something* is coming?"

Tyler smiled a little bit wider, knowing his pitch had just been caught. He said, "Precisely! You got the picture Marx. I knew you would, *that* is why we're talking right now."

Charlie continued, "Okay then. So, when the thing everyone thinks is coming doesn't come, *this* is my concern. I have never lied to my audience, Tyler. When we haven't been able to deliver an answer to a mystery or a theory, I've always told them that up front and usually why the thing will *never* be answered. When something is a bottomless pit, which I've told you Cadence Moore is, I tell my listeners it's a bottomless pit so they know what they're getting.

"Credibility for us is life blood and if we lose it on this podcast series experiment, we lose it for the radio, too. I'm just trying to make you understand the biggest reason why your short-term goal may not be worth the long-term consequences. What makes you so sure when they realize they've been hoodwinked like a gang of sorry chumps, they won't say fuck you to us, fuck you to WHHW, and fuck you to UPR?"

Tyler considered this sincerely. The time between Charlie's question and Tyler's response was a solid thirty seconds, which in the room and in the moment felt like an hour. Tyler finally said, "Because... fuck... because, Marx. Because I believe in *you* and I know *we* can do this. For Christ's sake, Charlie, this shit is the difference between the men and boys. We take a risk, we make history, we grab a big audience, and we get a chance to do much bigger things on much bigger stages on much bigger days! That's what we do! That's what people who are successful do! So, let's stop being pussies and just fucking *do* it!"

- 3 -

Charlie had to be careful how he proceeded. Tyler was a friend but he also held the strings, the marionette strings as well as the purse strings. Charlie said, "Tyler, I hear you... every word. But I need you to hear me too right now. I am not questioning your judgment... I'm just questioning your approach. What if we looked at some alternatives? You want an unsolved case?

I've got plenty… and those plenty have lots of loose leads dangling that me and my team could sink our teeth into and actually solve. It damn sure wouldn't be the first time."

Tyler would indulge him for a moment, even though in his mind it was going to go down his way and this special was Cadence or nothing. When Tyler was set on something, that something was going to happen. He said, "Okay, Charlie, tell me what unsolved cases you have in mind."

Charlie let out a sigh of relief and smiled slightly. He was about to start talking when Tyler held up a finger. Tyler added, "Oh… but before you do that, my time is short and so is yours, so, I hate to waste any of it for either of us. As you list off these unsolved cases, make sure you only mention the ones that a massively successful film has recently been made about. That way, I can make sure the attention we need for our special will be the same whether we focus on Cadence or not."

Charlie visibly sank in his chair. He said, "Tyler, you know I can't do that. Nothing I'd be able to solve in time for a podcast series is going to have the national prominence of Cadence Moore. But, you said it yourself; Barnes and Angstat fucked up the movie and didn't solve anything. Do you want us painted with the same stain those two idiots are currently being painted with?"

Tyler smiled. He said, "Charlie, they can stain me any color they want as long as the eventual color it all turns into is green. Barnes and Angstat may be a couple of jerks but they're rich jerks, Marx, and they're jerks who currently have a bigger audience for their product than either of us have for ours. So, if you're gonna sit there and tell me it's a better idea to dig up Katie Marsh or Herman Jackson (two missing children whose parents had alleged ties to occult activity in New Mexico), then be prepared to tell me how we're going to monetize that. If you want to sell me on another conspiracy theory… like a podcast about deadly vaccines or a podcast about mass shootings being orchestrated by the government to create a police state… well again pal… tell me how we turn the crap into cash. If you can't do that Charlie… then stop wasting my time and let's get back to talking about how you're gonna produce the Cadence Moore special."

Tyler was studying Charlie's face and knew he had nothing to say. Tyler had simultaneously stumped him and sold him, using cold hard logic as his weapon. He could now reel him back in a little and get some more buy in. He said, "Look Marx, I'm not trying to be a douche. But, you have to check the naiveté at the door if you want to be part of something this potentially big. It needs to be a hit, Charlie. It needs to connect with an audience. If you want to stay true to your art form and die with every shred of your credibility intact, then that's fine. But if you make that decision, you're not going to make this journey with me, and WHHW is as high as *Underground Broadcast* is ever gonna get. I'm not threatening and I'm not bullshitting. I'm being honest. It's Cadence or bust pal... Cadence... or... bust. You got it?"

What could Charlie possibly say? He had his marching orders and he had to move ahead. He didn't like it at all and he thought it would fail, but as someone who understood loyalty as well as logic, Charlie wasn't going to say no to Tyler Reubens. He owed this man his career and if Tyler wanted to take a huge risk and was asking Charlie to climb aboard, he had no choice but to go along. He shook his head and said, "You're the boss, boss. Let's fucking do it then. I've said what I had to say and you said what you had to say. At the end of the day, you sign the checks and you gave me my name... I won't say no, even if I think it's a terrible idea. If we both lose our shit on this, you'll owe me a shot... every night... for eternity."

Charlie really didn't like it. He really didn't like it at all. He knew the odds of solving the Cadence case were next to impossible and his credibility was definitely on the line. (If Charlie only knew in this moment how severely he was about to risk his own credibility and his career, he likely would have choked).

Tyler slapped him on the shoulder and said, "Shots, every night forever... you got it Marx. But I have a feeling, you'll be the one buying drinks when all of this is over. I wouldn't lead you to the cliffs, Charlie... I'm leading you to the tippy top. Believe that!"

Charlie didn't respond. He just extended his hand and sealed the deal. What the hell had he just agreed to?

- 4 -

UNDERGROUND PODCAST 1: (Official Transcript) Intro

Charlie Marx's Underground Podcast: Episode 1 (Intro). Original Drop Date: November 1, 2013. (Brought to you by United Way of Life, courtesy of Tyler Reubens, this program is funded and sponsored by WHHW, a subsidiary of Universal Public Radio)

(Narration by Charlie Marx) Welcome friends to the *Underground Podcast.* I am your host, Charlie Marx. The late-night hour is upon us weary travelers. Mysteries abound and the truth alarms sound… bringing out the seekers in every single town. Rest easy good friends… you have reached the final end… of your desired destination.

This is the place where we lift the curtain of accepted reality, and look deeper… down into the depths of the stories that permeate our consciousness. Yes, weary travelers, you can now take a rest, put your feet up, and plug in your minds. The investigation has begun, and it's gonna be damn good fun!

This series is the most important program in the history of our show which you have up until now known as *Underground Broadcast*, but here we are now… arriving up to date with the rest of society, and we find ourselves in podcast world. This podcast tonight is in fact the most important program of my career. Those of you just stumbling across this by accident may be asking yourselves why that is.

Well travelers, we will begin our quest to answer one of the most perplexing and legendary unsolved riddles in the annals of modern crime. We will finally dig up the answer to the question that has haunted the masses for years.

We will reveal the specifics of how one Cadence Moore, a beautiful young college circuit-singing sensation, just on the brink it seemed, of breaking out into mainstream American mega stardom, on one tragic night just disappeared without a trace, never to be seen or heard from again.

Seekers of knowledge, sailors of the dark information seas, my listeners one and all, that all comes to an end. During this series, we will definitively answer the question: Whatever happened to young Cadence Moore?

Legally, I must state a disclaimer, so I will state it now. Anyone listening to this should be of legal age and younger downloaders may find the violent subject matter, mature content, and strong language of this program offensive. We will be running on a several second delay during our live special and the worst language will be edited, but the podcasts will air in their entirety. You have been warned.

Okay, then... with our disclaimer out of the way, let's get started. Like any momentous occasion, the theme of our show tonight must fit within the appropriate boundaries of weight and substance, and truly be worthy of discussion on our biggest program. What better subject to focus on than a story which has never offered a satisfying conclusion... a true mystery of our time?

The Cadence Moore story captivated mass audiences when it first came to national prominence on the weekend of Cinco de Mayo in 2002, and recently the story was plastered right back onto the speeding windscreen of the world with the release of a fascinating, albeit flawed, documentary made by a Mr. Barnes and a Mr. Angstat, who will both be heard from during this series.

But, in spite of all the media coverage and a movie about this case, there has still never been a true end-of-the-story answer to all the speculation, evidence, and shreds of footage.

Todd Barnes and Michael Angstat tried during the making of their film to come up with indisputable proof that they'd found their man, but they failed. Some may disagree with that statement and to those people I will say this. Their film, which is highly entertaining, never accomplishes its true goal of solving the case. It simply succeeds in publicly accusing one man and presenting sensational images to support that accusation.

So, it is that we find ourselves here, with four podcasts and a live radio special to burn, in which we will pick up every clue, film strip, blood trail, and eyewitness statement, turn them all sideways, and see what no one has ever been able to see before.

When it's over, I want you all to leave this series feeling like pioneers who finally came upon the smell of golden roses on the cliffs of El Dorado with enough sense left in your minds to call this a mystery solved.

With those words my good men and women, we begin our descent, down into the depths of pure adventure, skulking through caves and digging out trenches, to arrive on the other side with provable findings, and some real facts about the greatest mystery we've ever seen since Dallas in '63. We shall answer the question… and arrive on the knowledge shore with glistening waves, pounding and pure, and we will know where it ends, and open the door to see what indeed ever happened to young Cadence Moore.

2

The World in Weeks
is a Different World

Tyler Reubens, Charlie Marx's mentor and the guy who talked him into this special to begin with, called him at his home at seven o'clock in the evening. This was the night of Charlie and Dillon's diner meeting with Bastard Bill (much more on that later). Charlie had for weeks now been in a state of frenetic preparation and hadn't worked this hard at any point in his professional career. He was going all the way to make this podcast series and eventual live radio special as great as it could possibly be. During this preparation, Charlie had begun lying and he'd been lying huge. Guests had been booked under false pretenses and he was hoping everything would come together before it was over. If not, Charlie Marx's career would be over.

But, in spite of the lunatic gamble he'd committed himself to (much more on that later as well), Charlie was prepared to go down swinging in his attempt to achieve the impossible, the solving of Cadence Moore's murder. Now the reality of the corporate process was about to crush his enthusiasm and zeal for doing what even *he* had not until recently believed could ever be done.

Tyler Reubens called to drop a bomb. He knew he was about to rock Charlie's world but he began his unfortunate news in the always positive tone he tried to start every conversation with. He said, "Hi Charlie. Look, I know you planned on having some significant time before the Cadence Moore special aired live on UPR, after all the podcasts were in the can. Well, I hate to do this to you buddy, but we have to push your deadline up. Don't flip… we can work with it. Just listen up. Here's the scoop pal.

"The week we planned for your live radio special, the culmination of all the podcast shows, has presented a complication. BBC rigged up a whole week of programming that we're contractually obligated to air… right in your time slot. I know it's crap but I don't call every shot and you know that. Look, I don't know how this was missed Charlie and I don't know what inept asshole dropped the ball, but I made the deal with you so I'm prepared to take the heat for it. My mistake… I didn't know there were any complications afoot, but now I'm aware that there are. Apparently, there is some serious nonsense happening in jolly old England and our limey pals won't feel too good about getting preempted. When the fuck anything actually happens in England I don't know, but they don't like getting gypped… so we're screwed here.

"But, hey, before you freak… we arrived at a compromise. They've got jack shit for the next three weeks. I know your special's gonna make money and I want it to happen. I'm in your corner on this thing. So, I went to bat for you. The big boss wanted to just cancel the special and have you guys record the final episode as a podcast. But I requested a meeting and stuck my neck out. (Tyler loved reminding a person how often he stuck his neck out for them… it had to make one wonder what that meant, if it meant anything.)

"I talked to Art Winston… who's usually impossible to reach, but he green lighted two hours for three weeks from today. If I'm honest, I'll tell you… had we not already spent what we did on promo spots and media ads, I can almost guarantee you he wouldn't have green lighted shit. He would have told us to forget the special and stick with the podcasts only. Needless to say, we worked around that hurdle, but it has to be the final episode, the live special for the radio. That means, and I'm not telling you anything you don't know… all the podcasts need to be in the can at that point… like almost a week ahead, so podcast deadline is just about two weeks. You guys have been working like dogs, you and Dillon and the rest of the crew, and I'm sure you've already got some great shit ready for me. But two weeks for completion, Christ I know that's a lot to ask, Charlie, but that's where we're at. Once those bad boys are ready for download, you fellas can go live for that two-hour stretch and button this whole thing up."

Charlie was literally vibrating with anger and fear in his office chair. He could not believe what he was hearing.

Tyler was in the zone. He was selling his protégé on a fucked up and impossible change of plan. At the same time, he'd already thought up a new angle and was in sales mode. He said, with an excited yet authoritative tone, "So, here's the plan. We've already advertised the shit out of it! People know it's coming and lucky for us, we never went into specifics on how the podcasts would be made available for download… thank god for that! I'm saying we release those bastards for binge listening, all at once… get some major download action and have people clamoring for the live radio show. We'll bum rush the fuckers and they'll buy it… I know they will.

"It would have been great to have the podcasts air one by one, week after week, just like we planned, but that's not the deal anymore. It's better that way if you think about it. Look at the TV shows coming down the pike this year and next year. You know the buzz in the television industry now man… they're going to release the whole season at once, that's the plan, that's the future. People watch it when they want. But if your fans know the final episode special is coming… the ultimate spoiler if you will, they *will* listen to those damned things rapid fire so they are up on all the goods before the finale hits.

"The way we're structuring it now, the fans will feel forced to listen as quickly as possible. Charlie, I know this upsets your plans but take it from me… it's the only shot you have at getting this thing aired. You best eliminate the fluff and be prepared to jump right in because you have gone from having months to having just weeks and I hope you're a fast worker because you don't have any other options my friend." Tyler took a breath and waited for the meltdown he knew was coming on the other end of the phone.

Charlie went into a rampage. The Charlie Marx who'd sat across from Tyler Reubens only a month before was not the same man talking to him on the phone this night. Charlie's sanity was starting to wriggle apart at the seams. He'd pulled so much together in an incredibly short time and he'd caught two mind blowing breaks with Budgie Bailey (a possible prison confession) and Bill Mattingly (a cop prepared to assist in potentially illegal ways) and in his mind, was so close to solving Cadence that he could taste it.

That was impossible just a few weeks ago, and now it was a potential reality. How could anything in this entire world fuck that up? Charlie heard the words coming out of Tyler's mouth and could not believe them. His thoughts raced, "Giving me fourteen days to finish everything and be ready to go live a week after that? To complete all my interviews and finish my scripts? I booked the guests in record time and Jesus, the scripts for the podcasts alone I planned on taking at least another month. Now, I have two weeks? Fuck that!"

Charlie yelled with more passion than he'd ever yelled anything in his life and he yelled it at a man he'd previously never even raised his voice to. "Tyler, you can't do this! There is no way on earth I can be ready in two weeks! Do you know how much work is going into this? The special is two live hours, Tyler, on top of the four goddamned podcast episodes which are supposed to grab all the interest! I can't just whack that off in a motherfucking day! You *know* that... you've been in my shoes. This shit takes months! God, if done poorly, each one takes weeks! You've got to do something... I swear to god you've got to do something because two weeks... that just can't be done!"

Tyler, well-practiced in these types of affairs and knowing when he needed to be a friend and when he needed to be a boss, simply stated, blank and lazy, "Yes, Charlie, I do know what your position is. I've been in your position and I know. If it were up to me, I'd give you the full-time period you needed to create your masterpiece. But I'm not in charge, Charlie. Art Winston is. And Art Winston wants to keep the limeys happy. So, please don't mistake this call as a situation where I'm trying to find out if you're okay with my scenario. I'm not asking you, Charlie. I'm telling you... this is how it is. You either have the podcasts in the can within fourteen days or your two-hour special, which I'll remind you is an impossible thing to get on UPR, well buddy... that whole thing goes right up in smoke unless you deliver on time.

"Like I said, I already know they'd sign off on producing two more pod-casts instead of the live special, you know... finishing up that way, but we both know the live special is where it's at. That could conceivably pull the biggest numbers this station has ever done and might be one of the biggest specials UPR has ever seen. That's not bullshit either... even if that out-of-touch Winston has no clue about it. Get it done, Charlie! I know you can! I'm hanging up now. I hate to be the wicked messenger but that's what I have to be tonight. Make it happen Charlie... make it happen or regret it forever. I still have faith!"

Charlie was dumbstruck. Tyler was about to hang up on him after selling him on this whole idea, against Charlie's better judgment, and then because of corporate pressure, rolling over and screwing things up in an astronomical way. Charlie completely lost his shit, desperation filling every one of his veins. He screamed into the receiver, ignoring the bullshit and all the rest, wanting Tyler to hear the blind passion he had for this case. "Wait! Don't hang up that son-of-a-bitch phone! There's something I didn't tell you!"

Tyler was silent for a moment... most definitely because he'd never heard Charlie speak to him in this way. He held his composure and calmly asked, "And, what is that Charlie? You seem to have misunderstood the part where I told you I was hanging up now."

Charlie still yelling said, "Tyler, if you make me finish this in two weeks, you could be fucking up the biggest program you could have possibly ever dreamed of!"

Tyler laughed but Charlie's tone and that comment had pissed him off. "Marx, I always love your hyperbolic rants on the air, but this is me you're talking to now. Who do you think you're hustling? I brought you in on this deal and we're doing it my way. My way has to work with UPR's way... that's business. So, before you start telling me about the biggest programs I can possibly dream of, let's take stock of things.

"You're doing some podcasts and a two-hour show on your favorite conspiracy and hell, I am looking forward to it... I know you'll make it entertaining and great, which is why I chose you for this assignment in the first place. I'll remind you of that once again. It's going to get major download action and big numbers when we hit live air. It will be great for all of us. I'm still looking ahead at the finish line. We're still going to accomplish the original goal. But Christ, Charlie... don't view this as more than it actually is and don't tell me I'm missing out on the biggest shit I could imagine because I can imagine a lot okay?"

Charlie fired back, "No, Tyler, you didn't let me finish. I am not saying it will be the biggest thing ever aired on UPR or anywhere because it's my show and I think it's great and all that. We *solved* the thing. We got a lead that no one ever dug up, we got new cops involved, and it turns out that we have the answer that no one else could get in over a decade. This is the biggest mystery of the 21st Century, right? I mean, that's how you yourself ordered it to be marketed in the ads. But now, it's the biggest mystery... *solved*... live on UPR. Does that change your mind, you corporate shilling bitch?" Charlie knew he was playing with fire after uttering the biggest lie of his life and calling his boss a bitch, but his feelings told him if he didn't push Tyler as hard as he could, this would all be for naught. Charlie had to make him understand.

Tyler remained silent. Even in his silence Charlie could feel his fury from the other end of the line. Tyler did not enjoy being called a bitch, especially by someone he'd built from the ground up all by himself, who was now disrespecting the hell out of him. But he was very smart and had a great gut for leads and information. Tyler's gut, which had a direct line to his brain, knew Charlie had something to say so the silence continued. He'd heard all the fish stories there ever were to be heard and he'd invented half of them himself. But he definitely picked up on something in Charlie's voice that he couldn't ignore. He paused a moment longer and said, "All right. I'd like to slap the shit out of you right now, forgetting where you came from. But I haven't ignored my instincts in fifteen years and I won't ignore them now. I think you may actually have something but you need to understand, it's not as simple as you'd like it to be."

Tyler was breathing heavily on the other end of the line and it was painfully obvious he was super pissed, but he was also *thinking* and in that thought process there was a logic that refused to ignore Charlie's confidence (mostly a fabrication) in the story he was hearing. He breathed a few moments longer and then said, "Here's how it works then. If you want me to put my ass on the line with Art Winston, and I mean for real, asshole, then you need to give me details pronto. No details... no deal. I can't market this as us actually solving Cadence Moore... not hinting that we may have solved it... not implying that we may have solved it... but actually marketing the fact that we have solved the Cadence case if I don't know we've solved anything. No details... you got fourteen days and that's the end of it."

Charlie believed he was about to suffer from exploding heart and head syndrome, which he'd be the first person in history to experience... but he could feel them both getting ready to burst. Tyler had just made the one demand he couldn't meet. Three-man secret... that was the agreement, and Tyler would make four; worse yet, Art Winston would make five.

When it comes to three man deals like the one Charlie and his producer Dillon had made with Bill Mattingly that very afternoon, five men is a universe. If they fucked that up with Bill, he'd go to the news himself and leave Charlie Marx and this whole series in the dust. Charlie was going to try and bullshit Tyler, which would be no easy feat since Tyler is the ultimate bullshitter himself. He said, "Tyler... I *can't* man. Do you have any idea the magnitude of this investigation? Even the detective we're working with hasn't told his cop buddies, not even his superiors. He's going to have press in a sealed room so this thing can be revealed right on the air without leaking out first. But I can't reveal anything now except to say that we've solved it, Tyler. We've known each other a long time and I've always performed for you in a big-time way. I'm asking you... based on our history... just trust me and get me some more time. You'll be glad you did... so incredibly glad that..."

Tyler cut him off. "Wait one second right there, Charlie Marx! I have shared things with you that could have gotten my ass charbroiled and I trusted you to keep it to your goddamn self! And now... *now*... when you think you've got some heavy shit, you're gonna shut me out? Fuck you, Marx! I built you from brick one. I made your career. We've been colleagues, but more important, we've been friends! Now tell me what is going on!"

Charlie was standing on a land mine and he knew it. He knew damn well what Tyler was saying was true. But he also knew that all the confessions Tyler had shared with him over the years had been cathartic venting sessions or the safe revealing of facts that had already been verified and ready for press and which Tyler was just dying to spill. Charlie also knew *Tyler* knew all of this and the conversation they were now having was a test if there ever was a test. Charlie wasn't going to bend. And he knew Tyler would respect him for it, no matter how pissed he became in the process.

He said, "Tyler, all I can say… no… I could say a lot, but all I *will* say is this. Over the last god knows how many years, you've told me what you wanted to tell me *when* you wanted to tell me it. You've shared what was safe or what was timely for you to share. C'mon man, you weren't doing me favors, you were working out your own issues and I was a good and trustworthy sounding board. So, don't try to sell me like you gave and gave and now I owe *you*. Dude, I love you and will always be indebted to you. But, I'll tell you this now, brother… I know *who* and *what* you are. And I'm about to show you what *I* am. This is red hot and you're not gonna get it at this moment in time. Not because I'm pulling a power play or trying to or whatever, but because if I tell you, and in effect tell Winston, then this whole thing is fucked. Be as offended as you want by the implication, but the bottom line is you're gonna wait until I'm ready to tell you and because you're smart and because you know good business… you're gonna let me roll with it!" Charlie's heart was skipping beats left and right and as soon as the last words left his lips, he felt as though he was surely going to pass out. The stress of the last few days and this current moment was starting to overtake him. He steadied himself on the arms of his office chair to keep from wobbling right out of it. His lips were tingling.

Tyler said nothing but Charlie could hear that he'd dropped the phone on the other end and was currently smashing things in his office. Boy, oh boy, things were getting real. The situation had never been so escalated between them. After what seemed like an eternity, Tyler finally picked the phone back up and breathed into it like a wasted fifteen-round fighter. He was speechless, he was sweating… but he was still on the line… that was the key point.

Charlie could tell from Tyler's continued presence on the other end of the line that he was going to let him ride on this… at least a little bit, regardless of how furious he was. Tyler knew if nothing else that Charlie believed what he was saying and he had enough credibility with Tyler that belief still meant something (even though said belief was a sham). Tyler finally shouted, "Marx… just shut it! Shut your mouth. Let me just ask you a question so I can clarify… you're not going to give me details that I can go to Winston with? You have the nerve to tell me right now that you're not giving me fucking shit?"

Charlie sighed, knowing this could be the end of the whole thing but also knowing that if he caved it would be over anyway. He said, "I *can't* Tyler… we're keeping this between us and the cop. That's the deal and if I fuck that up, my whole angle will be destroyed and this special will be nothing more than a goddamn opinion piece, just like Barnes and Angstat's piece of crap movie! I will not let that happen. (He was screaming again.) And, *you* can't let it happen either! If you were in my shoes, you'd be saying the same shit, word for word! Jesus, do what you've always done and have the balls to take a risk!" Charlie could hardly believe the words were his own… a goddamn maverick, building his entire house on a deck of cards… a deck of lies. He had nothing!

Tyler was quiet for one second longer. He said, "Marx, if you give me no details then we got nothin' else to talk about. Winston has spoken and Winston's will be done… he's god here and god does what he wants."

There was silence on the other end of the line. Charlie wasn't giving him a thing. Son of a bitch, he'd trained this fucker far too well. Tyler hesitated… knowing he was about to concede at least a tiny little shred of something. He knew very well in the pit of his own stomach Charlie Marx was on to something and he wished he knew what the hell it was. Had Charlie uttered even a grunt, Tyler would have probably won the game and told him to eat shit. But Charlie blinked last. He said nothing. Tyler considered the situation and the potential that may or may not have been a reality. He finally said in a defeated but disgusted tone, "I can push it *one fucking week* and one week only."

Charlie, still pissed but knowing he just scored a point, thought, *I got him*! Tyler went on, "Nothing truly crucial is happening in that time and

I know just from the general vibe of things that I can buy you that one week if you're going to deliver something. But listen now, Marx... harder than you've ever listened in your life. If I buy you a week, and more significantly, I start marketing this series and the special as a solution to the Cadence Moore case and you don't deliver on that promise, I guarantee you, asshole... it *will* mean the end of you, I'll *see* to it... friends no more.

"But, I'll *do* it because like I said in our first meeting, and I don't take that lightly, I *believe* in you... even though you're a piece of shit!" He took several deep breaths. Swallowing pride in the process of doing business was not always easy. "Now, let me be clear. If I bump you till the last possible time I can, which is in my ability to do and I *will* do it if you choose to go this route; if the conclusion doesn't turn out the way you say, there is no safety net. Your career dies and doesn't get a second chance to live. Are you willing to risk that? Are you willing to risk your career? I will come back from it... maybe slowly and with egg on my face, but I *will* come back. I will make it clear that I was lied to and I will sue your ass to put an exclamation point on that shit. I will come back. *You* won't, I promise you that! Are you willing to take the risk, I'll ask you one more time?"

Charlie knew Tyler was both the savior and the destroyer in this scenario so he controlled himself just a few more seconds even though his fists were balled and he was ready to combust. He said, "So, four weeks until live air is the best I'm gonna get if I don't spill every detail I've got working behind the scenes? That's what you're telling me? You promised me months and now I have four weeks to go on air with the finale?"

A full minute elapsed on the call with nothing but labored breathing and static to pass the time. Tyler having finally regained most of his composure simply said, "That's what I already told you in fact, Charles. And fuck you as well."

Charlie managed one last phrase before he hung up on his boss, after the tensest conversation he'd ever been a part of in his entire career. He'd won a battle on this call but he was still mad as a hornet. Tyler and his bosses had fucked this potentially beautiful (fake) thing up beyond recognition.

It was supposed to be so much simpler in the fantasy world Charlie had recently been building for himself. But he also knew he himself had complicated things beyond all reason with his deceit and his ego. Tyler's corporate maneuvering was simply par for the course. Charlie was pissed all the same. He said, "Then four weeks it is, and all I need is a miracle. Thanks so much for fucking me straight up the asshole tonight, Tyler. I do so appreciate your support. Have yourself a good night and feel free to fuck yourself, too, while you're at it."

- 2 -

Charlie slammed the phone down. As soon as he did, he was beset with a sour sting in his belly, telling him he'd just wrecked everything. He hadn't expected this. He hadn't expected a complication from UPR on top of everything else and he panicked. He blew it. Charlie had been the one who was so careful in the initial meeting with Tyler. He'd warned about credibility being lost. He argued for a new story. He worried about lying to his listeners. Where had that guy gone? Why did he just react without thinking?

But wait, wasn't that mostly his anxiety talking? He wasn't an idiot. He knew Tyler wasn't going to can him for what he said. Tyler knew he was upset and understood. He identified with Charlie, having been a radio host all these years himself, having dealt with impossible deadlines and unforeseen complications for a decade and a half. Tyler also half believed Charlie may have solved the craziest crime of this generation, based on Charlie's own sales pitch to the master himself. Charlie knew he'd beaten Tyler in a verbal game of chicken... but that didn't make him feel any less rage. Four motherfucking weeks... just when he thought he may have caught some career-making breaks.

Now on top of it, he just told Tyler Reubens he solved the case. It all came flooding at him at once, every one of the insane decisions he'd made in the past few days. Charlie Marx was depending on the hearsay of a guy his convict cousin Rydell knew who knew another guy who may have killed Cadence Moore. He was depending on the assistance of a dirty cop. He had lied to the guests booked for the show. And now he'd lied to Tyler Reubens.

What had happened to him? How could he be so stupid? He loved his life, he loved his show. He was now dangling it all between two fingers over a raging fire. Why?

Charlie stumbled to one knee on his office carpet. He was dizzy. What had he just done? That was it. If Bailey was full of crap or Bill Mattingly was playing them... Charlie was fucked. His whole career was fucked! Everything was fucked!

He nearly burst into tears but instead he punched the glass of rum and coke he'd prepared for a nice easy evening of work. It shattered all over the floor as it hit the low end of the wall. Poor Marjorine, the cleaning lady, was going to spend her morning picking up the shards of glass from his temper tantrum. Charlie was just so pissed and scared he couldn't help it.

He had already been fraying at the edges of every one of his nerves just putting the show together. For god's sake, almost no one knew it yet, but in the past few days he'd mortgaged his whole life for a fucking girl who disappeared ten years ago. Why? Why would he gamble everything on a case that he himself called a bottomless pit just weeks before?

There was only one answer. He knew what it was but couldn't understand how quickly he'd adopted it as truth and risked everything on it. It was the answer he kept coming to as he'd been building this world of fantasy around him. The answer was this. He was doing what he was *destined* to do... there was nothing else to it.

At some point over the last several days when leads and opportunities (all of which were possibly useless dead ends) started popping up out of nowhere, Charlie had been infused, it seemed, by some wayfaring spirit... a reckless crazy spirit which was convincing him to press on toward solving Cadence, even though it flew in the face of all rational thinking and was very likely pointing him right off the edge into career suicide.

This may have been delusion and over-inflated ego, but some mad section of his mind was buying the idea that he was put on this earth to solve the Cadence Moore case. Everything that had happened, from the new leads to the cop to Tyler Reubens talking him into it in the first place... all of it... every single thing was pushing him toward his destiny. Did he really believe it? Whether he did or didn't was irrelevant now... he was committed.

No matter how deep into the pool of insanity he was currently immersed, Charlie still had programs to produce. When it came to said programs, Charlie planned on having time and now time was the one thing he didn't have. Art Winston had seen to that. Charlie didn't know what he was going to do. His entire world was threatening to collapse... collapse on the lie that he was telling everyone... the lie that could kill his career and probably would. But he would keep moving forward. It was the only direction he had left. He may have been marching right into the belly of the beast in blackest hell, but forward he would go.

Charlie Marx was trusting his instincts. His instincts would lead him to ruin or lead him to Valhalla, but he was going to trust them all the same... going backward was not an option anymore.

- 3 -

UNDERGROUND PODCAST 1: (Official Transcript)
Part 1: Charlie Explains *Moore to the Story*

Charlie Marx's Underground Podcast: Episode 1 (Part 1). Original Drop Date: November 1, 2013. (Brought to you by United Way of Life, courtesy of Tyler Reubens... this program is funded and sponsored by WHHW, a subsidiary of Universal Public Radio)

(Narration by Charlie Marx) Cadence was a girl who never came back home again. For all the theories, accusations, and conjecture that have been floating across the airwaves and pages of news magazines for years, it all still boils down to a very sad story about a little girl lost; never to find her way, always silently pleading for the next 'would be' detective to solve her mystery and bring her justice and peace.

At the time of her disappearance, Cadence's story ignited a national media frenzy of rabid interest, only to eventually fade into obscurity when real answers were never found and the public lost interest, as they are prone to do. The problem with this mystery was the fact that very little was actually known about the true circumstances surrounding the night in question. A disjointed mixture of eyewitness testimony, memories of friends and family, and a maddening video tape, which may or may not have had anything to do with Cadence Moore at all, combined to create a vague, puzzling, and ultimately unsolvable mystery.

Even after all had been given time to preach about their personal views and their half-informed opinions, no official conclusion was ever drawn and the public was left with little alternative other than turning the channel and moving on to more easily resolved conflicts and issues.

Yet Cadence Moore remained conspicuous by her absence in the world. She just never showed up again. Most intelligent observers decided within six months of the time the story broke that poor Cadence was obviously dead and the world would probably never learn the reasons why. Lots of these Occam's razor leaning folks begin moving on at this point and just accept the official version as the best version. Yet for a select few answer seekers, the official word is usually a lie. There's *always* going to be a 'Badge Man' on the grassy knoll or a Building Seven being imploded by design. These men and women see things that not everyone else is able to see... sometimes because they can't and sometimes because there really is nothing there *to* see.

But because of the special vision these truth seekers feel they have, they are compelled to conduct their own exhaustive investigations; replacing missing facts with fat opinions, and eventually coming to a conclusion that allows their restless thoughts to lie dormant for at least the amount of time it takes them to catch a few winks of sleep at night.

Two such answer seekers were Todd Barnes and Michael Angstat, who at the time of the incident were a couple of twenty-year-old college drop-outs, watching life float by in the hazy smoke rings twirling about their broken down dusty apartment. They finally heard their true purpose come calling when the Cadence story broke in the national media. They slowly became obsessed with the Cadence Moore mystery and made it the mission of their lives to find the answers that no one else could.

Years after the story had been long forgotten by the media and the folks that walk the city streets in apathetic bliss, Barnes and Angstat took it upon themselves to pour over every last detail available in the case, and create a documentary film which conclusively and definitively (or so the taglines read on their movie poster) solved the Moore disappearance.

It had been ten years since Cadence Moore's disappearance when Todd Barnes and Michael Angstat began the final edit on their film. They had followed the story from day one when the startling news first broke that a popular young singer was missing and no one seemed to know why or how it had happened.

When the news outlets and the public moved on to more pressing and current dilemmas, Barnes and Angstat never wavered; always wondering and theorizing about how a girl who was loved by thousands of young adults and seemingly had a dream life and very few enemies, could somehow get wiped clean off the slate of the Earth, vanish without a trace, and eventually become forgotten altogether.

Cadence Moore, whom neither Barnes nor Angstat had ever met, became as important to them as their own blood relatives and some would say even *more* important as time went on. When their initial attempts at figuring out the mystery with simple daydreaming and coffeehouse discussions proved to be ineffective, they decided that something had to be done to keep the mystery alive, albeit on a much smaller scale than the national prestige it had experienced for a brief time. The solution they came up with was to start their own web site called Seekers.com, and create a blog which was dedicated to conspiracy theories, ideas, and all thoughts in general about the Cadence Moore story. They called the blog *Cadence Moore to the Story*, and it attracted significant online attention.

The blog was a haven for controversy lovers and conspiracy theorists. There was certainly still a small smoldering ember of interest in Cadence Moore and even though some of the comments that made it on to the blog were outright lunacy, it also allowed well-spoken and smart young people a place to sound off on the subject and offer well thought out opinions and theories, some of which had never even been considered when the story broke nationally.

Comments from the blog were actually a major source of leads and information in Barnes's and Angstat's quest for the truth. They followed every scent and uncovered every stone until they were able to piece together a coherent and fascinating film that revealed what *they* felt were the true facts of the story.

To say their finished documentary created a hornet's nest of debate and an ocean of renewed interest would only be scratching the surface of reality. The success of the film caught many industry pundits completely off guard. No one seemed to have seen this coming. No one expected a low budget documentary made by two novices to become a sensation. So how did it happen?

Well, first and foremost, Todd Barnes and Michael Angstat are very smart and that was the prominent force behind the film's success. Since Cadence Moore's name hadn't been a fixture in the public memory for a decade, Barnes and Angstat knew they needed a powerful hook to reel people back into the obsession they had all let go of years before; not to mention all the new young viewers whose first and only exposure to Cadence Moore would be their film.

Barnes and Angstat accomplished this by putting together an admittedly brilliant film trailer. (Roll film trailer with my narration for listeners.) The trailer begins with flash images of Cadence singing on stage, her pop tunes blaring over the sound of thousands cheering.

A professional voice actor begins narrating, "Cadence Moore was an idol to thousands of college students across the Northeastern United States. She overcame the tragedies of her youth to become a music sensation. She inspired young people to reach for the stars and let no one stand in the way of their dreams. Cadence Moore had the whole world in her hands. But on Cinco de Mayo 2002…"

At this point the narration stops and an electric guitar rendition of Beethoven's *Moonlight Sonata* begins playing over the soundtrack. The opening images of Cadence singing in concert are literally torn away by giant news headlines slamming into view with black and white pictures of

Cadence smiling right under huge letters screaming "SINGER CADENCE MOORE MISSING, FEARED DEAD!"

Another headline blasts into frame, "DFU CAMPUS IN SHOCK AS POLICE CONTINUE SEARCH FOR CADENCE MOORE!"

And yet another, "IS CADENCE MOORE STILL ALIVE? HOPES DWINDLE AS WEEKS PASS BY!"

The electric Beethoven continues playing over shots of Cadence smiling, laughing, and singing as quick cuts of interview sound bites, most taken completely out of context, by the way, start firing one after another.

Darlene Bethany (Cadence's roommate and best friend): "I literally said to myself, I'm gonna kill this bitch."

Stephanie Chambers (another best friend): "I'd never seen either one of them so drunk and I knew this could end real bad."

Detective Meghan Cocuzza (Investigating Officer): "There was blood in her boyfriend's car. I didn't have to think too hard before drawing my conclusions."

"Darlene Bethany: "How could something so stupid cause a person to act out violently toward someone they love?"

"The professional voice actor continues as Moonlight Sonata reaches its crescendo, "Events spiral out of control. A famous and beautiful young woman is stolen from the world, never to be seen or heard from again. What happened to Cadence Moore? People all over the world have asked this question throughout the last decade. Now... Todd Barnes and Michael Angstat take you deep inside the Dusklight Falls College Campus scene for a never-before witnessed look into the events leading up to the disappearance of Cadence Moore in May of 2002. Your question remains... What happened to Cadence Moore? Prepare to have your question answered! *Moore to the Story*, a film by Todd Barnes and Michael Angstat, coming to select theatres this fall."

One last interview sound bite closes out the trailer. It is Detective Meghan Cocuzza saying, "I can only hope someday the world finds out the truth about what happened to the poor girl."

Like I said, this was a brilliant little piece of business. Barnes and

Angstat took comments out of context and they came up with an answer that may or may not actually be the correct answer, but one thing is for certain. The trailer for this film stirred up enough renewed interest in the Cadence Moore case that people came out in droves to see it in theatres.

Barnes and Angstat firmly believed, based on their own research efforts, that Cadence's boyfriend at the time of her disappearance, one Jamison Kelly (who was now a successful sales rep for the HANDLER Corporation) had murdered Cadence in a drunken rage after finding her wandering the streets in the wee hours of May 6, 2002.

Once they had this idea branded into their minds, Barnes and Angstat shamelessly piled on mountains of so-called evidence which supported their theories about the murderer. It was at this point that their film became less documentary and more sensationalized opinion piece. Anything and every- thing that could have possibly even hinted at Jamison Kelly being the guy that killed his girlfriend and got away with it was shoved into the final film.

But regardless of how thin the bulk of evidence was that Barnes and Angstat were spewing out reel after reel in the film, the one shining and damning legitimate point remained; a tiny smear of blood *was* in fact found in Jamison Kelly's car after Cadence disappeared.

Of course, this had been addressed and dismissed at the time of the disappearance because there was not nearly enough blood to determine that Cadence had even been injured, let alone killed in the car, and Jamison also provided a reasonable explanation to police.

As unpleasant as it was to share at the time, Jamison admitted that sev- eral days before she vanished, he and Cadence had sexual intercourse in the car while she was on her period and the tiny smear of blood found on the seat was menstrual blood. Police ended up dismissing Kelly as a suspect when no hard evidence of murder could be tied to him and his whereabouts on the night in question were accounted for by several people, giving him what appeared to be an airtight alibi.

Remarkably, the DFPD never tested the blood found in Kelly's car to make sure it was Cadence's blood, or even to make sure it was menstrual blood. Once Jamison admitted the blood belonged to Cadence, it didn't seem necessary to the DFPD to test it anymore. Combining that with the fact that Kelly had an alibi during the time the disappearance is said to have taken place, DFPD decided not to pursue this blood evidence any further.

This decision has become a legendary botched maneuver on the part of the DFPD and has been pointed to as evidence by some who believe a larger conspiracy was at work. Kelly was dismissed as a suspect and was allowed to walk away a free man whose alibi had saved him from arrest and a murder charge.

This dismissal of Kelly by police mattered little to Barnes and Angstat who went out of their way to focus on hearsay and wild theories that made Jamison look as guilty as a cat with day old mouse stench on its breath. Their documentary was incredibly persuasive and for those not intimately familiar with the facts of the case, it was easy to become convinced of Kelly's guilt just based on the film alone.

The truth of the matter is that once a person is found guilty in the court of public opinion, they are forever marked with the stain of their dirty deed, whether the deed was theirs to live with or not.

The documentary, titled *Moore to the Story,* was premiered at the Horizon Film Festival in Twenty-Nine Palms, California. It won the award for Best Documentary, and Barnes and Angstat both received honorary mention in the Best Director category. Much of the talk coming out of the festival was centered on Cadence Moore and the two young "It boys" who had come out of nowhere and hit a home run their first time at bat.

Due to the buzz from Horizon, the film, which was supposed to have a very limited release in art house theatres of major population centers, instead was released nationally and became a massive success.

It also created a shit storm that Jamison Kelly and his family were not at all prepared for. They had the right to sue for slander and defamation. They had the right to make public statements professing Jamison's innocence. They could do and *did* do a number of things to combat the damaging effects of the Barnes and Angstat film, but the cold harsh truth for Jamison was this; unless he could somehow find a way to prove that Cadence was either alive and well somewhere in the world, or that she was killed by some other means than his own hand, he would forever be branded a cold-hearted murderer who drunkenly killed his own beautiful girlfriend and simultaneously robbed the adoring public of their future superstar singing idol.

With the release of *Moore to the Story*, a decade after that dark sad night in Dusklight Falls when she seemed to literally vaporize into the atmosphere, Cadence Moore was now a national obsession once again.

- 4 -

UNDERGROUND PODCAST 1: (Official Transcript)
Part 2: It Had Been Ten Years

Charlie Marx's Underground Podcast: Episode 1 (Part 2). Original Drop Date: November 1, 2013. (Brought to you by United Way of Life, courtesy of Tyler Reubens… this program is funded and sponsored by WHHW, a subsidiary of Universal Public Radio)

(Narration by Charlie Marx) Jamison Kelly shared the following recollection with *Underground Podcast* when we reached out to him and told him about the series we were in the middle of creating. For a solid chunk of time now, Jamison has been obsessed with the idea of having a forum to clear his name, since it has been dragged through pig slop and filthiness ever since the release of the film *Moore to the Story*, in which he is blatantly accused of murdering his girlfriend.

Jamison Kelly finally showed up in studio after my overbearing sales pitch had managed to get him in our chair and ready to talk. This had not been an easy task. Jamison shifted around uneasily waiting with frenetic anticipation for the potentially damning questions coming his way.

Jamison had been nearly impossible to convince as it related to speaking with us at all. My producer Dillon took care of most of it but just as quick as Jamison had agreed during the first conversation, he backed out just as fast, only to be coaxed back again by Dillon.

Then, when we were forced to postpone the interview due to scheduling nightmares with UPR, Jamison had cancelled again before my assistant Marianne had convinced him to still appear. Now twelve hours before our scheduled interview, Jamison was balking again. I decided that this was just a matter of needing to turn the man's perspective around. I called him and delivered one of the most intense sales pitches of my lifetime, just to get him to show up. Jamison was understandably paranoid with the hit piece *Moore to the Story*. Now that he was here, he was wrestling with a fear that told him he'd made a mistake. He looked directly in my eyes. He said, "Listen, if you guys want me to be completely honest in this interview I need some assurances, okay?"

I looked down at the silver-plated name tag I had on my desk right beneath the microphone which bore my name and gave me what I liked to believe was some kind of aesthetic legitimacy. *Charlie Marx*, the name, stared at Jamison from the placard. I looked at Jamison with a friendly smile and said, "Mr. Kelly, I can give you all the assurances you need, but you should know right now the only reason we're talking is because I think the conclusion drawn in the Barnes and Angstat movie was pure and unadulterated crap. We're doing this program to clear the air and come up with better conclusions, so really that makes us your allies on this subject and being honest with us is in your best interest, friend."

Jamison just shook his head. He was *so* defeated as a human being and his faith in all others was at a literal all-time low. He said, "That sounds real nice guys, but I still need my assurances. I need you to agree that when I start talking, you will not interrupt me and you will allow me to finish, no matter how long-winded I may be. The previous team of so-called journalists who investigated this case has done me a fair bit of damage, to say the least. So, I need a promise from you both, don't cut me off and you need to allow me to talk. We'll be fine if that part of the agreement is not messed with. I guess I just feel the need to say that now into a microphone and for you to answer into a microphone. If paranoia is an unattractive quality, you'll forgive my ugliness in the interest of pressing on."

I thought for a second. I already knew Jamison had signed a release (with the right of refusal) but was stricken with a pang of panic as though

I didn't know this. I made a very slight gesture toward Dillon with an expression that screamed my question and he reacted immediately and without hesitation, pantomiming the rapid signing of a document and he nodded his head rapidly. So, I knew we had Kelly but he was scared and trusted no one. I also knew he was bringing all this up because he still wanted to believe in the word of his fellow men. He signed the paper because he desperately wanted to be on air again telling his story. And even though he knew assurances would be useless once he signed on the dotted line and we delivered the one thing we promised (an answer to the mystery), he was feeling us out so he could discover if we were the type of people he'd actually open up to rather than the alternative, which would be guys who might fill in the gaps with fantasy. Jamison just wanted to know if we were safe to talk to.

I felt for Jamison Kelly, deeply and honestly. And even though I didn't control how all this went down, I made up my mind then and there to do the best goddamn job I could do to get his story out there, in its unadulterated form, true to its facts and solid to its conclusion.

Kelly looked me again right in the eye, so I did the same and answered him. "You'll have all the time you want to answer me, Mr. Kelly, as long as you answer every question I ask. Deal?"

Jamison smiled, apparently feeling as though I'd satisfied his major concerns. He said, "Deal… now if you will, let me tell my story… from the beginning… the way I need to tell it."

Thank Baby Jesus that little part of this interview was over. Now it was time to get the man talking and find out what the hell we were dealing with, and also find out if this man had anything to do with the main issue at all. I didn't even need to ask the first question. I simply said, "Jamison, the floor is yours. Tell us your story."

Jamison began, "I had a dream a little while ago. In my dream, I stood at the edge of the shoreline. The salty ocean water washed over my sand-encrusted feet. My thirty-year-old reflection looked up at me from the green hazy water, a little smoother than the real thing. In this ocean water visage, I could have passed for twenty-five. The oversized pores of my nose and the tiny crow's feet around my eyes were not as clear in the rippling reflective as they would have been in my bathroom mirror.

"In reality, I was getting older and felt it. In every creak of my knees and every twinge in my back, I felt it. I came down to the shore most of the time to reconnect with those sensory memories deep inside, which conjured up some former younger self inside of me and allowed me to feel like a kid again, for a while.

"In the days of my youth, I spent many a weekend at the beach and every time I walked down to the ocean now, I remembered the fire in my soul and the relentless force which drove me further in every facet of life back then. With one sound of a crashing wave and one solid whiff of the sea air, I could immediately recall young love, young passion, and every one of my young man's dreams. I remembered all the good things and rarely gave a thought to the bad or the very bad.

"But today was different. As soon as I walked up close enough to the water to get my feet wet, a soft familiar voice began speaking to me from behind. The voice did not seem to be forming words at first. It was just humming a monotone and strange sounding tune. Then it said my name, 'Jam-i-son.'

"I felt a chill that cramped up my gut. I looked up and out into the never-ending horizon of water and thought, *this is not happening*. In spite of my mental denial, the voice continued. Once again, it spoke my name, this time with more urgency and a hint of anger, 'Jam-i-son!'

"I listened intently and looked to the ground again. I kept my head down and my eyes closed because I couldn't bring myself to turn around and look at the young girl who was addressing me from behind.

"I had come down here to relax. I wanted to de-stress at my little vacation house, which provides an oasis when I need to escape from a tough week at work. I wanted to take a few deep breaths, smell the salty sea air, and feel the cool water between my toes. Soon I would return to my porch where a tall glass of iced tea would be waiting for me, and my wife and children would soon join me for a cook out.

"But, *this* would not be a relaxing day. This would be a day when my buried past, left out of sight for a decade, would finally return to haunt me. The girl that walked up behind me on the beach had not come for small talk. She had come to ask me the question I didn't have an answer for. She had come to find out why she'd been forgotten while I lived on in bliss with my beautiful wife and children.

"The girl who walked up behind me on the shore was a dream girl. She was a dream girl because she lived in dreamland, and dreamland was the only place she could communicate with anyone anymore. I didn't realize it at the time, but I was fast asleep in my waterbed, my wife's head resting on my chest, and the beach and sand were merely images floating through my subconscious dreaming mind.

"In life, the girl who now spoke to me as I looked out over the dream ocean had been known as Cadence Moore. She had been my college sweetheart… my first true love.

"Cadence had been gone for years now, lost in some unknown darkness, but she somehow found the strength to come back for me. She came back for answers and she wasn't leaving until she got them.

"Unlike the young lovers who on those long-ago college nights held each other tight like human life rafts, never wanting to let go, gazing into each other's eyes as though they were staring into a warm and inviting sunset, the two people who now stood on the dream beach had absolutely no warm or inviting connection between them.

"I was afraid to even look behind me at the girl who was radiating such anger and pain that I could feel the sting of it prickling the back of my neck like a heat rash.

"Cadence put her hands on my shoulder causing me to shiver and utter a strange moan of fear and disgust. She spoke coldly, but with the hint of long bruised feelings softening the bite of her words, 'What did I do to deserve this? Why did you stop looking for me? You promised me, wherever I was, you would never stop searching. Why did you lie?'

"When I couldn't bring myself to respond, Cadence decided she no longer wished to address me from behind. She violently spun me around and slapped my face which shocked me into opening my eyes. She screamed, 'Why did you lie!?!' I was about to answer, but all I could get out was, 'Cadence, I tried... '

"My words were cut off by the change in view. Cadence Moore's lovely nineteen-year-old face, contorted in anger and pain, but free of the stress wrinkles and age lines that decorated my own face, disappeared and was now replaced by the stained-glass skylight in my bedroom. I was shaking with nerves and sweating like I'd fallen asleep in a sauna.

"It had all been a dream. The love of my life, gone and forgotten for years, had not really found my home and grilled me for answers I couldn't provide. No, it was all just a dream. I'd been here the whole time, resting in my bed only inches away from the woman I'd married and become a parent with.

"My vacation home in Ocean City, New Jersey was still a place in which I could find peace and serenity. The rest of the world may have become sharks in a feeding frenzy while I was the chum being tossed in the water for the snapping jaws to consume, but my home was still a sanctuary.

"My wife Kim looked at me. She could see the fear in my eyes even beyond the thin façade of temporary relief that had briefly glazed them over. She put her hand on my cheek and asked, 'What's wrong? Are you okay?'

"I shook my head and returned the cheek-rubbing gesture to my wife. My relief was quickly transitioning into anger as I determined the cause of this unpleasant evening in dreamland.

"I looked at Kim and said, 'Those assholes are wrecking my life, you know that? You and the kids don't deserve to deal with the pain this is causing us. It should have never been made! I'd love to skin those motherfuckers alive! I don't think I'll ever get a good night of sleep again. They've ruined me, Kim. They have fucking ruined me!'

"In a very uncharacteristic moment, I was overcome by the rushing back of forgotten feelings mixed with my own anger and fear. I began to sob suddenly and uncontrollably. This scared Kim because it was completely unlike me and she had no idea what to say. I buried my head in Kim's lap while she pleadingly asked over and over, 'What were you dreaming about, please tell me, what *was* it?' I didn't know where to begin so I didn't. I continued to cry in my wife's lap and she eventually stopped asking what was wrong. She just held me and let me vent my emotions. There really was nothing else for her to do."

This is the end of *Charlie Marx's Underground Podcast Episode 1*: Tune in to Episode 2 for the continuation of the Cadence Moore story.

3
The Origin Story

When it became apparent to Charlie that he'd have to rush every aspect of this project due to the impossible deadlines Tyler had laid on him, not to mention the gigantic grievous lies he'd decided to heap upon his already stressful situation, one thing became crystal clear in his mind. He had to tell Cadence's story in a way that was not only different from the Barnes and Angstat film but different from *anything* that had come before.

When Charlie set out writing the Cadence Moore "origin story," as he referred to it in conversations with Dillon, his primary goal was to flesh this girl out as a person, not just the cliché she'd become in the years since her disappearance. This was a girl who'd suffered abuses more terrible than most can possibly imagine. But Charlie was determined not to just play connect the dots with Cadence's life story.

Sure, she had been abused. Sure, she had been promiscuous. Sure, she'd acted in accordance with traits some in the mental health field would say were par for the course with victims of the type of abuse Cadence had suffered. Yet, in spite of all this, she was *not* a cliché. She was a person. And more importantly in Charlie's mind, she was a person who was no longer around to speak for herself or defend anything she'd said or done within her lifetime. The situation at hand left *that* job in the hands of Charlie Marx and he took that job very seriously.

The first podcast episode had already been written and recorded when Charlie got another call from the man who'd become his least favorite conversation partner in the world, Tyler Reubens. The call came in at 9:30 in the evening. Charlie had recorded the first portion of the Jamison Kelly interview that very morning and would record the second portion the next day. This left him some writing time. He wanted to continue writing the origin story for Cadence, from start to finish, in chapters… just like a novel. He was already about halfway through.

Charlie was convinced he needed to tell the entire tale of Cadence's journey from childhood to stardom in order for the real weight of her experiences at DFU to resonate as clearly as it needed to with his listeners so they could connect on the deepest level possible with Cadence Moore. Only then would they be ready to follow this case through every detail and dead end, rooting for a resolution all the while.

Tyler began the conversation as he began every business conversation… professionally and calmly. Noticeably gone, however, was the playful and enthusiastic tone he'd almost always projected in every discussion he'd had with Charlie Marx for years before the tensions between them had exploded and strained the relationship beyond repair.

Tyler was not a happy man. He felt betrayed and disrespected by his once favorite protégé and he was also frustrated and unsettled by the fact that he was being kept in the dark about the supposed new facts Charlie had uncovered in the case. But Tyler was still always a businessman before an everyman and he had made a personal decision to bury the anger and resentment he felt whenever it was necessary to talk business with Charlie about the project. Tyler couldn't do business when he was emotional, and when he allowed his anger toward Charlie into the forefront of his mind, he became emotional and this put him at a disadvantage. He would not let that happen again.

In spite of Charlie proving himself a miserable prick and ungrateful asshole, Tyler respected the man's talent and his track record. He would let this ride as long as he could if all signs continued to point toward eventual success. If signs ever started pointing elsewhere, Tyler knew he could save his own reputation and permanently bury Charlie Marx's six feet under. For now, he would play the game. Without *playing* the game, he couldn't *win* the game and winning the game was what Tyler Reubens was born to do.

Tyler spoke halfway through Charlie's uttering of the word hello, "Charlie, I have some concerns about the treatments you sent to my secretary."

The treatments in question were summaries of the podcast outlines which Tyler demanded be sent to his office every few days so he had an idea of the progress being made. This demand was made after their last tumultuous phone call. Tyler had agreed for the moment that Charlie could leave any "classified" information redacted but if he didn't have a perspicuous (Tyler's word) view of how these episodes would look, he'd be inclined to pull the plug and wash his hands of the whole thing no matter how hot Charlie's big lead might be. Yes, this was a bluff in a way, but Tyler was prepared to do just that if Marx pushed him much further without some significant results.

Tyler continued, "I will give credit where it's due… I think you're building a decent intro into everything with what I read in the treatments for episode one… your lead in and the description of the film… so far its good radio… or podcasting… I guess that's what we're doing here."

Charlie, listening on the other end of the line and bracing himself for another verbal brawl, silently thanked god that Tyler was above all else a radio man and a storyteller who could not resist a great narrative. This was the part of Tyler's personality which would motivate him to let Charlie take this as far as he needed to, even as he cut Tyler out as much as possible. Charlie was counting on that part to hold out until this was all over. Whether it would or would not… only time could tell.

Tyler went on, "Credit where credit is due as I said, however, the first half of your Cadence background story for episode two… I have to say… it's gotta be dialed back in a major way. This isn't a pornographic podcast we're doing here, Marx. You can describe Cadence's past without going into this kind of detail. Not sure what you and your guys are going for but it's too much, trust me."

Charlie interrupted, "Tyler, I'm hearing you clear on that and I'm willing to make specific changes, but I must ask you, isn't the benefit of the podcast medium that we don't have to be as careful as we would for a radio piece?"

Tyler answered, affecting annoyance but really feeling none. He hated Charlie at the moment, but they were engaged in a chess match and this was just another move. He said, "Fabulous, that's what I was hoping for on this call… an argument. You want to go down this road again with me Charlie?

You sure? I'm pointing out an important bit of constructive criticism as your boss and as a professional who has done this much longer than you. You want to just cool the combative shit talking bit and listen to someone who happens to be smarter than you?"

Charlie heard something in Tyler's voice which told him it was time to concede a point in their battle. He'd hit some haymakers and had Tyler on the ropes when he got past that first call. It was time to drop the gloves and let Tyler land a couple of solid jabs to get back some equilibrium. Charlie said, "Yeah, you're right. I'm sorry. I know you don't like me right now Tyler and I know I've been a pain in the ass to deal…"

Tyler wasn't having it. Without raising his voice, he stopped Charlie in his tracks. "Oh… oh no, Marx, that's not… no, you're not doing that. You're not going to play nice and make me feel like you learned some kind of valuable lesson. You aren't as good a manipulator as you think you are. You can shut that shit down right now. I'm calling to tell you this. Dial back the detailed descriptions of abuse or else I'll fuck with podcast two in a big way and podcast three may not happen at all. That would stomp this whole thing into the ground and neither of us wants that. Just do what I say and we'll be fine… for now. Dial it back."

Charlie knew there was only one response in this moment in this conversation. He gave it. "I got it, Tyler. I'll dial it back. I got it."

Tyler said, "Good, you got it and I got shit to do. Send me the new treatments by tomorrow. You got a long night ahead of you, I guess."

Tyler hung up the phone and when he did, he smiled slightly. He wasn't happy but he enjoyed Charlie falling back into line a little. He enjoyed knowing he still held the strings, even though his puppet was dancing on its own every now and again. What Tyler didn't know was that Charlie was, in addition to being a reckless and impulsive half-crazy crusader these days, just as good a manipulator as he thought he was.

Charlie knew Tyler was mad as a wet wasp and needed to feel like he still had control of the wild dog his protégé had recently become. In order to make Tyler feel like he was still in control and also accomplish exactly what he wanted with the Cadence origin story, Charlie had concocted an over-the-top and salacious description of Cadence's childhood, with gratuitous details about the horrors she experienced at the hands of the man who should have protected her and shielded her from the world, but instead had poisoned her to the core of her being.

Charlie planned on telling the story in a horrifying way and including all the details, but he knew if what Tyler saw first was such an extreme version that he'd be forced to order changes, Charlie could acquiesce and still end up with the story he wanted. Tyler fell for his bait and bit the hook bloody with both cheeks. Now Charlie could get to some real work. The student had learned his lessons well.

- 2 -

UNDERGROUND PODCAST 2: (Official Transcript)
Part 1: Ten Years Before

Charlie Marx's Underground Podcast: Episode 2 (Part 1). Original Drop Date: November 1, 2013. (Brought to you by United Way of Life, courtesy of Tyler Reubens... this program is funded and sponsored by WHHW, a subsidiary of Universal Public Radio)

(Narration by Charlie Marx) We will hear much more from Jamison Kelly during this series. But before we hear the rest of Jamison's tale, we will bring all of you up to speed about the girl this entire project is focused upon. For those of you not familiar with Cadence Moore, and for those who are familiar with her, we will now begin the most comprehensive review ever undertaken on the story of Cadence's early years... all the way through to her singing career and college experience, ending with the night she disappeared from this earth. Only when we have established who this girl was and what she meant, can all our listeners truly appreciate the scope of this entire case and the importance of seeking an answer to the mystery.

Ten years before Todd Barnes and Michael Angstat were finishing up the final cut of their documentary, Cadence Moore was living a life that most young girls dream of. She was a successful regional recording artist; her first hit, "Goldfish Chaser," had recently been released and bought in dizzying numbers by the college crowd, and her live show was selling out campuses all over the Northeastern United States.

Cadence had grown up in upscale Wyomissing, Pennsylvania, a rich suburban oasis where the wealthy and superior better men raised their families on streets lined with Japanese maples and wooden picket fence loveliness.

She could have written her own ticket and followed any career path her heart desired. Cadence was the only daughter of HANDLER Corporate Executive Darien Moore and his wife Collette. She had a brother, Morgan, who was a troublemaker and small-time criminal as a young man; but, who in later years was groomed to follow his father into the corporate world of HANDLER Rental.

Cadence had no desire to follow her father into business. In fact, while she had more money being thrown at her via a weekly allowance than she even knew what to do with, Cadence did not get along with her father.

She was rebellious, as most teenage girls will tend to be, but this was no simple case of angst. Cadence despised her father for a very specific reason, although this reason was not known to anyone else outside the Moore household.

In the aftermath of Cadence's mother Collette's death of complications from double pneumonia, her father Darien was an emotional wreck and in the immediate period that followed, he descended into a black swamp of alcoholism and severe depression.

Darien began leaning on Cadence to take care of the house and the family's needs. Cadence balked at this pressure for the most part and did everything in her power to get out of the house whenever possible. She was destroyed inside by losing her mom, but Cadence did not want to replace Collette as surrogate housewife and mother to the Moore men. She had dreams to pursue and she was going to go after them, no matter how much residual pain and loss she had to bury in the process.

Cadence knew she wanted to do something monumental which would change the world, but *how* she planned on accomplishing this was a mystery to everyone, including her. Like many kids who come from privilege and possibility, Cadence had a desire to do something big but no actual plan for execution.

She had started singing sporadically at school talent shows and local county fairs over the previous few years and was beginning to carve out a reputation in the greater Reading, Pennsylvania area as a very good singer who had some real potential.

But behind the everyday façade Cadence projected in school, during performances, and to her friends, there was a dark and painful burden that no young woman should ever have to carry.

Only four months after her mother's death, Cadence was (and here I must add 'allegedly' as a legal pleasantry) the victim of the most indecent and, well let's just say it for what it is, fucked up act that any parent could ever engage in.

Darien Moore, Cadence's powerful and intimidating father, had gotten abysmally drunk one night and when his daughter arrived home from her girls' ensemble chorus practice, he pulled her inside before the door was even shut. Darien threw Cadence onto the living room sofa and proceeded to rip off her clothes and rape her.

Morgan Moore, the troubled son of Darien and brother of Cadence we mentioned previously, wrote at great length about this event (which he partially witnessed) in his journal, which was later stolen by a friend who was curious about the case and decided to play amateur detective.

The fact that Morgan witnessed this event only a few months after his mother's death, sheds some clear light on the issue of why he was such a delinquent as a young man, likely trying to exorcise his buried demons through petty theft and juvenile hijinks.

Cadence, for her part, never spoke to anyone about what her father had done to her and very likely continued doing to her for a significant length of time after the first incident. She spoke often of hating her father and wanting to run way. She told those close to her that she wanted to become a singer and travel the world. She constantly spoke of running away.

But it was always in the context of seeking fame and fortune... never with the intent of escaping the monstrous activities going on in her very own home. She was apparently too ashamed to ever come out with the truth about the sexual abuse. So, it remained a secret.

She never told anyone… except the lined notebook pages of her diary, so those feelings remained inside her own heart. They may have made her feel dirty and useless and sometimes even suicidal, but she kept them to herself just the same. One can only imagine the mental and emotional burdens she carried with her for the rest of her short and tragic life. One can only imagine the scars that never healed, and probably never would have… even if Cadence was still here with us today.

These insights into the mind of Cadence Moore became available through interviews with school friends and neighbors, and also when Cadence's own diary was seized as a piece of evidence at the height of the investigation.

It is very odd reading passages in her diary now. She never comes right out and says what happened in any kind of clarity. Even in the private written account of her own life, she could not bear to write out the horrible events she'd been forced to experience.

Vague references to what Darien had done are clear enough to decipher and understand, but it certainly says a lot about the kind of shame Cadence carried around, considering she could not even spell out the full truth in her own journals.

Cadence withdrew from almost everyone during the months the abuse was most prevalent. She had very few close friends, and even the ones she did have were never let in close enough to know what she was really going through.

Also, since her self-esteem had been all but eviscerated, Cadence became very promiscuous and began sharing her body with just about anyone she found the least bit interesting, and some who probably didn't even fit that description.

Still, despite all of this one has to ask, why didn't Cadence come forward about the abuse? Was it simply paternal intimidation? Was it because she didn't want to be publicly humiliated? It was almost certainly both of these things on some level.

But, in addition, another chapter of this story reveals a deeper reason for Cadence's public displays of playing nice and her aversion to blowing the whistle on her father. Darien Moore was doing everything in his power, which was wide-reaching and considerable, to give Cadence exactly what she wanted most—a ticket out of her home town and into the wide world— riding on the success train of a teenage singing career.

Darien got Cadence booked at every county fair and talent show gig he could find. He also spent five thousand dollars to send Cadence into a recording studio with a backup band of talented studio musicians to record a demo of songs she had written.

"Goldfish Chaser," the little tune that would bring Cadence her biggest amount of fame, was among the songs she recorded during that first session. The song, although not a musical masterpiece by any stretch of the truth, displays some rather impressive composing and writing skills for a girl so young who had never even traveled beyond the city limits of the town in which she was born.

Was Darien doing all this to keep Cadence quiet? Was he shelling out hush money to keep his family name clean? Or had Darien, in his grief and confusion, imagined Cadence as his new wife in the aftermath of Collette's death and began pleasing and satisfying her in the same way a husband might with his wife?

He doted on her and fed her artistic pursuits as though they were his top priority. Yet, with all the lavish spending he forked over to support Cadence's burgeoning career, he still seemed to have no conceptual understanding of the unspeakable damage he was doing to her psyche on a regular basis.

Regardless of their complicated motives, Darien and Cadence forged ahead and took Cadence's very local name and reputation to the highest levels they could achieve. The next step after recording the demo album was to find a label that would distribute it.

Darien ravaged through his various networking connections that had been forged over years of sales work for HANDLER. He finally found some-body who knew somebody as the old story goes. This connection put Darien in contact with Matt Bridges of Nighthawk Records. A meeting was arranged.

Matt Bridges was willing to speak to *Underground Podcast* for the purposes of this series and he offered some very intriguing observations about the state of Darien and Cadence's relationship at the time and about Cadence's personality, in particular.

Matt recalls, "I was working out of a tiny office in Allentown, Pennsylvania at the time. I had discovered a few decent young acts in the previous few years and had gotten some of them up to the level of local stars; local meaning within the State of Pennsylvania. One of the groups at that time was *Invisible Red Suns* who went on to become a national success at least for a year or so. One might say Cadence would have been my second great discovery, as I make quotes with my fingers, because I really never discovered her at all.

"My boss at the time, Paul Edwards, comes up to me one day and tells me a dear friend and investor in the *Nighthawk* label was referring a young singer to us. Paulie told me her father was Darien Moore, who was a dear friend of our dear friend, and she should be given a chance to sing for us and we should strongly consider working with her. Since Paulie wasn't the type to endorse shitty musicians sight unseen, I knew this guy Moore must be very connected and it would be in my best interest to hear the girl sing, pay her some compliments, and do what my boss told me to do from there.

"I'm no idiot and there is a lot of nepotism in the music business, but I figured if this kid is really god-awful, it won't matter if we distribute her. Her recording will die a quick death and she'll never be heard from again. Why we would want to have our name associated with that I never could understand, but, in this business, when the boss lays down a decree, you follow that decree or they find some other schmoe to replace you and that schmoe will follow the decree anyway."

We asked Matt if he was surprised that Cadence had talent when she finally did perform for him. He smiled and said, "Well, she didn't have a whole lot of real talent, but she definitely had charisma and I knew we could train her to be what we needed her to be. I was just glad she wasn't like so many of these rich kids who get a free ticket to the label office because they've got a powerful daddy, and then they stink up the place. Plus, I was really affected by how passionate she seemed to be. It was odd though. Cadence, cute little thing that she was, came up to me after the session and said, 'I want to get out of here so bad and anything you can do to help me, I'd forever be indebted to you for.' I thought it was real cute, ya know. I thought it was kind of quirky and it made me laugh.

"But, the strange thing was, Cadence was acting real flirty after she said it, almost like she was trying to seduce me into supporting her. She touched my shoulder and even brushed her hand on my thigh when she walked away. I was thirty-three years old and married at the time, but Cadence seemed to think she could seduce men and get what she wanted. I have to assume that was the case anyway. Maybe I'm reading into it too much. Of course, Daddy Darien was nowhere around at the time or I don't think she'd have ever done that. He seemed to have a real powerful control over her."

We asked Matt to elaborate a bit on the supposed control he personally witnessed Darien having over Cadence. Matt told us, "Well, it was weird. When he was around, Cadence would be very proper and polite and barely ever say a word. As soon as she would start to speak, Darien would quickly shush her and take over himself and say whatever he felt was appropriate to say in the given situation. He was like her manager, father, controller, and whatever the hell else you want to call it.

"She also seemed to fear him. That was disturbing to watch. When she'd speak and he'd interrupt, as he always did, she would wince slightly, almost like she was afraid he'd crack her in the face if she didn't shut up. Most of us felt there was some type of deep-seated control relationship going on and possibly even some physical abuse; but, I'm ashamed to say, we're not in the business of rescuing little girls from big mean ogre daddies. We're in the business of making stars and we knew, relatively quickly after she first performed an audition, that we could make this girl a star."

We had a final question for Matt. We asked him if he regrets not doing anything about the perceived abuse he and others felt Cadence might be enduring. Matt, who throughout our interview had been jovial and at ease, quickly tensed up and even teared up as he left us with a rather haunting final word on the subject.

Matt said, "I really do think... well, I don't know what I exactly think about it, but… it sucks, because she was so young and really just wanted to be a singer and get the hell out of her hometown. She didn't know how to deal with the situation she was in at home. She also didn't have much self-respect because she'd shamelessly flirt with all of us when Darien wasn't around, like she thought she could manipulate us through her sexual charms which makes sense given all that's come out in the media about the abuse she went through.

"I just thought it was sad. I thought she was better than the circumstances she found herself in. Plus, considering what happened later, I almost wish we'd never agreed to distribute her. If we'd turned her down that day, obviously realizing this situation was all kinds of fucked up, then maybe… I don't know… maybe she would never have gone to that college, and maybe what happened… I don't know… just never would have happened. She could have gotten counseling or something. I just wish one of us would have had the balls to push her in that direction instead of filling her head with more confusion and false hope that she was being fed her dream and all was going to be great for her. That, for me… that's the shit I'll carry with me to my grave. I feel partially… I feel, ya know… responsible in some way."

- 3 -

So, what can we gather from the information we've reviewed so far? The first conclusion we can draw seems rather obvious, doesn't it weary travelers?

Cadence had a sick, controlling father who abused her in the worst way possible. When she went off to college, he feared she would get to the point where she didn't need him anymore and she may start talking about the filthy writhing skeletons in the closet of the Moore family.

So, the logical next step in conspiracy would be to venture the following theory. Darien Moore could have used his long reach to arrange the permanent disappearance of his own daughter. After all, he still had Morgan, the pathetic damaged son who was not strong enough to walk away. Morgan was going to be the sales success and successor Darien demanded that he be. Cadence was a potential problem. And once she achieved her first taste of success with "Goldfish Chaser," Darien's best efforts to keep her happy could eventually backfire on him.

He boosted the beginning of her career, but with Cadence off at college and already having achieved a level of fame, it seems certain that Darien Moore must have wondered at some point... would Cadence need him much longer? And, if Darien started having these thoughts, is it reasonable to assume he also started having thoughts about how he might deal with the Cadence problem?

Were these private fears enough to drive the man to have his own child murdered? The sexual assaults that he is alleged to have committed are terrible, but murder is an entirely different matter. Darien Moore was capable of a lot, but was he capable of *that*? This question has been asked many times. Let's examine it.

If you only know the part of the story we've just been through, it seems obvious and natural to list Darien Moore or a hired associate of Darien Moore as a prime suspect in this case. Well, for those who seek obvious answers and simple conclusions, you will not find them looking in the direction of Darien Moore. This man seemingly had little in the way of sanity, capacity for love, good sense, or kindness; but, what he did have in abundance were alibis on the weekend of Cinco de Mayo, 2002.

We would like to be able to put the smoking gun right in his creepy incestuous hands, but it's not that simple. Darien Moore, contrary to the theories of many, may not have worried about Cadence as a potential problem at all. His actions certainly don't indicate that he did.

Just as he had moved on from his deceased wife to Cadence, he moved on from his daughter to Marianna Paulson, a forty-two-year-old alcoholic secretary working under him at HANDLER, whom he quickly married and moved into his home when Cadence went off to college. It was not a major transition since, according to several coworkers, he'd been enjoying Marianna on the side for years anyway.

Darien now had a new wife and threw himself with furious abandon back into his work. He'd leveraged ridiculous control over Cadence's success, and it seems he was confident that she needed him, his connections, and weekly allowances to live the life she was beginning to enjoy living.

Remarkably, it appears in Darien's mind that Cadence was a non-issue. He felt he had full mental control over her and she needed him desperately to cling to the success he'd handed her on the proverbial silver platter.

Okay, now when dealing with mysteries like the Moore case, it is important to play devil's advocate and really talk through a theory before casting it aside. Let us pretend for just a moment that Darien *was* worried about Cadence becoming a problem. Let's say he *did* make the decision that she had to go or else he could be ruined. We'll also say these feelings drove him to commit murder. If we allow all these points in our scenario, the one question left is this. Could he have done it?

Darien Moore earned two promotions within a year and a half of Collette's death. HANDLER sent him traveling and as one of their top earners, he went all over the United States. In fact, Darien was on a business trip for a sales conference in Milwaukee, Wisconsin the weekend in which Cadence disappeared, Saturday, May 4 and Sunday, May 5 of 2002 (Cadence was officially last seen on May 6 a little after midnight, but the car ride to the place of her disappearance began during the last minutes of May 5).

The other two family-connected suspects in this mystery, Morgan Moore and Marianna Paulson, both accompanied Darien on this trip to Milwaukee. Morgan was there for the old meet and greet with some important folks and Marianna was there for arm candy purposes.

The whereabouts of all three were verified countless times by a dozen individuals. There was simply no way any of the three could have made it from Milwaukee, Wisconsin where they were seen by many at a dinner party around 9:00 p.m. on May 5, back to Dusklight Falls, Pennsylvania where Cadence attended school and was last seen that night, and then back to Milwaukee where all three were again seen at a nightclub bar a little past 2:00 a.m. on May 6. For that to have happened, one of them would have had to make a bare minimum twenty-three-hour round trip in less than five hours. It simply wasn't possible. There wasn't enough time... not by any stretch of the imagination. And, if any of you travelers are thinking plane ride... you can land that shit right now. Every major, potential, and bottom rung airline that would have even been a possibility for travel to Dusklight Falls... all of them were checked by anyone who ever took a stab at this case and none of the three names appear anywhere on passenger lists, wait lists, or otherwise.

This physical impossibility of direct involvement by Darien, Morgan, and Marianna did not stop a significant number of conspiracy theorists over the years from still pointing the accusatory finger in Darien's direction. If he didn't do it himself, then he must have had someone else do it for him.

To be sure, aside from Jamison Kelly, who was by far the likeliest suspect in the court of public opinion, no one else in this real-life drama comes anywhere close to having the same level of suspicion surrounding them as Darien Moore.

Before we move on to the college experience that Cadence jumped into after her burst of initial singing success, it is probably best to close the book on Darien, temporarily at least, since his name will surface again in our further investigations.

As things stood at the time, Darien could not be found guilty of anything since he, his wife, and his son had airtight alibis for the entire weekend in which Cadence went missing, and there existed no evidence tying Darien to anyone else who may have harmed Cadence on his behalf.

- 4 -

As we close out this part of the story for now, one might ask, what ever happened to Darien Moore after Cadence went missing and his shameful family affairs became public fodder? Well, when the Cadence story broke nationally and the private journals of Morgan and Cadence were both released to the press, Darien Moore was forced to accept a severance package from HANDLER and end his thirty-year association with the company.

HANDLER simply would not stand for all the negative press surrounding Darien and, in reality, surrounding Darien and Cadence, since one of their own not only was being accused of incestuous relations with his daughter, but was also a prime suspect in her disappearance since anyone with a brain could deduce that just like there being more than one way to skin a cat, there are plenty of ways to get rid of someone without getting one's own hands dirty.

Darien could have easily hired someone to do the job, allowing him a beautiful alibi that no one could deny, while still accomplishing the goal of making his troublesome daughter go away forever. Whether or not this actually happened is a matter of debate. All available evidence seems to indicate that Darien Moore had no intention of harming Cadence, and felt his control over her would keep her quiet.

Regardless, with all the suspicion surrounding Darien, HANDLER had no choice but to offer a severance package and get him out of their company as quickly as possible. There may have been a chance of them forgiving Darien being a suspect in the disappearance, considering no solid evidence of his guilt had surfaced. But, they certainly were not going to forgive the charges of incest and abuse. There was plenty of evidence of that.

As a PR gesture, and as a means of avoiding a lawsuit from Darien for wrongful termination, HANDLER agreed to keep his son Morgan on in a high-profile sales role. The Moore name could live on in the company allowing Darien to begrudgingly go off quietly into the night, not wishing to make a lot of waves, risking his son's future success.

Marianna stuck around for about a year after all the murder fervor had blown over, and then she was off to her next sunny stop in life, a few hundred thousand dollars richer from a tasty divorce settlement she was able to sink her teeth into.

Darien, most of those close to him would agree, had just grown too tired and weary to even fight it. His reputation was in ruins and he'd lost the only thing that defined him as a success. The quicker Marianna hit the bricks, the sooner he might find a little spot of peace. The king just simply had no more fight in him and he was relinquishing his throne to anyone who could withstand the harsh judgments of life. He'd decided he no longer cared.

Morgan Moore worked at HANDLER for the next three years. The first year he put up impressive numbers and tried to do the Moore family name proud, not that the name ever had any chance of recovering from the infamous stain it would always be associated with. After that first year, things started to decline for Morgan. He became less and less successful, and was eventually fired for lack of performance. Unfortunately, Morgan never could reconcile the pain splotches in his heart and mind; they were too deep and bright to ever wash out.

Morgan took a fistful of pain pills one night and chased them with a bottle of Puerto Rican rum, forever removing himself from the agonizing plane of Earth he so purely had come to despise.

Darien Moore still lives a modest and quiet life in Wyomissing, Pennsylvania. He was able to hold on to his home and, according to his very few remaining close associates, he passes the days away playing solitaire and watching old movies on his computer. Darien cuts quite the ghoulish lonely figure nowadays, living by himself in a dark empty house, surviving off some very unimpressive monthly installment checks from HANDLER, and eating TV dinners by a false fire place.

Darien Moore became a broken man, barely eking out a daily existence. Most would say, and actually have said on several occasions, to a nicer guy it couldn't have happened—a matter for the courts of public opinion to ultimately decide.

Although we reached out to him, Darien Moore, through his lawyer, refused to speak with *Underground Podcast* for this special.

- 5 -

UNDERGROUND PODCAST 2: (Official Transcript)
Part 2: The College Year- First Installment

Charlie Marx's Underground Podcast: Episode 2 (Part 2). Original Drop Date: November 1, 2013. (Brought to you by United Way of Life, courtesy of Tyler Reubens... this program is funded and sponsored by WHHW, a subsidiary of Universal Public Radio)

(Narration by Charlie Marx) Cadence Moore had scored a hit record with "Goldfish Chaser," and the management of Nighthawk Records was all too eager to send her out on a publicity tour and a concert run of college campuses where she could connect with the audience who was buying her single in stupefying numbers. These young people, so eager and so enthusiastic, seemed to provide the vulnerable base for the lightning rod to strike... the strike of light which had set Cadence's musical career ablaze.

During the summer tour after her high school graduation, Cadence played sixty-eight shows across the Northeastern United States, selling out small college campus civic centers and theatre halls.

College students are notorious for blind devotion to small acts that they feel they've discovered and Cadence fit the particular bill at that time. She was greeted with an enthusiastic welcome at every campus she visited and "Goldfish Chaser" was quickly earning her enough royalties to pay for a full ride at any college she saw fit to attend.

Some have asked over the years why Cadence wanted to attend college at all. Wouldn't it have made more sense for her to focus on the concerts and making more records? Well, if any of these people had known Cadence Moore on a personal level, they would have been fully aware of her obsessive desire to escape, not only the greater Reading, Pennsylvania area of which her hometown of Wyomissing was a part, but the confines of her family unit and the controlling and smothering grip that Darien held over her.

With these facts in mind, it is not surprising in the least to learn that college was a top priority for Cadence. She needed to get away and live many miles from the scene of psychological shattering crimes in the town of her birth. In the midst of her concert tour, which was increasing her fame with every single show, Cadence was getting the opportunity to sample the local flavor of dozens upon dozens of northeastern college campuses and the unique micro culture which was threaded throughout each one of them.

When the summer tour after her graduating year was over, Cadence had decided that Dusklight Falls University in Dusklight Falls, Pennsylvania, which offered a small-town atmosphere with unique ambience about 100 miles outside of Pittsburgh and four glorious hours away from Reading, was the place for her. She loved the vibes in this small-town wilderness which housed an impressive university, well known for its arts and music programs.

Dusklight Falls is one of the most interesting spots in all of western

Pennsylvania. It is named for its haunting waterfalls on the outskirts of the southern end of town. The hills that silhouetted the entire town sloped drastically into a river surrounded by small cliffs and several beautiful waterfalls.

The effect of the water hitting jagged rocks and misting upward offered a spooky vision at the edge of Dusklight Falls, and when tourists entered the town from the south, the falls were the first thing they saw. When dusk would arrive each evening, the falls glistened and almost glowed like a landscape out of a ghostly dream, the mist rising and spreading its wet wings across the town.

Cadence Moore had played Dusklight Falls Arts and Culture Center in August of her summer tour. She absolutely fell in love with the feel of the place and when she learned of the arts and music programs the university had to offer, she made a final decision that this was where she would attend school and set up the next launching pad for future success.

As we alluded to previously, royalties from her hit single would have granted Cadence free and clear access to just about any college she saw fit to offer her patronage. However, Darien Moore would not hear of the notion that Cadence would pay her own college bills.

He forked over the entire tuition bill, four years in advance of the time in which Cadence would have earned her degree. Cadence got a free ride, while still being allowed to horde her massive royalty earnings from "Goldfish Chaser" sales. Seriously folks, are you not witnessing a horrifying control-based relationship here?

Just when you think you have it all nailed down, you find out you still can't see the whole picture. Darien remained in control of absolutely none of Cadence's money. He'd set up funds and investments for her, but his interest in her success was not coming from a financially driven angle. He literally never made a dime from any of her fame. His interest in Cadence's career was purely and simply about control. The hand that feeds should not be bitten, so say the mythologies and truth tellers of our time.

Darien subscribed, it would seem, to this theory and felt the best way to keep Cadence under his control was to keep feeding her pursuits and artistic desires; so, regardless of what the actual situation was, Cadence would always feel dependent on him.

Cadence was reaching a point in which she could more or less guarantee herself a status of being set for life, granted she had at least one or two more hit singles and Darien kept the living expenses covered for the next few years.

This was another move in the mind control game Darien had been playing since the night he first… allegedly—of course, we must add, since parasite lawyers would love to throw darts at our pictures and drain our cash accounts—we're talking about the night Darien is said to have raped young Cadence, mentally fucking her up for the rest of her life.

Control was what Darien Moore was all about, so the more dependent Cadence felt on his money, the easier time he had in manipulating her to keep quiet, do his bidding, and god knows what else.

- 6 -

Cadence's entry into Dusklight Falls University was like a royal river ride in which a princess lady from a faraway land, displaced from her own kind, sailed into a small wilderness village attempting to live among the locals in the primitive ways of their custom.

The response she got from fellow students at DFU was probably very much like the way villagers would have reacted to a royal presence invading their familial zone and pretending to be just like them. The reaction Cadence received generally came from three categories of students.

The first category was comprised of fans, some of whom bothered her incessantly for autographs, discussions of music, and maddening requests for her to listen to a tape containing their own musical masterwork, usually recorded in a dorm room on a shitty cassette player which they were sure would be the next big sensation in music if someone just gave them a break and put it in the hands of a record company executive.

The second category was comprised of the aloof and suspicious students, the types who would think, 'Who is this girl, this star, masquerading as a regular person, as if she weren't swimming in champagne and using hundred dollar bills for toilet paper?'

These young folks were working their way through college so they might someday make a comfortable living. They assumed Cadence was already making boatloads of money… she must be… after all, she was a music star. Why would she be posing as a person who needed to go to college and better herself and her situation? These students looked upon Cadence as an unwelcome invader and she got plenty of dirty looks and cold shoulders as she made her way down the hallways from class to class.

The third category was made up of everyone else. These kids really didn't care a whole lot about Cadence Moore one way or the other. They were attending school for their own purposes and while some felt it was kind of a cool novelty to have a celebrity in their calculus class, Cadence's presence didn't affect them very much in their daily lives.

All three categories made up the welcoming committee she faced at DFU, overbearing fans, the judgmental and jealous types, and everyone else who could really take her or leave her. So how did she react to this environment?

Cadence Moore, for all of her emotional baggage and insecurities, actually seemed to have a revelation of sorts shortly after arriving at DFU. She simply ignored those who snubbed her, put up with those who annoyed her, and tried to focus on people who accepted her at face value and reserved their judgments for what they actually witnessed.

Cadence had very few friends back in high school. At that time, she was withdrawing from everyone and trying not to lose her mind from the horrors of her unhappy home. While she was promiscuous in high school, becoming intimate (according to her closest classmate Claire Forman) with somewhere in the neighborhood of forty people before the end of her senior year, as has been documented in several different outlets. Cadence never got truly close to anyone and appeared to desire what was inside of her heart to stay where it was, not even venturing out for any venting sessions with a best buddy or chatty girlfriend.

Yet, after some time had passed, Cadence began to change. Once she arrived at DFU she was free, at least geographically, from Darien and the rest of the Moore family. This separation helped her slowly explore what lay outside the prison of the person she'd been, and assisted her embrace of a new opportunity to be whoever in the world she wanted to be.

After all, the students in Dusklight Falls had no idea she was the damaged little girl from Reading, Pennsylvania, faking confidence and a sparkling smile on stages across the state. They saw her simply as a celebrity classmate and some of them wanted to know more about who she really was.

For Cadence, this was a chance to invent someone completely new. She didn't have to be the damaged and soiled person she detested anymore. She could be anyone she wanted to be. She had this revelation and realized she had the freedom to control the version of herself she let people see.

Once she made this important self-discovery, only one question remained. Who would this new version of Cadence Moore actually be? That question can be answered by the girl who eventually became Cadence Moore's best friend, Darlene Bethany. Darlene was starting her sophomore year at DFU when Cadence arrived. She happened to randomly be placed in the same dorm room with Cadence and the two became almost instant friends. The way this happened can best be explained by Darlene herself.

We interviewed Darlene for this podcast and she helped us reconstruct a clear picture of DFU and Cadence Moore as they were a decade ago.

Darlene Bethany is a thirty-year-old administrative director for the Lehigh Valley Airport in Allentown, PA. She is married to Dennis Ulrich, a chef and restaurant owner with whom she has two young children.

Darlene has come a long way since her sophomore year at DFU, and has worked through a lot of emotional turmoil since that time to attain the domestic happy home life she currently lives. Obviously, the people closely associated with this story carry with them some deep scars and Darlene may have some of the deepest.

She has never spoken at length about the Cadence Moore case or her involvement in it. She had initially agreed to appear in *Moore to the Story* but pulled out after only a few minutes into an interview when she took a severe disliking to Michael Angstat and his line of questioning.

She felt Michael was being rude and callous when referring to Cadence and also felt the entire theme of the Barnes and Angstat film was one of sensationalism and lies, rather than an honest attempt at having justice served to whomever was truly responsible for Cadence's disappearance.

The fact that Darlene Bethany was one of three people who were the last known human beings to ever see Cadence Moore alive made her a necessity for inclusion in Barnes and Angstat's film. Since they only had ten minutes of usable footage, they included sound bites from the aborted interview throughout the film and its trailer to make it appear as though Darlene's presence throughout the documentary was larger than it actually was.

Darlene was very disappointed in the finished film and angry at herself for ever agreeing to be a part of it. It took some major convincing from myself and the *Underground Podcast* team for Darlene to finally agree to participate in our program.

She explained some of the reasons for her hesitation during her interview. "I was worried, based on my experience with that film, that this was just another attempt by the media to make a spectacle of Cadence's disappearance, and not be concerned with the truth. Being someone who loved Cadence for the brief time she was a part of my life, I just wasn't going to stand for someone attempting that again and using me to do it.

"I wanted no part of anything like that, but when you guys showed me the format for this show, I liked that it seemed to be playing fair with everyone involved and showing Cadence's life from all angles. I thought the film was a disgrace filled with lies and offered no help in solving anything.

"I was also told by you, Charlie, that *Underground Podcast* and the team of researchers working on the film actually solved the case and would reveal the new information during the radio special. If this turned out to be true, which I had my doubts about and still do... but if it is true, then I not only was *willing* to be involved... I *wanted* to be involved."

I asked Darlene if she believed our team when we told her about solving the case. She responded, "Well, no, to be honest, I didn't. However, Charlie, you and your producer, Dillon, I believe, came to my home. Your lawyers drew up an agreement which basically stated that I'd have a chance to see the new information right before it aired, which I'm holding you to by the way, and if I didn't think it had validity, I would have the right of refusal for any of my comments to be included in the show.

"I never thought to have such an agreement drawn up with Barnes and Angstat and I kick myself for it to this day. In the case of your show, I guess it's okay to tell your listeners about this… I agreed to sign a confidentiality agreement, so when I'm told about the red-hot news you guys say you discovered, I won't be able to tell anyone else without penalty of legal action and million dollar fines. I figured anyone making me sign something like that at least believes what they have is the real deal. After all that was done with, I agreed to do your show and I feel good about it. As of now, I haven't seen the new information you say you've uncovered, but I'm hoping for the best; and, if I don't like what I see, then I suppose no one will ever hear this explanation, or anything else I have to say about the subject."

People listening to this probably wonder why Darlene, or anyone, for that matter, didn't insist on seeing our new information before beginning the interview. That was a condition I laid out.

My guests were going to find out what we knew, but not until they told their stories. Indeed, the caveat in our contract protected them so at least they knew they had rights to have their comments pulled from the show if they didn't like the solution we revealed to them.

Aside from confidentiality concerns, my guests *not* knowing was very important because I felt strongly if any of the interviewees knew about the information we'd uncovered, it would affect their state of mind and their comments about the part of the story they were personally involved in.

For the sake of the interview and the overall quality of our presentation, the conversations had to take place before anyone was allowed to be let in on our evidence.

Now, by the time you weary travelers tune into the live radio special (see your local UPR affiliate for the details), all participants *will* have been allowed access to our new evidence. I was banking on convincing all of them since any pulled interviews would wreak havoc on the final program. But that's how much I was willing to wager that what we found had finally cracked this case wide open. That wager may have been reckless and stupid on my part, but I had nothing else to work with, so I went with it.

Back to my conversation with Darlene. We were very interested in hearing about her first recollections of meeting Cadence Moore, and also to hear her perspective on the type of person Cadence was at that time.

We hoped she could offer some clarity about how the Cadence Moore she knew in Dusklight Falls contrasted to the girl who left Reading, Pennsylvania an emotionally twisted victim who was juggling newfound fame with old, painful wounds. Had Cadence been able to reinvent herself successfully? What persona was she offering the students of DFU and particularly her new roommate?

Darlene Bethany recalls, "My first feeling was excitement. I absolutely loved the song "Goldfish Chaser." It was probably my favorite song at the time it came out… this was like right before Cadence enrolled.

"My very good friend Stephanie Chambers and I actually went to see Cadence at the Arts and Culture Center when she toured through the previous summer. So I was stoked to be sharing a room with her. I couldn't wait to see what she was like.

"My first impression of what she was like? I have to say, it was kind of weird. I mean, for the first few days she was cordial and friendly, but seemed a little withdrawn and scared to open up or talk to me about anything.

"But it only took maybe a week and she seemed to change drastically. Like one day she just woke up and her personality turned on. She… it's like she made some kind of personal decision to let down her defenses and embrace her new environment.

"I've had ten years of perspective on this now so after seeing everything that came out in the wake of her disappearance and looking back at my own recollections of our college year together, I think Cadence woke up one day and realized she just didn't have to be *that* girl anymore if she didn't care to be. Cadence could be who she wanted, and no one would know the difference a half day's drive away from home.

"When that personal moment happened for her, I think it was maybe a week, maybe even less than that, I found Cadence to be interesting, curious about life, and really funny. She definitely didn't take the fame thing too seriously. She laughed about the way certain kids at school were treating her and the strange questions she'd get. But, really, she just seemed like a normal girl who knew she had achieved success and was proud of it, but was look-ing for something more out of life.

"She, I think, found so much satisfaction and enjoyment in attending school far away from home, being this new person she had either invented or was burying deep inside for years, and just living life. More importantly... she was living life for herself... not for her father or her deceased mother anymore... it was just *her* living for her."

Underground Podcast was also able to speak with Stephanie Chambers, another one of the last three people to positively see Cadence Moore the night of her disappearance. Stephanie currently resides in Tucson, Arizona where she lives with her young son whom she shares custody of along with her ex-husband, and works as a logistics supervisor for the MRM Company.

Stephanie was Darlene Bethany's best friend in the year before Cadence arrived and the two friends became three after Cadence. Stephanie under-standably lost touch with Darlene Bethany over the last ten years, as any reminder of the terrible feelings both girls carried with them about the eve-ning of Cadence's disappearance was something they wanted to avoid, and their friendship became a casualty of the tragic situation.

During the process of trying to procure them both as guests, I suggested an on-air reunion of Stephanie and Darlene. I thought it would make great radio... well, audio I suppose is the correct term, and I also thought it would help convince them both to give me a solid agreement to do the show. After some brief hesitation, both agreed it was a good idea and felt it was about time two old friends stopped avoiding each other over bad memories.

We were ready to roll. I interviewed them together and it was fasci-nating to see two former best friends, estranged for a decade, come back together and finally get some closure on a subject that had brought each of them significant pain.

There was a mist of mixed feelings floating around our studio during the joint interview. Joy, painful recollection, awkwardness, and eventually gratitude and relief made for an incredible conversation.

After we finished, Darlene and Stephanie both separately came up to me and told me how happy they were that they'd made the decision to participate. Darlene told me she had faith that I'd do the right thing with this presentation and she'd be let down personally if the *Underground Podcast* version of this story descended into a typical media murder drama, taken down to the lowest common denominator. I made her a promise that I'd do everything in my power to avoid that happening.

The last remaining piece of the three-person puzzle our team would have liked to put together could not join us. Steve Willis, the boyfriend of Darlene Bethany at the time of Cadence Moore's disappearance, sadly passed away from a head injury he sustained while cliff diving in Fiji the year after his college graduation.

Steve Willis, aside from being one of the last three people to officially see Cadence alive, is important to this whole story for another reason. It was Steve Willis who became the catalyst for a volatile argument between Darlene and Cadence which began on the evening of May 5, 2002 and ended badly in the early morning hours of May 6 when Darlene kicked Cadence out of her car for what Darlene and Stephanie both said they felt, at the time, was shameless flirting with Steve.

All four were heavily intoxicated and as most people can attest to, emotions and reactions can become grossly exaggerated in the heat of drunken confrontation among young people.

Darlene became convinced that Cadence was disrespecting her by overtly flirting with Steve Willis and things came to a head when Darlene's car, an '87 Olds which was being driven by Steve at the time, was stopped at a traffic light at the intersection of Painted Sky and Neversink roads in Southern Dusklight Falls.

Cadence allegedly kissed Steve, as a joke she professed to Darlene when angrily questioned about it. Darlene felt Cadence had gone way over the line and became incensed, which caused her to slap Cadence violently across the face and force her out of the car. Steve Willis, acting on the very clearly stated wishes of Darlene, peeled out and sped away, leaving Cadence alone in the road, drunk, and far from the dorm.

Stephanie Chambers, who sympathized with and supported Darlene Bethany at the time of the incident, remembers how things got started that night. "We were all partying at a place we called The Basement, which was an actual basement of a frat house I honestly can't remember the name of anymore. It was Cinco de Mayo and everyone was getting completely plastered. Cadence was there with Jamison Kelly, her boyfriend, and Darlene was with Steve. I was prowling around looking for a date for the night but having no luck. I was the one who initially suggested we all take a drive out to the Falls and have some drinks on the rocks overlooking the water.

"The Basement could get real hot and smelly after an hour or two and we were getting kind of sick of the whole scene. Darlene and Steve wanted to go. Cadence wanted to come too, and she would have brought Jamison, but he'd been drinking heavier than any of us, and was too drunk to make the trip. He told Cadence to just go without him since he was gonna crash soon.

"This didn't sit well with Cadence. She'd expected to get laid that night when the party was over. She was acting pretty frisky throughout the whole night and you could tell she was pissed when Jamison declined the Falls invitation so he could sleep it off. Jamison wasn't going to make the little after-party she had in mind because he was literally almost passing out from drinking too much.

"I know those documentary douchebags passed around some stupid theory about how he was faking it and was just trying to forge an alibi for himself. But please, take it from someone who was there. I didn't just see Jamison acting drunk… we all saw how much he was drinking and if he faked that, then I guess all of us were faking it too since our drinks were being made from the same bottles of liquor that his were. That would be a lot of collective faking from people who have no reason to fake things together. I always thought that was ridiculous. Anyway, Cadence came with us and Jamison didn't. I knew Cadence was very drunk, based on how she acted during the car ride. It wasn't her normal behavior. For all the rumors of how promiscuous she was when she was younger, she never showed that side to us in college.

"She was in a long term serious relationship with Jamison and as far as I know, was always faithful to him the entire time they were together. But that night, between a combination of her drunken state and her frustration with Jamison for cancelling on their bedroom after-party, she was acting way out of character."

Darlene Bethany has a similar memory of what led up to the late-night car ride to the Falls. "Like Stephanie said, we were all pretty tired of The Basement and wanted to go somewhere else. It wasn't the first time we'd done that either, gone to the Falls late at night that is. We all used to go out there with our boyfriends or as a group. It was the local hangout for most people in the area, but late at night, you'd usually have some solitude since kids didn't frequent the rocks over the Falls very much at two o'clock in the morning.

"Anyway, my point is that Stephanie suggesting that wasn't something out of the ordinary. What *was* out of the ordinary that night were two things, Cadence's behavior once she got in the car, and the fact that Jamison Kelly got so drunk.

"First, it was very weird for Jamison to get hammered. I mean, it was college, we all got toasted on the weekends to some degree, but Jamison was usually the DD, and even when he wasn't, he'd have a few drinks and call it a night. So, the fact that he was so completely intoxicated that he pretty much passed out was really odd for him.

"That's what Barnes and Angstat hopped on when they made their film. I'm sure they talked to plenty of our former classmates and locals around the campus. They all would have probably told a similar story about Jamison not being a big drinker. And, of course one conclusion leads to another. If he was drinking so much, he must have been upset and what would have made him so upset? Well, he must have fought with Cadence. So, if he fought with her then he probably killed her. Then they said he was faking how drunk he was and had planned on killing her earlier in the evening... seriously, with no evidence at all they threw these things out there. I mean, that's how ridiculous their accusations are in that film."

Stephanie interjected, "Yeah, it was dumb... because like I said, if you want to talk to someone, talk to people who were there and saw Cadence and Jamison in person that night. If Cadence had fought with him to the point where he was drinking himself into a stupor and there was enough anger between them to result in a murder, why then would she be asking him to come with us to the Falls?

"It's like these guys… Barnes and Angstat don't consider annoying logic like this and they just pick up on random points different people bring up as afterthoughts, then they take those little comments or thoughts and create a whole story. The only problem is the story they came up with was a fictional story."

This interjection by Stephanie gave me an opportunity to ask her what seemed to be an appropriate question. I asked why she agreed to full participation in *Moore to the Story* if she felt this way. Darlene had quit within a few minutes of starting her interview but Stephanie completed an entire two-hour conversation for the film. Stephanie was not pleased with my question and became somewhat defensive.

She said, "I don't appreciate that question because you're insinuating that I'm changing my tune depending on who I'm talking to. I'm giving you the same thing I gave Barnes and Angstat which is my honest recollection and my honest opinion. If you don't appreciate that, I'd be happy to end this interview before we get even a few minutes in. Would that give me some credibility in your eyes?"

We, well I should be honest here and say *I,* since I was the one conducting the interview with her, felt badly that I'd offended Stephanie and made it clear I wasn't questioning her character. I just wanted to know why Barnes and Angstat had managed to keep her happy enough to complete a full interview when Darlene had quit within an hour. What was different about the way they had acted with Stephanie? That's what I was really getting at.

Stephanie took a breath and calmed down. She continued, "I don't mean to get all upset, but I don't want you insinuating that I'm turning on someone in your interview who I was very happy with when I did their interview. The reason the *Moore to the Story* interview went like it did was because Todd Barnes treated me with courtesy and was never disrespectful when talking about my friends Cadence and Darlene, or Jamison Kelly who they ended up calling a murderer by the end of the film. I think they probably would have had better luck with Darlene if Todd Barnes had conducted her interview as well. Apparently, Michael Angstat is kind of a jerk and was confrontational in his questioning. If I'd been them, I probably wouldn't have had him conducting any conversations.

"I think at this point, anyone with a brain would question the overall judgment of both men. They turned out a film that can be torn apart very easily by anyone with an inside knowledge of the case. But luckily for them and unlucky for everyone who was personally involved and cared about the truth, the public ate up their film like cherry pie and believed every detail since it's easier to do that then to do any research yourself. They made an entertaining lie and that's all they made. Now seeing what they ended up with, I'm as ashamed and upset as Darlene that my name was ever associated with it. If I could hit the rewind button I wouldn't have done the film."

I asked Stephanie if she had doubts about the *Underground Podcast* version of the Cadence Moore story and she said, "I really don't trust anyone when it comes to this case anymore, Mr. Marx… and if you guys turn out a piece of crap filled with more lies, then I will just as passionately berate and insult your show as I do now with the Barnes and Angstat movie.

"But I'm not just going to sit by quietly and avoid speaking up when the opportunity presents itself. Darlene Bethany is not a rich woman. Stephanie Chambers is not a rich woman. We don't have the power or the finances to go out and make our own film about this. If we did, I'm positive neither one of us would talk to anyone like you or Barnes or Angstat ever again. But like I said, that is not a realistic possibility and I will not sit by silently. It's important to all of us who knew Cadence, and who knew Jamison for that matter, that the truth comes out. Until it does, I'll continue to appear on programs, do interviews, and offer my own little contribution to solving this thing."

I returned the trajectory of our conversation to the late-night car ride to Dusklight Falls. I asked Darlene what she remembers about the car ride itself, specifically the way Cadence was acting when she first got in Darlene's car.

Darlene began to recall the details of the evening and became emotional. She tearfully recalled, "I'm sorry, this is hard for me to talk about because… well, it's the last time I ever saw my best friend and I've never gotten to clear the air with her and apologize for the fight. Stephanie can tell you, for a year straight, we were all inseparable. We went to parties, went to shows, and Stephanie and I were Cadence's biggest fans, sitting in the front row at her concerts and shouting for her. I loved her. In one night, our friendship turned sour and I made a snap decision based on anger and jealousy."

Darlene began sobbing at this point and we had to pause the interview for a few moments while she composed herself. She continued, "The reason this is so hard is not just because I can't make it right with her now, but because... I know if it hadn't been for me kicking her out of the car... let's face it... the truth is she would have never disappeared. She would have come back home with us that night and we all would have laughed about it in a few days.

"Instead of that, I kicked her out and she's never been seen again, except by the person who killed her, or kidnapped her, or whatever god-awful thing actually happened that night. That's the worst part, I mean, after all these years none of us knows what really happened. And I know you said you and your team have solved the case, but others have made that statement before and until I see proof of that, I will still be tortured by not knowing where Cadence is, whether she's alive or dead. We all have had to assume by this point that she's dead, but not knowing has just been total... yeah, I have no other way to say it... it's been torture. And I've punished myself for being responsible by putting Cadence in that position.

"That was part of the reason Stephanie and I drifted apart. I couldn't handle any reminders of that night. I broke up with Steve a month later, too. I didn't want to think about it and seeing either one of them brought it all flooding back every time. I ran away from it, and... it... it's been the biggest regret of my entire life. I truly hate myself for what I did that night and not a day goes by where I don't wish I could take it back."

Stephanie Chambers felt the need to console Darlene and tried to lift some of the burden off her. She said, "Darlene, I know we haven't seen each other in almost a decade, but I completely understand what you feel. I promise you, I regret what happened that night, too. But the fact is... it wasn't your fault. I was right behind you bitching Cadence out and telling her to get the hell out of the car. You weren't alone there... and remember, hindsight is 20/20. But, if you take that night by itself, not wanting to speak ill of someone who is very likely no longer with us, realistically Cadence was completely out of line with the way she was hanging all over Steve. She was mad at her boyfriend for falling asleep in a drunken haze and she was also completely drunk. She wasn't thinking clearly and she let her negative personality traits come out. She was all over Steve to the point of kissing him, which he resisted; I remember very clearly.

"Any normal girl at that age, in that situation, would have reacted as you did… and as I did, for that matter. If any of us had a clue about what would have happened, we obviously would do things differently… but we had no way of knowing. You have to see that, Darlene."

Darlene put her arm around Stephanie and hugged her. She said, "I appreciate you saying that and my rational mind tells me the same thing. I know I didn't do it on purpose. But it's agonizing to know that one decision you made on a drunken night in college resulted, whether directly or indirectly, in the disappearance and probably the death of your best friend. That fact makes it impossible for my emotions to believe what my rational mind tells them."

It was both mesmerizing and touching to see two old friends, separated by a decade naturally assume positions of comfort and support with one another. I knew this was difficult for both women, but I couldn't help but feel happy that we got them together for this show.

I tried to take things in what would hopefully be a happier direction at this point in the interview. These girls had some very enjoyable times together in school. One night should not eliminate all the happiness that came before. I wanted to get Darlene and Stephanie's remembrances about where the relationship between Cadence and Jamison Kelly first began.

- 7 -

Stephanie immediately laughed and Darlene smiled and put her hand over her eyes. Stephanie spoke first, "Uh… yeah… well that's an interesting one because I actually dated Jamison… or should I say, *we* dated Jamison for about a week and that directly led to Cadence meeting him and completely falling for him."

I had to admit this was the first time I'd heard anything about Darlene Bethany or Stephanie Chambers ever dating Jamison Kelly. I broached the obvious question, "If that's true, I'm shocked that it's never been mentioned previously. I would think this would be a rather significant detail to gloss over in every major covering of this story."

Darlene laughed and said, " Well, now let's not get too far out into left field on this. When Steph says we dated him, what she means is that we each literally went on *one* date with him. And I hate to say it, and no offense to Jamison if he happens to be listening, but these were not dates either one of us would have put on the top ten list of greatest dates we've ever had.

"Jamison was an unusual guy back then. He was kind of awkward and shy and not the best conversationalist. I learned later that he always felt like an introspective person who probably did a lot of solitary thinking. But after he took both of us out to dinner in the span of a week, I think Stephanie would agree we laughed for hours recalling the details of our dates. He was just so damned awkward and would stumble over all his words. I recall Stephanie even saying he spilled a drink on her."

Stephanie burst out laughing and confirmed, "Oh yes, that's true, you're remembering right. We went to Mickey Benz Barbeque Pit and he ordered a Shirley Temple which I thought was the weirdest drink for a twenty-something college guy to order. And, I remember he had tiny spots of barbeque sauce staining the cuff of his shirt. He was gesturing wildly with his hands while he droned on about a physics theory he was working on and in the process, he knocked the glass of Shirley Temple all over the table and all over my brand new white pants.

"And... that was the end of that date. I yelled for the check and told him I had cramps. He was so nice, though, and I shouldn't have been such a bitch. We did eventually become close friends and he was a very sweet guy."

Darlene continued, "Let's just say Jamison hadn't yet found his way with women and Steph and I had each been in college for a year and we were no strangers to having some casual sex with guys. Jamison was totally the opposite. He viewed dating a girl as some kind of old-fashioned courtship. He was overly polite, overly careful, completely scared, and just not up to our speed at all.

"As Steph mentioned, he was a very nice guy, and between his stuttering, he actually did manage to say some interesting and intelligent things. He was just not the right fit for us; we were into excitement and confident party boys. I met Steve a few weeks later, so I was back off the market after a brief period of availability.

"But, I guess we're supposed to be talking about how Jamison met Cadence. Basically, when Steph and I were finally done laughing about our evenings with Jamison, we decided that he'd already had a shot at two girls in our little group, and it was Cadence's turn to take a crack at breaking down Jamison's confused and awkward exterior."

Stephanie added, "Remember, this was kind of just a joke... like we both have dated this strange boy so it was only fair for Cadence to step up to bat and try to hit the same curveball we took swings at. The funny part was, Cadence agreed to go out with him and after one date she came back and told us she thought he was adorable and had major potential. Darlene and I just about fell over with laughter, but Cadence got irritated and insisted she wasn't lying. She really liked him.

"Now that I'm older and have lived a little bit, I understand the reasons for it. I think Cadence probably related to his introverted and socially awkward nature. What Jamison projected externally, I think Cadence felt internally, so they kind of had a bond right away."

Darlene nodded her head, "I never actually thought about it that way, but you're probably right. I figured she looked at him like a little challenge... someone she could mold into what she wanted him to be, but when you say that, it makes sense. She was a closet introvert and obviously had some emotional issues, so he probably seemed like someone she could bond with. What really threw us all for a loop was the way Jamison changed after they started dating. It was almost an overnight transformation. After a few weeks of dating Cadence, Jamison became a different person altogether. It's amazing what a little positive attention from a female can do for the confidence of a young guy. The stilted awkwardness Steph and I had seen was all but gone. Replacing the shy and clumsy guy was a quirky but funny and engaging young man who was a lot of fun to be around. I think he needed Cadence to bring that out in him."

Stephanie thought back on the relationship between Cadence and Jamison. "If any of these cynical people out there who point the finger of guilt at Jamison could have seen him and Cadence together back then, there is no way they'd ever believe he would have harmed a single hair on her head. He really loved her, and she was the first girl I think who gave him what Darlene was talking about... some actual positive attention. Again, I'll repeat... I was there and I know what I'm talking about. You can take this to the bank, Charlie Marx. If there was one person in the world who wouldn't dream of hurting Cadence Moore, it was Jamison Kelly."

This is the end of *Charlie Marx's Underground Podcast Episode 2*: Tune in to Episode 3 for the continuation of the Cadence Moore story.

4

The Scene is Set

Tyler had a weakness for whiskey and a weakness for friends. Despite his own resolve to avoid any emotional interplay with Charlie Marx in their little chess match, Tyler was still a sucker for the bottle, just like his protégé, and when the liquor began to flow, so did the emotions.

Tyler Reubens lived in a world of stress. He was balancing an attempt at a personal life with his girlfriend, managing the madness of his own deadlines and story threads with *United Way of Life,* in addition to all the bureaucratic bullshit and headaches that went with his role as a programming liaison between UPR and WHHW. This stressful existence, which he'd begun to accept as normal, was the backdrop for the current melodrama playing out between himself and Charlie Marx.

Not only was Tyler fighting through the red tape and antiquated understanding of the UPR brass trying to push for the podcast series and special, but he was being cut out of the inner circle of information by his own boy, his own student, and he didn't like it. More precisely, Tyler hated it. He hated it not because he was egotistical, although he was. He hated it not because Charlie had committed a transgression that Tyler himself never would have dreamed of committing, because he would have. He hated it not for a host of reasons one might imagine. Of course, he didn't like it for all of those reasons, but Tyler hated it for only one. He hated it because it hurt.

Tyler was producing a series of programs he was confident would explode with the public and become a huge success. He'd personally decided on the Cadence Moore case and he'd personally handpicked Charlie Marx above all others to sit at the helm of the ship. He didn't have to do that. He could have gotten anyone. He could have approached Artie Rothstein or

Barry Shearing. Shit, he could have brought in Allen Jones or Daryl Thicke as hired guns… both well-known conspiracy hosts much more relevant in the mainstream than Charlie Marx had ever been. He could have studded his show with names and legitimacy and made the whole sales pitch to the UPR suede shoe boys a hell of a lot easier.

But, he trusted his instincts, something he'd always done and something which had always paid off. He knew Charlie was sharp as a tack and he had built the man's career himself, giving him every break he'd ever had in radio. Who better to put in charge of an experiment he was creating. If this thing hit, not only would Tyler's series be a smash, he'd have a new star on his hands… a star that would certainly bring new ears to future podcast runs which culminated with live radio specials, some of which Tyler had already been formulating in his mind.

And Charlie, that fucking ingrate, what did he do? He bit the very hand that fed him! Charlie should have been licking the footprints Tyler left in the dirt. But instead of that, he had fought him at every step of the way, and to add insult to injury, he'd cut Tyler completely out of the supposed big lead he'd discovered which would crack the unsolvable case. Of course, Tyler understood this was the way it worked sometimes, and some leads were as delicate as colossal towers made of flimsy cards. Any wrong move could send them crashing into smithereens, rendered useless. But he wasn't some boardroom schmuck. He was Tyler Reubens. He was Charlie's friend. He was Charlie's mentor. Here was Marx, sharing secrets with his little under-study Dillon Balast and some ass monkey cop, but closing the fucking door of the treetop clubhouse right in Tyler's face. What the fuck was that?

The whiskey sours were going down like cool water after a desert trek. Tyler had a rare day off the following day and was cutting loose. He had earmarked the night to read over Charlie's notes for podcast 3, an in-depth description of the night of Cadence's disappearance. After getting through half of it and making his own notes, Tyler had planned on calling Charlie and telling him what to change.

But he'd decided that he'd worked enough that night and it was time to chill out and forget about UPR, WHHW, *United Way of Life*, and

Underground Podcast for a while. Tyler's girlfriend Marquise was presenting a paper at an East West Philosophy conference in Honolulu and he had the house to himself for a few days. The timing seemed perfect to blow a couple of hours getting intimate with a bottle of whiskey and sleeping it off through the entire next day. That would go quite a way toward a proper decompression... something Tyler Reubens was in dire need of. He could worry about life and that piece of shit Charlie when it was time to work again.

Somewhere between his sixth and seventh drink, Tyler decided a phone call was indeed in order after all. Charlie needed to hear a few things and he needed to hear them now. He'd fucked up bad with Tyler and it was time to fuck with him back and let him understand a couple of things. Emotions were his enemy. Tyler knew this. But emotional and irrational soft voices in one's head had a way of taking on the role of commanding officer when the drinks were poured.

Tyler picked up his phone and dialed Charlie Marx's number. It was 2:00 a.m. and if he knew anything about his good buddy Charles, he knew he was not asleep at this hour and he was likely putting down a few himself. Charlie picked up the phone after Tyler had called him four times. Charlie shook his head and looked at the receiver. Tyler was not leaving a voicemail. He wanted to talk and talk they would. Charlie knew damn well that Tyler knew he would be awake and if he didn't pick up, Tyler would know he was intentionally dodging the call which would add another layer of bullshit on top of the mounting pile that already separated them.

Charlie was aware he had no choice, so he picked up and said, "Still keeping late hours aren't you, Tyler? What can I do for you, boss?"

Tyler laughed softly. "Oh, now don't be so formal, Charles. We both know you're not above telling me to go fuck myself or calling me a bitch when it suits you. This isn't really a business call anyway... it's more... a social call. Well, I guess you could say it's both. I want to have a word with you. You owe me some answers. I guess you could say it's time for you to give me something... what I've got coming to me... for everything I've done for you."

To just about anyone else, Tyler's rate of speech would have sounded normal even if his words were odd. But to Charlie Marx, no stranger to the drunken waste lands of the career alkie… Tyler's almost imperceptible slur was unmistakable. He was half in the bag, but good at hiding it. Really good at hiding it, that is, from most people. Charlie knew the approach with drunk Tyler had to be different from the approach with sober Tyler. Sober Tyler hated him currently, but drunk Tyler was probably sitting at home recalling some of the good times and asking himself how things got this way. That is what had propelled him into action to call Charlie in the wee hours. He really did want answers. He wanted explanations.

Charlie would give him what he could and hopefully smooth things out between them. Tyler as an ally was much more beneficial than Tyler as an adversary. Charlie wouldn't lead him to the pot of gold, but he could at least point him toward the rainbow far off in the distance. Maybe that would be just enough to get Tyler back in the friend zone again. Maybe that would be just enough to remind him that Charlie was only doing what he'd been taught to do while attending the Reubens school of leads, intel, and info. These thoughts sped through Charlie's slightly boozed up brain in the span of four seconds or so.

He began, "Okay… you've done a lot for me… let's face it… you've done everything for me. So, what is it you believe you have coming to you, Tyler?"

Tyler, still with a smile in his voice, said, "Ah, yes, the direct approach from a very direct man. I like that. You have some answering to do Charlie. You fucked me buddy. You fucked me up bad with this shit and I'm ready to talk about it. I won't be ready to talk about it tomorrow, just like I wasn't ready to talk about it yesterday. I'm ready to talk about it now so we're gonna talk. And then we're not gonna talk about it again."

Charlie said, "All right. That's fair enough. What are we talking about then? You tell me. You want an answer… then ask me a question."

Tyler laughed, "Well, look who has a bad case of amnesia. Look who has forgotten obvious things. You know obvious stuff, Marx… like how people who have made our careers are not expendable goofs we can cast aside and use *only* when they are of use to us. That's an obvious thing. Oh, another obvious thing… when you have no reason to distrust someone, you continue trusting them… unless, of course, they give you that reason… then you can stop. But, if they don't give the reason, you just go right on trusting them. That's the unspoken deal… and that's how business is done between men. You my friend… you did real bad business with me."

Charlie answered honestly, "Yeah, I suppose I did. I had my reasons, Tyler. I sincerely did. But you're right. It was bad business to do with you. And I'm sor—"

Tyler snapped at him, "Shut up… shut that right up, Marx. Don't apologize. You do that and I'll lose the last pathetic bit of respect I still have for you. I just want to know why. That's a simple question. So, give me a simple reason now. Why? Why was Dillon Balast and this cop of yours worth trusting while I was simply too much of a liability? Why was I the guy you had to keep in the dark? I *made* you man. I made you and taught you every lesson you ever learned. The instincts that are telling you I'm not to be trusted are the instincts you developed learning under *me*, goddamn it! I told you what stones to uncover and what leads to bury. I told you who to trust and how much to trust. And somehow, you end up putting me on the no-fly list? I'm not worth your confidence? How the *fuck* does that work?"

Charlie could hear the hurt in Tyler's voice. He never would show this during a normal conversation, especially about anything business related. The whiskey had loosened his lips and he called tonight as a friend… a wounded friend. Charlie was still sharp enough to know he had to handle this carefully. The lines were blurred for Tyler now, but they were not blurred for Charlie Marx… not really anyway. This was an opportunity to make things right… at least a little bit more right than they'd been since the lie, the rush job, and the arguments had driven a fat wedge right in the rib cage of their friendship.

He finally answered. "I trust you, Tyler. I didn't tell you one piece of the puzzle and here's why. Look dude, you have more responsibilities than I ever hope to have in my career. You juggle a lot of shit and you serve a lot of masters. If I told you what my lead is, the risk taker in you would jump right on board with me. But the businessman in you would be compelled to get corporate approval to run with an angle like this, and you'd want a contingency plan in case it all turned out wrong."

Tyler interrupted, "And he admits it folks. He's been full of shit all along. Thanks Charlie… at least you're telling the truth now."

Charlie continued, "No Tyler, it's not shit. If it was shit, I wouldn't be running with it and you and I both know it. But because I know you and because I know there is still a big risk taker in that heart of yours, I told you what you needed to know. I told you I had cracked the case… I just didn't tell you *how*. Now, the risk taker in you can't help but ride with me because your instincts demand it! You taught me well and you know I wouldn't fall down a fucking rabbit hole and get lost in wonderland while our careers burned down above ground. (It was still amazing to Charlie how convincing he could be spitting out lies like this. Jump right down a rabbit hole he had and their careers were already probably starting to smoke up above). If I told you the details, I not only would be breaking my tenuous agreement with our detective, but I'd be saddling you with information you would have a compulsion to share with Art Winston… not because you can't keep a secret… not because you're untrustworthy… but because you'd see it as another angle, another piece of leverage, and the time would come when you'd use it. Tyler, you can't tell me that's not 100% true. I couldn't let that happen because the cop we're dealing with could take our entire lead and run with it on his own and you, me, and this whole show would be sitting there watching the parade go by."

Tyler was silent for a few seconds. "Wow, I guess you've got me figured out pretty good don't you? You know I'd have to run an angle at some point with your secrets. I guess you know me better than I know me."

Charlie said, "I know you… yeah I do."

Tyler said, "Well, do you know *this* about me?"

Charlie asked, "What's that?"

Tyler answered, "Do you know how good I am at spotting the exact moment when a poor schmuck has started grasping at straws because he has nothing else to hold on to?"

Charlie was slightly rattled by that. He said, "I imagine that's something you'd be pretty good at by now, sure. But that really doesn't have anything to do with me… even if you think it does… or you'd like to think it does."

Tyler laughed, "Oh yes, I'd like to think that, wouldn't I? How about…

I don't think it at all… I *know* it. How about that?"

Charlie, although he felt he was still in the driver's seat, was unnerved by Tyler's tone. Charlie was, at the bottom of it all, a liar and a fake… hoping the gamble of his life was still going to pay off. But a liar always has his guilt and fear to drag behind him, like Jacob Marley's chains in *A Christmas Carol.* His paranoia needed to know, so he asked, "How about *what* Tyler? What is it you think you know? What makes you think I'm grasping at straws and not playing this whole thing close as fuck to the vest… just like you taught me?"

Tyler laughed even harder. He knew, even in his altered state, he was getting to Charlie… and he liked it. "I'll tell you… I'll tell you what. I'll tell you what by asking *when*. How about this *when*? When did you become a sitcom writer?"

Charlie didn't understand. "What? What the hell does that mean?"

Tyler said, "Why don't you not ask another question until you answer mine? When did you become a sitcom writer?"

Charlie was getting pissed, "What does that mean, for fuck's sake? I'm not a sitcom writer… so I don't know why you're saying that. Is this your drunken critique of my podcast 3 notes? If that's what it is, then let's get back to business on this business call. You told me we were having a social call so I didn't know I'd be receiving constructive Tyler Reubens criticism."

Tyler said, "It's both kinds of calls. I believe I told you that already. So here you go. My critique… is… this. Your description of the incident is fascinating and well written. It will come off great. It will come off great… as a great rip off of the Barnes and Angstat movie because none of your details are original or new."

Charlie defended it. "Tyler, we've got to bring the listeners who haven't seen the film up to speed and the incident story is the essential piece of the whole series, so it was kind of unavoidable to have in there; don't you think?"

Tyler said, "Oh sure it was… but was it unavoidable to include what the other guys had already done, and then as your own contribution, you take the listener on a fascinating trip into the college exploits of a guy named Jimmy Derek who no one gives a fuck about, and then you write another sitcom about a bickering married couple? This was the groundbreaking, mind-blowing material you came up with to separate our series from *Moore to the Story*? Forgive me for saying it good buddy, but my mind's not blown. I'm left here wondering if you are trying to pull my leg and tell me I'm left in the dark, because, as you claim, you knew I'd be compelled to squeal to Winston when all the while you kept me in the dark because you yourself are stuck in the darkness. Maybe you don't have any lead to crack the case and your desperate ass is stalling and praying for a miracle. Is that really why you begged for more time? So, you could just sit there a while longer, as Leonard Cohen might say, waiting for the miracle to come?"

Charlie felt every muscle in his body tense up and his heartbeat went into overdrive. The sweat beads dripping from his temples tickled his cheeks and he gave himself a painful pinch to the gut as he tried to think of how to tackle this accusation. Had Tyler seen right through it the whole time? Had the lie been that easy to spot? No, he couldn't think like that. If Tyler knew he was full of garbage, he wouldn't have been so butt hurt about being cut out, and he wouldn't have entertained half of the shit Charlie had been putting him through. He also wouldn't be continuing the project. He'd have pulled the plug by now. This was a psych job and a good one, but Charlie would not blink.

He said, "Okay... I see. I see what you're driving at. Well, I hate to disappoint you, Tyler, but I have very good reasons for writing what you call sitcom episodes... *very* good reasons."

Tyler said, "You do then I suppose... and you should suppose I still have very good reasons for saying you're full of shit, partner."

Charlie raised his voice slightly. "You can mock my formats and call them sitcoms. You can say I'm grasping for shit, but goddamn it, Tyler, do you really think... on top of the ridiculous deadlines you laid on this project, that I'd have the time or the desire to stall and take a little sideline journey into the exploits of a frat boy and a dishonest married couple if it didn't have a fucking point? Like I did it just for fun?"

Tyler raised his voice in return. "Then why don't you make the fucking point... with me, right now. Make it! Sell me on the point... before I point you in the direction of the unemployment line."

Charlie laughed, "C'mon man, don't even go there with me. If you were gonna can my ass, you'd have done it right after I cut you out. You don't plan on doing anything to me because you want to see how this turns out. You know me very well, Tyler, but I know you too. So, here's what I'm going to do. You hate me for cutting you out… you hate me a lot for cutting you out completely. Let's try something different. How about we go for this? Let's move toward you liking me a little for cutting you in partially."

Tyler said, "How about not? How about the business of liking you is a business I'm retired from."

Charlie ignored him. "It's clear to me now. The Mintz and Derek stories bug you. They don't seem to belong because Barnes and Angstat disregarded them. You think I'm pulling at the last thread or two that they forgot about because it's the only original angle I have to run with. Well, you can think that and you can be dead wrong."

Tyler said, "I'm not always right. But, I'm *usually* right. I'm not usually wrong and I'm *never* dead wrong… and you know it Marx."

Charlie smiled, "There's a first time for everything. Why don't you hear me out and you can make up your own mind about how dead right or wrong you might be. Here's how it goes. I'm going to ask you some questions and I want you to answer me. Don't think too hard. I'm not debating you. Just answer me. First question: Who did Barnes and Angstat tell their audience the murderer was?"

Tyler was more than buzzed and decided he'd play along for a little while. He mockingly answered, "Hmm… let's see, if I remember correctly, I believe that was that nice young Jamison Kelly boy from Dusklight Falls, wasn't it? Wasn't he boyfriend of the year or some shit?"

Charlie kept on. "And if Jamison had an alibi, then he makes a pretty shitty murder suspect, doesn't he?"

Tyler feigned a dumb southern drawl, "Why, golly, I'd say you might just be on to somethin' son!"

Charlie continued ignoring Tyler's bullshit, knowing if he made his point, Tyler would understand… no matter what a dick he was trying to be. "Okay, alibis for murder suspects are bad. If Barnes and Angstat are telling a story which ends with Jamison being a murderer, then any parts of the story which point away from him as a suspect really do need to be disregarded, don't they? What the fuck do you think the Mintz, Derek, and Hummingbird scenarios do for Jamison? Don't answer that... I'll tell you. They make him look a lot less guilty, Tyler—*that's* what they do. They cast potential guilt in all sorts of directions that don't necessarily lead to Kelly's dormitory door."

Tyler, without a hint of sarcasm, said, "Is that really all you've got, Charlie? Is this what it comes down to? You're doing a counter piece to the movie and claiming Jamison's not the guy? It was some other guy... some other girl... some nameless, faceless person who we don't know shit about, except that they're not Jamison Kelly? Wake up, Marx! This isn't new ground you're blazing either. Just because Barnes and Angstat didn't cover it doesn't mean every one of these scenes hasn't been covered a hundred times. I know all of these stories and so do a million people. Why does Charlie Marx talking about them make them somehow fresh... like fresh evidence for exonerating a wrongly accused man? Wait... don't answer that... I'll tell you. It doesn't."

Charlie realized something in that moment. He'd been baited. And he'd bitten. Tyler was going to challenge him on his supposed sitcom writing because he wanted Charlie to give up what it was all pointing toward. Tyler sold him day one on the approach of challenging Barnes and Angstat's conclusions. That wasn't a problem for him. Tyler was trying to snake the big lead right out of Charlie's mouth. Marx made an on the spot decision to allow himself to be reeled in. He'd give Tyler something. He'd give him enough to back him off and shut him up. "Right, it doesn't. It doesn't offer anything fresh at all."

Tyler was surprised. "Well, someone is feeling honest tonight, aren't they? I have to say I was not expecting that from you."

Charlie said, "Oh, I think you were boss. I think you expect quite a lot out of me and that's why you know goddamn well I wasn't about to bet the entire pig farm on Derek and the Mintz family and whatever actually happened at that diner. You know me better than that. You know what I'm doing."

Tyler said, "Pretend for a minute that I don't. Tell me. Tell me what you're doing, Marx. Fuck... I might even be able to help you. Imagine that fantasy... a mentor actually helping his mentee. I know, seems like a foreign concept to someone like you. Go ahead... tell me something I don't know."

Charlie smiled, "Sure, why not. Okay, boss, here you go. I need some points of contention for my interview with Barnes and Angstat. Including parts of the story in my format that they ignored in their film will be a natural segue to introducing these parts of the story into the interview, and hopefully getting a rise out of those two idiots. But don't be a fool, Tyler. Realize this. The Mintz family, Derek, the Hummingbird... all of them... and the rest of it for that matter... all the retreads from the film... means to an end... all means to an end."

Tyler asked, "What end? It's time to put up or shut up, Marx... what end?"

Charlie answered, "The end that leads to the murderer of Cadence Moore."

Tyler was silent. Charlie heard him breathing and taking several long pulls on his bottle. Tyler wanted him to keep talking but Charlie remained silent too. Tyler was forced to talk first. He needed to know. "Charlie, you fuck. Tell me what you have. Tell me now. Give me a fucking name."

Charlie said, "I'll give you no such thing and I've already told you why."

Tyler needed it. "Then give me what you can give me."

How many emotions can swirl in the mind of one man at any one given time? Charlie didn't know the answer to that question but he knew what was going on in his head might give the world record a good run for its money. Here was the dormant lie, ready to awaken, ready to serve its purpose again. Here was also his friend and boss, drunk and vulnerable, and truly wanting to be let in on the secrets Charlie was supposedly dealing in. Guilt, anxiety, annoyance, caution, plotting, ego, remorse, and regret all swam around haphazardly like tadpoles in his brain. He finally said, "Hypothetically..."

Tyler grinned wide and downed another swig. He got him.

Charlie continued, "Let's say there's a guy. And let's say this guy knows some bad people. These bad people know other bad people. And let's say one of these bad people knows what happened to Cadence Moore. If such a bad person existed... they could potentially be located and interviewed. They could potentially have supplied missing information that, to this date, has not been public knowledge. Let's say this bad person lives in a cell. Let's also say that someone else lived in that cell at one point. Now, Tyler, do you think that the hypothetical person who hypothetically lived in that cell with another hypothetical bad person who hypothetically knew yet an additional bad person who hypothetically knew *me* was Jamison Kelly?"

Tyler was still smiling. He said, "Probably... not."

Charlie said, "Then you know what you need to know and when this is over you'll be glad I played this exactly how I played it. Until then, what do you say you let me get to work?"

Tyler wouldn't give Charlie the satisfaction of a pleasant end to this conversation. He knew he'd gotten everything he was going to get and for the moment, he would live with that. At least he knew his boy was on to something. If it wasn't true, then either Tyler's instincts were on the fritz or Charlie was a better liar than he'd ever imagined. For now, he'd bet on truth and operate accordingly. He said, "You're a piece of shit, Charlie... a memorable one at that, which is good because it will make it much easier for me to never forget any of this." Tyler hung up.

Charlie winced at the sound of the line clicking. But he smiled a second later. Operation "Shut Tyler Up and Keep Moving Forward" had been a rousing success.

- 2 -

UNDERGROUND PODCAST 3: (Official Transcript)
Part 1: The Incident

Charlie Marx's Underground Podcast: Episode 3 (Part 1). Original Drop Date: November 1, 2013. (Brought to you by United Way of Life, courtesy of Tyler Reubens... this program is funded and sponsored by WHHW, a subsidiary of Universal Public Radio)

(Narration by Charlie Marx) Now, my friends and fellow travelers, I feel it necessary to take a slight break from the college exploits of Cadence Moore, the relationship with her friends and her relationship with her family, as well as her romance with Jamison Kelly. I promise we will return to all this in due time.

But timing is everything dear listeners and to avoid the risk of destroying the tension of this podcast series, I fully believe we must deviate at this point and describe the incident of Cadence Moore's disappearance. We will still be having some in-depth discussion with Darlene and Stephanie, as well as Todd Barnes and Michael Angstat. In addition to all of that, we still have a lot of fascinating conversation with Jamison Kelly waiting in the wings for all of you to sink your wisdom-loving fangs into.

But now comes the time when it is imperative to bring out into the open, for all of those who don't yet know or haven't heard the story, the details about the incident that drew us all to the dance this evening. The nucleus of this incredible story lies in the actual disappearance of young Cadence Moore.

The circumstances surrounding it are still shrouded in mystery, but we have enough details that have been gleaned from police interviews and reports, the Barnes and Angstat film, and tons of random details from other sources to give you all a hearty helping of reality and truth on the particulars of this tragedy.

Let's summarize what we've already been through, giving you all time to make your own decisions and draw your own conclusions. Here's what we know:

Cadence Moore came from a dysfunctional family of the highest order. She used the financial support of her wealthy and demented father to forge a singing career, and scored a hit song on the college circuit with a charming little ditty called "Goldfish Chaser."

She rode a little success wave, and could have conceivably surfed that wave all the way into the national success shore, had it not been for the events that followed.

Cadence bravely entered Dusklight Falls University, dealing with the cold and suspicious welcoming of the student body. She made very close friends with some nice girls named Darlene and Stephanie and she got herself a steady boyfriend in the form of one Jamison Kelly.

All seemed to be going well for her when one night, after a drunken car ride during which she allegedly behaved inappropriately, Cadence engaged in a fight with her best friends and was dumped out of the vehicle, left to her own devices, drunk and miles away from her room. No one has ever seen her since.

So what do we know about the period of time *after* Cadence was kicked out of Darlene's '87 Oldsmobile? Unfortunately, up until the very recent time, the answer to that question is… very little.

Here is the generally accepted version of events, based on agreement from the largest number of people with intimate knowledge of the facts of this case. Cadence is believed to have exited Darlene's car around 12:30 a.m. on May 6. She most likely walked in circles of frustration for a few moments, and then sat on the curb adjacent to the Painted Sky Road and Neversink Road intersection.

She is thought to have spent about an hour there since the next sighting of someone resembling her occurred at 1:30 a.m. One can only speculate as to what she was doing. She could have been just sitting there with her head in her hands, maybe crying a little. Maybe she was still upset with Jamison and now with Darlene and Stephanie. She may have also just been trying to sober up a little before she made her next move.

Since we cannot know for sure what she was doing in the immediate moments after being ejected from the car, let's focus on what we do… almost conclusively… know for sure.

The place in which the next Cadence sighting probably occurred was Andy Notch's Mini-mart in southern Dusklight Falls. We will continue to use terms like "alleged" and "possible" when discussing assumed sightings of Cadence Moore after she was kicked out of Darlene Bethany's car. The reason for this is because none of these supposed sightings have ever been properly validated as a factual encounter with Cadence.

We will only be focusing on two such sightings… perhaps three, depending on how you interpret them since the multitude of alleged encounters with Cadence the morning of May 6 (everything from wild parties in which she is said to have stripped on the table for a crowd of unruly drunks, to fist fights she had in an alley with a teacher from school who'd given her an F on her last paper) have been completely discredited or shot full of holes by police. They do not even warrant further mention on our podcast.

The next most probable person to have seen Cadence on May 6 is a gentleman named Andy Notch, owner of the aforementioned mini-mart.

Andy Notch, a thirty-five-year-old self-proprietor, claims to have seen a young disheveled looking woman matching Cadence's description entering his store about 1:30 a.m. on the morning of May 6. We invited Andy, who these days owns a used book store in Pittsburgh, to offer his memories of this infamous evening.

The way Andy recalls things: he was immediately sympathetic to this young girl who entered his store. "It was pretty early into my third shift when I saw this young chick stumble in; she couldn't have been more than twenty. She had that puffy-eyed late night look you see with a lot of these girls in a college town. Some boyfriend dumped her or hit her… or maybe she drank a bit too much or snorted some coke and couldn't handle it.

"Either way, she looked real strung out and upset. I tried to talk nice to her and even offered to make her a sandwich on the house since she looked so damn bad, and believe me that isn't something I do often. For whatever reason, this girl didn't seem in the mood for conversation and just said thanks anyway and told me what brand of cigarettes she wanted me to ring up so she could get the hell out of there.

"I did what she asked, rang up the Pall Malls, and wished her the best. She meekly thanked me and then left my store. The last I saw of her, she turned left out the exit door. That sidewalk leads out to the dumpster out back, but there's also some parking and the streets beyond just over my little patch of grass. So, what became of her after she bought the cigarettes… I can't say."

We wanted to know about any details Andy was able to provide us. These were questions already asked by law enforcement, Barnes and Angstat, and many others, but we wanted to see if Andy had anything new to offer.

I first asked if he had any recollection of how Cadence, or whoever this mystery girl was, actually paid for her cigarettes. Andy replied, "Normally I wouldn't have the slightest idea since people are coming in and out all night long. But in this case, like I told the cops years ago, I do remember how this chick paid. She paid with crumbled up dollar bills which were stained blue. That was odd enough to remember."

If the girl had paid with a credit card, it would have been easy to verify whether she was, in fact, Cadence Moore. But since she paid cash, there is just no way to conclusively say who she was. Some convincing evidence is to be found in the fact that Andy Notch recalled the bright blue stretch pants she was wearing at the time, which were also commented on and confirmed by Darlene Bethany and Stephanie Chambers.

As per the memories of several people who came in contact with her that night, Cadence was wearing a pair of metallic blue stretch pants. So, when Andy Notch describes the 'shiny blue jobs she was sporting which probably dyed the money the same color,' one would assume he did very likely encounter Cadence Moore that night.

Certainly, this blue money could have been checked by police for fingerprints, couldn't it? Unfortunately, as is normal in his business and in transactions throughout the rest of the morning, Andy Notch apparently handed all that blue money to a random customer when making change so it, if it ever existed, was not available for analysis by police.

In pursuit of verifying the assumption that the cigarette girl was Cadence, we asked Andy if he could describe her features. He already commented on her puffy eyes and disheveled state, but we wanted to know if her physical description, beyond the pants she was wearing, matched Cadence to a tee.

Andy laid it out for us. "Yeah, I remember her well. I couldn't do this with any customer, but between the blue money and the fact that cops swarmed my joint and asked me a million questions within two days, the memories of this girl stick out brighter than all the rest. I can tell you what she looked like. She... not to be a pig or anything... but the chick was built like a damned brick shithouse with flowy blonde hair and bright blue eyes. That's why her eyes looked so pronounced and puffy... they were so blue that every single blood vessel and red swell stood out like a sore thumb.

"Of course, I do also remember the jerk who threw an egg at my window a few minutes later. He was somebody I thought I recognized. A guy who looked just like him would come around every few weeks, and he'd always ask for food. I'd always refuse. Like I said, I'm not usually as generous as I was with the young chick that night. I guess when I refused that bum the last time, he got all pissed off."

We will discuss this 'jerk' fellow who egged the mini-mart in a moment. However, let's discuss Andy's description of the girl who bought the cigarettes, blonde mane of hair and bright blue eyes. Anyone who has ever seen a Cadence Moore music video or even a photograph of the girl would be able to tell you that this description, if not of Cadence, could have been describing her twin, since the bright blue eyes were a trademark of the young singer and she did have a long blonde mane of hair.

Since no one listening to our podcast this evening is a fool, it seems logical to go on the assumption that Cadence *did* run into Andy Notch in his mini-mart the morning of May 6. If this is the case, then we should have a trail to follow and from the mini-mart we know she must have gone somewhere else.

But without the ability to verify, number one, that it was 100% for sure Cadence Moore who entered Andy Notch's store, and number two, what became of her afterward, it makes this trail a rather cold one to follow.

What we do know is that Andy Notch, being a very economical fellow, did not have a security camera so there is no footage of Cadence checking out at his register. Lucky for all of us, and also for those of you who know where I'm going with this, (mind-numbingly frustrating for all of us) the security camera was running two blocks down at the Tarynco gas station.

Sadly, two blocks is a long way when it comes to security camera clarity. There does exist a very hazy and blurry video, taken by the gas station camera, of the side lot of Andy Notch's Mini-mart. What this camera picked up has been played on countless news programs over the last ten years. This hazy film is one of the most viewed pieces of documentary footage since the Zapruder masterpiece just before the triple underpass.

So, just what does this video show us, and what light can it shed on Cadence Moore's disappearance? Likely, none at all, but that will not stop us from discussing it since this scratchy and blurry security film has become as synonymous with this case as Dusklight Falls and "Goldfish Chaser."

- 3 -

The Tarynco security camera is time stamped. The first footage of interest picked up by the camera begins at 1:45 a.m. on May 6. Now this is very weird because Cadence is generally accepted to have entered Andy Notch's Mini-mart at 1:30 a.m., almost to the minute.

Remember the mystery girl assumed to be Cadence had walked around a few moments and was also offered the free sandwich before she bought the cigarettes. This is important because even though there was no credit card transaction when the girl bought her cigarettes, there was a register history requested by the Dusklight Falls Police Department, and that register history shows a purchase of $2.80, the exact purchase price of a pack of Pall Malls at the time, taking place at 1:34 a.m.

Now, if this is true, and if the girlish silhouette shown on the Tarynco security camera leaving Andy Notch's Mini-mart on May 6 is, in fact, Cadence or at least whoever it was that bought those Pall Malls with blue dollar bills, then how could she have exited the mini-mart between 1:35 a.m. and 1:36 a.m. and be picked up on the Tarynco security camera leaving the store almost ten minutes later?

It just doesn't make any sense. To complicate matters further, there is no person shown leaving the store at all between 1:35 a.m. and 1:36 a.m. on May 6. Now, granted the Tarynco camera only filmed one side of Andy Notch's Mini-mart, so the Pall Mall customer could have gone out the other end and not been picked up on the camera at all. The reasons why most people believe the person shown in the footage is Cadence Moore are interesting. First, the silhouette (and that is truly all it is… to say it was anything more would be wishful thinking) does resemble the way Cadence is said to have looked at the time. The girlish figure's legs look tight and thin, no sign of baggy pants or a skirt. Either the figure was bottomless or wearing very tight pants… something like blue stretch pants would fit the bill in this case, as would any pair of stretch pants or very tight jeans.

Second, Tarynco franchise owner Ashley Prince was interviewed by DFPD and offered a statement indicating that the time stamp on the camera was not accurate and was off by as little as five minutes and as much as eight minutes, depending on whose watch you were looking at to compare with.

So, if we take the most extreme estimate of eight minutes fast, the camera would have picked up the figure at 1:37 a.m. real time, a solid three minutes after the girl exchanged her blue money for the Pall Malls. So, what was she doing for three minutes before exiting the store? We asked Andy if he remembered her lingering around, perhaps looking at the magazine rack, or maybe touching up her make-up. Andy Notch answered honestly, "I can't be sure, and if I say anything to the contrary, I'd be making it up for the most part. I know she paid with blue money. I know she had long blonde hair and bright blue eyes. I know she looked all strung out. And for some strange reason, I remember her positively turning left out of the door when she exited. Could she have gone to the bathroom in the back before she left? Did she hang around a minute to check out the *Twinkies* or the magazines? I really don't know... I'm not saying it didn't happen... I just don't remember."

So, let us go on the assumption that the girl was Cadence, and she did hang out a few minutes in Andy's store before exiting at 1:37 a.m. The door Andy refers to when he remembers her exiting to the left is in fact the door picked up by the Tarynco camera.

It is important to note that no one in the twenty minutes preceding the time Cadence was allegedly buying her cigarettes was filmed entering the mini-mart from this door. So, even if it was Cadence who was filmed leaving, she exited from a different door than she entered. If it was not Cadence, then whoever it was also did not exit the same door they entered and Andy doesn't remember anyone else at all, for what that is worth.

If the person filmed leaving the mini-mart was in fact Cadence Moore, then what does the Tarynco video actually tell us about what may have happened to her?

- 4 -

The following is a complete time line of the Tarynco camera on May 6, 2002 (factoring in the eight-minute margin of error) from 1:37 a.m. when it picked up the girlish figure leaving Andy Notch's store until 1:50 a.m. when it filmed a girlish or womanish figure entering the frame briefly, only to be dragged off camera abruptly, never to return.

At 1:37 a.m., a girlish figure appearing to be wearing a tight pair of pants and a tank top or tight T-shirt (also consistent with Cadence's reported wardrobe on the evening in question) is filmed leaving Andy Notch's Mini-mart, heading toward the dumpster and the patch of grass leading to another parking lot, and beyond that, Dallas Boulevard (one of the main drags in Dusklight Falls).

At 1:39 a.m., two children (assumed to be kids since they were half as tall as the girlish figure and jumping around in play) are filmed walking down the sidewalk toward Andy's mini-mart, shortly thereafter followed by two adults thought to be the parents of the children. The four of them enter Andy Notch's store.

At 1:41 a.m., the same four people, two adults and two children, walk up the same sidewalk on which they entered from, presumably returning to their car. The two adults are carrying a bag in each hand and the children each are carrying something that resembles a cola or bottled water.

At 1:43 a.m., a husky figure, possibly a homeless man or woman, lumbers up to the window of Andy Notch's store. This person bangs on the window... waits a moment... then motions with their hands. A moment later, the person puts both hands in the air and shakes their head.

At 1:44 a.m., this same husky figure throws an object at the store window, possibly an egg or a small stone. Some very faint residue can be said to appear on the window of the mini-mart. The person gestures once again in an aggressive posture and then skulks away in a frustrated manner, back the way they came toward the dumpster and the parking lot beyond.

No activity is seen at the mini-mart location until a strange flurry of motion appears on camera beginning at 1:50 a.m. At 1:50 a.m., a girl or woman—it's impossible to tell which since only half the body is ever seen on the film—briefly enters the frame and then is jerked back suddenly.

A viewer of the film can see a slender arm and leg, as well as a flip of long hair. This two-to-three-second period of film has convinced a great number of people that the actual abduction of Cadence Moore was caught on video.

There are a few problems with this theory. The first of which is the fact that there is no way to conclusively say this figure is Cadence Moore; in fact, there is no way to say for sure that it's even the same girlish figure filmed leaving the store at 1:37 a.m.

The second problem is one of logic. Why would this girl, even assuming it was Cadence, come back to the mini-mart, thirteen minutes after she exited? She already bought cigarettes and left. Why come back?

Now, some might agree there are just too many questions here and put the suspicion to rest with those two points; however, something very odd must be added to the story here. When police checked this area two days after Cadence was reported missing, they found a pack of Pall Malls, with one cigarette missing, behind the dumpster at the top of the sidewalk from Andy Notch's Mini-mart.

Police tested for prints on the pack and unfortunately found nothing, so the light rain that occurred around 9:00 a.m. on May 6 obviously rendered any prints that may have been on the pack useless.

Did Cadence Moore, or whoever the girl who bought the Pall Malls actually was, drop her newly-bought smokes in a clumsy drunken mishap, and then attempt to go back to the mini-mart to purchase more?

If this happened, and for simplicity's sake, we'll just call the girl Cadence as we continue the discussion, then one could reasonably assume it was Cadence Moore caught on the Tarynco video, walking toward the mini-mart side entrance door before being dragged off by some unseen force.

This leads to at least one obvious conclusion. The homeless man or woman, or whoever this husky figure was who panhandled, threw a rock or an egg at the mini-mart window, and then flipped off Andy Notch before storming off, was still in the vicinity when Cadence returned to the mini-mart, presumably to buy more cigarettes.

After all, the husky, supposed homeless figure was last seen at 1:44 a.m., only six minutes before the girl or woman was dragged out of the camera's view.

Was this person hanging out by the dumpster, scrounging for food, when they saw a pretty young girl show up? Did they decide on the spot that they were still hungry, but this time for something other than a bag of chips or some beef jerky? Did this homeless person abduct Cadence and do something terrible to her?

Okay, I realize this is a stretch and supported by only weak circumstantial evidence, if you can even call it that. But let's assume this is exactly what happened. This would be an easy solution to the mystery... the homeless ghoul snatched up a drunken, confused girl, robbed her or molested her, and then killed her.

So, if that's what occurred, why would we have been faced with this relentless mystery that has lasted more than a decade? Well, I'll tell you friends right now why this scenario has more holes in it than a flyswatter.

Number one... there was no... I repeat... no blood found anywhere near Andy Notch's Mini-mart. If this homeless person really did drag her off the sidewalk and kill her, then why didn't police find any blood anywhere near the scene? I mean, let's not forget, the person was presumably some kind of homeless hobo, so it's not like there was a getaway van idling a few yards away for him to jump into.

And if there was no getaway car, the hobo would have had to drag Cadence through the streets, kicking and screaming, in the process of bringing her back to some hidden lair in the sewers. Common sense would dictate that someone, anyone, at nearly two in the morning would have witnessed this scene and reported it to the police.

Now, if one wishes to stretch the bounds of reasonable conjecture even further, let's just say for the sake of argument that this person dragged Cadence off the sidewalk and brought her back to the dumpster where he assaulted her and then strangled her to death.

The next step for this murderer would be to discard the body. But wait, maybe the hobo just didn't care. Maybe he figured he got what he wanted from this poor girl and just left the scene. It was almost a solid two days before the authorities did any kind of exhaustive search of the area. The hobo could have made it to New Jersey on foot by that point.

Okay, so we're assuming the hobo makes it away scot free... but we're forgetting something. Why didn't the police find Cadence's body? We know the hobo couldn't have dragged her away to some sewer lair without being seen. So, he would have had to leave her in the dumpster, right? Well then why wasn't she still in there when police did their search?

May 6, 2002 was a Monday. Trash day in the borough of Dusklight Falls happens to fall on Mondays and Thursdays. So, if Cadence was killed and thrown in a trash dumpster in the very early morning hours of May 6, then we know about five hours later her body and the contents of the dumpster would have been picked up by the garbage truck and taken to the local Lime Street Landfill, the place where all Dusklight Falls waste eventually ends up.

It just so happens that the DFPD actually followed the same line of thinking that we just ran down here. They believed that the "homeless person" who caused a slight commotion outside the window of Andy Notch's Mini-mart was a definite person of interest.

They also naturally followed the circumstantial evidence that we just did and decided it was very likely Cadence was abducted near the scene and then disposed of in the dumpster, where she would have been picked up by the garbage trucks on Monday morning.

The DFPD, led by Detective Meghan Cocuzza, questioned all involved including Andy Notch, Ashley Prince of Tarynco, and Jordan Philips, the driver of the garbage truck which made the pickup outside Notch's store.

Andy gave the DFPD the breakdown of events he has already rehashed for us here. Ashley Prince guided Meghan Cocuzza through the timeline that was picked up by the Tarynco security camera. Jordan Philips told the police he did not notice anything odd about the mini-mart pickup; no strange sounds, no weird feelings, no anything.

Sadly, and frustratingly, the DFPD did not elect at the time to interview the security guard or sanitation workers from the landfill and incredibly did not do any kind of search or investigation there in the days following the disappearance.

Only after three months had passed since the disappearance, due to pressure from the local public, did the police perform an exhaustive search of the landfill premises, and when they did, they found nothing.

Now, as I mentioned, the Lime Street Landfill we're discussing is the destination for all the garbage picked up around Dusklight Falls. It's not like whatever was picked up on May 6 would not still have been there, somewhere near the middle, covered with three months' worth of soil and foam, but still there nonetheless.

The question is, would the search team really have dug as far as they needed to find every bit of garbage dumped on May 6? The odds of this have been questioned by a great many people over the years.

Regardless of whether their search effort was as exhaustive as claimed, the search team ended up finding nothing. Most will agree this three-month delay was a major bungle on the part of the DFPD, almost as glaring as their decision to not test the tiny blood smears in Jamison Kelly's car.

To her credit, Detective Meghan Cocuzza has kindly agreed to be part of our program tonight and explain where the DFPD was coming from at the time.

"The honest truth is… in the first few days at least, we had bigger fish to fry. In those crucial days, we had so many leads from so many people who claimed to have seen a blond-haired girl on May 6, and these people were *absolutely sure* it was Cadence Moore. I can't tell you how many times people claimed they would have bet their lives on the fact that they saw this girl, or talked to her, or had sex with her, or what have you.

"We had all kinds of weird people claiming to have the missing link that would tie everything together. Nearly all of these stories turned out to be bullshit which we were able to ascertain within a few minutes of speaking to these people and seeing their stories fall apart after a few questions from police who had more answers than they did.

"But, my point is… we were coming from a point of zero knowledge and that meant we had to follow each of these leads and devote at least some time to them.

"Unfortunately, once we realized there was no blood or physical evidence at the mini-mart scene, and that includes hair, bodily fluids, and everything else; and also, once we'd questioned the driver of the truck and he claimed to have heard nothing odd when emptying the dumpster, our team made the calculated decision to move on. When I say our team, I must clarify this, which I will do in a moment.

"First, as far as the landfill goes, it's important to point out that we did search it eventually and we found nothing. If someone dumped a body there on May 6, we would have found it three months later. We did an exhaustive search and would not have missed human remains; I can assure you of that.

"But backing up to the time immediately following the disappearance, we moved on from the landfill scene and pursued Jamison Kelly and his blood-stained car. That to me was the smoking gun in the whole case. And to my great irritation and regret, we didn't investigate that properly either.

"I must be clear on this. I think my superiors in the DFPD were scared of this case. They preferred it to be of an unsolvable nature, with deniability on our part about whether she actually disappeared in our jurisdiction or somewhere else after being picked up by some random person. We never found a body, so for all anyone knows for sure, Cadence Moore was driven right out of town that night and is still walking the Earth to this day.

"This was much more attractive to them than making it clear the murder of a celebrity happened right within the city limits of Dusklight Falls. How high up the pressure to squash it came from, I'll never know, but pressure was coming from somewhere and it was immense pressure.

"When we didn't test the tiny smears of blood in Jamison Kelly's car, to me the whole investigation became a bit of a joke. But they all knew what was going on. They knew this was a case of love gone wrong. Yet we didn't test the blood and we stopped pursuing Kelly altogether when he offered his very shaky alibi, backed up by a few friends, and we didn't have the blood evidence to even prove him a liar.

"This supports my opinion that the DFPD wanted to squash the case. I believe this based on what my superiors directly told me, and based on the fact that they threw red tape at me for over two months before public outcry for justice and the bad media coverage made it impossible for them not to search the landfill.

"They didn't want to do it! They would have never searched that landfill site if their hands hadn't been forced. Like I said, the first few days we had more pressing matters. But, after a week, I was already hounding them to search Lime Street. They finally caved in and did the search.

"The whole time they'd been telling the media we were searching everywhere, even the sewers. That never happened and the only places we searched were above ground; that is until the landfill three months later.

"I don't work for DFPD anymore, which is why I'm so candid in my comments to you and your program. But I *was* a member of that team and I know the vibe in the station was that this was a passion crime, simple as that. Yet when the time came to prove this assumption, my superiors looked the other way and decided to put this case in the morgue so it could slowly rot over the next few years.

"Move on to the next crisis, and put this one on ice. Except for a word or two, I have just recounted verbatim what I was told by more than one superior officer at the time. If that doesn't tell you they wanted this thing to disappear, then I don't know what would.

"What it comes down to is this. We never found the body in the landfill. I personally oversaw that search and believe we would have if it was there, even three months later. So, if Jamison Kelly killed Cadence Moore, as I believe he did, her body was disposed of somewhere else... maybe buried in the woods, maybe driven to another location by an accomplice; God only knows. But, we never found her so it's all speculation at this point."

Detective Meghan Cocuzza, formerly of the DFPD, offered us a wealth of interesting and valuable insight which I assure you faithful and sharp-eared listeners, we will return to as we move along here.

However, we still have to address some other possibilities that revolve around the mini-mart scene and the security camera. There are still some additional theories that need to be examined. Not to mention, we've only discussed the first credible alleged Cadence sighting after she was kicked out of Darlene's car. There were more to follow and we must look at those as well.

- 5 -

The next theory we shall examine here which has gotten a ton of play in conspiracy circles and was part of the Barnes and Angstat film, *Moore to the Story* (although not in a good way) revolves around the family of four who entered the mini-mart at 1:39 a.m. after Cadence left, and who came away with a few bags and some bottled water or cola for the kids.

This family was picked up by Tarynco security cameras and unlike the Pall Mall girl who paid blue money for cigarettes, this family paid their bill with a credit card.

It turned out that this family was actually the vacationing Mintz family from Pittsburgh, on their way to Vero Beach, Florida, who happened to make a sightseeing side trip to Dusklight Falls to see the spooky mist-ridden falls in the early hours of the morning. The transaction history revealed that Misty Mintz, wife of Jared Mintz, had paid with her credit card for a few wrapped subs and some soft drinks for her family on their road trip.

The timing of their entrance and exit to and from Andy Notch's store brings with it some questions that have to be addressed. First off, did the family see the mysterious Pall Mall girl leaving the store as they made their way from their car in the rear parking lot of the store to the mini-mart itself?

Secondly, could it actually have been Misty Mintz who was filmed being dragged out of frame on the Tarynco camera? After all, the family would not have been far out of the area at 1:50 a.m., and it's possible they forgot an item at the mini-mart and returned to purchase it.

Were Misty and Jared simply fooling with each other? Is the famed footage of the girl being dragged out of frame simply a husband and wife joking around, delirious from driving too long?

Third, the fact that this family was in this general area at the exact time the abduction of Cadence Moore very possibly took place, makes them a person... well, people of interest. Did they offer a lift to a strung-out looking young girl? Were they really a car load of creeps who decided to randomly snatch Cadence out of thin air and kidnap her?

While this last theory seems extremely ridiculous, we must leave no stone unturned. So, for the sake of clearing this portion of the mystery up once and for all, we at *Underground Podcast* reached out to the Mintz family for answers, which they provided for us.

Unfortunately, the Mintz family no longer exists as it did in 2002. Jared and Misty Mintz divorced a year after their cross-country road trip and brief foray into Dusklight Falls. Their two children, Alexis and Austin, are both now nineteen- and twenty-one-year-old college students who have no recollection whatsoever of the night in question. The fracturing of the Mintz family has also had some *very* interesting effects on their memories. Both Jared and Misty remember events from that evening extremely differently, which leaves many studiers of the case baffled as to what their exact involvement, if any, was.

Before we hear from the Mintz clan, it is appropriate, at this time, to review the conclusions Todd Barnes and Michael Angstat drew from their presence in this story. It's simple, they don't believe that Jared and Misty *were* present in the story. Barnes and Angstat figured the Mintz family for a couple of liars who made up the whole story for attention.

The reason they gave for interviewing Misty and Jared at length for their film was apparently just to discredit them and eliminate their whole story from the evening's events. They believe that aside from buying some hoagies from the same store Cadence Moore had probably been in a few minutes earlier, they had no connection to her whatsoever. That would mean Barnes and Angstat could move right from the mini-mart scene to Cadence returning to one of the dorms (either by Jamison picking her up or by some other means.)

Before hearing from Jared and Misty, it's also important to make one note about the 'Cadence murdered in the dorm' theory. Darlene Bethany, Cadence's roommate, stayed at her boyfriend Steve Willis's dorm the morning of May 6 and would not have been present to verify whether or not Jamison Kelly brought Cadence back there.

Darlene also wouldn't have been there to verify if Jamison was waiting in the dorm all along and killed Cadence when she returned. It is known for a fact, confirmed by Darlene, Stephanie, and Jamison himself, that he did have a key to the room and could have entered it if he pleased.

Barnes and Angstat, in their embracing of this theory (Jamison killing

Cadence in the dorm after either picking her up on the street or waiting there until she got back) have chosen to ignore myriad other details, including a credible sighting of Cadence at the Hummingbird diner and an alibi that Jamison had which is hard to argue with. But, we'll get to that in time.

So, what does any of this have to do with the Mintz family, and why would Barnes and Angstat have shrugged off their remembrances? Well, the problem with those remembrances is that Jared and Misty might as well have been through different evenings in parallel universes because their individual recounting sessions of their time in Dusklight Falls simply do not coexist with one another in any rational way.

Let's start with Misty Mintz. These days Misty is a medical transcriptionist living in Exton, Pennsylvania. She was legally divorced from Jared Mintz in very early 2004, following a several month-long separation. She has since remarried and lives with her new husband, Ryan Kozuch, and their child, Lindsey. She shared custody of Alexis and Austin with Jared Mintz until the two children were of age and could decide who they wanted to spend their time with.

In her interview with us and in the conversations she had with Barnes and Angstat, she states that the family did make a side trip to Dusklight Falls to get a good look at the falls in their creepy wee-hour state, with spray rising and moonlight glistening. They were on their way to Vero Beach, Florida and wanted to see all the great sights along the way.

After seeing the Falls in all their moonlight glory, Misty remembers the family was hungry and came upon Andy Notch's Mini-mart. They bought sandwiches and drinks and then returned to their car. She describes in great detail seeing a young blonde-haired girl wearing blue leotards and a black tank top pacing back and forth in the parking lot behind the mini-mart.

Neither Misty nor Jared had any idea who Cadence Moore was as they were unfamiliar with her brief success as a college singing sensation. To Jared and Misty, she was just some lonely lost girl. They both agree on this point.

Misty felt sorry for the girl because she looked troubled and lost. Jared allegedly at this point suggested that they offer the young girl a ride. However, understandably, Misty says she was hesitant because of the two young children they had in the back seat, and not having a clue who this troubled girl was or what she may have been wrapped up in. Misty said she convinced Jared it was best to move along, and move along they did.

In this way, Misty's story matches Barnes and Angstat pretty closely. They claim to believe the Mintz family probably never saw Cadence at all which makes their version of events free of complications. Considering they were in the vicinity of the mini-mart within two minutes of each other, Cadence and the Mintz family not crossing paths is not an assumption one can make with any kind of confidence.

Back to Misty. In an effort to avoid moving into territory that was too personal and may have had nothing to do with the Cadence mystery, I asked Misty if it would be okay for me to inquire about the nature of her split with Jared.

To me, and to many others who have followed this case, the fact that Jared and Misty Mintz split up a seemingly happy marriage a year after the events that occurred in Dusklight Falls on the night they just randomly happened to be passing through, seemed just a tad bit coincidental, considering that, at the very least, they encountered Cadence Moore (or her doppelganger) pacing around a parking lot on the same night she went missing forever.

Misty said she understood my reasons for asking and she was okay with responding. "You know what... it's the strangest thing. I remember this girl like it was yesterday and I remember my exact words to Jared when he suggested we give her a ride. I said, on the off chance that she's not crazy or on drugs, there can be no wholesome reason why a girl her age is wandering around at two in the morning. I feel bad if she's in trouble, but we have children in this car who need our protection more than she does. Keep driving, Jared.

"But, Jared was persistent and he said we shouldn't be those typical scared Americans who think every lost soul on the roadside is a serial killer. He even brought the kids into it and said it would be good for them to see their parents reaching out to help someone in need. I emphatically told him that if he picked that girl up, he would be gaining one passenger and losing another… me. So, Jared huffed and puffed and gave me the silent treatment, but we moved along and that's the last we ever saw of the girl in the shiny blue leotards.

"A little later, we get a call from an officer of the DFPD asking us what we saw that night and grilling us about why we were there so late with young children, did we pick up a passenger along the way, and do we know anything about this girl's disappearance. It was really a complete interrogation.

"I told them we knew nothing, but we did see someone that matched Cadence's description. I told them the truth and said my husband wanted to pick her up, but I wouldn't let him. Then we drove on and continued our vacation."

I tried to politely remind Misty that she hadn't actually answered my question. Why the break-up of their marriage so soon after this family vacation? I knew the answer in my mind, but as a good investigative journalist, I wanted to hear it straight from the source. I probed Misty again and she elaborated on the specifics of the divorce.

"I was getting to that, Mr. Marx. As I told Mr. Barnes when he spoke to me, what really shook the foundation of our marriage and the reason why I just couldn't trust or believe in Jared anymore was because he lied. He lied so terribly, I plainly couldn't fathom it. And, in the process of lying, he put our whole family in jeopardy. If it were true that we had picked her up, then we would have conceivably been the last people to see her alive; therefore, we'd be suspects in her disappearance.

"Remember also, the national news story was just exploding at this point and was all over the place. That is why I committed the details of this night to my memory. I just couldn't brush it off like it was another pit stop on our vacation. We came within a few yards of a girl who disappeared forever, and may have been the last ones to lay eyes on her besides the person who accosted her.

"With all this blazing on the news, and the fact that we had done nothing more than look at Cadence Moore, if it was *her* to begin with, then I ask you, Charlie… why would anyone voluntarily bring that kind of heat, attention, and suspicion on their own family?"

I told Misty Mintz that I did not have an answer for her that could explain it. If Jared was indeed lying, it would seem a very stupid maneuver, and it would absolutely have brought strong suspicion down on him and Misty.

Because this is such a ridiculous thing to do, and considering that no one in their right mind would actually do it, my natural tendency is to entertain what Jared had to say and not eliminate the possibility that it was Misty who was lying, possibly out of fear for her family if they were tied to the disappearance of a famous young singer.

Was Misty Mintz lying about the evening's events so her family would be as far removed from the case as possible? Let's turn our attention to the statements made by Jared Mintz about May 6 and his encounter with Cadence Moore. When both sides are heard, I will leave it to you listeners to decide which person you find more convincing.

Jared Mintz recalls, "This is a really awkward period for me to talk about, because the direct aftermath of these events led to my marriage ending and also to me being seen as a possible murderer. I want to be clear with you guys, my honesty in telling this story has not helped me one bit. I know my former wife in the past has accused me of being a liar who made the whole thing up to get some fame and attention; but, it's not true.

"The truth is, the ties my family and I have to this case have really fucked up my whole life. I never made a dime from telling this story. Every interview I've done has been on a volunteer basis when I was asked to comment. I also have not been given any endorsement deals from Nike or guest TV spots, so I'm guessing that this fame I so ferociously desired didn't exactly work out for me.

"The truth is, I told everyone exactly what happened that night, including the police; and, a decade later I told it to Todd Barnes and Michael Angstat who made an even bigger circus out of the whole thing. And now, if you need me to tell you, I'll tell you too. I have never been afraid of the truth."

I thanked Jared for his direct comments and told him for the sake of this podcast and listeners who have not been familiar with the Barnes and Angstat movie, it would be best if he could run through his story again. He agreed and began telling me what happened that night… from his perspective.

"Okay, first and foremost, I'm not blind, Charlie... I've seen the film and I know what my ex-wife Misty has stated about what happened. I'm here to tell you... Misty has her own reasons for lying... but she is still lying. Make no mistake, I understand her desire to leave the family out of it, but a lie is not something we should ever feel the need to resort to. If what goes out there into the media is ugly, but it is still part of our truth, then there is no shame in taking responsibility for it, especially when you consider this whole thing happened because I was trying to give a girl a simple ride back to her home. Isn't that what most people would do?"

I felt the need to be honest with Jared on this point and tell him no, most people probably wouldn't have done that. There is a reason why folks these days are scared to pick up people on the side of the road. You just don't know what will happen to you and it could mean your life. It's not like that hasn't been the case before. When you consider that they did have two kids in the car, I had to tell Jared that if what he says is true, I think he made a risky and dangerous decision.

Jared replied, Yeah, well... you know what, I just wasn't raised like that. I wasn't raised to mistrust everyone. I was raised to give a fellow a chance and unless he proves otherwise, you treat him as a decent man and with the respect a decent man... or woman deserves. So, when it came to the girl in the parking lot, this is, more or less, the way it all went down. We walked into the mini-mart to grab a few snacks. We came back to the car and that was the first time, once we were in the car and ready to drive away, that we saw the girl I assume was Cadence Moore... since the girl we saw seemed to match the description that was beamed out all over the place a little while later.

"Anyway, we saw her sort of pacing back and forth and stumbling a little. I said to Misty that we should pick this girl up. We should give her a ride home since she looks like she's having a rough night.

"As you know, my wife was not into that idea at all. She basically threatened to leave the car and start walking with the kids to the nearest bus station if I dared to pick this girl up."

I had to say, at this point in the interview, I was amazed by how close the stories of Misty and Jared were until this very point. If someone was lying, you'd think they'd be lying from moment one… but not in this case. Here is where it goes off the rails.

Jared continued. "I thought about just driving away to keep the peace in my marriage, but I felt so bad for this girl. I don't know how else to say it… she just seemed so… depressed. Before I drove off, I leaned my head out and said, hey there… you all right, sweetheart? Do you need any help?" Well, she must have taken me to be some kind of creepy old stalker because she started walking away. Just like that, she took one look at me and split. What I did next really pissed my wife off. I stopped the car, put it in park, and then got out and followed the girl. I wanted her to know we were just trying to help. I figured if she could see the kids in the car, she might feel comfortable and let us actually help her."

Even though I already knew this story, as I was listening to Jared recount the tale, I was shocked by how inappropriately he acted. Yelling at a drunken young girl and then chasing her? It all seemed like madness and a sure way to scare a person. I asked Jared if, looking back, he found his own behavior to be strange.

Jared answered. "To most people, I guess I did act weird. But honestly, like I said before, I just wasn't raised to fear people. I saw a kid who needed some help, or at least looked like she did, and I reached out to help. Going after her may not have been the brightest move, but I just wanted to catch her and show her we were safe and could get her home.

"What ended up happening, she got up to the sidewalk next to the minimart. I grabbed her by the arm and pulled her very gently toward me. I told her it's okay, I want to help you… I'm not a crazy person or anything. My family is right down there in the car. I just wanted to offer you a ride because you looked lost.

"The girl… Cadence, I assume… was freaked out but she did come a tiny bit closer to me and then froze. I pointed toward the lot to my car. She followed my finger with her eyes and saw my family sitting there waiting. By this point, Misty was out of the car looking up at us shaking her head. She was so livid with me over this. But Cadence, or whoever this young lady was, agreed to walk down to the car and check out the situation. I think seeing Misty comforted her since serial killers didn't usually travel with their irritated, bitching wives in a beat up old station wagon.

"We got down there and Misty, despite how angry she was with me, asked the girl if she was all right. She offered some of her sandwich if the girl was hungry. Eventually, the girl conceded to let us help her. We drove her toward the campus but she asked to be dropped off at a diner... I remember it as the Cardinal or the Blue Jay or something, but I guess the Hummingbird was the actual name. She said she wanted to go there because she was hungry. Strange since she refused half the sandwich Misty offered her. I just figured she felt weird about taking food from people she didn't know.

"She said she'd call a friend from there and then go home. So, we dropped her at the diner and then drove away to finish our road trip. We never saw her after that."

Jared and Misty tell very different tales. My gut tells me that Jared's story is just too out there and makes him look very bad, so there has to be some truth to it. Otherwise, why would someone lie and make themselves look like a creep and an obvious suspect in the process. Almost everything Jared did in this story seems a little off and casts a negative light on his character. For that reason alone, I tend to believe him. So, the question becomes... well, who are we kidding... the question becomes three questions.

Number one, why are the stories of these two spouses so different, and whoever is lying, why do they feel the need to do so?

Number two, if Jared is telling the truth, where did Cadence go after being dropped off at the Hummingbird Diner in Dusklight Falls? And, supposedly, when she got there, Cadence phoned someone which also raises questions about which friend she would have phoned since she was not Miss Popular on this particular evening.

Number three, if Misty is telling the truth, then why did Jared lie? Is he somehow connected to this on a more sinister level? Did he pack his family into a hotel a few miles down the road and then come back to hunt for the young lady? That can be put to rest because credit card receipts and guest registers at every hotel within thirty miles were checked and the Mintz family does not show up anywhere.

We can even pull a number four out of this. Why did Barnes and Angstat assume that the Hummingbird was not the destination in which Cadence and the Mintz family parted ways? What evidence exists to support the theory that the Mintz family drove Cadence all the way back to campus? Perhaps none. Perhaps it is possible they just drove off without interacting with her as Misty claims. We will be discussing this with Barnes and Angstat a little later in our series.

Let me get my opinion out there now since these details and accounts from several different folks on this dark night in Dusklight Falls really just confuse the whole issue. I share this opinion not as an ill-informed emotional response since I have followed this case as close as anyone since it first broke nationally; and, it is very dear to my heart. I think a smart person can connect the dots here.

I believe Misty Mintz is lying. Detective Meghan Cocuzza also believed this and the DFPD went with John's story, considering the Hummingbird owner Todd Crist's account backs it up to a large extent. It seems strange that Misty would be willing to appear in a documentary film and a podcast about a case she was lying about simply to distance herself from it. Why would someone do this?

I have to believe Misty Mintz feels that it would have been best if she told her husband Jared to keep driving the morning of May 6. She didn't do this or at least did not succeed in her attempt to do this and what happened, happened… period.

Now, why hang on to a lie for over a decade? Once Misty made her false statements to police, she was forced to back these statements up since, if she backed off on them, she'd allegedly be considered a liar and a suspect which is the exact thing she was trying to avoid.

So, she appears in the Barnes and Angstat film and on our podcast. Why would a woman seek out this type of attention if she knew her whole story was a lie? I believe strongly that Misty is terrified at the notion of being associated with the murder of a young woman and she never wanted to deal with this in the first place.

But now that it has happened and she is involved, she feels the need to back up her prior statements and continue to distance herself from any guilt or suspicion while trying to make Jared appear as a glory hound and a liar. Again, this is an opinion… not an outright accusation on my part.

But let's just say ol' Charlie has called this one correctly. Let's assume Misty is lying for valid reasons and justifiable motives, but lying nonetheless. That would mean that Jared Mintz is telling the truth. He *did* yell out to Cadence Moore in a parking lot and she ran away from him.

Preposterously, Jared ran after her and pulled her back toward him to show her that he was safe and she had nothing to fear. She ended up in his car and was probably being driven back to campus when she suddenly decided she was hungry. She was not hungry enough to eat the sandwich Jared's wife was offering or the one Andy Notch offered her for that matter, but she was hungry enough to insist on being dropped at the Hummingbird Diner.

I know friends… that detail is a little strange. I would imagine her motives for wanting to go to the Hummingbird were not exclusively hunger-related as the next part of the story will explore. Likely what caused Cadence to insist on the diner drop off was not food. One might believe she wanted to get back in touch with her own people, probably not Darlene or Stephanie on this particular morning, but very possibly her boyfriend, Jamison Kelly. Do her actions in the diner, if she was ever there at all, lend credence to these beliefs?

Let's look at it. She enters the diner after being dropped off by the Mintz family. She sits down to have a cup of coffee and smoke a few cigarettes (if she had any left, that is, since we cannot forget the abandoned pack of Pall Malls missing only one) and maybe she even ordered an omelet to soak up some of the booze she had consumed.

- 6 -

Let's not get too far ahead of ourselves here. This is not the Charlie Marx conspiracy theory hour. I am not here to convince you that what I think, or at least used to think, is correct. But there is some strong evidence that

Cadence Moore did arrive at the Hummingbird around this time on May 6.

Todd Crist, the sixty-five-year-old manager of the Hummingbird recalls the events of May 6 with surprising clarity. I say surprising since there is really no reason for Todd to have remembered the events of the morning of May 6 any clearer than any other morning, save for the fact that police questioned him at length within a week of the disappearance, which could have imprinted the whole thing into his memories. But the day itself was not unusual and Cadence (or the doppelganger) did not do anything strange while in Todd Crist's establishment to make him think something was up.

What follows is Todd Crist's remembrance of the whole situation. Todd generously agreed to speak to *Underground Podcast*. He was never contacted by Barnes and Angstat since they choose not to acknowledge that Cadence ever visited the diner and all involved parties are lying or mistaken about this detail for some reason. (This type of mentality did not do Barnes and Angstat any favors when people accused them of omitting facts that didn't fit their version of events.)

Todd Crist tells us, "This was a typical Monday morning crowd. When I say Monday morning, I mean real morning since the crowd at this point is pretty much made of truckers passing through, insomniac college professors, and drunken kids trying to soak up some beer. It was my typical crowd at three in the morning on a Monday. I remember this young blonde girl in blue stretchy pants and a black shirt. She was real nervous and agitated. She ordered a burger and ate only a quarter of it. She spent most of her time on the payphone in the back. I had a clear view of that from where I stand behind the counter. I noticed she was making a few calls and seemed agitated, almost like she was trying to get ahold of several people and they were not picking up. That's just my guess on the thing; she may have been agitated for another reason.

"At any rate, she finally must have contacted someone because she dropped a few bills on the counter, not blue bills by the way, I would have remembered that. She paid for her barely eaten burger with a couple of regular looking bucks and then split.

"She was out in the parking lot for a few minutes smoking cigarettes she just bought out of my machine (more evidence that the abandoned pack of Pall Malls at Andy Notch's Mini-mart belonged to Cadence) and then someone came and picked her up. I remember this distinctly. Headlights flooded the lot, she got in, and the car drove away. I remember it all very clearly, although I couldn't see what type of vehicle it was or who was driving."

I had to be straight with Todd Crist since he seemed to be straight with me in his recounting of events of May 6. I told Todd that it seemed peculiar that he remembered these facts with such clarity since cops did not visit him for over a week and there was really nothing weird or unusual for him to remember about his encounter with Cadence.

He even claims there was no blue money used for payment. So, I had to ask Todd what he thought of accusations thrown his way over the years that he had just made up details of this evening so he would have some attention bestowed upon himself and some notoriety for his diner.

Todd smiled wide and let out a little chuckle. "Hey, I didn't agree to do your show so I could impress you with some tall tales. I agreed because I'd really like to be part of the effort to figure out what happened to this little girl who disappeared. For those who think I'm lying, let me tell you this, I have a photographic memory. Since I was a schoolboy, this has been the case. I say this because I've run my business in a college town for damn near thirty years. In that time, there have been thousands of people coming in and out of my doors. It seems strange that I could remember one more than the other. I'll give you that.

"But, I'll point this out. Cops visited my joint a week later and questioned me and I had to recall details from seven days before. It forced me to focus and remember details. I'm sorry if people can't understand how I could do that, but I did. I remembered this night because it had recently happened and I recalled the details because I was forced to remember them.

"Like I said, I have a photographic memory. If you ask me what happened two days ago, and I focus on that time, I can remember in surprising detail every little thing that occurred. I have nothing to gain from stretching the truth here. What I told you is what really happened. You can take this for what it's worth. It does me no favors no matter which way it's sliced."

We pulled some points from our interview with Detective Meghan Cocuzza of the DFPD about their research and investigation into the Hummingbird Diner and any involvement it has in this case. Meghan recalls, "After speaking to Mr. Mintz, it became clear to me that we better question the workers of the Hummingbird at the time of this event so we could glean any possible connection to the case we were working on.

"I spoke to Mr. Crist, the owner of the diner. He seemed like someone who was telling the truth and I took what he said very seriously. Keep in mind, if Todd Crist is telling us the truth, then Jamison Kelly may have picked up Cadence Moore from the Hummingbird Diner on May 6, and this may have directly led to her being murdered.

"If he picked her up from the diner and then killed her in his car or either one of their dorm rooms, then we had the evidence right there in the vehicle to connect all the dots. Kelly was dismissed as a suspect when some very convenient things happened.

"One, he came up with the menstrual blood excuse to explain the tiny smear of blood in his car. Second, he was given convincing and verifiable alibis by friends who claim to have seen him around this time. Third, the DFPD determined that there wasn't enough blood in the car to prove that Cadence had been killed or even injured in it, so it warranted no further investigation or testing... which also conveniently fit into their plan of squashing the case altogether.

"But even to this day, I can't think of any other scenario or any other suspect that makes more sense than Jamison Kelly. Let's be honest here, Jamison could have picked Cadence up from the diner, killed her in one of the dorm rooms, carried her out to his car, already dead from strangulation or some other blood-free means, and then drove her to her site of burial or hiding.

"Jamison would have had to hide her body at that point. Where he allegedly hid it is still unknown, but if that's what happened, then the blood we found may have been an unintentional head wound or scratch wound that bled in his car while he was transporting Cadence from the site of her killing to the site of her disposal, burial, or what have you. He would have *had* to make up the menstrual blood excuse to explain away this unplanned complication of blood in his car.

"And, to be frank, we made it easy for him because we never tested it. That was the grand screw-up of this whole mess. I will never understand it. It still keeps me awake at night, if you can believe that. I've been in the law enforcement business for fifteen years and this still gives me fits.

"Jamison's car is long gone now. He sold it to a junkyard a few months after the investigation, claiming that he couldn't hold on to it due to the emotions involved, which, if you ask me, is more evidence of his guilt. It's been sold for scrap since then rendering any further investigation of the car impossible.

"This is where I think the DFPD totally went off the reservation and my superiors developed their exit plan from the case they wanted nothing to do with. God, we could have proved Kelly an innocent or a liar with a simple blood test. Here we have a police department that will spend $3,500 a month on food for the station functions, entertainment for parties, and reimbursing mileage for stakeout officers. But, we couldn't be bothered to spend a pathetic pittance on a simple blood test?

"If we would have tested the blood in Kelly's car, we would have known if it was menstrual in nature. Menstrual blood is different than regular blood because it contains traces of uterine wall lining. If we would have been able to prove the blood was menstrual, then Kelly's excuse would have been proven true. If we proved it was not menstrual in nature, then Kelly would have been proven a liar.

But, my superiors at that time felt that since there were only a few smears of blood in the car, not nearly enough to prove a murder had been committed there, it was not worth pursuing since Kelly had what they felt was an airtight alibi, and he also already told us a believable story about having sex while the girl was on her period. It is a real travesty that we never confirmed this.

"The rationale of my superior officers at the time was that even if we determined that this was Cadence's blood, there was not enough of it to prove murder had taken place. I protested until I was blue in the face. As I mentioned a second ago, I made it clear that regardless of the amount, if we proved the type of blood was not menstrual in nature, then we could prove Kelly was lying, which would have been damning to every one of his other claims about that night.

"My superiors really screwed up the whole investigation. I believe to this day that they felt from a PR perspective, a strange and unsolvable disappearance of a national celebrity was better than a confirmed murder in their University town of a national celebrity and one of their own students. I will never understand their decision or where all the pressure to make it disappear was coming from; but, I will always feel that we could have done a much better job than we did. I just want to be clear here… it wasn't for lack of trying on my part."

Meghan Cocuzza has been very forthcoming about her opinions and conclusions in this case. She believes Jamison Kelly was the killer of Cadence Moore even though her superiors felt the need to cast away this possibility due to what they publicly called a lack of evidence.

Todd Barnes and Michael Angstat's surmising of the situation points in the same direction Meghan Cocuzza's conclusions do. The only difference there is that Barnes and Angstat chose to ignore the Hummingbird scene completely.

So, what is keeping the public from lapping up these Kelly-as-killer theories like sweet broth and going about their happy lives? Just what exactly are the glistening rocks in the ocean of assumptions that keep sprouting up to make folks believe Jamison is innocent and others are responsible for this dirty deed?

Let us examine these so-called airtight alibis being pointed to by many a conspiracy theorist throughout the years. There are people who claim to have seen Jamison Kelly the night of May 5, and even the morning of May 6. If these people who provide the alibis are speaking truthfully, then it isn't humanly possible for Jamison to be in two places at once. So, I suppose it is essential for us to look at these alibis and determine if they hold any water.

- 7 -

One of the strongest pieces of evidence pointing in the direction of Jamison Kelly's innocence comes from Jimmy Derek, who at the time was a college student at DFU. He currently resides in Cleveland, Ohio working as a late-night radio disc jockey for KLFM 99. Jimmy is not married and has no children.

Back in 2002, he was attending DFU pursuing a degree in Communications and was a good friend of both Jamison Kelly and Cadence Moore. He was also at the Basement party the night of Cadence's disappearance. Jimmy tells us, and us alone, since he did not get an invite from the Barnes and Angstat team during the making of their film, (more fodder for the accusers who claim the doc team ignored facts in favor of their own conclusions) he remembers things very clearly from that evening.

Jimmy explained, "Listen, bro, I have heard all this shit about Jamison being a murderer and all. Let me tell you this… I can give you the straight story right now. That dude never killed anyone. He loved his girl, man; I can tell you that for sure. That's why he was drunk as shit the night she disappeared. She had fought with my boy, Jay, and he was so distraught that he drank like I've never seen him drink before. I mean, he was really upset, bro. I hadn't seen him like that ever.

"I knew it had been a bad fight. He thought they were gonna break up. I remember him telling me after she left the party that he knew she was gonna dump him since he was too drunk to go with her, and she was already pissed about the fight earlier in the night. Jamison didn't know what to do. He was so fucked up that he couldn't have left the campus, and he also knew Cadence was ready to dump his ass because he wasn't paying enough attention to her.

"That was what the whole fight was about. Jamison told me right after it happened. But when she asked him to come out with her and her friends, he was so far gone, he just couldn't. He needed to go to bed. He had to crash because he'd gone too far with the drinking and was just totally blitzed, man.

"He ended up sleeping in the bedroom of the frat dude that lived at the Basement house… Zach Burns, I still remember him. He was the guy who let Jay take his room. He could tell Jay was screwed and needed to sleep it off. So, it was about one o'clock in the morning, man, and we put Jay to bed. We saw him enter the room and he didn't come back out.

"A few hours later, way after Cadence and her friends left, I went up with Zach Burns to check on my boy Jay and he was sleeping like a baby in Burns's bedroom. He hadn't even made it to the bed. He was crumpled over on the floor like a drunken scarecrow. But he was there man, plain as day.

"I tell you this, without a shadow of a doubt, bro, he was there and he wasn't going anywhere. Zach could tell you the same thing if you ask him. When we put Jay to bed, he was fucked… barely able to stand anymore and he slumped down on the floor like a bum. What was he gonna do, come back to life like a zombie and run a mile to his dorm to grab the car and then pick up Cadence at a diner so he could murder her?

"I know to some folks this kind of shit seems reasonable. But listen, he was only worried about not getting dumped by his girlfriend… a girlfriend who was also a beautiful celebrity, which to a dude like Jay who wasn't exactly a ladies' man, was a big deal. The last thing on that boy's mind was killing her. I can't say it any clearer than that."

Jimmy Derek and Zach Burns both told DFPD officers stories that seem to match up perfectly with the account Jimmy has gone through for us here. It appears that Jamison was, in fact, drunk as the proverbial skunk and not in the type of shape required to get his car, drive to a diner or another dorm, and then murder Cadence Moore. So, why still the doubt from Meghan Cocuzza, Barnes and Angstat, and thousands of other people?

Well, let's travel around this a little. Zach Burns and Jimmy Derek both submitted statements to the effect that Jamison Kelly was sleeping it off in Burns's bedroom the night of Cadence's disappearance. I asked Zach Burns directly to appear on this podcast, but he unfortunately declined. He told me he had no interest in rehashing shit from a decade ago, and if his statements to police were not good enough, then he didn't know what to say.

So, we are forced to rely on Burns's testimony to DFPD and take it for what it is worth. He did conclusively state that he remembers putting Jamison Kelly to bed around 1 a.m., and then going into his bedroom around 4 a.m.

and seeing Jamison slumped over in a heap on the floor.

If this is true, it seemingly takes Kelly out of the running of possible suspects since Cadence (or the doppelganger) was picked up from the Hummingbird between 2:45 a.m. and 3:00 a.m. on May 6.

If Jamison was sleeping in the bedroom of the Basement house since 1:00 a.m., and was seen again by Jimmy Derek and Zach Burns there at 4:00 a.m., how did he slip out of sight around 2:45 a.m. without anyone seeing him, walk to his car, pick up Cadence and murder her (either in the car, his dorm, or her dorm) and then come back to the Basement to sneak up in the bedroom by 4 a.m.?

First, this is not possible to do without being seen. There is no back door out of the bedroom he is alleged to have slept in and the front door leads right to steps which go downstairs to the main room above the Basement, where many kids were still actively partying and hanging around. So, if he walked out of the room, someone would have seen him.

If Jamison did, in fact, leave the room and didn't walk out the door, he must have climbed out the window. This would require him to either jump two stories to the ground which could have injured him, or he would have had to fashion a rope out of the bed sheets and scale down the side of the house, just like in a teenage comedy movie.

If this is true, then when he came back to the Basement house, unless he suddenly developed the power to fly to the second floor, he would have had to either climb back up the makeshift rope and back into the room (very difficult to accomplish in real life,) or re-enter through the front door of the house.

This party reportedly was still hopping at 4:00 a.m. and it's not logical to think that nobody saw Jamison come back if he entered through the front door. Remember, many eyewitnesses from the party were questioned by police and none of them claim to have seen Jamison Kelly after he was taken to bed at 1:00 a.m.

But, let's just play devil's advocate and argue the point that Jamison Kelly could have left the Basement without being seen and he did pick up Cadence from the Hummingbird. At that point, we can surmise that the fight from earlier in the evening segues into part two and a new fight begins.

Jamison gets annoyed with Cadence all over again and becomes so angry that he strikes her hard or chokes her, maybe in the car or maybe when they get back to one of their dorm rooms. Cadence, all of a sudden, is dead and Jamison is freaked out and has no idea what to do. So, he dumps her body in some secret location, goes back to the Basement bedroom to sleep it all off once again and then he denied the whole night's events for the next decade.

Some have argued it seems ludicrous that, if he killed Cadence, Jamison would have returned to the Basement bedroom afterward. But, we know he was there because Zach Burns and Jimmy Derek both claim to have seen him there at 4:00 a.m.

And, even if Burns and Derek have their timeline all screwed up, Zach Burns submitted a statement claiming that Kelly was still in the bedroom at 9:00 a.m. Monday morning and he shook him awake and demanded he go home. So, why would Jamison have returned to the Basement at all?

Well, if he really had planned to kill Cadence from the start, it would make sense that he'd return to that particular bedroom to maintain an alibi. If he could sneak out and back into the room without being seen, then at least two people (Burns and Derek) would claim that he was there the whole night.

Now, the second possibility is that Jamison was asleep all along in the Basement bedroom and had no connection whatsoever to the disappearance of his girlfriend. Someone else was responsible for Cadence going missing and Jamison simply awakened the next day as clueless as everyone else wondering what happened to the love of his life. Okay, so let's follow that track.

We will go with the notion that Jamison sleeps as innocent as a baby during the crucial points on this early May 6 morning. Then he awakes to the horror of knowing that his girlfriend has gone missing. Following this line of thinking, we know that someone else is responsible for Cadence's disappearance. And if this is the case, then we have not yet even touched the surface of this mystery.

We know this. Todd Crist, owner of the Hummingbird, saw a car's headlights float into his parking lot and that same car picked up Cadence or the girl who was her twin. Todd could not see what type of car it was, so we don't know if it was Jamison's vehicle or not.

But, for now we're assuming Jamison was sleeping through all of this, so he could not have been the driver. If not Jamison Kelly, then who in god's name was the driver of the car that provided the floating headlights Todd Crist spoke of? This question has been on the minds of conspiracy theorists for over a decade. We must narrow down the suspects here.

As we have shown, the first and most popular suspect in the minds of Barnes and Angstat, Meghan Cocuzza, and many other followers of the case is Jamison Kelly. But as we have already painstakingly reviewed, the statements of both Jimmy Derek and Zach Burns seem to take Kelly out of the picture. We're going to leave him out of the picture for now. If he didn't pick up Cadence from the Hummingbird, then who did?

Second most likely suspects are Darlene Bethany and Stephanie Chambers. Regardless of the fight in Darlene's car, we can reasonably guess that the next people besides Jamison on the Cadence Moore dialing list (going on the assumption she was trying to get back in touch with her people) would have been either Darlene or Stephanie. She did not have a ton of friends at school and Darlene and Stephanie had become like sisters to her.

Let's assume that Cadence called her recently very pissed off friends, and they took pity on her and decided to go pick her up and presumably make up like pals. While it does not seem completely out of the realm of possibility that at least Darlene would have been angry enough at Cadence for kissing Steve that she killed her in a drunken crime of passion, there are already problems with this theory.

First and foremost, both Darlene and Stephanie state that they went back to campus after the car fight with Cadence. Darlene stayed with her beau, Steve Willis, and Stephanie, the victim of a failed night of hunting for young boys with companionship on their minds, slept alone on a futon in the same dorm room.

Two students, Melissa Wilder and Regina Bucks, both claim to have seen Steve Willis, Darlene Bethany, and Stephanie Chambers walk into the St. Phyllis dorm (where Steve Willis lived), go into Steve's room, and close the door.

So, if these girls returned to Steve Willis's room, were seen by several witnesses, and have no memory of seeing Cadence again, it seems a major stretch to think that they somehow exited the dorm without being discovered, drove back to spring Cadence from her exile, killed her and dumped her, and then denied this fact for the next decade.

Third most likely suspects and the next most likely candidates for a 3:00 a.m. phone call from Cadence Moore would have been members of her own family. This presents a gigantic complication, of course. The three members of Cadence's family who would have been accessible on this day were Darien, Morgan, and Marianna. All three were seen by several people at a dinner party in Milwaukee, Wisconsin around 9:00 p.m. on May 5, and all three were again seen at a nightclub bar (The Wasp of Wisconsin) a little past 2:00 a.m. on May 6. There just wasn't enough time for any of them to be in Dusklight Falls, Pennsylvania to pick up Cadence from the Hummingbird at 3:00 a.m. the morning of May 6.

But, what if… as some have suggested, Cadence *did* get a hold of someone in her family by phone, and what if this family member, sensing danger and possibly even some really bad press, decided to make a few calls and send a "familiar face" to pick up Cadence. But, instead of taking her home, this hired goon dragged the young girl out to the wilderness and disposed of her like an animal?

This third option should not be dismissed immediately as lunacy. The truth is that Darien Moore had plenty of contacts, both savory and unsavory, in and around the Dusklight Falls area. He could have instructed one of his unsavory associates to grab up his daughter and forever erase her from the possible threats he had to deal with from there on out.

You all will recall Darien helped Cadence choose her college and it's not totally out of the realm of possibility that he had a rogue's gallery in the general proximity that he could call on at any given time to do his bidding. So, to take this far-fetched notion a little farther, we'll assume that Darien, or Morgan, for that matter, could have gotten in touch with the right person on the right night and arranged for Cadence, the problem child and trouble maker, to be taken care of forever.

If this is what happened, we must assume that the floating headlights driving into the Hummingbird parking lot had come for Cadence and were there for one reason: to escort the young star to her doom.

What evidence is there to support this theory? Truthfully, almost none. It is known that Cadence had a very complicated relationship with her family and it is a real leap of faith to think she'd even contact any of them on a troubled evening such as the one she was experiencing on May 6.

The girl had already confided in the paper bindings of her diary as to the reach of her rage against the daddy who loved her too much, the brother who barely existed, and the new step-mother who was nothing more than a glory-craving whore in young Cadence's mind.

But, what if it was actually true? What if the unthinkable occurred? We already know that Darien occupied a strange and prominent place in Cadence's life. What about the thought that at her darkest moment, she called on her controller, her oppressor, and her commander to help her out and rid her of all the uncomfortable complications?

Well, if this is how Cadence disappeared, we know the extent of Darien's or Morgan's involvement in all of this would have been as simple as calling in a favor over the phone. This favor would have involved either a gallant protector sent to take the young girl back to safety, or an individual who would permanently erase Cadence from the history books, thus eliminating the one questionable factor in the seemingly perfect life of the Moore clan.

The reasonable answer here is that the Moore clan was not involved at all. I say reasonable because it just doesn't add up if we examine the wild theories of hired gunman or hired protectors to save Cadence from a bad night of drunken revelry.

If the hired goon was put into action by Darien to silence the young Moore from spitting out dark secrets, then why was all this other activity, like a skyrocketing singing career, fame and notoriety, and a college experience allowed to occur without incident while one drunken phone call from a diner convinced Darien to put an end to the Cadence problem? That doesn't really make sense if you think about it.

I simply do not believe the Moore family would have felt the need to call in any favors to silence the drama of a typical obnoxious college chick who flirted with the wrong boyfriend.

Again, I must ask you good listeners to probe further with some basic questions. If the Moore clan had no good reason to become involved, and Jamison Kelly, Darlene Bethany, and Stephanie Chambers all have rather strong alibis, then what indeed happened to young Cadence on that strange night in Dusklight Falls?

- 8 -

This would be a prime opportunity to reveal another detail that complicates things even further. Cadence Moore allegedly used a payphone to call whoever she called from the Hummingbird. Why would she do this when we know that she routinely carried her cell phone with her, you might ask? Since the cell phone was found with her other belongings in her dorm room when police conducted their search, that question is an easy one to answer. For whatever reason, she did not bring it with her that night. How wonderful it might have been for all of us, especially those with an actual real-life connection to Cadence, had GPS tracking capability in her cell phone been able to pinpoint her exact location throughout the morning of May 6.

Some have tried to point to the payphone usage as evidence backing up the notion that Cadence was trying to hide her communications, at this point, in some desperate attempt to disappear from Dusklight Falls altogether, and wishing for no one to follow her. This seems a crazy theory on its face since leaving her cell phone behind in the dorm would have forced her to make calls by some other means. But the idea of her wanting to leave town, while at first may sound ridiculous, becomes not so ridiculous when you consider what the payphone records did eventually tell us.

It is possible, even likely, that Cadence thought that her phone communications could not be picked up or recorded if she used a pay phone. This is a common misconception shared by many people. The truth is, going back quite a few years, it is very possible for police to find out what numbers were called on a public payphone, even though a large portion of the general public still assumes that using a payphone makes your calls anonymous and untraceable. So, what did the DFPD do? Well, we must look no further than Detective Meghan Cocuzza who led the investigation into Cadence Moore's disappearance.

Meghan tells us, "We did follow the diner lead and we pulled the public payphone records to see what calls were being made between 2:45 a.m. to 3:00 a.m. on May 6. Here is where it gets bizarre. The girl assumed to be Cadence Moore did *not* call Jamison Kelly, Darlene Bethany, Stephanie Chambers, Darien Moore, or Morgan Moore on the morning of May 6. She called no one in her familiar or familial circles.

"She made one call to Cricket's Pizza Shop, at 2:36 a.m. on May 6, which seemed to make no sense at all considering she was at a diner already. However, we did find out that a friendly acquaintance of hers, Barry Rainfield, did work at Cricket's as a delivery boy and she may have been trying to get in touch with him. However, we interviewed the night manager of the 24-hour pizza joint and he told us that Barry was not working the evening of May 5 into the morning May 6.

"The next phone call Cadence made was to the Falcon Link Psychic Service. This call was placed at 2:41 a.m. on May 6. We contacted Falcon Link to find out what they remembered, but they incredibly do not record their own phone calls which seems crazy since most companies record their calls as evidence to protect them from lawsuits. Apparently, whatever the Falcon Link psychics were preaching was so far out that it seemed a better option for the company to keep no phone records than an actual account of what they are feeding people. This is simply my opinion. Regardless, Falcon Link provided us no leads, whatsoever.

"So, we move to the next call, the one that really, I think, sheds some light on this whole matter. The next call made from the Hummingbird payphone was to the Dusklight Falls Municipal Bus Station.

"Was she looking for a way out of town? Was she planning to return home to her clearly dysfunctional family? No one can say for sure, but this call to the bus station indicates that Cadence was not planning on sticking around Dusklight Falls, especially considering that she'd had a terrible fight with her friends and was quarreling with her boyfriend.

"It is with certainty that we can state if Cadence was making calls from the Hummingbird, she *did* call the bus station, but did not call Jamison, Darlene, Stephanie, or her own family. We can also clearly state that if Cadence had wanted to buy a bus ticket, or any other kind of ticket that might have crossed her mind, such as a plane ticket, she only had cash and left all her cards at home (the cards and her wallet were all found back at her dorm room). This means she would have had to pay for said ticket from her dwindling supply of cash unless she first went back home. This return to her dorm does not seem to have happened, at least as far as any verifiable evidence is concerned. Why it didn't happen is another question and, in her drunken logic, there is no way to determine conclusively what Cadence was thinking in this moment."

Meghan Cocuzza's description of these events does raise a worthy question. If Cadence didn't call Jamison from the diner and he was the guy who killed her, how would he have known to drive to that specific location to find her?

Meghan was prepared for this question. She replied, "The Hummingbird diner was the most popular diner in Dusklight Falls for kids, drunken or stoned, or what have you, to visit for a late-night meal. It would not surprise me in the least that Jamison was searching for his girlfriend and came up empty in several popular late-night sites such as the Hossler family-owned pool hall, at least a dozen different bar parking lots, from Ginger's to Willy Ray's or a bunch of others, the '50s-inspired Burger joint, Bobby Socks, and the public park. Lots of places yes… but almost like an amusement park map to anyone familiar with the Dusklight Falls nighttime landscape.

"To assume Jamison would not have eventually reached the Hummingbird is very short sighted. I assume he *did* eventually go there through process of elimination. When he arrived, he probably couldn't believe his luck when the very girlfriend he was searching for just happened to be standing right out in the parking lot smoking and waiting for a familiar face."

Meghan Cocuzza once again adds more fuel to the fire burning in support of her theories. However, I want to discuss a little further this fact that Cadence paid for everything in cash on this day. We know all the purchases made by Cadence Moore or her twin on May 6 were paid in cash. Meghan also verified that Cadence's wallet and several credit cards were found in her dorm room after the disappearance.

It's important to remember this. From the cigarettes at Andy Notch's store to the burger at Todd Crist's Hummingbird, Cadence was shelling out cash. It is very possible, as I alluded to previously, that she spent too much cash and because she did not have her credit cards, she could not pay for a bus ticket, even though she did call the station probably hoping to be quoted fare prices in the $10 to $20 range.

Well, unlike Falcon Link, calls to the bus station are recorded. DFPD did some exhaustive research and pulled a call from the recording system of the Municipal Bus Station from 2:53 a.m. on May 6. The contents of this call are less informative than we would hope. In fact, the entire call consists of the following brief dialogue. A young girl who sounds an awful lot like Cadence Moore asks, "How much would I have to pay tonight, like in twenty minutes, if I wanted to go to New York... Manhattan?" The dispatch phone rep for the bus station pauses and some papers can be heard rustling. The phone rep replies, "A line to New York City will be leaving at 6:00 a.m. and the fare will be $75." The young girl concludes the conversation with, "Well, you can go get fucked."

We can deduce from this phone call that Cadence wanted to go to New York City, perhaps thinking she could transfer her fame to a new place in the Northeast and start over once again with new friends and a new audience. She may have even been advised to do this by a psychic friend from Falcon Link.

When she was informed that the fare was $75, Cadence's reply indicated she was very unhappy. She likely did not have $75 on her and had no way to get back to campus. She could have walked back, but it was nine miles. The bus station was a mere mile and a half from where she stood at the diner. She probably figured for ten or twenty dollars she'd be able to ride out of Dusklight Falls forever leaving all her newfound troubles behind. Obviously, this is not what happened.

It is well understood that many college kids leave their wallets and cards at home when they go to a party. So, if Cadence spent too much and did not have enough cash for a bus ticket, we must then assume she went out into the parking lot and smoked some cigarettes, trying to come up with a plan B.

At this point, a car pulls into the lot and picks her up. We have no idea who the driver of this car was but we do know that if it was Jamison Kelly, Darlene Bethany, Stephanie Chambers, or an associate of Darien Moore, then this person would have had to have some premonition of future events or have been lucky to find her there through process of elimination as Meghan Cocuzza would like us to believe.

We can safely say this because we know no calls were made from the Hummingbird informing any of the possible suspects of Cadence's current whereabouts. We are left to believe that either the driver of the car was not one of Cadence's close friends and just showed up at the diner randomly... or the driver was a close friend or associate and that person has some psychic abilities they never bothered to tell anyone about.

I realize Meghan Cocuzza has argued that the Hummingbird was a popular night spot and eventually someone searching for Cadence would have found her there. But let's not forget, this is barely more than an hour after she was buying cigarettes at Andy Notch's store. Was that enough time for one of her close friends or a family-hired goon to come up empty at all the popular spots and end up at the Hummingbird where Cadence just happened to be waiting?

I respect Meghan Cocuzza a great deal, but I have problems swallowing this theory. I believe that if *any* of these suspects really picked up Cadence, then they must have just magically known she was at the Hummingbird waiting to be picked up. Does this really sound right to any of you? I didn't think so. It doesn't sound right to me either. So... since it doesn't sound right... we have to keep searching for an answer that does.

5

The Longer It Goes,
The Worse It Gets

The phone was making an annoying buzzing sound every three minutes or so. Charlie had finally managed to fall asleep after his late-night conversation with Tyler and his defense of the sitcom writing he'd been doing. Somewhere in the hours between that call and the annoying buzzing now coming from his phone, Tyler Reubens had finished reading Charlie's treatments for all of Podcast 3 and Charlie had conked out.

Tyler tried calling him a dozen times and finally gave up hope that Charlie, the consummate night owl and hard drinker, might still be awake. Tyler was also mangled. Charlie knew he'd been drunk when they last spoke, but now Tyler was in the outer reaches. Tyler left him a voicemail, a very long voicemail, before he himself finally retired for the evening in preparation for the pounding headache that awaited him in the morning... the pricey penance for decompressing by way of the bottle.

The buzzing of the phone on the nightstand finally succeeded in cutting through the cobwebs of Charlie's slumber. He picked it up and saw he had a voicemail from Tyler, and now that he was up it would nag at his mind if he tried to go back to sleep. So, his only choice was to listen... listen to the drunken but wise rant of the man he'd learned everything from.

Tyler, speaking too close to the phone, repeating himself, and slurring badly, began his diatribe. "Marx, the Kelly interview is fucking great! You hear me? Fucking great! You don't deserve compliments but your questions and the directions you took him in... all of it is fucking great! I'm a man who'll say I'm wrong when I say I'm wrong and I'll call it right down the middle when you're right you're right. So, this is me... this is me telling you... you are right!

"But here's the part where you need to listen to the guy who is more right and better at this shit than you are. You probably don't know the land mine you're standing on. This is such a delicate balance… like razor wires, Marx… and I'm telling you there is only one way and one way only to play this now… here's how it must be; I'm gonna tell you. (Charlie had to laugh, even in his groggy and irritated state, at the sheer drunken exuberance in Tyler's words).

"You better sell the shit out of that first date, man. I mean highlight that and make sure it's a key point of the interview. You can edit out a lot of other shit to make sure it's fleshed out, but you gotta sell that because it's your meet-cute and the audience will think that's where he fell for her. They gotta feel that!

"Next thing, when they're in the room and she wants to bang and he's too messed up… you can hear in the guy's voice, that and when he's out there at the party and they're fighting… that's when you got to… when that fucking audience, man, they gotta hear the hurt in his voice. They gotta know how much it bothered him. He wasn't looking to kill her, for fuck's sake… he was terrified to lose her. When he sees her in there shakin' her ass for other dudes, you gotta sell that shit… it was killing him. Not killing him like he's pissed and he's gonna strangle her… but it was ripping him up. They gotta feel that, too!

"The stalking shit with the other singer, it's too fascinating not to include, especially hearing him tell it. But, it makes him look like a creep and a weirdo and, if you wanna clear this fucker's name and shove him outta the way to make room for the mystery murderer you think you've found, you got to be fucking careful with that shit. (Tyler was yelling now.) If you don't edit it right and highlight the exact right parts… it's gonna indict him, not clear him. You heap suspicion instead of sympathy right at his feet and that's not what we need. He did it all for love, Charlie! The audience… they gotta feel that the most!

"Now listen to me. I may be drunk, but I'm still smarter than you, and I'm better at this than you are. We need to make sure, if nothing else, this episode is done right. I want full treatments. I mean full shit, Marx; don't try to throw up more smoke. Edited and completed scripts and formats…

on my desk. We're gonna play nice with each other for now because you're an asshole and you don't know it, but you need me… and you need me bad when it comes to this episode. This isn't a request. You'll have those to me in the next three days and I'll make sure it's done and edited right."

Charlie heard every inebriated word and knew every one of them was true. If this podcast series was a film, the Jamison interview was his hero shot. If he didn't light that shot in just the right way and edit the dialogue at just the right moments, Jamison wouldn't be the hero of anything. If Jamison wasn't the hero, he'd be the villain.

If the audience didn't buy Jamison as the hero, they would not be ready to take the ride Charlie was planning to take them on, the one he needed them to go on if they were going to stay with him to the very end. If they didn't take that ride, then the whole series would collapse under the weight of a botched execution. His own lies had already insured there were plenty of things this series and his own career were at risk of collapsing under, and Charlie Marx would be damned if botched execution would be one of them.

He stood up, smoked a cigarette, put on the coffee and started working. He shipped off the entire completed transcript and format for the updated and polished second portion of Podcast 3 to Tyler's office two days later.

- 2 -

UNDERGROUND PODCAST 3: (Official Transcript)
Part 2: The College Year: Second Installment

Charlie Marx's Underground Podcast: Episode 3 (Part 2). Original Drop Date: November 1, 2013. (Brought to you by United Way of Life, courtesy of Tyler Reubens… this program is funded and sponsored by WHHW, a subsidiary of Universal Public Radio)

(Narration by Charlie Marx) Jamison Kelly agreed to an interview with *Underground Podcast* for several reasons. First off, he had never been given a national forum to speak about his feelings on the Cadence Moore disappearance, namely because he was not interviewed for the Barnes and Angstat film, *Moore to the Story.*

Jamison has been fingered by a great many people over the years of being responsible for Cadence Moore's disappearance and probable death. What exactly does Jamison think of all this? Jamison Kelly sat down to speak with *Underground Podcast* and he shed a lot of important insight on this subject.

Jamison told us, "This whole thing, this whole horrible thing, has really been the most significant experience of my life. I'd love to be able to tell you that my children's births or my marriage, or even my successful sales career would rank higher on the list of important things in my life, but it's impossible to say that. Imagine yourself as a man who is trying to live a good and decent life but is constantly reminded that he is presumed to be a murderer in the minds of millions of Americans.

"The truth is, I am horrified by this more than you could imagine. I truly loved Cadence Moore. She was the girl I first fell in love with in my life. This is no small thing. She became the most important person in my world for a brief time.

"Jesus Christ, I would have died before letting anything happen to Cadence. It breaks my heart when people claim I'm the one responsible for it. I've already confided to you and your show that I continue to have nightmares which torture me and I'll explain a little later how this obsession with finding the truth almost landed me in prison on stalking charges."

I gently probed Jamison for more details on the stalking subject. This was highlighted in *Moore to the Story,* but we will get to the revelations coming out of my direct conversations with Jamison as we proceed here. But first, I think it's important to recall some of the details of the time and see from Jamison Kelly's eyes what Dusklight Falls and his college experience looked like to him.

"I'll tell you, Charlie, I was kind of a geek when I first entered DFU. I was a complete nerd in high school and I came into this new adventure with wide eyes and a clueless mind. I had no idea what I was in for. I made a couple of buddies right away. Jimmy Derek for one was a guy who went out of his way to make me feel welcome and part of his group.

"I was glad for it, too, because I didn't know what to do myself to make friends. Jimmy made sure all his friends knew me and liked me. Even if they didn't, he made sure they acted like it. I still don't know why, but I think Jimmy saw something in me... something that reminded him of himself or people he liked. I don't know, but he seemed to think I was one of his people and he had my back from Jump Street. I love that guy to this day for that. Believe me... college life can be tough for an awkward person like me and I owe Jim a lot for taking me into his little crew.

"He was a good friend, Jimmy Derek. He used to like how I'd explain complicated physics concepts to him. He thought it was cool that I knew about this stuff and could help him understand by explaining it in laymen's terms. He was a real laid-back, cool guy and he had lots of friends. After a little while, Jimmy's friends became my friends and things were going very well.

"I was hanging with Jimmy and his boys. I'd always been terrified of girls. Jimmy must have had three or four girls at a time wanting him, and he was totally unfazed by it all. He just took it like a normal thing in life. These chicks who wanted a piece of Jimmy were just minor complications in his mind. He paid attention to ones he gave a shit about and ignored the rest. Some of these girls who were ignored would turn their attention to the rest of Jimmy's crew.

"I distinctly remember this one girl. She just ran through all the guys (excluding me, of course, since I couldn't even look at a girl straight in the eyes without getting a panic attack) like a bull and must have slept with six dudes in a week. She seemed determined to show Jimmy that he made the wrong decision by ignoring her and wanted to make her mark by presenting her special blend to all the members of Jimmy's club.

"As it was, most of them enjoyed her but kind of felt like she was a loose cannon. They liked her when she was near and then cursed her name when she was gone. Let's face it, she was the prettiest girl any of them would ever have a chance at, and they knew it.

"Instead they pretended to all think she was a psycho and Jimmy was right to cast her aside. This was the way you kept the peace in the Jimmy Derek gang. You fed the ego of the leader and sang the same song he was singing no matter what. He was doing favors for all of us and raising our social statuses, so we supported him without fail.

"The truth was, all of those guys were lucky to enjoy the benefits of Jimmy Derek's table scraps. We would have been alone by ourselves had it not been for the connection with Jimmy. In fact, Jimmy is the reason I met Cadence Moore in the first place.

"In the beginning, I had some awful and just ridiculous dates with Cadence's roommates that Jimmy set up. I remember all of this very clearly. Darlene Bethany was chummy with Jimmy. He convinced her to give me a chance. We had a very awkward date and when she decided she had no interest in what I had to offer, she somehow convinced her friend Stephanie to give me a try.

"All I can say about that date is that it was a catastrophe. I remember spilling something on her and the look on her face, if it could have been translated into English, would have sounded like, 'I hope you die a fiery death and I hope you die it soon.' I really couldn't blame her. I was horrible. I eventually did become good friends with both of them. I knew they were nice girls, but I also knew I blew it in so many ways that I couldn't even begin to count them all.

"As weird luck would have it, these two chicks must have seen something interesting in me because they recommended that their famous friend Cadence take a chance and try me out, as well. Either that or they found so much amusement in my goofball bullshit that they thought it would be an amusing lark to hook her up with me. I can't be sure, but I prefer to believe the interesting theory… just for ego's sake.

"Whatever the real reason may have been, I got a chance to go out with Cadence Moore, an honest-to-god celebrity music star. I think I was the first guy at college to have a real date with Cadence. No one had even dated her yet, if you can believe that. Most guys acted weird around her because she was famous and they didn't know how to handle that.

"Cadence and I went on one date and, in spite of my awkward nature, she seemed to like me. I was just being myself and she seemed to dig it. It's funny… the biggest hit I had with her was a comment about Marble

Works. I hadn't learned from my previous dating failures with Darlene and Stephanie. I was once again talking physics, the exact thing to do when you're trying *not* to impress a woman; but, I was going into my theory about the expanding Universe and the fact that it really wasn't expanding into anything but simply moving into circular formations upward and downward, kind of like Marble Works.

"At that point, Cadence grabbed my arm and smiled the most beautiful smile. She looked at me with those crystal blue eyes and yelled, 'I love Marble Works. I used to play with them for hours. Thank you, Jamison! You just made me realize that I totally understand the universe now.'

"All these years later, I can only surmise that the reason she was drawn to me was because my social awkwardness and strange ways made her feel like she found a kindred spirit. She felt so out of place, like an outsider, around almost anyone she met in college, including, I believe, her own roommate and best friends."

It was remarkable how close Jamison's theory on Cadence's attraction to him matched Stephanie Chambers's thoughts on the subject.

Jamison continued, "Cadence took me on like her pet project and told Darlene and Stephanie that she thought I was cute and they had missed the boat on me. Cadence saw something in me that she didn't see in the other guys at DFU campus. I think she saw something real in me. We had a second date during which we went miniature golfing and played arcade games at Zinn's Park in the suburbs beyond Dusklight Falls.

"She kicked my ass really bad in everything we played together. I remember we were playing air hockey and she beat me, no shit, 7-2. I had to laugh at my own pathetic performance. Cadence started doing this little victory dance and doing ridiculous karate kicks in the air. I deadpanned and looked at her and said, 'You know Cadence, I think you might truly be evil.' Without missing a beat… Cadence danced over to me and looked me right in the eye and said, 'You know, Jamison, I think *you* might truly be evil, too… and cute.' Then she kissed me.

"It was the first kiss I'd ever had. As Cadence kissed me, I felt like the world was teetering on its axis for a second. Something strange and wonderful had just occurred and I knew I was in love. And to be honest with you right now, I believe she may have been in love, too. Just like that.

"I know it sounds stupid to say that when I'm just recounting little details, but if you could have been there, and could have felt the electricity between us, it was something unbelievable, like a hidden truth and we both discovered it together. We were a couple after that."

I asked Jamison if it was difficult to talk about these exciting times when they first met, considering what happened later. He replied honestly. "Yes, it is. It sucks, because if I could go back to that moment right now in Zinn's arcade... I would, you know... I would go back there without any hesita... You know, I don't know what I'd do. I'm happy now in my current life and I have a beautiful wife and kids. This trip down memory lane just really packs a strong punch, you know?"

I found it interesting that Jamison almost stated that he'd go back to the arcade at Zinn's Park and to his date with Cadence Moore if he had the power to do so. This date and Cadence still carried tremendous emotional weight with him. And, I'm sure that if given time traveling powers by the gods, Jamison would go back to that moment on Cinco de Mayo in 2002, and make sure both he and Cadence Moore were safe in a place far, far away from Dusklight Falls. And, I challenge anyone in his position to say they wouldn't feel exactly the same way.

However, as someone who is trying to live a peaceful life with his wife and family, it is understandable why Jamison hesitated and did not complete the sentence he started.

I decided to change the subject. I asked Jamison what the fight that night at the Basement had really been about. We've heard commentary from Jimmy Derek, Darlene Bethany, and Stephanie Chambers on this subject, but, I felt it necessary to reach out to one of the actual participants in this late-night argument to see what really occurred. Jamison was silent for a moment and then answered my question.

"That night has taken on almost a dreamlike quality in my memory... a bad dream for sure. First off, I was drunk as all hell and really don't remember things in stark crystal detail. Now, when I really try to recall all that happened, it comes in flashes of images.

"The first flash I can provide is when Cadence and I arrived at the party. We'd eaten dinner in my dorm room. We made out for a little while and then proceeded to trot on over to the Basement party. I remember her clothes, as everyone else also seems to remember, these tight blue stretchy pants and a tight, torn black tank top.

"Then I remember us entering the party and spotting Jimmy Derek behind the makeshift bar. Jimmy spread his arms like an eagle, let out a giant smile, and yelled, 'My People! My dear sweet people, Cadence and Jay! Come drink with me right now.'

"We must have had a few drinks with Jimmy, but, I don't remember them. The next flash I can recall is Jimmy and Cadence dancing together, this weird little two-step deal, when somebody put on *Bloody Mary Morning* by Willie Nelson. Little did this joker at the controls know that Jimmy secretly worshiped and wanted to be just like Willie Nelson. By this time, I was already getting tipsy. All I remember is Cadence and Jimmy doing what seemed to me a strange dance.

"After that, people started to calm down a little and everyone was just feeling good, stoned or drunk, and hanging out. Cadence tickled my chin, which I notoriously couldn't handle and started giggling like a baby. Then she looked me square in the eye and said, 'Let's go upstairs.'

"We went into one of the spare rooms in the Basement frat house. Cadence brought out some of the fantastic weed we'd purchased from our common pal, Jimmy Derek, and we started smoking. I could never handle the shit very well… especially back then. With any more than one or two hits, I'd become the super hero of the relaxed and stupid, or else the poster child for paranoia.

"I had my couple of hits and Cadence started kissing me down the neck and on my chest. My head fell softly on the pillow and I soon committed the ultimate sin of boyfriends everywhere and briefly dozed off. Now, you must keep in mind, Cadence was feeling a lot of love for me in this moment and expected to feel the… I guess… rewards for such devotion, so she was pissed that I just fell asleep like it didn't mean shit. I was so screwed up, but that didn't make it any less of an indiscretion on my part. She took it very personally.

"The next flash of memory that I have is getting slapped really hard in the stomach and Cadence screaming at me. She yelled, 'You lazy, pathetic, little son of a bitch! I could go down there right now and fuck any guy I please. What makes you feel so entitled, you bastard!?!'

"Remember something right now. Cadence was a complicated individual and she had demons that she sometimes couldn't control. I never, believe it or not, had any kind of extended conversation with her about it. She chose to keep that part of her past hidden from those closest to her. I assume she didn't want to bring it out into the light and be associated with something that shamed her. But, I can tell you these types of buried issues do end up causing some problems. Namely, when Cadence felt rejected, she reacted very strongly and very ugly. She thought I was disrespecting her and I made her feel worthless by not responding to her. Honestly, I had just gotten too fucked up too quickly and fell asleep.

"Again, I say these things ten years later with a disconnected perspective and years of media mentions of her horribly abusive past. So, my little psychoanalyzing profile on Cadence says that rejection caused her to act irrationally and go seeking comfort wherever she could get it. I feel kind of sleazy even making this comment because the girl is no longer here to provide a counterpoint, but this is how I feel about it.

"She flipped out on me when I fell asleep. Then she started screaming at me about how I never paid her any attention and acted like she was here to please me and gain nothing for herself. After all, she was a celebrity at the time and I was just this lucky geek who happened to be graced with her presence and intimate relations.

"Her ugly side was painting our relationship as something I should have felt lucky to be involved in and something she could leave at any second without batting an eye. I have a flash of Cadence storming out of the room and slamming the door so hard that she knocked plaster off the wall. I fell back asleep and only stumbled down into the Basement a little later once my weed-induced haze had a chance to float off me.

"When I got downstairs I remember seeing something that really bothered me a lot. Cadence was hanging all over people. She was moving from one guy to the next, desperately trying to give herself some valida-tion after what she perceived as a rejection from me. Keep in mind, this was all very odd because our three-month dating stretch was filled with pretty much nothing but good times. We'd never had a serious argument. This night in the Basement was weird and strange. I wasn't prepared for it. I loved Cadence and really couldn't understand why she was doing this to me.

"She was the first girl I ever made love to… I'll be honest about that. People who have never been in love use that phrase to describe the banal act of having sex. She'd had sex before, but she'd never made love; I believe that wholeheartedly. With Cadence, I did truly make love, and it meant some-thing. I thought that then and I think it now.

"Our relationship was filled with *nothing* but good and decent times. I'd sit in the front row seats with Darlene and Stephanie at Cadence's concerts. We were so goddamn proud of her. We screamed the loudest and held our hands higher than all the rest.

"I bragged to anyone in the crowd within earshot that this chick was my girlfriend. Most of them laughed at me and told me to fuck off. Then Cadence would bend down from the bandstand during a musical solo and plant one on me. I'd look back at some of these guys who had laughed at me, and they'd be smiling and coming over to pat me on the back and shake my hand. They'd yell, 'You are a fucking stud. You are the king!' It was funny; no one seemed to believe a nerdy-looking, gangly dude like me was dating this beautiful college singer who could have had any guy she wanted.

"Darlene, Stephanie, and Cadence used to love going to Dusklight Falls, the actual falls I mean, once or twice a month. When we'd go there, the three girls would bring their current boyfriends, which included me, Steve Willis, and whoever Stephanie was currently putting up with in her quest for the perfect boyfriend.

"We'd go to the Falls late at night, too late for any tourists to be hang-ing around. We'd sit on the rocks overlooking the rushing cascading water. The couples would kind of drift off behind bushes, although not really. We could all see each other from where we were. We had unashamed sex with our mates, and then proceeded to smoke a joint that was passed around like candy and philosophize on life, existence, and anything we felt like discussing.

"Steve Willis was a chef at a local Italian restaurant not far off campus. He had this little propane grill he'd always bring along. I thought he was the greatest. Steve was this rock solid laid back silent type of guy. He'd come in with the perfect one liner or he'd come out with some crazy statement that was more interesting than anything everyone else was saying. But aside from that, he never said a word. That's what was so cool about him. He only spoke when he had something profound to say.

"He was a great guy. It's a shame what happened to him a little later. I could see why Darlene liked the guy so much. Steve would always bring along little steaks, or burgers and dogs. He'd fry them up as we hung out on the rocks. We had our own little late-night hideout by the Falls and we'd eat Steve's cooking and just chill out like tomorrow didn't matter.

Eventually, after everyone had their fill and we were ready for sleep, we'd all stumble into our cars and head back to campus as the dawn was coming up. Little casts of light behind the clouds would illuminate the way home, and when we finally laid our heads down on pillows and closed our eyes, the sun would be making its way out for the first time that day. We usually didn't see it, unless we had class... and those school days following Falls nights, my friend... oh man... they were painful."

- 3 -

Jamison was painting quite the attractive picture of the late-night Falls barbeques he experienced with his college friends. It makes a person wonder how such a tightly knit group of friends could be undone and destroyed after one drunken night and one fight in a car. Yet, that's exactly what happened. Let's hope Jamison can make these murky waters just a tiny bit clearer for us.

Jamison continued, "I tell you all of this because I want to make it clear that Cadence and I had a fun and healthy relationship at the time that all this horrible shit went down. We were not a drama-prone couple and the fight we had that night in the Basement was the first real one we'd ever had… I'm not kidding, either… that was the first time I'd seen her truly mad. And I didn't like it. She was scary when she got that pissed. It gave me a chance to see the rage that boiled underneath her daily façade."

I was intrigued by Jamison's recalling of the relationship he shared with Cadence Moore back in Dusklight Falls, but as a journalist trying to move this story forward, I pressed him for more. I brought the conversation back to the moment when Jamison, recovered from his weed-induced sleep, came back down to the Basement room to see Cadence hanging over every guy in sight, including Jimmy Derek who was trying without success to move her in another direction. If anything, it appears Jimmy was loyal and didn't want anyone to think he was moving in on a buddy's girl.

Although I had agreed to let him speak uninterrupted, Jamison accepted that we were sticking to the meat and potatoes version of this story and even said, "I'm sorry; I was going on a little tangent there. This whole story is full of layers and I feel like if some of those layers aren't explained, the conclusions become too automatic and based on sound bite information instead of truth.

"But, if you need to talk about the party itself, then I will tell you. I went downstairs and expected to find Cadence hanging out with Darlene and Stephanie. They were there, of course, but at the time were off doing their own thing. Instead of finding Cadence bitching to them about what an ass I was, I found her cuddling up to every college dipshit in sight. These guys she was getting up on were mostly drunken, college assholes, typically not the type of guys Cadence would even give a second look to. But, on this day, she was out to prove a point.

"I must admit, it angered me. I marched down there; keep in mind I'm not Mr. Wild West looking for a gun fight. But, I was not okay with seeing my girl getting way too close to a bunch of other dudes. So, I stormed over and pushed this guy, I don't even remember who he was, and then I grabbed Cadence by the arms and swung her around to ask what the fuck she was doing. This shames me now as I was taught never to lay your hands on a woman. But, I was hurt and pissed and I wasn't thinking straight.

"I think that grabbing my girlfriend's arms contributed more to the rumors of my involvement in her disappearance than anything else. This may not be true, but it feels true to me. She looked at me and that defiant little smirk she'd had on her face when I saw her from the staircase was gone. She was shocked I grabbed her hard and yelled at her. She almost looked like she was going to cry.

"I looked her dead in the eye and said, 'We're going outside now.' She didn't argue. She just pulled away and then headed toward the veranda. I followed her and we both lit up a cigarette. We didn't speak for a few minutes. Neither of us knew what to say; we smoked in silence. This was the beginning of my undoing that night. Jimmy saw me fighting with her and then saw us go outside to smoke, and felt like he should do something.

"Jimmy came out a few minutes after we did. He had two strong drinks of triple vodka, club soda and lime. He gave them both to me and then smiled at Cadence who he was nearly as close to as I was… although strictly as a friend. He flashed a little doobie and touched her cheek. He said, 'Take it baby… love your boy again and end this.'

"Cadence forced a smile and took the joint. She passed it back and forth with Jimmy for a few minutes. She looked over at me as I was chugging the last of the second drink in the hope of floating away until morning so we could pretend this never happened. Tears began welling in her eyes. I wanted to just hug her and kiss her right then and show her I loved her more than anything, but, all I could manage was to remain standing and not stagger around and fall on my ass. She said, 'Let's go to the Falls and forget about this bullshit.'

"I really wanted to, but, I just couldn't. I had just chugged two triple vodkas after smoking up, and had six or seven beers before that. I was fucked, no two ways about it. I couldn't even walk, let alone ride in a car for fifteen minutes to the Falls to eat, smoke more weed, and have sex. There was just no way. I was drifting away by the second.

"I told her in a desperate slur, 'I love you Cadence… I'm sorry but I gotta go to bed. I can't take any more tonight. I want to see you in the morning for breakfast. We can start over and forget all this shit." Cadence made it clear this was not what she wanted to hear. She looked at me with those ice blue eyes and said, plain as day, 'Tomorrow seems like something you feel is coming without a doubt. Maybe there won't be one for us... then what will you do?'

"This was probably nothing more than a cryptic statement made to threaten me or guilt me into doing what she wanted. But after everything that happened, I'll never get that phrase out of my head, because for her there really wasn't a tomorrow." Jamison fought back tears before continuing.

"I couldn't even manage a small reply before taking a step backward and falling on my ass. Jimmy tried to catch me to no avail. I landed in a large potted plant which tipped under my weight. Cadence threw the rest of her joint at me and smiled something that looked more like a snarl and said, 'Go to bed Jamison. I'm outta here.' Then, she went back inside.

"I managed to pull myself up to the window of the door after she went back inside. It seemed like everyone she ran into was putting a shot in her hand. I don't know if word spread about our fight but those little fuckers at the party just seemed hell bent on trying to get her completely drunk, most likely so they could move in and then brag about banging a celebrity girl.

"It really makes me want to cry telling you this, in this studio with a goddamn microphone stuck in my mouth, but her little shuffle through the drunken and generous shot givers, that was the last time I ever saw Cadence.

"I don't want to remember her that way. I wish my last memory of her was from one of those magic Falls evenings, or maybe one of our goofy dates. But seeing her drunkenly sashay through the mass of inebriated idiots on her way to ditching me was not the way I would have preferred to part ways with the first love of my life.

"I watched for ten or twenty seconds as Cadence went back to the party, then I collapsed on the veranda again. Eventually, I drifted off to sleep. Jimmy dragged me over to the corner so I wouldn't get stepped on by smokers stumbling about, and then he went back inside. He knew I was completely gone and his peacemaking efforts had failed. So, he left me alone to sleep it off.

"When I woke up, I staggered back into the party. Cadence was gone. I started running in circles like a lost and lovelorn jerk and going up to people and asking if they saw Cadence somewhere. They all laughed at me and pushed me off in another direction. I couldn't even see straight at this point, and every one of their pushes made me stumble and fall into someone else.

"In my little tornado spin through the masses, I finally ran into Jimmy Derek. He caught me off another push I'd been given and held me up straight. Then he gave me a hug and said, 'Jay, she'll come back to you, bro... just give her time to cool off.'

"Jimmy, the saint that he was, dragged me back out to the veranda and let me just spout off all this incoherent gibberish until I couldn't talk anymore. He must have listened to me for an hour... I don't know; maybe it was only ten minutes, but it felt like a long time.

"Finally, I just kind of drifted over to one side. Jimmy got one of the frat house boys to give me his bedroom. I took three crooked steps in the direction of the bed but ended up on the floor. The next thing I remember, it was daylight and Zach Burns, who I later found out was the guy who offered up his bedroom, was telling me to 'get the fuck out and go home.'"

I asked Jamison if he had any recollection of getting up during the evening. He replied, with some irritation, "Well, that's what is supposed to have happened right? I supposedly faked my drunken stupor so I'd have an alibi. Then I snuck out a window or some bullshit and went to find my girlfriend who I was determined to kill since we had one argument. I guess I found her, god knows where after she'd been kicked out of Darlene's car, and then dragged her to her dorm room and killed her.

"Or, better yet, I killed her in my car and then got rid of her body in some fantasy location that no one has ever found. That wonderful little theory comes from the blood found in my car, and let me tell you since this has bothered me for years, man... the blood in my car... the supposed smoking gun that implicated me in her murder, we're not talking rivers of blood here. We're talking a few small spots which I've already explained the origin of, and I'm not going to disrespect Cadence by going through it again."

I could tell I'd hit a nerve with Jamison and wanted to keep things cool. I apologized for my general phrasing. I was very interested in hearing, from his point of view, how he remembers things *after* he fell asleep, drunk in Zach Burns's bedroom.

Jamison said, "Like I told you, I don't remember anything between collapsing on the floor and waking up to Burns telling me to get out. I know it is the perfect fodder for conspiracy-loving assholes, and a cop who should know better, to paint in a missing timeline. But, that is the truth, and I have two people who have gone on record confirming it, two people who… hmmm… strangely were never contacted by Barnes and Angstat when they made their work of fiction.

"As far as what happened after that, I drunkenly waddled home, tripping over my own feet, and got about another five hours of sleep. I skipped my day classes and just slept it off. I did make an evening class which Darlene was also in, so she can tell you I was there. You can ask her if I looked like someone who had just spent the night killing his girlfriend and burying her in some ditch."

As part of my interview with both Darlene and Stephanie, I did, in fact, bring this part of the story up. I asked them to tell me when they next saw or spoke to Jamison Kelly and what that conversation entailed. And, since no one had seen Cadence since the early morning hours, did he seem worried, upset, or strange in any way?

Darlene recounts, "I didn't see Jamison until the next night. Well, I guess it was the same night, but about sixteen hours later. We had an evening philosophy class together. I saw him in class, and he still appeared hung over. I asked him if he'd talked to Cadence. He said no.

"He asked me if I'd taken her home last night and I explained what happened with the fight in the car. Jamison seemed worried at this point. He left right after class, which was weird for him because he usually hung around with me afterward and smoked a couple of cigarettes. He told me he had to go see what was up with Cadence. I was worried at this point myself since we hadn't heard from her all day and no one seemed to know where she was. I tried to push the whole thing out of my mind, but it wasn't long after that police came and I just knew in my heart something terrible had happened."

Stephanie was not able to shed any additional light on the subject because she didn't see Jamison Monday night; but, she may have revealed some valuable information about Jamison's state of mind when she did eventually see him. She told us, "Unfortunately, I don't know what Jamison was up to that next day. I didn't see him until Wednesdays, usually, when we had a Chinese language and film class together.

"Normally, if I ever saw him before Wednesday, it was because we were partying together with the rest of the group. When I did finally see him on Wednesday of that week, he was totally freaked out. Keep in mind, this was a whole two days after Cadence got out of Darlene's car and she hadn't been heard from since.

"Jamison told me he'd already contacted police, which I knew because they'd already been out to interview us early Wednesday morning. I think her road manager and agent had called the police way before Jamison had, because Cadence wasn't answering her phone.

"When I saw Jamison, I hugged him and said, 'Don't worry Jay… you know how Cadence can be sometimes… she probably blew town for a few days because she was mad at all of us. She gets moody a lot.' Jamison started to protest and said he never saw Cadence very upset or moody… not before that Basement party.

"I did think… I have to admit… that it was really weird for him to say he'd never seen her upset or moody. He was dating her. For some reason, she never apparently showed that side of herself to the boy who was supposed to be closer to her than anyone.

"I thought that didn't quite add up. But, hell, who am I to say it wasn't true. Maybe she just didn't want to show him any negative sides of her personality. Maybe she was trying very hard to be someone else in front of Jamison and please him as much as she could.

"I don't know and she's not here to ask so there's really no point in discussing it. No matter what, though, Jamison was surprised and hurt by the way she'd acted at the Basement party and now he was out of his mind with worry since she'd disappeared. I tried my best to reassure him that Darlene and I had both seen her dark moods, even if he hadn't.

"I told him I was sure she just needed a break and she'll be back soon. 'Try not to let your hair turn gray over it, buddy.' Jamison could not let go of his fears though. He said he had a horrible feeling that something very bad had happened to her and he didn't think he'd be seeing her again.

"Now, this is what I was talking about before. People make these little judgments about what they think must have happened, but, they don't bother listening to people who were there interacting in person with Jamison or Cadence.

"When I saw how worried Jamison was, I knew beyond a shadow of a doubt that he had nothing to do with Cadence's disappearance. I already knew this because I saw how drunk the poor guy was Sunday night and it was clear he wasn't going anywhere.

"But even forgetting that, let me tell you. Just as I know there are planets in the solar system and just as I know there is a god watching over us somewhere up there, I know Jamison Kelly is innocent and wasn't capable of hurting Cadence Moore.

"This is a feeling that cannot be denied, especially since, as I will remind you again, I was there with these people when it all happened. So, I know better than the big mouths who have weighed in on the subject."

Returning to Jamison's comment, I asked, "Considering that your closest friends have protested the conspiracy theories and have come out, loud and confident, regarding your innocence, what do you think it is about you that gives them this type of assurance that you could not have hurt Cadence Moore?"

Jamison Kelly got a little exasperated with me. I could tell that these questions were all hitting nerves. He said, "Well, the main reason why my friends got the vibe that I was innocent is because I *am* fucking innocent, Charlie! I didn't do it. I would have never dreamed of doing it. I know this ruins a good story for a lot of heartless people, but I can't explain the truth in clearer terms. I didn't do it."

I pressed even further, hoping not to break Jamison and push him to a level where he chose to end the interview. I asked, "What do you think your friends and others who were around you in those first days following the disappearance would say about your state of mind?"

Jamison said, "I think that's obvious. My state of mind was one of worry and heartbreak. I not only was scared for the safety of my girlfriend, but

I was upset and sad because I didn't know if I'd ever have a chance to set things right with her after our fight.

"After a few more days, I started to pray. This was probably a week later when it was becoming more apparent with every passing day that Cadence was gone and not coming back, the result of some horrible and violent act I can't even imagine. So, I started to pray.

"I wasn't praying to god since I've always been on the atheist side of that particular fence. But, I was praying to Cadence, wherever she was, begging her to come back. That wasn't working too well for me. About a month later, even less than that, I guess, after it was major news across the nation and we were all resigning ourselves to the idea that Cadence was dead, I prayed once again and promised her that no matter what, I would never stop searching for her. I'd bring her justice if someone had done this to her."

This was delicate territory, but I felt the need to inquire a tiny bit further. I asked, "Jamison, I say this with respect, so please don't feel attacked. How do you feel about those promises and prayers today?"

He looked at me with an angry and befuddled expression, almost like he didn't hear me right but thinks he understood what I said. Jamison's response was not as angry as his look. "Charlie, how do you think I feel, man? I feel like a failure. I feel guilty. I feel like I made a promise I couldn't keep because, as we sit here today, (unless the latest little theory you're promising everyone you have turns out to be true) we still don't know what happened to her. I never searched hard enough to find her and I never brought her any justice.

"So, you ask how I feel? I think the nightmare I discussed with you earlier should be pretty clear. I am haunted by guilt and may never get over it. That's how I feel."

- 4 -

Jamison was extremely sensitive when being asked about the night in question. I'd asked everything I needed to know and I got his response. Whether he is being truthful or not, what we just heard was Jamison Kelly telling his side of the story, which he's never had the opportunity to do on a public platform of this scope.

I moved on to what happened after college. "Jamison, what happened after graduation from DFU? I know how difficult finishing out school must have been after Cadence disappeared, but, I'm very curious about what happened after school was over? What was your first move out into the real world? Did you remain friends with Darlene, Stephanie, and Jimmy? Please fill in the gaps of what became of Jamison Kelly between his time as Cadence Moore's boyfriend and the time he became the man who sits before us today, a very successful and wealthy sales executive who supports a beautiful family in a beautiful home."

Jamison smiled and said, "Well, thank you for that compliment. I'm getting a little worked up as we talk about this, but you have to understand, this period of my life was a true living hell… not the overused living hell phrase that people drop all the time, but an honest-to-god torturous period of pure hell. I loved Cadence more than anything. And, in one moment, she was gone… taken from me and from everyone (Jamison snapped his fingers) just like that.

"But, I managed to move past it. I was in counseling for a very long time… about four years altogether, and I learned that we can do nothing as human beings when things happen out of our control, except move on… keep moving to the next day… and don't stop living. This may sound trite, but the advice worked very well for me.

"I worked through most of my feelings about Cadence. Obviously, not all of them which I'm sure you'll ask me about as we continue talking. But, I got over enough of them that I graduated from DFU and got a job right out of the gates with HANDLER, which everyone always likes to point to as being weird since Darien Moore and Morgan Moore worked there, too. Well, HANDLER is a big company and it was mere coincidence that I found my first job out of college there. Within seven years, I moved up from phone rep to shift lead, to Supervisor, to Manager, and finally Director of Sales. From there, I earned my last promotion a year ago, and now am the Executive VP of sales for the company.

"HANDLER has been great and has never used my past against me, which cannot be said of Darien Moore since they distanced themselves from him as soon as it became clear the evidence of his horrible acts was likely all true. I have cleared this interview with them, by the way, and as long as I tell the truth, I feel pretty secure that they will not try to hang me with it… as long as I tell the truth. HANDLER is looking for this to go to bed as much as I am… well, at least on the surface. They just want it to go away… who wouldn't?

"In my case, my immediate superiors were smart enough to see the Barnes and Angstat movie as a fictional hatchet job. They called me in for questioning and some internal investigation, but as soon as I told them my side, that was good enough for them. Their reasonable judgment was proven when I received my last promotion, just as the Barnes and Angstat movie became hot news everywhere. The marketing department did a blog story for our website in which I spoke a little about Cadence. My superiors went on record to say they support me one hundred percent; and, according to law enforcement, I am not a suspect in this case, regardless of what a movie is telling people. Of course, we had to block comments on that blog since Barnes and Angstat conspiracy supporters blew up the site with accusations and bullshit.

"My boss's boss, Jeremy Wenrich, did some local press explaining that an internal review had been performed and they were standing beside someone they considered a loyal and valuable part of the team. He also said he was confident the true nature of this crime would become public knowledge one day.

"I can't thank HANDLER enough. My bosses, the people who knew me and still bet on me gave me a chance, even as the masses began cursing my name. They even pulled strings with the legal department and got me referred to a great lawyer so I could start the process of suing those sons of bitches who made the movie, until they have to walk around the slums offering to work for food. Their day is still coming; I can promise you that. They've damaged my name, reputation, and mind… you can be damn sure I'll be damaging their wallets.

"But moving on, successful sales career aside, I met my current wife Kim during my last year at DFU. She was living down there with friends but not attending class. She worked at a bookstore and I'd go in there all the time to read physics books... the one's I always impressed girls with by talking about them on dates.

"I kid about this, of course, but the cool thing was... Kim was as into that stuff as I was. We would talk for hours and have coffee after she got off work. We never dated while I was in school, but when I was about to leave and go back home... she gave me her number and made me promise I'd call her.

"I was back home for a few weeks going out on job interviews and got a call from Kim. She was laughing and said she had to resort to stalking me because I didn't keep my promise about calling her. I laughed and actually came out with a clever response which was totally unlike me with women. I said, 'Kim, you won't believe this, but I was just dialing your number when you called and interrupted me right before I could hit the last number.'

"She thought I was funny. We arranged to meet at a halfway point and we went out to some movies together. We dated off and on for a month, and then it got serious. I was having feelings for Kim, the first of any feelings like this since Cadence. I already knew Kim liked me. The sting of losing Cadence was still there in my mind and heart, but I was trying to move on, just like my therapist had advised.

"I guess I took moving on to a new level, because within three months of her calling me at my house, Kim was pregnant with our first child and we were engaged. I had just started on the phones with HANDLER and life was moving very fast; so fast, in fact, that I was almost able to forget about Cadence... almost, but not quite."

Jamison gave us an interesting look at how his new life had begun... but what I wanted to know was why Cadence still hovered over his new life like a shadow, refusing to be forgotten.

Jamison was honest. "Charlie, I tried really hard to forget her... but I couldn't. I felt like part of moving on was forgetting her and if I didn't do that, I'd never be free. Even though I swore to her that I'd never stop searching, it was clear to me and everyone else by this point that she wasn't coming back.

"I had lost touch with almost all of the DFU crew. I hadn't spoken to Darlene or Stephanie since we graduated. I think part of that is because we're all connected to this horrible event, and seeing each other brings it all back every time. I rang up Steve Willis a few times right after college but he lost his life not too long after graduation, which is just a terrible and sad thing to have happened to a nice guy like him.

"Really, the only person I remained in contact with was Jimmy Derek. He was such a good friend and helped me in so many ways. At one point, he was working as a radio DJ and got dumped by the station manager. He was out of work for a little while and I tried my damndest to get him into HANDLER but he just didn't want to do it. I could have started him at double the salary he was making, but Jimmy had a gift for entertaining people and that's what he was happiest doing.

"So, he stayed in the radio game and eventually landed a much more lucrative job hosting a show on politics and other random subjects. You know, I'm actually a little surprised he didn't beat you to this show, Charlie. A series on an unsolved disappearance, especially of a person he knew well, seems like the kind of thing Jimmy would have been all over. Did you talk to him for this?"

I told Jamison, "Absolutely. We completed our interview with him a few days ago and he has not changed his tune from when he first talked to the DFPD right after the incident."

Jamison smiled, "I'm not surprised. I wouldn't have expected Jimmy to change his tune because he's an honest guy and a good friend. Anyway, I've gotten way off topic here. You asked me what kept Cadence in my memory, and what kept me from being unable to forget her.

"The thing here is that no one from the DFU days was even around me, except Jimmy's occasional phone calls or lunch meetings we'd have every few months. But Cadence *was* there… I mean like a presence of her followed me. I could still feel her, even years later. This led me to have nightmares, like the one I described earlier, one of hundreds. I can only guess this whole event was just so heartbreaking and shocking that it stayed with me and never let go."

I figured this was a good time to bring up the other subject Jamison alluded to earlier. I asked, "Jamison, again, with respect… how did this presence of Cadence Moore, and the memories you couldn't let go of… lead you to a place where you were almost put in jail for stalking a woman?"

I will state for the record since not all our listeners are aware of this story. This woman you were accused of stalking, she was actually a college-aged singing star named Lita Marie.

"Jamison, to many folks this looks very odd and frankly very bad. This seems to push a lot of suspicion toward you. Please tell us what happened with Lita Marie so our listeners will understand and you'll have a chance to clear the air for everyone."

Jamison took a deep breath, "Okay, listen… this whole story is embarrassing for me because I just wasn't thinking straight at the time, and I… I did some really stupid things. It all started when I was watching television. It was some show Kim had on, a music show where they do a countdown of whatever the top music picks are that week. Anyway, this video comes on. I couldn't tell you what the music sounded like or anything. I just remember this singer, Lita Marie. She had piercing blue eyes and they were, I don't know how to say it without sounding completely nuts, but it was like I was looking into Cadence's eyes. No, it wasn't *like* looking into Cadence's eyes, I *was* looking into Cadence's eyes. I became sure in that moment watching the screen that Cadence Moore was alive and she was pretending to be this other person, Lita Marie.

"Keep in mind that at this juncture in my life, I was feeling the pressure of having to meet sales numbers at HANDLER, drinking way too much every night, and Kim and I were experiencing our first taste of marital conflict.

"When I saw that girl's eyes, it was like looking back into a time machine and seeing Cadence Moore right there in front of me. I was smoking a lot of weed at this point, too, in addition to the heavy drinking. Kim didn't know the extent of it, but I was kind of whacked out of my mind on a nightly basis. To say I wasn't thinking straight would be an understatement. As I said earlier, I never could handle the stuff.

"I started having dreams where I saw those blue eyes in the sky and

I was driving this huge big rig for some reason, following those eyes and moving toward Cadence. I must have had thirty dreams between the time I saw this video and the time I met Lita Marie for the first time. I was literally obsessed with those eyes. I couldn't let it go."

I had to point out the obvious questions that have occurred to most people who are aware of this story and I hoped Jamison could explain. "Jamison, it seems very peculiar that you would come to this conclusion. While Lita Marie does have piercing blue eyes, she bears only a passing resemblance to Cadence Moore. Plus, the strangest thing about this is that Cadence would have been in her mid-twenties by this point, since you saw this video in 2007 when Cadence would have been twenty-three or twenty-four years old."

This singer, Lita Marie, for those of you who don't know, was a bit of a one-hit wonder who disappeared by 2008 or so and hasn't had a hit record since. But, Lita Marie was only seventeen years old when she made that video. "Jamison, some have questioned your judgment when you mistook a seventeen-year-old girl for someone who would have been a good six or seven years older. What made you so sure?"

Jamison shook his head, "I can't really tell you in a way that makes a lot of sense, Charlie. It was the eyes... the eyes convinced me. They were an exact match. Yeah, she looked a little different and had brown hair... but my mind began working overtime in rationalizing all that. I started thinking she disappeared on purpose. She was done with me and done with her friends from Dusklight Falls. So, she decided to get a little plastic surgery, after all she had plenty of money, and she became this other person."

I persisted with the logical arguments many had over the years. "Okay, Jamison, I can see how this rationalization made you think you were on to something, but some big questions seem to have eluded you... or at least eluded you at that time. The biggest one would be this. Why would a girl who tried so hard to disappear from DFU, and make people think she was dead, intentionally pop up five years later as a college singer who is being seen by millions of people on television? This seems a strange thing for a person to do when they're trying to disappear."

Jamison nodded, "Look, I realize this now. I was a fool for thinking the way I did, but I wasn't in my right mind. I became obsessed with those eyes and everything flowed from there. I started filling in all the blanks. Cadence was sick of her life, and decided to become something else. Then, in my little fantasy, she missed performing and singing, so she went back in that direction, only as a different identity. Plus, I figured even though Cadence would have been in her mid-twenties, it was possible she could pass for a seventeen-year-old. She always did look youthful, so it's not out of the realm of logic that she was pretending to be as young as Lita Marie actually was."

I said, "I'm hearing that, Jamison, but these questions are still overpowering. The second one which is hard to explain away is the fact that Lita Marie has a whole backstory. She has parents. She has public records. She existed and lived a whole seventeen years before making that video. Did you realize during your period of obsession how many people would have had to lie and be part of a if Lita Marie was, in fact, Cadence Moore? Lita Marie's supposed parents, her siblings, her teachers from elementary school, talent scouts, her friends… the list literally goes on and on."

I pushed too hard with my last comment and Jamison pushed back. He slammed his hand on the desk and yelled, "Goddamn it! What did I say to you? I was a fool for believing it. I wasn't thinking straight. Jesus, it wasn't like I was trolling around on IMDB reading Lita Marie's biography and trivia sections. I probably should have and I could have talked myself out of the craziness of it all. But I didn't. I saw those eyes and became obsessed. I admit that. A happily married father saw eyes on TV that reminded him of a love lost and I lost my damn mind for a while. I had to see for myself, so I didn't talk to anyone about it. But I came up with a plan… a plan only I knew about. I secretly purchased a ticket and backstage pass to Lita Marie's next concert which was all the way in Clearwater, Florida and I went there."

I interrupted him at this point, partially to calm Jamison down by taking his side on something. I didn't want him to feel attacked but these eight hundred-pound gorillas in the room needed to be escorted out. I was trying to be as delicate as possible, but I'd struck another nerve. Now I had to bring him back a little.

I said, "I think that's important to point out here, Jamison. The phrase 'stalking charges' sounds huge and ominous. But, in reality, the contact you had with Lita Marie was not actually that much. Am I correct about that?"

Jamison took a deep breath and when he continued speaking his tone was more even and relaxed than before. I'd managed to get him back and would have to watch myself from this point on… which was rather difficult for me to do, weary travelers, as you'll soon see for yourselves.

Jamison continued, "As I said, Charlie, I bought the ticket because I had this overwhelming feeling that no matter how unrealistic it was, I had seen Cadence again and she was alive and well. I had no other choice but to go see for myself.

"I mean, think about it; if I had been right, and damn it I know I wasn't, but if I had been, it would mean the love of my life was still alive and I could go see her and touch her again. I mean really, man, it was crazy. It took me a long time to heal relations with my wife after this since she was rightfully pissed and terribly hurt by this whole ridiculous thing.

"You ask how much contact I had with Lita Marie? I met her only twice. The first time I met her was in Clearwater at the concert. I told you I bought tickets and backstage passes and then drove all the way down, telling Kim I had a sales conference.

"I sat through her concert and even then, it dawned on me that she really didn't sound like Cadence when she was singing. But, I figured again that Cadence altered her voice, just the way she altered her looks and identity. I know this is the rambling of a psychopath, and I can't argue with that. But you want the truth and I am giving you the truth.

"I sat through the songs and then made my way backstage. After twenty minutes, I still hadn't seen her. She finally did come back to the backstage area. I was hanging around by the catering table munching on little pigs in a blanket while Lita was talking to other fans, local newspaper reporters, and her management people. She turned a corner and I got my first glimpse of her. She seemed to be the same height as Cadence and I could make out her blue eyes from thirty feet away.

"I quickly made my way over to her and got as close as I could, about six feet from where she stood still talking to people. The electricity and nervous energy I felt coursing through my body at this point were literally overwhelming. I yelled out, 'I told you! I told you I'd never stop searching! I knew it was you as soon as I saw those eyes. I knew it!'

"Well, needless to say, Lita Marie was startled by my outburst. She looked me right in the eyes for a second and I didn't see recognition, I saw wariness. She said, 'Um... hey buddy if you're talking to me, I don't think I am who you think I am.'

"The last thing I said was, 'Cadence... Jesus Christ, it's me! Cadence, I know it's you, you can stop this now.' Lita Marie looked at me like she was scared I was going to pull out a gun and shoot her or something. She yelled out for a guy named Werner, who was her security man. The next thing I know, I'm being dragged out of there and thrown out in the street by this giant man who was not very gentle with me to say the least."

I really wanted to probe into the actual state of Jamison Kelly's mind during this period. I asked, already knowing the answer before I did, "Did this experience, getting kicked out into the street and this girl who you thought was Cadence Moore acting scared and ordering you to be removed, help reality set in at all for you, Jamison? Or, did you start to rationalize more?"

Jamison looked down at the ground and was silent for a moment... he looked ashamed. He said, "It probably should have... but I have to say it did not. I became convinced that Cadence was just surprised by me showing up unexpectedly and she didn't know what to do, so she panicked. She didn't seem to recognize me, but I convinced myself I had just surprised her and she was desperately acting like she had no idea who I was. After all, she went to a lot of trouble to disappear, in my fantasy world.

"So, I... well, I found a way to go see her again. I figured if I could catch her in more private surroundings, then she wouldn't feel the need to keep up her charade. I looked at Lita Marie's tour schedule and it turned out she was touring Reading, Pennsylvania a few weeks later which is close to where I lived at the time in Ephrata. I bought more tickets, but this time instead of backstage passes, I had another idea.

"I asked around and easily found out who was handling the catering at this particular concert. All I had to do was call the Sovereign Center in Reading and claim I was a logistics coordinator from the corporate office who needed directions for one of our trucks. Just like that, the Sovereign Center rep asked me if I was coming from our factory and I said yes. Then she said, 'If the truck's coming from Tasty Town on 5th Street, all you have to do is follow… and she went on and on from there. That's how I learned that Tasty Town was catering.

"I got to the concert early that night, about four hours early. I went to the backstage area… Lita's tour bus hadn't arrived yet. I had a bag with me filled with rolls that I had actually just bought at Jack's, an Italian restaurant in town. Between the rolls and the fact that I had dressed in black dress pants, a white shirt, and black bow tie, with a name tag that had *Tasty Town* and the name Ben under it, that was enough of a ruse to convince Sovereign Center security that I was with the Tasty Town catering company.

"He let me backstage, right into her dressing room (marked by a lightning bolt and star with her name through it on a stick-on banner) and I started arranging the rolls on a banquet plate by a make-up table. I told a guard, 'The rest of my team's out front getting things together. They'll be back in a bit, but I want to get this part done before security has to seal it off.' No disrespect to the guy, but what an awful security guard. He just nodded and walked away. I disappeared from there quickly and hid in a closet until the concert was over, probably six hours later.

"The closet was huge. There were giant black sheets of cloth that they use at concerts and events to cordon off different areas. I covered myself with one of them and hid in the back corner. I was sweating like a hog and cramping horribly because I was still and silent for so long, trying to avoid being seen. When Lita's security team did eventually sweep through the room a while later, I heard them open the closet. My heart just about stopped. I was convinced in that moment they would discover me and I'd be hauled downtown, probably after first getting the shit kicked out of me. But, they never saw me.

"The concert finally was over. I could tell by the crowd noise and a faint muttering of 'Thank you, Reading, you guys are the best.' I waited in the closet and listened. Lita hung out for a while signing autographs, schmooz-ing, doing her whole deal. Finally, after what seemed like a year, I heard the click on her dressing room door. She said, 'Thanks Werner, give me like twenty minutes, okay?' I had already cracked the door a few minutes before and as I slowly approached, I could see into the room. I saw her go in and sit down in front of the dressing room mirror. She let out a deep sigh and stretched her arms out. I made my move.

"I whispered, 'Cadence.' Lita whirled around, terrified and shocked. I barely got out my next words, 'We're alone now, you don't have to keep up the act. They can't hear us.' Lita let out a murderous shriek. '*Werner, get in here now... help me!*' Before I knew it, a gigantic man, the same guy who dragged me out before in Clearwater, was choking me around the neck with his huge arm. It felt like an anaconda was choking the life out of me.

"Werner dragged me outside and knocked me down on the ground. He pulled a gun, pointed it right at my face, and screamed in a very unfriendly manner, 'Stay the fuck down, you loony bastard! The cops will be taking you in a minute.' I was scared at that point, and tried to get up to run. Werner stomped me in the back of the head, almost knocking me out.

"The next thing I remember, I was in the back of a cop's car being driv-en to the Reading Police Station. They put me in one of the interrogation rooms and a rather nice officer named Bobby Williams sat down with me and asked what the hell I was doing in Lita Marie's dressing room.

"I actually cried, Charlie. I simply hung my head and cried like a baby. I think Bobby was about to give up when I started explaining who I was and why I was there. After about forty minutes of talking about Cadence and the fact that I was haunted by her disappearance, I tried to explain that I was sure Lita was Cadence and I just wanted to talk to her.

"Bobby must have felt sorry for me because, amazingly, he let me walk out of there that night, but not before a very long lecture and an even longer phone call with Lita Marie's security team. They did end up getting a protec-tive order issued against me, but after Bobby told them the story, they de-cided not to pursue any further charges. I understand my picture was passed around to every security team in every building where she performed for the next year. And, I was required to check in with Bobby Williams every week so he could report, as my volunteer babysitter, that I wasn't getting into any trouble. I can't overstate this. I owe that man a lot. My insane behavior could have wrecked my whole life and I could have been in a lot more hot water than I was. Bobby Williams is a hell of a man in my opinion and someone I'll always be grateful to.

"Over the next few weeks, reality started to set back in and I realized how crazy and foolish I'd been. Kim was livid when she first found out and didn't understand why, even if it *had* been Cadence, I felt the need to go behind her like this and sneak around to rekindle some old romance from the past.

"I tried to explain it better than that, but I knew Kim was right. She had every reason to be angry and she left me for two months until we talked things out and got back together. It was a terrible dark time for me. HANDLER at least was left out of it because none of this made the papers. I was sure this would be front-page news. I guess it turns out that crazy fans bothering celebrities is not all that newsworthy or else nobody from the police or Lita Marie's team contacted any reporters, so I was saved from a possible firing by HANDLER. I already worked there and had all my background checks so the PFA order didn't end up being something anyone knew about until years later, and by then it didn't mean much anymore.

"As for Lita Marie, I felt horrible for scaring her like I did. When I got my wits about me and researched her a little, I realized she was not Cadence Moore. I really *was* a creepy weird stalker who scared this poor girl half to death. I even wrote her a letter of apology. I cleared it with Officer Williams first and he insisted on reading it and mailing it himself to make sure I didn't add any psycho stuff to it.

"I don't know if Lita Marie ever got my letter, but if she's listening now, I just want to say I'm sorry for scaring you. I did it because I thought I'd gotten another chance to see Cadence Moore alive again and it consumed me, through and through."

I let Jamison know at this point that *Underground Podcast* did interview Lita Marie, who is currently working as a producer in California, helping other young artists make recordings. Lita used the power and notoriety of

her one major hit, a song called "Planking on the Tracks," to shift into another career. We reached out to her and she responded and agreed to do the
show. She discussed the letter Jamison Kelly wrote to her. She also discussed
how, after seeing *Moore to the Story*, she doesn't quite know how to feel
about the man who once stalked her from a dressing room closet.

Lita explained to us, "When it first happened, I was really scared. This
random guy who I'd never seen before just showed up at two concerts. At
the second one, he made it all the way to my dressing room which really
freaked me out because, number one, it was really creepy, and number two,
it showed me that I had major holes in my security arrangement.

"My bodyguard, Werner Sternzog, a gentle bear of a man to those who
were close with him, but a straight up beast if you crossed him, had to drag
this guy out into the street on two separate occasions. The last time, in
Reading, Werner was forced to pull a gun on him.

"A few months later, a letter was mailed to my fan club address. My assistant, Randie, called Werner and asked to speak to me. She said, 'Lita, I
wouldn't normally bother you with this kind of stuff, but I think the guy that
wrote this letter is the same dude that Werner had to rough up in Reading.
Do you want to know what he's saying in this letter?'

"Obviously, I *did* want to know since I think a sick part of our human
psyche demands that we embrace madness or something. I told Randie to
give me the abbreviated version. She said, 'All I can say is this guy seems
to be awful sorry for all the trouble he caused, and on top of that, he has a
hell of a back story.'

"That made me pause. I started to think it may be worthwhile to read
his letter. Don't ask me why because I don't know. I'm glad I felt this way
and insisted that Randie fax the letter to me in Austin, Texas where I was
currently touring. When I read the letter, I was overcome with a feeling of
empathy for this man. I felt sorry that he lost his girlfriend. I wasn't really
familiar with Cadence Moore, even though I'd heard the story over the years
since it was such a huge deal at one point. In fact, my Dad was pretty much
addicted to the case when it was national news. But, I really felt sorry for this
man, Jamison Kelly. He became convinced that I was Cadence Moore and

all he was trying to do was reconnect with a love he had lost.

"I let go of all my anger and fear about the creepy stalker who scared me. All I could do now was just feel sorry for the guy. I stopped short of writing him back because of a little voice in my head that warned me if this guy really was a creeper with a good story made up to tug on people's heartstrings, I shouldn't encourage him to write more, or even worse, show up at any more concerts."

I told Jamison Kelly about the comments Lita Marie had made. They seemed to relieve him. Jamison smiled and actually shed a few tears. He said, "Charlie, it's good enough for me that the girl I terrified by being an out-of-control lunatic actually has enough human decency to realize I was lost and desperate at the time. Lita seems to understand why I did what I did, and that alone makes me feel a lot better. I certainly didn't mean to scare her or make her feel threatened. I was just out of my mind and thought I had another chance to see Cadence again. I'm relieved things didn't turn out worse because, based on my behavior, they certainly could have."

I had one final question for Jamison Kelly. I first thanked him for being so up front and honest with us, and for doing the show which I know was not easy for him. My final question for Jamison was asking him what it felt like to be tied to this so closely, branded a stalker and a murderer, and still somehow find the strength to go on with his daily life and the raising of his family. Jamison extended his hand to me to shake and I returned his gesture. Jamison went on to say, "Being tied to the disappearance and possible murder of Cadence Moore has been the single most significant event I've ever experienced.

"As mentioned earlier, I will be suing Barnes and Angstat and making them pay for the slander they perpetrated on my name. But, as far as the general public goes, I'm still the guy waiting in the shadows to snatch up his girlfriend because I'm mad with jealousy. That's been the hardest part since the initial police investigation and the subsequent documentary piece of shit produced by Barnes and Angstat.

"You ask me how I have the strength to go on. I don't really know how to answer you except to say that I have no other choice. I have a wife and kids who need home and shelter, and I have no choice but to provide it. But my reputation out there in the world is terrible and stained with guilt. Two irresponsible filmmakers made it their mission to smear me and point the finger in my direction because they needed an ending to their film.

"So, I want to use this last statement on your show, Charlie, to let everyone know I am not the monster I've been painted out to be. I loved Cadence Moore more than anything and when she was taken, my life dissolved for a while. I managed to rebuild that life after a long time, but I still have my scars and that movie brought all this stuff back to the surface. It has given me fits of insomnia, nightmares, fear, and frustration ever since.

"I want to leave your listeners with this. Don't believe everything you read and hear because it's the details *not* included that tell the story. I can tell from my time here with Charlie Marx and *Underground Podcast* that all the details, at least the ones I have control over, have been included this time. When you listen to this, please consider everyone and everything in this presentation. Then, you are welcome to pass judgment and make your own decision. Charlie, I appreciate the time very much, and I want to say I am indescribably thankful I met my wife, Kim. I've been fortunate enough to raise a family with a woman who has more patience and compassion than anyone on the planet. She deserved better than the husband I was for a while and I'll spend the rest of my life trying to be the one she truly deserves."

Thank you very much, Jamison Kelly. I hope this experience has done some good for you and I anticipate your reaction to our final conclusions.

This is the end of Episode 3 of *Charlie Marx's Underground Podcast*. Make sure you tune in to the final podcast episode in which Todd Barnes and Michael Angstat are interviewed as we move to the finish line and the live special in which the Cadence Moore mystery will be solved live on UPR!"

6

The Final Podcast and the Live Special Looms

UNDERGROUND PODCAST 4: (Official Transcript)
Part 1: The Diaries of Cadence and Morgan Moore

Charlie Marx's Underground Podcast: Episode 4 (Part 1). Original Drop Date: November 1, 2013. (Brought to you by United Way of Life, courtesy of Tyler Reubens... this program is funded and sponsored by WHHW, a subsidiary of Universal Public Radio)

(Narration by Charlie Marx) As we move along here with our final podcast in the series, please remember that we still have our conclusions to review. We have an answer to the mystery we've been dissecting tonight and before this series comes to a close, you all will know what happened to Cadence Moore. This is not a theory. This is an answer that we can prove beyond any doubt.

However, for this conclusion to have any resonance and for you to accept it for the fact that it is, we have to go over every detail, every theory, and every so called "fact" that has come before.

With that in mind, we still have some major players to speak with, most notably Todd Barnes and Michael Angstat, the filmmakers who rekindled the national flame of this case with their documentary film, *Moore to the Story*. But before we speak to those gentlemen, we must look a bit deeper into the mental state under which Cadence Moore lived her life before she entered Dusklight Falls University.

There is no better way to do this than speaking to Cadence Moore herself. Sadly, it is not possible to interview Cadence Moore, but what we can do is probe into her thought process by reviewing the contents of her diary.

We will also be looking at some excerpts from Morgan Moore's diary, which shed a lot of light into the mental struggles he was battling with when he finally decided to end his life precisely at a time when success was just over the horizon for him.

I must get something out of the way first. Many have criticized me, within the programming family of Global Media Cooperation, UPR, and the *Underground Podcast* team themselves, not to mention fans in general who were aware that we'd be revealing diary excerpts during this show. To these folks, I say two things.

First, Pandora's Box was already opened when the diaries were discovered and their contents flashed across several different media outlets. Second, while reading off the private thoughts of deceased persons who no longer can speak for themselves is a shady operation to be sure, it also is the only way for the voice of a victim to be heard.

Not to review these diary findings would be a disservice to Cadence Moore, and to be honest, Morgan Moore as well, since he was forced into a situation he did not create and had to deal with the mental anguish that resulted from it.

So, if you want to call me shady, I welcome your accurate opinion. But, I care less about being shady than I do about Cadence's story getting told correctly and fairly, once and for all. For that to happen, some necessary pieces of this puzzle are the very thoughts and feelings of Cadence Moore herself. We will be rounding out the reading of these excerpts with commentary by Cadence's closest associates, so we will hopefully achieve a balance that ends up being fair and just to everyone involved.

I want to address briefly how these diaries were made public in the first place. Cadence's journal, hidden in the attic of the Moore family home and obviously not known to exist by Darien (otherwise he would have gotten rid of it for sure), was seized as a piece of evidence when Cadence disappeared and the investigation was in full swing.

Morgan Moore also kept a diary, but he kept it with him all the time and it was not seized by police when the house was searched. However, Morgan's diary was stolen by a young neighbor and friend of Morgan's named Paul Woodsen.

We tracked down Paul Woodsen, now in his late twenties and living in Tuscaloosa, Alabama working as a substitute school teacher. We asked Paul about the circumstances leading to his possession of Morgan's diary. We wanted to find out if Paul had to resort to extreme measures to attain the diary or if Morgan had made it easy. The answer to this question I believe speaks volumes about whether Morgan Moore wanted this information made public. After speaking with Paul, we believe he did.

Paul explains, "Morgan really wanted me to have it, I think. I know this sounds like the rationale of a thief, and to a certain extent it is, but I know Morgan wanted someone to know he had it and would not have objected, I think, if someone came into possession of it and let the words get out to the public.

"During my visits with him, we'd usually be playing video games and talking comic books. I was a few years younger than him, but he didn't have a lot of friends. He hung with a bad crowd and did stupid things, but he wasn't really friends with those guys. They were his connection to bad decisions and destructive behavior and that was about it. But when I hung with him, Morgan liked it because we had the same interests in more innocent and fun things. Morgan could be a cool guy when you got to know him.

"One time, after the whole house got searched when Cadence disappeared, Morgan started telling me that he had a diary and the cops never got hold of it. Morgan said, 'God, if the cops knew what was in here, certain people would already be in handcuffs.' This piqued my interest and I asked him to let me see it, but he said it was private and only for his eyes. He said he shouldn't have even mentioned it. But then he made a big show out of putting it on his bookshelf in plain sight. If he was worried about someone taking it, he certainly didn't take many precautions to avoid that.

"A day or two later I was hanging out with him again and he took a break from our video game. I can't remember for the life of me now what we were playing, but he got up to go use the bathroom and I took my chance to snatch the diary. Later that night, I read what was inside and I went right to the cops.

"They found it to be faulty evidence, I guess, because even after they had handwriting experts compare the writing with Morgan's writing and it matched, just like it had with Cadence when they cross checked the handwriting in her journal, it was still just the writing of someone and not verifiable as facts.

"That was true with Cadence since she wasn't around anymore to validate any facts. But Morgan was still around and he could have verified every word in that journal. I wanted him to and I begged him to, but he got all pissed at me for taking it and said I should never show my face at his door again.

"It sucked that I lost a friend, but I still somehow felt that Morgan would do the right thing. For some reason that I'll never understand, he denied that any of his writings were true and said he made everything up. Obviously either Darien got to him and promised him the world to keep quiet, or he was just so intimidated by his dad that he couldn't speak out against him. I don't know what it was but it kept him from talking.

"I think the guilt from holding back that information and dismissing everything he wrote as lies was a big part of the reason Morgan ended up killing himself later. He couldn't stand that he lied and didn't even speak out for his own flesh and blood while the monster who controlled both of them was getting away scot free… if not with murder, then at least with the incest and abuse.

"That was a lot for Morgan to carry around. I never did get it though. I'd made it so easy by taking the diary and releasing it to the cops. All Morgan would have had to do was confirm it and the police could have investigated Darien on criminal charges, not just related to the disappearance, but everything else that went on before that."

I interjected and made the point to Paul that maybe it wasn't as easy as he thought for Morgan to give up his father. I said, "Paul, you certainly did make things more direct for Morgan. He now just had to simply say yes or no to the allegations written in his diary. But when you say it would have been easy, I have to believe Morgan was controlled on many levels by his father and had been bailed out by him on several juvenile crimes and the punishments that should have followed them. So, saying it would have been easy to come forward… I just don't know if that's accurate."

Paul nodded, "I know what you're saying. I also know it wouldn't have been easy because on some screwed up level Morgan loved his dad and idolized him. I know it would have been hard for him to sell Darien down the river. But what I meant was I made it so easy by putting the truth out there. Morgan couldn't even be blamed for blowing the whistle. All he had to say was that the diary was true. But he didn't.

"Morgan kept quiet and denied the whole thing and the cops couldn't use it to put Darien in jail. But, thankfully, someone from the police force went into business for themselves because the media had it within weeks of me stealing it, and I never gave it to any media people. I tried to do things by the book... well, aside from stealing it in the first place.

"But within weeks the diary was plastered everywhere, so somebody in blue got a big payday out of it. Not to mention, Cadence's journal, which the police were in possession of from moment one, also got the press treatment. Something tells me the transfer of these books to the television sets of the world was not made on the simple basis of uncovering truth. Like I said, somebody got paid."

- 2 -

Okay, so now we know how the diaries of Cadence Moore and Morgan Moore were made public in the first place. Let's examine what is contained within them. First, let's take a look at some of the excerpts from Morgan Moore's diary.

His journal begins before the incest incidents and really goes into a lot of his feelings regarding his mother's death and some of the crimes he was committing to get back at society or whatever his motivation was for doing them.

We will not focus on these excerpts heavily, but I find it prudent to at least consider them in the overall picture because Morgan's state of mind had a lot to do with his behavior and his eventual end. None of the entries are dated so we can only guess at the timeline. Also, we are calling these entries first, second, third, etc., but we skipped several entries in between and are only focusing on the ones we find most relevant. One of our staff radio actors, Walt Collins, is doing the narration here.

First entry: "Fuck this world. I can't fucking stand the stupid asshole looks I get from people in school. I hate them all. They have no idea what real tragedy is so they just fake these stupid sympathetic looks at me in the hallway. Like I'm so sorry, I know this must be so hard. But they don't know fucking shit. They all should be dead. If I had the fucking balls to go to jail for the rest of my fucking life, I'd go into school tomorrow and start shooting every single person who gave me a stupid look right in their fucking faces. Then I'd get to see what a real horrified look was like on their faces."

Second Entry: "My only relief is writing in a fucking diary like a teenage girl. Fuck it. It's better than fucking counselors. Dad made me see one for one appointment just to see how it goes and I told him when it was over that if he ever makes me do that again I'd run away and he'd never see me again. Dad is trying to be cool but he's just as fucked up as me and he can't show it to anyone. I told him to just leave me alone. I said he should give himself a chance to be fucked up for a while like me since, if he didn't, he was really just a liar. He looked at me with a stupid look of confusion or pity or whatever fake emotion he was trying to show and just walked away. I hope he leaves me alone soon. I really can't stand how he tries to fix me when all he does is stay up all night until 5:00 a.m. drinking gin. He's drunk all the time, but I'm the one that needs the counselor. That makes sense... sure it does."

Third Entry: "Me and Cadence went to the lake today. We got stoned as motherfuckers and it felt good. She's younger than me, but Cadence is the closest thing to a friend I have now. She understands what this feels like. We got stoned and then threw a picture of Mom into the lake. I don't know why but that felt like the right thing to do. I want to help Cadence through this but I don't know what the fuck to say."

Fourth Entry: "I am the smartest motherfucking thief that ever lived. Okay, dear fucking diary, let me tell you how to pull a goddamn robbery. It's so easy. I will never get caught because I'm smarter than everyone else when it comes to this shit. Okay, dear diary... here goes. This is how to rob a convenience store using a dog, a bag, a track suit, and no weapons.

"First, I dressed up in some preppy shit I stole out of Dad's closet, a little sweater and some khaki shorts.

"Second, I put on a snap button wind suit from my track days. All you have to do to pull this shit off is tug hard and it all snaps off, pants and jacket, within a second.

"Third, I pick the Pheasant Hill Convenience store right out in the boonies, only a five-minute walk from my house. This place has a little woods behind it and you can easily stay hidden back there if you're trying to pull some shit. I put my backpack on and my tracksuit on.

"Fourth, before I left the house, I put Lucy our beagle in my backpack. She was all freaked out and was whining but I left the zipper open for her to breath. She only weighs like ten pounds and isn't heavy to carry. I put biscuits in the bag so she'd be entertained and not bark while I walked to the store. I also stuffed a book in there, which comes in handy later.

"Fifth: I get to within one hundred yards of the store. I look around to make sure no one's watching. I sneak into the woods behind Pheasant Hill. I hung the backpack with Lucy in it from the branch of a tree so she won't try to jump out while I'm gone. I pull out a replica pistol that my friend Shane sold me for $12.00. It's fake as shit but you can't tell that by looking. I pulled a black ski mask out of my track suit pocket, put it on, and ran out of the woods into the store.

"Sixth: I run up to the register and pull out the fake gun. No one is in the store but me and the sales chick. I tell this bitch to give me as much cash as she can within ten seconds. She starts saying the register is all she can open but the manager only has access to the safe. I tell her fuck the safe and give me what's in the register. She hands me seventy bucks in cash and I tell her to get down on the ground and stay there for five minutes. I tell her I got a guy across the street watching and if he sees her move within five minutes, he's gonna start shooting at her from where he is. She gets down on the ground and is crying. I don't feel bad at all. This is a fucking riot!

"Seventh: The beauty of my plan. I run back out to the woods. I rip the track suit and mask off, use the mask to wipe off the fake gun and throw all of it into the woods. Then I pull Lucy out of the backpack. She was whining and freaking out at this point again. I hold her leash, which was attached to her the whole time. Then I stuff the seventy bucks into the wallet I was keep-ing in my khaki shorts which I had on underneath the track suit the whole time. I picked up the backpack and put it on over both shoulders. I leave the bottom part of the woods with Lucy on her leash, about two hundred yards from where I first entered, and start walking on the street like any other preppy douche bag just taking his puppy for a walk and I head back toward the Pheasant Hill Convenience store.

"Eighth: For this to be truly perfect, I wanted to get stopped by a cop. Well, the pigs didn't let me down. I got about a quarter mile past the Pheasant Hill store and I was stopped by this fat retarded-looking cop. He asks me if I know anything about the Pheasant Hill getting robbed. I tell him I just went past there and didn't see anything. Was anyone hurt, I ask? This fat ass isn't satisfied and tells me to please open my back pack just so he can be sure. I open up the back pack and it contains two dog biscuits that Lucy didn't eat and the book I'd brought along, which was *The Grotesque Majesty of it All* by F.S. Star. I told the cop I brought the snacks for my dog and the book in case we decided to stop. The kicker was when I asked if there was anything I could do to help. He said, no that's all right, enjoy your walk. But please do call us if you see anyone around here wearing a black track suit. I told the pig, sure officer, I'd be happy to.

"This is fucking incredible. Misdirection, that's what it's all about. That's how you pull off a fucking crime. Go into the place with a black suit on and a mask. Come out of it looking like a preppy asshole walking a dog and no one suspects you. I spent the seventy bucks on two pornos, a carton of smokes, and a seafood dinner at the Salty Lobster. It was the best dinner I ever tasted."

Fifth entry: "I guess the smartest thief of all time didn't work. I'm so fucking stupid. I was thinking I was hot shit after my robbery. So, two days after, Shane and I decided to try again, only this time we robbed the Weathers Grocery store. Well, Weathers doesn't have woods behind it and I also wasn't smart enough to bring the dog this time.

"So, we go in there. We're back at the candy racks and we put on our masks. If we went in there with them on, we wouldn't have been able to surprise everyone and catch them off guard. Shane walks out first and pulls a gun on the cashier. All the other customers and cashiers freeze and look over. Well, this cashier starts handing Shane the money. I come out of the candy racks and start telling all the customers to give me their wallets, just like the criminals in *Pulp Fiction* did. All of them do it.

"I'm thinking we've got this shit wrapped up and we're gonna triple my take from Pheasant Hill. So, in our black masks, we leave the store and start running across the parking lot. Our friend Katie was waiting in a car two streets down. All we had to do was make it to her, ditch the masks, and we'd be home free.

"No sooner do we get out of the parking lot, a cruiser comes barreling down after us and the pig pulls his piece and shouts at us to get the fuck down. Apparently, as I was collecting wallets, every fucking cashier hit their panic button, even though we told them to get down on the ground. They must have been able to reach the button from there, because cops were on their way before we even left the store. Katie must have figured it out and drove away after a few minutes.

"Shane and I were stuck at the police station for four hours. Dad came in finally and talked to the cops. Then he talked to Shane. After like two more hours he finally came over to me and told me we were going home. He must have paid off the cops to keep certain parts of the story out of their reports and he must have promised Shane a hell of a lot for him to shut up. If not that, I don't know what he did, but I walked out of there like none of it happened. It's been three weeks and I've heard nothing about it. Dad saved my ass and I guess I shouldn't put it on the line anymore. I just find it hard to give a fuck. I really don't give a fuck about anything."

Sixth Entry: "I thought that my life was already fucked up. But what I saw tonight is the most fucked up thing anyone could ever see in their whole lives. I know it wasn't a dream, but I wish it was. I was sleeping and I woke up to a bunch of thumping around downstairs. So, I went down there and I see Dad stumbling off the couch with his fucking pants down. Then Cadence crawls off the other end and she's crying. Cadence was naked. I looked away and tried to make sure I was really awake. At this point I yelled at Dad and said what the fuck's going on? He looks at me and says, go back to sleep Morgan. Cadence got drunk tonight and I am making her take a shower because she stinks like liquor and puke. Go back to bed.

"Here's the deal… Cadence may have been drunk but I saw her on the couch naked and I saw Dad with his pants down. I know what the fuck he did. I'm gonna kill him if I ever see this kind of shit again. I swear to god."

Seventh Entry: "Dad has been fucking Cadence. I've walked in on it now three times. Tonight was the last straw. I came down when I heard the noises. Then, I actually saw him doing her. I ran over to the couch and punched him in the face. He fell on the floor screaming at me. I told Cadence to go upstairs because I was gonna teach Dad a fucking lesson. She ran up to her room crying.

"I started kicking Dad in the stomach and he starts fucking crying and saying he didn't mean to and he couldn't stand losing Collette, and please forgive him and please this and please that. I yelled in his face that if I ever saw this again, I'd kill him. No better yet, I'd go the cops and they would do a test and he wouldn't be able to pay anyone off then."

Eighth Entry: "It's been a month since I caught them. Dad promised that this fucked up shit was going to stop and I think he means it. He also promised to get me a sales job making 50K a year if I just let this go. I'd be hurting Cadence worse if I talked. Dad promised he'd get her counseling and help her with her singing. Dad says he'll make everything right."

Ninth Entry: "I've been out getting drunk every night and tonight when I came home Dad was mad. He was fucked up, too, and he started screaming at me about how he saved my ass when I robbed the store and, if he snapped his fingers, he could bring every single charge back on me and I'd go to jail. He said I should remember who runs the show. Dad punched me hard in the face and started kicking me in the guts, just like I did to him when I saw him doing Cadence. I couldn't breathe and I puked on the floor. Dad pushed my face in it and yelled at me to remember who the fucking boss is. I cried on the floor like a baby. I don't know where Cadence was but I hope she didn't see it. Dad is so fucked up. I hope he fucking dies. I hate his sorry ass. But I need him if I'm gonna make 50K a year, what the fuck would I do… that makes me hate myself even more. Fuck everybody and fuck me, too!"

- 3 -

It is very powerful to sit here and listen to the words and feelings of Morgan Moore. I included his entries about the crimes he committed simply to illustrate that Morgan wanted very badly to take control of his own destiny and to assert his will on others. In the process, he got caught and his father had to bail him out of trouble. Even then, he continued to rage against his father's treatment of Cadence but when all was said and done, Morgan had to succumb to the fact that he needed his father's help and silence was the only way he could get it.

It seems at one point Morgan made it his mission to protect Cadence and teach Darien a lesson. But as soon as Darien struck back, at least from what we can pull from these writings, Morgan backed down and pretty much gave up.

Darien convinced Morgan that he had the ability to put Morgan in jail if certain favors he called in were uncalled all of a sudden. Logic dictates that Darien wouldn't have done that since Morgan could have then revealed what he knew. But just like the control he practiced with Cadence, Darien knew how to manipulate his children.

He used Morgan's fear of getting caught to his advantage and kept Morgan from talking. He also used the temptation of a $50,000 salary to appeal to Morgan's weak character. With money, everything is made easier and Morgan knew this. He also did not seem able to resist it.

When the diary was made public and Morgan was asked to say yes or no about Darien's guilt, Morgan chose to say no and to keep his salary and job. I suppose one could make the argument that even though Morgan and Cadence appear to have been close with each other, Morgan knew he couldn't help Cadence anymore since she was gone, so he figured he better make the decision that benefitted him the most. That decision resulted in Morgan keeping his mouth shut.

It's a shame that Morgan did not keep a diary in the year after Cadence's disappearance. It would have been enlightening to see what his thought process was in the weeks and days before he took his own life.

I believe Paul Woodsen makes a solid point when he says the guilt Morgan carried around ended up being too much for him to handle and that is why he committed suicide.

Regardless of his criminal exploits, it's hard not to look at the situation and say that Morgan Moore was as big a victim in this whole mess as Cadence Moore was. While the circumstances of their fates are different, both of these people were once innocent children until life took one too many turns in the wrong direction.

Morgan Moore in the end is a tragic figure and one has to wonder what would have happened if he had gone to the police when the abuse first happened. Would Cadence have ever become a singer? Would she have gone to Dusklight Falls, the place of her disappearance? Would Morgan have ended up selling his scruples and honor for a $50,000 paycheck? One can only wonder, but what we're left with is the reality of what actually happened. And this reality is not a pleasant one.

- 4 -

Cadence Moore's diary has been talked about at great length over the years. While it contains no explicit references to the abuse she suffered, it is apparent from her references to the abuse and her state of mind at the time, combined with what we already have seen from Morgan Moore's journal, Cadence Moore was living in a nightmare.

Cadence's journal was seized by police when the search of the Moore family home took place after she disappeared. Darien lawyered up and tried to keep the diary from them, but to no avail. The diary was considered pertinent evidence and police were able to take possession.

After the Morgan Moore diary was delivered to authorities by Paul Woodsen, within a few weeks the media had taken hold of both diaries, and the contents were all over.

After that occurred, Darien began his descent into the dark and lonely world of a recluse. There was a cascading waterfall all around him. First, his daughter disappeared. Soon after, his second wife Marianna divorces him and takes everything she can get her hands on. Not much later, his troubled son Morgan takes his own life due to mounting pressures and unimaginable guilt.

Unfortunately for us and the story we attempt to tell tonight, neither Darien Moore nor his ex-wife Marianna agreed to speak to us for our podcast. Without the input of these two major players, it is impossible to really understand the whole picture from their end, so we're forced to be satisfied with our own assumptions.

Now we arrive at the point where we can talk to the girl at the center of this whole story. It is time now that we listen to the very words of Cadence Moore herself. With the reading of these diary excerpts, performed by our radio actor Tanya Gilliam, we try and find out what the mental landscape looked like from where Cadence stood at the time of her mother's death and the abuse that followed.

Like Morgan's diary, the entries we review here begin after her mother's death but before the alleged abuse from Darien Moore. Entries are chronological, but not all inclusive, as some have been deleted in favor of the ones we find most relevant.

Entry One: "I want to die. If I died today, right now, Mom and I would be together and I'd never have to face another day on this evil planet again. If I died today, all would be peaceful and tranquil for me. No father trying to force me into being a chipper, happy, stupid idiot. No brothers who are so fucked up they can't even see straight. No more teachers making me stay after class for little talks. No more kids giving me sympathetic looks when I see them. No more neighbors shaking their heads with pity as I walk by with my dog. No more anything. If I died today, I could finally live… in peace."

Entry Two: "All I want to do is get the hell out. I want to take my songs to the nearest publisher, have him make a few calls, and go touring around the world. If I have to spend another day in this house or in this town, I am going to explode! I hate it here. I hate everyone around me. There must be a better life out there somewhere. I have the songs… I just need listeners. Is that too much to ask for, god? You already took everything from me… how about giving me a fucking break, you narcissist?"

Entry Three: "I told Claire today that I didn't think I'd be seeing next year. She's usually cool but she got all preachy with me and even squealed on me to the fucking asshole school counselor, Mr. Schwartz. That guy had me in his office for like three hours until I finally told him I was just in a bad mood and didn't mean what I said. Little does that half brain know that I would kill myself any day if I knew it would improve my current life quality? My life sucks worse than anyone's. I challenge the arrogant bastard who thinks his life is worse than mine. I would ask this piece of shit… Have you ever been robbed of your plain old simple humanity? Have you ever been made to feel like a worthless dog? Have the people you thought you loved actually taken every ounce of pureness you had left in you and ransacked it like a fucking house burglar. No, Mr. Asshole preachy fuck… your life does not compare to mine. So, here's what I'm going to do. I'm going to hurt the next person who pisses me off. I don't care if it's my worthless piece of crap brother who couldn't solve a problem if his life depended on it. I don't care if it's my demonic father who thinks the world rotates around him and will stoop to any lows possible if he thinks he'll get something from it. I don't care if it's the gold digging slut who's been sniffing around the house lately trying to dip her claws into my father's money. I don't care who it is. I will kill the next son of a bitch that pisses me off."

Entry Four: "I haven't killed anyone yet, but I have a really good idea whose head is on the chopping block right now. I detest this world and the god who made it."

Entry Five: "Goodbye diary. Goodbye, Daddy, who died to me three weeks ago and shall remain dead. Goodbye, brother, who was good for some weed and not much else. Goodbye, world, who was so unfulfilling and useless. Goodbye, teacher, who is the stupidest of them all. Goodbye, Claire… I will miss you and love you. Goodbye, WORLD… hello Mom!!!"

Entry Six: "This god of mine has other plans apparently. I woke up in a puddle of my own puke last night, and I have the shakes which won't go away. I guess my little hellish journey is not yet over. So, what's next? Fuck if I know."

Entry Seven: "In trying to find my new purpose in life, I've decided that sex is nothing. I find it boring really, but it's a great way to get what you want.

I have fucked so many guys in the last month that I lost count. But really, who cares. They all bought me food, took me to movies, and showed me their little monkey version of a good time. I can deal with that."

Entry Eight: "I am going to be a singer. My pathetic excuse for a father has been guilted into making calls. He knows I would be the one to knock his whole kingdom to the ground. Oops... sorry Daddy, you fucked up and now you need to pay the fucking toll. You need to do what I want so I don't become a singing little bird and ruin your pathetic life. Darien is now making it his mission to get me where I need to go. If I have to use him and all his contacts to get what I want, don't think I feel the least bit bad about it. I don't even know real feelings anymore. All I know is what I want and I want that shit now!"

Entry Nine: "My songs suck, but it doesn't really matter. All songs suck, at least the ones that become popular. I went to visit some friends at Penn State and I went to this party where the girls I was with were swallowing goldfish... and then doing shots. So, I went back to my room, all stoned up and drunk and wrote this song called Goldfish Chaser. I swear to god, it's the dumbest song ever written but it's got a sweet melody which is all that matters. I think I just wrote my first hit. God, what a weird world this is."

Entry Ten: "Yes! I am a recording artist, baby! I just laid down my tracks for a demo being backed up by a bunch of professional musicians. Now Darien's going to be my little press agent and get this song heard by millions. If anything, he's a good salesman and I'll pull every drop of salesman talent he has right out of him. I'm running the fucking show now."

Entry Eleven: "Met with people from Nighthawk Records. We played my little demo of stupid songs, which honestly are good for today's taste, but just suck compared with any actual good rock band in the past. But, we have to start somewhere, don't we? I will soon be writing shit worth listening to, but for now I will be happy to write the bullshit that sells to the masses. My career is what it's all about now. Nothing else matters."

Entry Twelve: "Flirted with some dudes from Nighthawk, but they acted all weird toward me. I don't give a fuck anyway; they're old. They are promoting my single, Goldfish Chaser, and soon it will be all over everywhere."

Entry Thirteen: "I feel like out of the nightmare that is my life, I've finally found a way to achieve my dreams. Nighthawk got my single played everywhere and now I've got gigs set up for college campuses everywhere. They've put me with a band, roadies, and free trans. I just have to show up. I'm gonna be playing sixteen different campuses in the Northeast in the next year. I will not be stopped now. My destiny is set. I can't be erased from history anymore."

Entry Fourteen: "It's been a hell of a ride the past few months. I'm going to be attending college soon. I let Darien do all my talking for me, and above all else, the little fucker can talk his ass off. I am going to Dusklight Falls University. Dusklight is the coolest place by far that I've gotten to see on my tour. Now, I am one of their own. I will be attending classes, getting educated and cultured, and best of all, I will be out of Wyomissing forever. I didn't think life could be cool anymore but it feels kind of cool today."

This fourteenth entry was Cadence's last. It seems she did not keep up her journal writing while attending DFU. So, let's examine what we have read and what we can glean from it. Cadence's entries reveal a girl who was very troubled by the activities that went on in her household. They also reveal a girl who came to a point where she realized the world was ugly and unfair and wanted to leave it. But, it didn't work out that way and a bit later she was determined to use it for what it could give her. She used her abusive father to further her singing career. At some point, it seems, Cadence decided that life was not handing her what she wanted, so she was going to reach out and take what she needed.

She was abused by her father, abandoned by her brother, and irritated by her new stepmother, or at least at the time, the person who had designs on being her stepmother. So, what kept Cadence writing, and perhaps more significant, what caused her to stop writing once she got to Dusklight Falls?

First, here is what we can ascertain by reading her words. Cadence was very angry and felt isolated from the rest of the world. She attempted suicide, which obviously didn't go as she planned. Then, all of the sudden, she became singularly focused on her career. She used the networking contacts Darien had and she went to town trying to turn herself into a superstar. And the amazing thing is, that's exactly what she accomplished.

Within months, Cadence had become a singing sensation. She detested her own songs, even calling them stupid. But she accomplished her goal nonetheless. She became a singing star. It seemed like she was having fun and enjoying her new notoriety. She also made a choice to attend Dusklight Falls University right in the middle of all this. She was looking forward to the new direction her life was headed.

Cadence stopped writing at this point so we have no way of knowing what her actual state of mind was at the time of her disappearance. But we do know she felt compelled to keep pressing on in life when she got to DFU. I'm sure this moving forward mentality is what drove Cadence to make friends and continue her career until her untimely disappearance.

We reached out during our interviews with Cadence's best friends, Darlene Bethany and Stephanie Chambers, as well as her boyfriend, Jamison Kelly, to try and understand how her words, preserved for eternity in her journal, represented the Cadence they all knew and loved.

Darlene Bethany says, "Charlie, it's really strange hearing those words read back to me. These are words Cadence never planned on sharing with anyone, but here we are discussing it on the radio. It's really strange. All I can say is that none of it surprises me. I mean, this girl, this poor little girl, was forced to endure incest and abuses we can't imagine but still had enough character to overcome it all and turn herself into a success. This diary just makes me love Cadence Moore even more than I did before. Even as a naive eighteen-year-old, she knew what she wanted and was prepared to do whatever it took to achieve that. That's admirable.

"In my opinion, that is completely admirable. Let's face it, most girls in her situation would not have become what she became. They would have wilted under all the negativity and abuse and they would be damaged people. What did this girl do? She turned herself into a star. That, to me, says all anyone needs to know about Cadence Moore."

Stephanie Chambers weighs in, "Just listening back to that reading makes me want to go to Wyomissing right now, find Darien Moore, and just beat his face to a bloody pulp. He really was a monster. And her brother, that poor kid, he never stood a chance. His fate was sealed the second his father bailed him out of jail. He didn't know it, but he was a slave to Darien Moore after that.

"It's weird though, when we listen to this reading, we hear a girl who was so angry and unstable... but that is not the Cadence we knew. I mean, don't get me wrong, she wasn't someone to mess with and she could be a real bitch when you pissed her off. But, anyone that knew her could tell you she had a strength about her. She was not a little delicate flower that could break and fall apart with a simple touch or twist of the wind. Cadence had a presence and a solid strong center. She also wasn't a slut.

"That seems to be the position most of these media jerks have taken on her, but as far as I know—and I know a lot since I was the girl's best friend—Cadence had one boyfriend and one boyfriend only while she attended DFU, and that was Jamison Kelly. Aside from her weird drunken behavior the night we lost her forever, she never showed any signs of being unfaithful to Jamison or even wanting to be unfaithful to him. She may have gone looking for love in some wrong places in high school when she felt worthless and alone, but at DFU, she was committed to having a real loving relationship. I think if things had been different, she'd have eventually married Jamison.

"She really loved him, but, tragically, their relationship has been poisoned by time and by bad representation in a film. But, I was there, and these two loved each other. Cadence would have done anything for Jamison and I believe the opposite is also true. It's a crying shame that they never got to live out the life they seemed to be destined for."

Darlene Bethany agrees, "Yeah, what Stephanie said really rings true to me even now. We all knew Cadence was in love with Jamison and no one expected her to carelessly fuck any random guy that came around. That may be how she acted in high school while she was going through all of this, but that isn't the girl we knew. She obviously felt so strongly about Jamison that it kept her from doing things that may have been part of her very nature at this point.

"Regrettably, in the last minutes we got to spend with her, she acted very out of character and unfortunately this is what a lot of folks will remember when they discuss Cadence Moore. But there was a whole year before that at DFU and I choose to remember what happened in that year, and not what happened during the twenty minutes we spent in my car the night she disappeared.

"Cadence loved Jamison Kelly and it makes my heart feel warm and reassured to know that, in spite of her horrible struggles and the dark debased place she came from, Cadence was open and accessible enough to receive real love and she was able to offer it back to Jamison too. That's how I choose to remember the situation, and as Stephanie has stated many times tonight, you probably should take our word for it because we were there... and you weren't."

Jamison Kelly also commented on the journal readings. He offered, "It's so strange to think that Cadence went through all of that before I even met her. I have to be honest, when we were together, anything we talked about or laughed about, anything we debated over or discussed, they were all happenings of the moment. Cadence lived in the moment when she was with me. She made one or two cryptic comments while we were together, but not enough for me to even realize what she was referring to. I'd ask and she'd just say, forget it.

"The girl I dated, loved, and spent most of my time with back then was a girl who was honest, faithful, loving, and above all else, someone who lived for the moment she was experiencing, not some dark past. I take solace in the fact that she got to spend that year with us in Dusklight Falls, performing on stage and being part of our group, and part of something even more special with me.

"She deserved that year. She deserved many years, but at the very least, the brief sunshine of stardom, friendship, and happiness at DFU was something Cadence Moore deserved, considering what she'd overcome. I really loved her, and hearing this reading tonight, I won't lie to you, it strengthens that love."

It is illuminating to hear the musings of Cadence Moore's closest friends when they hear her story told and her words spoken. Cadence was an extremely complicated person and it really is a testament to her that she was able to achieve the success she did.

What Cadence and Morgan Moore had to endure at the hands of fate and at the hands of their very own father, makes them both, as I referenced earlier, tragic figures. It is heartbreaking to listen to their recounting of events and realize these kids were stuck in a strange hell play. It took the strength of a goddess for Cadence to overcome it, become a success (regardless of how much she was helped by Darien's money and contacts), and, more importantly, make lasting friendships and relationships at Dusklight Falls University.

- 5 -

UNDERGROUND PODCAST 4: (Official Transcript)
Part 2: Underground Podcast Speaks with Barnes and Angstat

Charlie Marx's Underground Podcast: Episode 4 (Part 2). Original Drop Date: November 1, 2013. (Brought to you by United Way of Life, courtesy of Tyler Reubens... this program is funded and sponsored by WHHW, a subsidiary of Universal Public Radio)

(Narration by Charlie Marx) Many of those listening to our podcast series have been waiting for the following segment above all others. These listeners know the story and have seen every magazine clipping, newspaper article, TV cover story, photo, documentary film clip, and exposé about the subject we have delved into on tonight's podcast.

The wildly popular documentary, *Moore to the Story*, by Todd Barnes and Michael Angstat, released last year, has become the accepted truth of millions of viewers. This documentary should be admired on many levels. It was the first piece of media that encircled the entire scope of the Cadence Moore case and established a clear and cohesive picture of the whole story. Not to mention, Barnes and Angstat's film was the catalyst for the name of Cadence Moore returning to national prominence.

It is imperative that we bring in these filmmaking gentlemen, or filmmaking assholes as Jamison Kelly referred to them earlier, and we discuss just what it is that separates their film from our podcast and examine what really happened to Cadence Moore.

Let us start this segment by discussing why it is so important in the first place. Number one, the reason Barnes and Angstat have been both showered with praise and littered with criticism is because they made a film which many folks took as the god's honest truth about Cadence Moore's story and her disappearance, while others have pointed to the film as an exercise in fantasy, trading facts for good fiction, while layering the whole thing in a veil of easily disputable lies. But any way a person chooses to slice it, Barnes and Angstat are the world recognized leaders of knowledge and research when it comes to the Moore disappearance and most of the general population still sees the material contained in *Moore to the Story* as the true story.

As we speak to Todd Barnes and Michael Angstat during this episode, I want to make it clear what we're after. We want these gentlemen to have their say when it comes to the film they created, and we want them to answer the criticisms that have befallen their film about factual inaccuracies, omission of information, and just plain dishonest journalism.

I realized that Todd and Michael had no real need for participating in our podcast outside of a desire to have a forum to defend their film against detractors. But they've had that forum in other arenas and could get an interview in many outlets even now if they wanted one. They didn't need our show. They participated with our series and, for that alone, I tried to treat them with the utmost respect when I interviewed them. But the tough questions did need to be asked and I am pleased to announce that this documentary team of movie makers were more than generous with their time, their recollections, and their willingness to discuss accusations against their film... that is at least... until the end of the interview.

I think when this segment is over and the podcast portion of this series is complete, you will all have a clear opinion on what you think about *Moore to the Story* and the men who made it. That is enough for me. Whether you are on my end of things or not, I want you all to feel like you have heard a discussion that made it possible to sift out facts from static and truth from tumbling twisting forest trees.

So, we must start with a first question if we're going to analyze a conversation. I spoke to Barnes and Angstat together, rather than alone. They seemed eager to defend their film and not rest easy in the face of stinging criticism. I do have to say, these guys have answers for just about everything, and unless you are a true student of the case, it is very hard to give them pause and make them think before answering. The confidence they have in themselves and their conclusions makes Barnes and Angstat hard men to argue with, but… I found a way.

- 6 -

I asked Todd Barnes my first question, which I considered an ice breaker, so I asked it with a smile. "Todd, your name shows up first in all the credits and media surrounding your film. Do you consider yourself the leader of your filmmaking team?"

Todd smiled and looked over at Michael Angstat, seemingly for some type of approval. Todd laughed and said, "Mr. Marx, our filmmaking team was built on joint offerings. We got into this together and we solved this case together, with a mutual desire to get to the bottom of what happened to an innocent young girl on a drunken evening in Dusklight Falls. "But, if you're trying to paint this in some kind of weird way, like I was the ringleader and Michael was just along for the ride, then that is just simply inaccurate. I will tell you, I was the one who brought this subject to Michael in the beginning. "Michael was very interested when I started talking, but he didn't really have a solid grasp on what the story was all about. When I filled Mr. Angstat in on what I thought was really going on, he became a devoted follower and seeker of truth, as you're so fond of calling your listeners, Charlie."

I kept smiling and pressed this subject a little further. "No implication intended, Todd. Sorry, that was my attempt at a lighthearted ice breaker. But, that being said, I think it is a worthy discussion when delving into the facts of this case, and first and foremost, the dynamics of your filmmaking collaboration with Michael. If you were the one who initially brought the idea and Michael joined up in the effort and movement to solve a murder, then I'd imagine your personal take on the case was the jumping off point for everything that followed. In essence, *Moore to the Story*, the conclusions drawn by the film, and the swarming controversy that followed it would be a product of your own initial ideas and feelings about the case. And then Michael Angstat put his own spin on everything afterward. Would you say this is accurate, Mr. Barnes?"

Todd Barnes shook his head and grinned while looking me straight in the eye. His demeanor was whispering, *I see what you're doing... okay, let's go there if you want.* He said, "I think you have an angle already, Charlie. And it's a weak one to be honest. You want to paint me as a mastermind of some sort and you want to draw Michael as the little follower who just did what he was told and assisted me in clipping some footage together. Is that right? Have I about covered your take on this?"

I never dropped my gaze from Todd's eyes, but I knew we were off to the races now and it was time to get down to it. I said, "Absolutely not, Todd. I don't intend to paint a false picture of things. I just thought it bore mentioning that your name is always listed first in any media mention of your film and I wanted to know why that was. I do not mean to insinuate that one or the other of you was the ringleader behind it all and the other was a simple-minded dupe or a gullible goof of some sort. But the question is worthy and I simply want you to answer it before we move on. Why was your name always out front in the media discussion of your work and your film?" What had started out as an ice breaker was becoming the first of many tense moments in this interview.

Todd looked over at Michael who was laughing hysterically for some strange reason. I took the opportunity to question Michael since I was getting nowhere fast with Todd. I asked, "Michael, do you feel slighted in any way when the mention of *Moore to the Story* is inevitably followed by the words, 'A film by Todd Barnes and Michael Angstat?'"

Michael replied, "Seriously, man, I don't think of these things. When credits roll or posters are printed, someone's name has to be first. I hear all the time about Hollywood actors throwing temper tantrums and making threats and demands if their names are not first on the credits.

"In my opinion, Todd's name can be first. I really don't give a shit. He was the one who first brought the thing to me. So, I really don't care if his name appears before mine in press releases and credit reels. The simple truth is our film hit a nerve with people and that wasn't by accident. Our film, regardless of whose name appears in front on the opening credits, opened up some eyes and forced open some closed minds and hardened hearts.

"I didn't think twice about whose name was up front on this movie. I just reveled in the fact that millions were now paying attention and maybe, if we were lucky, those masses of people would buy into our take on the case and the film would be a success. This started as Todd's project and he gave me a lot of creative leeway. I put my own stamp of ownership on that film and I approached everything that had to do with it, from interviews to editing, with my own take on things.

"My take on things… like this for instance. Todd didn't press as hard as I did with my interview subjects and he wouldn't have included certain dialogue in the final film if he felt it was too aggressive and extreme. But again, there was a reason why Todd decided not to make this film alone. He knew that his own personality and the restraints which are hard-wired into him would not allow certain things to happen.

"Todd did the smart thing and brought in a college buddy who was loud-mouthed and opinionated when it came to just about any subject. That is why I lost certain interview subjects and why the film almost seemed to argue with itself at points, like the narrative voice wanted to be polite but kept losing its cool and delved into a passionate rant. But that's what made it cool.

"I was the antagonist in our filmmaking team and Todd needed one. When we spliced the interview footage together and started crafting a film around it, it was obvious that a certain dynamic, like the one Todd and I shared, would be essential to the proper telling of this story. "I came in and presented a counterpoint and struggle for the viewer. It might have been inconvenient at the time, but Todd knew this was the right way to make a film.

We were working in documentary form, but we were still making a film. So, it was part of our modus operandi to present life and the struggles of life in a way that clicked with the largest number of people at a given time.

"When the film came out and the questions and criticisms came out with it, this was a hard period to live through for us. And a real credit to Todd is that he's defended me when every criticism of my work and my interview tactics was raised."

I found Michael's take an interesting one. I also wanted to make it clear that I was running no angle here and I just wanted to establish that when this whole thing began, Todd Barnes was the driving force behind it and the eventual film has Todd's signature on it more than all others.

So, with that in mind, I questioned Todd again. I asked, "Todd, now that we have gotten through our first tense moment in this interview (slight laughs from everyone when I said this), I want to move on and ask you about what drew you toward the Cadence Moore mystery in the first place. What was it that caused you to spend three years of your life making a film about it and several years before that running a web site dedicated to it? What about this case fascinates you?"

Todd thought on this for a moment and replied, "I'm glad our tense moment is over Charlie, but I'm sure it will make for fascinating radio or podcasting, or whatever you and your associates are doing here. I just want to say that Me Todd, the leader, and Him Michael, the foolish follower, are very glad to be able to assist you in garnering the highest ratings possible for your show. We'll be expecting a bottle of fine wine on every holiday from now on and you better not let us down!"

I laughed at Todd's little speech and said, "Noted. Bottle of wine for Barnes and Angstat, every holiday. Now if you could, good sir, please answer my question."

Todd smiled for a moment and then said, "Okay, it's a good question and I will answer it. What drew me to Cadence Moore wasn't just one thing. I was twenty years old when I first saw the news coverage explaining that a young singer had disappeared. I knew of Cadence Moore. In the few months I spent at Penn State, she was being played all over the airwaves with her

"Goldfish Chaser" song. Not to be crass, but I thought she was hot. My friends and I used to talk about how good looking she was in the video she did for her song. I actually liked the song too, which is weird because I'm not one to usually favor plastic pop crap. But I liked the single and I thought she was pretty, so I guess you could say I was a fan.

"Then suddenly, I'm sitting home one night after dropping out of college, smoking up a little and chilling out, and the news comes on and this huge headline scrolls over saying, 'SINGER CADENCE MOORE IS MISSING AND PRESUMED DEAD.' I still remember this headline clear as day. For some reason, when the story first broke, several news outlets decided to lead in with the line 'MISSING AND PRESUMED DEAD.' There was no evidence at that point to make it clear that she was dead. Only months later... when she was never found... did it become clear that she was probably dead.

"Anyway, I saw this news show, and I was hooked from that moment. Here was a famous contemporary figure in my own life, a girl my friends and I thought was cute, and we liked her music, and then out of nowhere she's missing and possibly dead.

"In the weeks that followed, all the stories and little tidbits of testimony and details from Dusklight Falls came flooding in and this wasn't just a simple disappearance; it was a genuine mystery and one that didn't appear at all close to being solved.

"No answers came and, little by little, the news coverage started waning. A few exposés were done, the best was probably from Brandon Baker Smith over in England. He produced an hour-long piece running through the facts and details of the case, with a few interviews from college administrators at Dusklight Falls, some people from Nighthawk Records, and the first public statement from Darlene Bethany who cried so hard during her interview that there was not much of it that could be aired. The problem with Smith's piece was that he had no ending. He did a really nice explanation on the facts as we knew them at the time, but he offered no conclusions of his own which I think hurt the final product.

"A year or two after the disappearance when no actual conclusions had been drawn by police and no details seemed to be coming in that could clear the whole mess up, the entire story sort of dissipated like smoke. The public lost interest because no answers were found and it became a literal unsolved mystery.

"But, I never lost interest. I never stopped wanting to know the truth, and soon it became the main focus of my existence to figure this thing out. I painstakingly went over all the available information and talked to whoever would entertain me; and, I pieced together enough about the case to arrive at a rough outline of what I believed probably happened.

"It was at this point that Michael entered the picture. He was a friend of mine who'd also dropped out of Penn State, and he was recently kicked out of his parents' house."

Michael Angstat interjected at this point, "I'm afraid I wasn't quite the success they had expected. I quit college and spent most of my days smoking herb and basically accomplishing nothing. Todd and I used to smoke up together and go to football games. I was sitting up one night finishing off a joint and listening to *OK Computer* by Radiohead which should be on everyone's top five of all time lists, by the way. So, I remember listening to it when I got the call.

"My Dad had flipped out on me that night and said I better be out in three days because they weren't supporting me anymore if I didn't care to try and support my own future. Todd called me and said, 'Hey, you know that Cadence Moore disappearance I was telling you about a while ago?'

"I asked, 'The video chick? Yeah, I remember it; you wouldn't shut up about it. What happened? Did they catch the killer?'

Todd very seriously said, "No Mike... they haven't caught anyone, but I think I know what happened and it's time to let the world know. Can you help me?"

"I answered him, not honestly giving a shit at that present moment, 'Well, I just got told by my parents that I can't live here anymore. I apparently am a waste of life and useless or something. Tell you what, Toddster, you let me crash with you a few weeks in your apartment and I will help you with any mystery you want.'"

Todd laughed and nodded. "Yeah, that's pretty much how I remember it happening. Mike didn't care at first. He vaguely knew who Cadence Moore was and knew she disappeared because anyone watching television back then would have had to know something about it. It was everywhere. Mike just wasn't all that familiar with the details of the case so it didn't mean anything to him at that point. But after he moved in with me, we would talk for hours about it and he became extremely interested, to put it mildly. He'd ask questions and I'd supply more facts and opinions. Soon, Mike became as devoted a follower of Cadence Moore as I was. He developed his own thoughts on the whole thing and soon we were bouncing ideas off each other, filling in missing pieces and little holes in the timeline of the disappearance until we felt we had an iron-clad version of how things had probably happened."

I interrupted for a moment and asked Todd, "Now when you came up with the conclusions you did, how much of the eventually-revealed facts in the case were actually out there already in the public? How much of this whole thing did you need to piece together in your imagination and how much of it was out there for you already in the form of established evidence and witness statements?"

Todd began to speak and said, "Well, lots of..."

Michael spotted a trap. He cut Todd off and responded, "If you're trying to ask when did we stop using evidence and replace it with our own opinions, then I will answer you. Never. Not during the website days, or during the making of the film. We never just ignored the facts and made shit up. You certainly have to use caution and inference to pull facts together but we never just stopped looking at the hard facts of the case and made up our own version of how we *wanted* things to be."

I responded quickly, "I'm not trying to say that."

Todd chimed in, recovered from his near fall into an alleged snare. "Actually, Mr. Marx, that's *exactly* what you said. You have made several comments about our film and about our replacing facts with fiction and such. What Michael is trying to say is that we never just said screw it. We never just got lazy or sloppy and tried to replace the truth with our own imagined version of events. That's what bothers me so much about all the critics and everything that has been said. I promise you, our main purpose was not to make a lot of money, or even make a great and interesting film. These were priorities but not our first priorities.

"Our first order of business was to find the goddamn answers. We wanted to solve the unsolvable and give Cadence Moore's story an ending. A girl that talented and beautiful should not have her life ended with a question mark and a 'whatever happened to' following her name around for the rest of time. So, we made up our minds to answer that question and we did the best fucking job we were capable of with years and years of hard and intense work.

"And when people, yourself included, Charlie, call us liars or hacks, it pisses us off because you weren't there with us during the process. You don't know how many sources we checked with, how many rocks we turned over, and how many hours, days, weeks, months, and years we stayed with this thing to make sure we got to where we wanted to go. This film represents our hard work and dedication and the conclusion we came up with did not appear in our film as a marketing ploy or a hook as some have said. We accused Jamison Kelly of murder because we believe Jamison Kelly to be a murderer. You can disagree all you like, but to call us liars or hacks because you don't like what we ended up with… well, I hate to say it so childlike, but that's simply not fair."

It appeared, at least based on these comments, Todd and Michael did truly come to care about Cadence Moore and her story. They both seemed frank and earnest when it came to their discussion of the film and what they did with it. Both men claim their conclusions were honestly arrived at through a painstakingly thorough search of available evidence.

And let us not forget, Barnes and Angstat were not the only ones who came to the conclusion that Jamison Kelly was the murderer. You'll remember, of course, the comments earlier in our podcast from Detective Meghan Cocuzza, head of the DFPD investigation team for the Moore case. She also believes Jamison killed Cadence. She didn't have the evidence to prove it though, and that lack of evidence problem is where I drew the opening for my next line of questioning. Meghan Cocuzza had that problem and so did Barnes and Angstat.

I resumed the conversation with the following statement, "Michael and Todd, it seems to me that you fully believe in your theory of events and have not intentionally tried to pull a fast one on the public by putting out the most sensational possibility just to get attention for your film. That much is clear to me already, just in the few minutes I've spoken with you.

"However, I think one strong point that most critics of your film and your conclusions would hold on to would be your simple lack of hard evidence. Meghan Cocuzza did not arrest Jamison Kelly, whom she believed to be guilty, because she was faced with the same nagging problem most folks think you guys are faced with, that being a severe lack of hard evidence to back up the Kelly as murderer theory."

Michael Angstat said, "Certainly Charlie, that is the one thing these doubters have going for them. There is not a *lot* of documented hard evidence, and I emphasize the words 'a lot' in that statement because, while there are not mountains of hard physical evidence pointing at Kelly, there certainly is *some* hard, physical evidence and I happen to believe that evidence is extremely damning to him. Let's be real here. Todd and I are not police officers. We do not have to be anchored down by tiny little glitches and missing trinkets in our evidence locker. We're filmmakers and we can take a look at the big picture and come up with the obvious. Jamison Kelly killed Cadence Moore.

"There is a wealth of circumstantial evidence to support this in the first place, but added to that, we're able to use our common sense and artistic license to piece a few sure things together and come up with facts that the DFPD never could procure for themselves. Questionable police procedure and shaky witness statements basically fucked their whole case, but it didn't fuck us. We had plenty of great testimony from people close to this thing and, as far as hard facts, when you look at the facts we present in the film, I challenge anyone to say they're not pretty fuckin' hard."

Todd added, "Exactly. We're prepared to answer any questions you or your listeners have about the film, Charlie. However, it's important for all of you people to know that our film is not a work of fiction. It's a carefully studied and researched documentary. Maybe the DFPD was not able to move on the lack of physical evidence. But when you add up all the circumstantial evidence out there and you add a bit of common sense to that, you end up not with an unsolvable mystery, rather you end up with *Moore to the Story*."

- 7 -

I said, "Gentlemen, I think you have made your point clear and our listeners have now had a chance to hear your honest appraisal of the film you made and a crystal-clear explanation of your motives. My listeners now also wish to be heard. I will reach into my vault of questions posed by the very folks listening to this podcast. I have already eliminated ridiculous or redundant ones, but the questions remaining are solid and should hopefully lead us down several interesting paths of discussion. So, please allow me to start with this."

- 8 -

Question 1: "'Why did you guys never bother to interview Jimmy Derek and Zach Burns? They provided an alibi for the man you accuse of murder in your film. Don't you believe that it was your journalistic responsibility to include their voices and try to refute their statements instead of ignoring them and pretending they don't exist? Your only mention of them in the film is a comment about two people who claim to have seen a shadow of a man who they want us to believe is Jamison Kelly. How can you ignore these two major figures in the story you made a film about?' That question comes from Sam Raymondler of Tucson, Arizona. Todd, that's a question I'm sure you've already been asked more than once. Can you please answer it now for *Underground Podcast*?"

Todd said, "Yes, it's a very good question. I agree with that Charlie. I'm happy I have a chance to answer it once again in a public forum. I can only hope after publicly answering this and any other questions you throw at us, it will cut down on people asking them in the future because, frankly, we're both tired of that. All you fine people listening to Charlie Marx's show today... please heed my words. This interview for *Underground Podcast* is going to be Todd Barnes's and Michael Angstat's final words on the subject of our film, or more specifically, criticism of our film. Going forward, if anyone wants to ask these questions again, Michael and I will refer you to the *Underground Podcast* web site and tell you to check out the archives. Then we will walk away from you.

"You know, I'm kind of excited for that to happen. Let's not waste any more time Charlie. Your listener wants to know why we did not interview Jimmy Derek and Zach Burns. I'll tell you why. I believe Jimmy Derek to be a liar. And, I did not want to have a liar confusing the truth in my film.

"Let's introduce a dose of reality right now. Everybody who's ever even read an article about this case knows that Jimmy Derek was Jamison Kelly's best friend. Don't you think it's a little convenient that he just happened to have provided the only alibi for Jamison? No one else can conclusively state that they know Jamison Kelly was in Zach Burns's bedroom during the time of the murder. So, why would we believe Jimmy Derek who was very likely trying to protect his best friend?

"Think about it, he already knew about the volatile argument Cadence and Jamison had. He also admits helping them both get stoned and drunk that night. I fully believe Jimmy Derek knew what Jamison was planning on doing, but probably thought he didn't have the nerve. The next few days come and go, no sign of Cadence, and Jimmy figures out his broski seems to have done a bad thing and now he's got to help him cover his ass.

"Either that or perhaps Derek knew what Jamison was planning and believed he *would* go through with it. Then after failing to talk him out of it, Jimmy decided to help him. You see, I say perhaps and maybe here. I cannot be sued for my opinion although you won't have success trying to convince Jamison Kelly of that these days. Either way, to answer the question, Jimmy Derek could not be considered a reliable truth teller and that is the reason he's not in my film."

Michael added, "Seriously people, how many times in murder cases do family and friends attempt to paint an alibi for their guilty loved one, and then later it is revealed that the alibis were bullshit, and just feeble attempts at covering up the truth. These well-intentioned people are close with someone who was capable of great evil and acted on it. They can't handle that so they begin lying.

"It's as simple as that. Christ, you remember... oh what the hell was the guy's name... I'm blanking... oh yeah... Ramirez, Richard Ramirez, the Night Stalker, his own father swore to his innocence and placed him at a birthday party or some shit when he was supposedly butchering some innocent woman. It was a total lie, but the father told it anyway. Like I said, these family members and friends can't deal with the fact that their kin or their good mates are capable of the worst violence imaginable and they lie to save the ass of their buddy and help themselves sleep well again at night as they continue to live in delusion.

"Plus, Jimmy Derek, according to several eyewitnesses from the Basement party, was all kinds of fucked up. He'd been drinking heavily and smoking up the whole night. How can we trust that his recollection is even worth a damn? For all we know, he could have dreamt the whole thing about putting his boy Jay to bed that night."

I was forced to interrupt at this point with something both men seemed to be ignoring. I asked, "All this is well and good, gentleman, but how can you make these blanket statements about Jimmy Derek and leave out the documented fact that he was not the only person claiming to have put Jamison to bed that night? Zach Burns made statements to police that he was there, too, and Jimmy Derek's story checked out. How do you both get around this issue when assuming Jimmy Derek is lying?"

Todd answered, "Charlie, for one thing, you know that's a ridiculous question. To think Michael and I are just ignoring Zach Burns's presence in this story or we somehow have never heard of him... it really is stupid. Of course, we know who Burns is. And, of course, we know what he said to police. And lastly, because we know what he said to police so well, we have reached a conclusion that Jamison Kelly was not sleeping in his bedroom at 4:00 a.m. on May 6, 2002."

I couldn't believe what I was hearing. I said, "Todd, that makes no sense to me at all. One would logically think that knowing Burns's testimony would lead a person to the exact opposite conclusion. Please explain further."

Todd smiled, "Of course. I'll explain as far as you'd like. Let's look at the actual statement Burns made to police. Number one, he told them he helped take Jamison to bed that morning. This we believe to be true. He also claims to have seen Jamison Kelly clear as day at 9:00 a.m. that same morning, and proceeded to kick him out and demand he go home. This we also believe to be true."

I shook my head and asked, "Then which part of this leads you to believe Jamison was not there?"

Michael became impatient and decided to take over. "Charlie, Todd is being very calm and explaining our take on this. You keep interrupting him, but maybe you'll stop that if I just lay it out for you real plainly. Forget Jimmy Derek because he was Kelly's best friend and his testimony alone has to be dismissed as dog shit, because his loyalty to his friend trumps his motivation to tell the truth. Zach Burns cannot be so easily dismissed. He was not a friend of Jamison and, in fact, kicked him out later that morning. He has no reason to lie, so his words should be taken seriously. Here is how we interpret his words.

"At 1:00 a.m. he remembers seeing Jamison Kelly's face and helping Jimmy Derek carry him to bed. At 9:00 a.m., he remembers seeing Jamison Kelly's face and kicking him out of the house. So, we have documented instances of Zach Burns seeing Jamison Kelly's face twice on May 6, eight hours apart.

"What about 4:00 a.m. is the question you now want to interrupt with. Well, I'll tell you about 4:00 a.m. Burns saw Kelly at 1:00 a.m., he saw him at 9:00 a.m., and at 4:00 a.m.; he saw a heap on the floor that could have been anyone. Have you ever thought about that Charlie? It could have been anyone. Burns and possibly even Derek assumed it was Kelly because that is who they put in the room and that is who was in the room the next morning.

"But at 4:00 a.m. they did not see Jamison Kelly. They saw a crumpled heap on the floor in a dark room. Neither Burns nor Derek ever mentioned turning on a light to verify that Jamison himself was lying on the floor. That never happened. So, the person lying in a heap on the bedroom floor at 4:00 a.m. could have been anyone in the whole world… it could've even been you, Charlie.

"Here is what we believe. One of two things happened here. In the first scenario, Jamison has a terrible fight with Cadence, determines that he wishes to do her harm, and then sets things in motion for this to happen.

"He tells her he's too drunk to drive with her to the Falls. He then makes a big show of how drunk he is to everyone who's around. Jamison sets it up so he is witnessed by many being carried off to bed by Jimmy Derek and Zach Burns, who, the next day, along with everyone else in the general vicinity, will claim that they know Jamison was in the Basement house drunk off his ass and not out somewhere in Dusklight Falls finding and eventually killing his girlfriend.

"Jamison hangs out for a while in the bedroom, planning his next move. A little while later, about 2:30 to 2:40 a.m., he slips out of the bedroom to carry out the murder. He slips back in when the deed is done. There's been a lot of talk about how he couldn't have done this without being seen, but as someone who has attended many frat parties, I can tell you with confidence that the attendees of these little soirées are not exactly what you'd call the most observant people after they've had a drink or two or ten. It's a fucking laugh riot to say Kelly couldn't possibly have left and returned without being seen. Of course, he could have!

"It's not like everyone at the party was on Jamison Kelly alert, ready to sound the alarm at first sight of his face. Jesus, even if someone had seen him, it's very possible they wouldn't have remembered it. And, if you don't like that theory, here's another for you.

"Scenario number two plays out like this. Jamison and Cadence have their fight. They get into it real bad and Jamison's all torn up about it. So, a while later, he's drinking more and more and Cadence asks him to come to the Falls. He says no. Maybe he's still pissed. Maybe he really was feeling too drunk and sick to go anywhere at that point.

"Cadence leaves with Darlene, Stephanie, and Steve. Jamison drowns his sorrows in a few more drinks. He gets to talking with Jimmy Derek. Now, his head starts to clear a little. The anger seems to be sobering him up. He starts talking to his idol, Jimmy, the guy he wanted to impress and was so loyal to, about all the things he'd like to do to that bitch. How dare she behave like such a whore. How dare she this and how dare she that. If she was here right now, he'd do this and that to her.

"Okay, you get the general gist of what I'm saying. Jimmy Derek realizes his buddy is in a bad frame of mind but he doesn't think Jamison will act on anything. So, they talk a bit more and then a bit more. Jimmy starts to believe Jamison isn't just venting anymore. Jimmy starts to get the picture. Maybe he tries to talk Jamison off the ledge. But it's to no avail. Kelly is furious and plans on taking action. Jimmy Derek now has a choice to make. He either takes steps to keep Jamison from doing something stupid or he helps him do something stupid.

"Based on the comments that have been attributed to Jimmy Derek over the years, Todd and I believe this is the type of young man who'd subscribe to the motto of 'bros before hos' to be quite blunt about it. We believe Jimmy would not have wanted to get his hands dirty, but certainly would have had his friend's back in such a situation. Again, we're not claiming that happened, we're just stating that this is an opinion that an observer of the case could potentially arrive at.

"In the end, perhaps Jimmy agrees to assist Jamison by helping provide an alibi, which he will swear to when questioned. It's possible they even set it up that Kelly would fall into a heap on the floor when they put him to bed. This way when Jimmy made sure Jamison was checked on later in the night, whoever he brought with him would see a figure on the floor and assume it was Jamison Kelly.

"They would assume this and they'd be wrong because, in our opinion, Jamison was somewhere else, somewhere far away from the Basement, doing unspeakable things in the night. Again, this is simply a theory and requires another person's involvement, because if Jamison was out and about getting up to a bit of murder, someone would have had to take Jamison's place on the floor when Jimmy arranged a check in at 400 a.m. to seal up the alibi.

"So, who was this other person? And did they know why they were being asked to lay there in a heap? Could Jimmy have just gotten one of his other buddies, already drunk out of their minds to agree to sleep it off on the floor of a bedroom? Would this other buddy even remember it? Would they have remembered it when Jimmy came in later that morning and told them they had to scram?

"Just theories but what we've just done here Charlie is lay out two plausible scenarios in which Jamison Kelly could have left the Basement, found Cadence and killed her, only to return to the Basement bedroom so he could be found the next morning."

I was silent for a moment… trying to fairly consider what Michael and Todd were theorizing. It was very troubling. So many questions… questions that seemed obvious, were still popping up left and right. There were major holes in the Barnes and Angstat theory and they needed to be addressed.

I politely inquired, "Okay, Michael. I hope you don't feel like I'm interrupting you now, but I do have some problems with what you just laid out. Problem number one: Jamison Kelly was close friends with Stephanie Chambers and Darlene Bethany. Both girls claim they've never seen Jamison as messed up as he was that night. When you say in your scenario number two that Jamison began to sober up while he bitched to Jimmy Derek and became angry, that doesn't make much sense.

"How does a drunken rant sober a person up? He would have had to be sober to offer a coherent enough explanation of what he planned to do and then conspire with Jimmy Derek to pull it off with a fake drunken pass out and a body double to take his place on the floor. I'm not sure how much sense this makes.

"Guys, I respect you and the film you made, and I also respect you as people and do not wish to offend you. However, I must call serious bullshit on these two theories. Let's look a bit further. And before I give you a chance to respond, which I promise I will do, I must address problem number two with your version of things. Problem number two is regarding this idea that Jamison Kelly could have escaped the Basement bedroom without being seen and then return to the same room hours later and not be seen again.

"You know we're talking about twenty or thirty college students, right? To say it's a laugh riot when people claim Jamison leaving without being seen is impossible… I just don't buy it. It's not a laugh riot at all… it's very feasible that if Jamison left and went through the front door, he would have been seen by someone and very possibly several people.

"Out of… okay, let's say even a conservative estimate of ten to twenty kids… you're saying not one of them would remember seeing Jamison come out of Burns's room or back into the room after they saw him dragged off to bed hours before. How is that even possible?

"Remember, just days later it was all over the place that Cadence was missing. Don't you think that any of these kids would have put two and two together and figure 'hmm, I saw Jamison leave the house after he'd gone to bed, and now his girlfriend is missing… hmm, maybe I should tell someone… ah, fuck it… I'll keep it to myself.' I mean guys, this is the problem with your film and this is what fans and students of the case have been pointing to as proof that you are making things up that could not have happened. Please tell me… how do you respond to that?"

Todd was quick to answer, probably sensing a quick and angry rebuttal from Michael was coming. He said, "You have pointed out some valid points, Charlie, and again, just like your comments about Zach Burns and acting like we weren't aware of him, you're once again acting like none of this has ever occurred to us. I have a question for you now. If there is no doubt whatsoever that these drunken college kids would have seen Jamison leave, and when news broke about Cadence it hit them that they'd seen Jamison leave, and that it was really weird and he must have killed her, and on, and on, and on… then you still have a major question to answer.

"Tell me, Charlie, why didn't anyone in that house who was interviewed after the fact, and a lot of them were so this isn't just speculation, come forward and tell reporters that they saw Jamison leave. You claim it's impossible to think they wouldn't have seen him if he left. So, if that's true, then how come none of them claim they *did* see him? How do you explain *that*?"

I shook my head once again in spite of myself. I didn't want to insult Barnes and Angstat because they were giving me their time and all three of us knew they didn't have to. I shook my head because this whole line of discussion was amazing to me. I had just finished saying that Jamison *couldn't* have left because someone would have seen him. Now Todd was asking me why no one came forward if they *must* have seen Jamison leave... like this was proof of something. In reality, what it meant was that beyond a shadow of reasonable doubt, Jamison *didn't* leave at all; he was in Burns's room the whole night, and someone else was responsible for Cadence's disappearance. That was the point I was trying to drive home.

It seemed so godforsaken obvious that Barnes's and Angstat's arguments were paper thin, yet they clung so close to them and professed total faith in their theories. I kept on course and tried to explain why this still didn't make sense and Barnes's and Angstat's arguments were actually leading in a direction opposite of their conclusions.

I explained, "Todd, Michael... you've made an impressive film which, regardless of whether people think it's crap or think it's a masterpiece, got a lot of attention and shined a well needed spotlight on this case. But my podcast serves a purpose too. It is a companion piece to your film in a way. You put what you put out there and people consumed it. Now I am putting something out there for people to consider when watching your movie, so it's important that we go over these points in exquisite detail.

"Okay, addressing this statement you've just made Todd. You asked me why none of the college kids at the Basement party came forward and admitted to seeing Jamison leave the room. I'm assuming you're asking this because you want to make it clear that it's very possible none of these kids *saw* Jamison leave, which would support your theory of events. Is that correct?"

Todd nodded, "Correct so far, Charlie."

I continued. "I thank you for that Todd. I ask you this as a counterpoint to your initial question. If kids at the Basement party never claimed to have seen Jamison leave the room, don't you think that could also be strong evidence pointing to the notion that he never *did* leave the room at all? Don't you think the fact that dozens of witnesses were interviewed and none of them saw Kelly leave the Basement house would indicate that he obviously didn't leave? Doesn't this seem the more direct conclusion... that he simply didn't leave... rather than saying the kids didn't see him leave because they were too drunk?"

Todd smiled, "Charlie, you make a decent point. But your assumption that these partygoers denied seeing Kelly because they didn't in fact *really see* him is no more credible or convincing than our argument that they never claimed to see him because they were too trashed to know what the hell they were seeing at all.

"Why is it so compelling for you to think the reason no one saw him is because he never left. What other evidence is out there to make you believe wholeheartedly that Jamison Kelly didn't do the deed? You seem to believe that any reasonable theory which ends with Jamison being guilty is just hogwash that should be dismissed immediately."

I replied, "I never claimed your theories were hogwash, Todd. But your reasoning for ignoring a total lack of evidence or eyewitness testimony regarding Jamison leaving the Basement so he could kill Cadence is very questionable. Am I saying it's impossible that Jamison could have left the Basement without being seen? Not really. But I have to go where the evidence points and for that to happen, I can't allow myself to become pulled in a strange direction by theories not grounded in fact.

"The kids from the Basement never claim to have seen Kelly after the fact, so that alone makes me think he remained sleeping on the floor of Burns's bedroom and didn't leave to kill anyone. There is simply no evidence to indicate that he did. But you guys refuse to acknowledge that because your theory demands Jamison is guilty so all evidence to the contrary must either be ignored or dealt with by introducing an alternate theory. Since you did not really deal with this point in your film, it is not unreasonable to say you ignored it. I don't see how this omission in the film can be construed as good journalism, my friend, respecting of course the fact that you're addressing it now.

"But I think that is what Sam from Tucson, our listener who posed the first question, was trying to get at. Please end this segment with your last words or thoughts on the subject gentlemen, and then we will move on to other questions."

Michael Angstat was sitting in his chair visibly seething. He was ready to pounce and ended this little segment of the discussion with a strong burst of energy. He yelled, "Fuck that, Charlie! Fuck that and fuck you! You're manipulating things now. Who are you to say what is credible and what is not? What gives you that right? We know no college kids claim to have seen Kelly, but we also know they were drunk off their asses at a frat party. You say it's not realistic for Kelly to get out of the room and back in the room a few hours later without being seen. But you make that assumption thinking there was a normal and well-adjusted crowd there looking for anything out of the ordinary.

"But there wasn't... there wasn't anything of the sort. That frat house was filled with drunken little idiots and it is beyond feasible to say that no one knew what the fuck was going on and no one saw Jamison when he left. I will repeat; no one has come forward and stated that they saw anything.

"You think this means there was nothing to see. I think, and Todd thinks it means that Jamison Kelly knew he had to be quick and sly if he wanted to get out and back in again without being seen. Maybe he covered his face. Maybe he ran out in a blur. Maybe be wore a hoodie or a hat. You aren't giving any of these possibilities a shot, Charlie, and I think that's because you do not want to go down this particular alley."

I decided enough was enough and it was time to move on. This point about the hoodie or a disguise was a good one, and I decided not to argue. I had to give some credit where it was due. At least that one possibility allowed a shred of credibility in the story these men were trying to tell.

It was time to press on. I said, "Gentlemen, thank you once again for your candor and your honest opinions. I really am excited, if for nothing else, about the lively discussion we've had so far and the great radio this will make for our listeners. Michael, I especially want to thank you because I've never had a famous filmmaker say, 'Fuck You' to me and now I can cross that off my bucket list."

Michael, in spite of himself, burst out laughing when I made this comment. In interviews, it's important to keep things as light as possible if you want your subject to keep talking. If they feel attacked or unappreciated, they will quickly clam up and your interview will be shit.

I continued, "So, now that you've made your position clear on the Jimmy Derek and Zach Burns issue, and you have laid out a potentially plausible theory about how Kelly could have left the room in some type of disguise, I want to move to another question from a reader of ours:

"'Mr. Barnes and Mr. Angstat, I liked your film a lot and I want to say that I also think Jamison Kelly killed his girlfriend. I think it's painfully clear when you look at the common-sense aspect of the whole case. He was a guy who fought with his girlfriend, was an emotional wreck, and was also heavily inebriated on the night of her disappearance. That description would fit many men who have been convicted of domestic violence, or worse, and I think that says a lot. My question is this. Why do you think Meghan Cocuzza, the detective in charge of the Moore disappearance was unable to arrest Kelly and charge him with murder? They supposedly had the victim's blood in his car already. Also, the night she disappeared, he had a terrible argument with her. Wouldn't these two facts alone warrant an arrest and a charge?'"

I smiled at Michael and Todd. I said, "I can see our honored guests smacking their lips like starving hounds, ready to answer this doozy of a question, which by the way comes from Tammy Whinstone of Coeur D'Alene, Idaho. Todd, what would be your response to this? It seemed that the DFPD had plenty of... at least circumstantial evidence to get Jamison charged up and processed. Why didn't it happen? Why did they let him go? I've interviewed Detective Meghan Cocuzza myself for this program and I found her to be very intelligent, well spoken, and experienced. It does seem strange that if she believed Kelly to be guilty, which she has gone on record claiming, that she wasn't able to make an arrest happen. Meghan herself claims that she was forced to let Kelly go due to lack of evidence. She wanted him badly, but her superiors made her drop the case.

"Primarily, she told me this decision was made because there was a general fear of the case in the Department and they wanted it squashed. They were eventually able to do just that which was based on their findings that there was not nearly enough blood in Jamison's car to prove that Cadence died there, and also because Kelly had a very strong alibi, which we've just spent the entire last segment discussing.

"Let's jump right on this. What do you guys think? Were there major mistakes made? Could the DFPD have arrested, charged, and tried Kelly...

eventually convicting him?"

Todd nodded, "Oh, believe me… I've often asked this question myself. In fact, I asked this exact question in the narration of my film. I will try to give you my take on things again. I believe the same things you believe about Meghan Cocuzza, Charlie. She is very intelligent and she's good at her job. But, unfortunately, in this case, there were some grave mistakes made.

"The first and most significant mistake made was letting Kelly go at all. They could have held him on suspicion alone, simply due to the evidence they already had. Who knows, if Kelly was guilty and he was given enough time to sweat after long and painful interrogations, he may have changed his tune and admitted what he did. That happens all the time. Criminals come in claiming they didn't, and when all is done and said, they end up admitting they did. That was mistake number one.

"Mistake number two was not investigating the landfill where the garbage from Andy Notch's dumpster and everywhere else in Dusklight Falls was taken. They waited too long to search the landfill site; it was pretty much a useless exercise in futility by then. Cadence's body may still be in that fucking landfill, buried under never-ending piles of rubbish, irretrievable and lost.

"Remember, Marx, there is no real strong evidence to validate the whole Hummingbird story at all, or the confused and conflicting ramblings of the Mintz family. So, for all we know, she was picked up right outside of Andy Notch's convenience store by Jamison Kelly, driven back to one of the dorms where he killed her. Then he dumped her in one of several hundred possible dumpsters in Dusklight Falls.

"What a pity it is to think about all these years later, that she was killed and discarded in that landfill… waiting to be discovered while the DFPD toiled around for months, rendering their eventual search of the landfill useless… that is, if the search was ever meant to succeed in the first place.

"It's possible Jamison was waiting in her dorm for her when she came back, but we believe he decided to go looking for her. He had murder on his mind and a feeling of murder is an impatient emotion. It's more reasonable to think that Kelly picked her up… possibly right outside the mini-mart…

and then returned to one of the dorms with her.

"One problem with the theory of the dorm killing, which I've had pointed out to me many times by less than informed people has to do with the security guards. Neither the security man at Jamison's dorm nor the security man at Cadence's dorm saw either one of them come back the morning of May 6.

"Now, that would have been really nice proof to have but we don't have it… so we're forced to fill in the blanks. It certainly doesn't mean they *didn't* come back as dozens of kids stroll into dorms around the country at all hours, sneaking past security because they've missed curfew or lights out. Like I said, the killing was done… probably at Jamison's dorm since that is the one place he could have had her alone with no one possibly there to see what he was doing to her.

"Could he have killed her in Andy Notch's parking lot? Likely not… remember the lack of any physical evidence there? Could he have parked along the road and did it in the bushes just as easily? Maybe, but that seems sloppy and probably would have seemed that way to Jamison, too. I think he wanted things to appear as normal as possible to Cadence so when he strangled her to death or whatever the means he used were, she would be caught by surprise. From there, the body had to be disposed of, which probably would have involved Jamison's car once again… and perhaps that little spot of blood that has gotten so much attention.

"That is also where mistake number three of the DFPD comes in. Although this mistake was not made by Meghan Cocuzza, she did everything she could to avoid this mistake, but to no avail. The DFPD chose to ignore the blood in Jamison Kelly's car because it was supposedly inconsequential and not worth pursuing, which to this day is one of the grand miscalculations in the annals of modern crime. They dismissed it on claims that it was not enough blood to prove a murder and the fact that Jamison had a so-called airtight alibi which proved his whereabouts at the time of the disappearance. When that happened, the case went south in a hurry and there was no going back.

"The one piece of solid physical evidence was pissed on and discarded and is now impossible to revisit in hopes of righting a decade old wrong.

So, yeah... I'd say there were some serious police work problems going on here, and those three points I've reviewed are the clear reason why Meghan Cocuzza couldn't get our friend Jamison locked up for safekeeping."

I probed a bit further, "You gentlemen believe the blood in Jamison's car was in fact the blood of Cadence Moore. If you do think this, is it possible in your mind that the blood was there because of sex during menstruation as Jamison claimed? Is that at least a possible reason for it to be there? Or is murder the only plausible reason it could have been there?

"And while I'm at it, why don't I just come right out and ask you both why the Hummingbird diner scene is all but ignored in your film and also ask why you have both publicly gone on record (including once during this very program) saying you don't believe the Hummingbird scene ever happened to begin with?"

Michael put both hands up in the air, indicating a gesture of surrender. He offered this, "Charlie, you are firing some serious darts in our direction now. Let's take this one point at a time. Your first question was about the blood in Kelly's car. So, we will address that first. Todd, why don't you offer our joint take on this since you are the more eloquent member of our little tag team."

Todd laughed and patted Michael on the back. He said, "Of course, stick me with the hard questions while you sit back and wait for your moment to sneak the good rants in. God, such a glory hound you are!"

This comment was made in jest and Michael smiled, but I couldn't help but notice a small expression of anger on Angstat's face when his partner was making these cute but benign confrontational comments.

Todd continued, "Let's discuss this menstrual blood. It was the one piece of physical evidence the police had and they chose to do nothing with it. All these years later, it still boggles the mind to believe such things are even possible. But in 2002, it is a matter of public record that the DFPD had blood in the car of the prime suspect and it is believed that blood belonged to the victim... yet no investigation was conducted. So, we really don't even know what we're talking about at his point.

"Let's just discuss the blood itself for a moment. The question Mike and I get asked the most is, (Todd mimicked this oft-asked question with a dumb jock sort of idiotic mumble) 'Why do you try to pretend the victim's blood was found in Kelly's car when no criminal investigation team ever proved or even pursued this?' Okay, so I will tell you.

"Michael and I have a motto in our line of business. There are no coincidences in life. Where there is smoke, there is fire. And where there is the alleged blood of a victim, there is probably also a murderer. Jamison Kelly fits the fucking profile to a tee, Charlie! He was Cadence Moore's boyfriend and he'd fought publicly with her that very same goddamn night! But we're supposed to believe that when police find some tiny traces of blood… I don't care if they were fucking microscopic… they find the victim's blood in Kelly's car, and they ignore it? I mean, does that sentence alone not make you shake your head in wonder?

"When you put your common-sense glasses on, that sentence alone pretty much indicts Kelly as the killer! He fits the damn profile, as I said. His whereabouts on the night in question can easily be called into question when you try just a little bit, as we've proven in the previous segment. So, I ask you Charlie, whether it be a miniscule spot of blood, or a waterfall of crimson nastiness, shouldn't the DFPD have investigated that blood and found out for sure if it belonged to Cadence Moore, and if it was in fact menstrual in nature?"

I couldn't deny the logic in Todd's statement. I answered, "Todd and Michael, I cannot fight you on this point. That the DFPD did not test the blood in the car is plainly a sham and deserves the condemnation it has received for a decade. If for no other reason than to prove Jamison Kelly a liar, this blood should have been tested.

"More than anything else in this case, the blood not being tested has added more fuel to the conspiracy story that's flirted around this thing ever since the beginning. If the test had occurred, 90% of the conspiracy theories out there would have been laid to rest. Actually, they would have never been theories in the first place since they'd have had no credibility."

Michael could contain himself no longer. He screamed, "Exactly! This is the whole point! The police work done in this case left too many unanswered questions, and if nothing else of what we say is true, that shoddy

police work alone demands that the public question every official conclusion the DFPD ever came up with, including… and I want to make this very
pronounced so I will emphasize this statement by repeating… including…
their conclusion that Jamison Kelly was innocent or at least that there was
not enough evidence to arrest him and try him."

On this point I was about to argue and could see Todd squirming a little
in his seat, obviously frustrated at Michael opening another door for debate.
Michael dealt in vague statements that could easily be questioned. Todd was
at least a little better at stating his points in a way that demanded admission
on the part of the debater that he had raised a decent point. Michael was so
hot-headed and impulsive that it was hard *not* to argue with his statements
since he left the door so wide open.

Before I could point out, or more accurately remind Michael of what
we'd already discussed, specifically all the points which led in the direction of there *not* being enough evidence to call Kelly the guilty party, Todd
stepped in. He said in an irritated tone, "Hold on… hold the fuck on,
people! We're not going down this same winding road again. We all know
about Jamison Kelly's alibi. Our main purpose in doing this show tonight
was proving to you and the public, Charlie, that there is reason to doubt
the official conclusions and start thinking in a totally different direction.
That is what we came here for and that is what we've done. We've poked
enough holes in the Kelly alibi theory to make it clear the DFPD fucked
up royally in their handling of events and evidence. What does that mean
you ask? And even if you don't ask, I'll tell you!

"It means that the conclusions I drew in my film (notice the ownership
Todd takes in this verbiage, making sure we know these are his conclusions
and the film they were revealed in belonged to him) were not mere crazy
theories born out of conspiracy or craziness. I have made a film, (Todd hesitated, seeming to realize he was leaving Angstat in the dust, and then cor-
recting his course), *we* made a film which attempts, and we believe succeeds,
in taking that other line of thinking and following it to its natural end.

"This is the road the DFPD never travelled down. And we have made it
clear and plain this evening what the reasons were for even beginning our

journey. We smelled a filthy rat from the start of it all, and we spent years of our lives trying to sift through the murky accepted bullshit and finding the real meat of the matter.

"Let us not fall back into a useless debate. Let's move on to other questions. We have satisfactorily answered young Tammy Whinstone's inquiry so what else does Charlie Marx's listening audience want to know? Let's hear it. We're ready for the next question. I can field this one, Mike. Just sit back and chill because I'm in the zone now, buddy!"

Michael laughed and pointed with both fingers at Todd saying, "Hey man… you said it all… keep sayin' it."

It was interesting to me that Todd jumped in the way he did when I was ready to pounce on Michael's statement about Jamison and the lack of evidence surrounding him. I didn't know if he was simply trying to avoid troublesome arguments and stay on task or if he was dodging conversation he was afraid to discuss.

The way Todd Barnes cut off Michael Angstat seemed to make it clear he was tired of the impulsive and abrasive remarks and probably found Michael much easier to deal with in their own studio, having the aid of editing, rather than in a live podcast environment where Michael's big mouth might get them in trouble.

Todd was ready to move on and was getting irritated. He badly wanted to change the subject, which I figured he would when he'd made the singular point he was able to make. With this in mind, I was prepared for a sudden change in direction. I wanted to get their take on the whole Hummingbird episode which they both have denied ever happened. Since it also happened to be a question asked by Tom Villecco of Round Rock, Texas, I decided to pose this one next.

- 9 -

I addressed Todd, the man who'd decided to take the whole interview over, directly looking him in the eye while I did so. My question was, "Todd, I know I have alluded to this, but it's also a nice segue to a listener question that echoes the same concerns. This is, I will reiterate, a listener question which is the precise thing you have requested.

"So, here it is. Tom Villecco, our man in Round Rock, wants to know, 'Todd and Michael, why do you guys feel so confident about the whole Hummingbird Diner episode being fake and never happening, even though at least two people, Todd Crist and Jared Mintz, have both sworn to it and stated their remembrances as pure facts in the presence of lawful authority?' Todd, your response please?"

Todd laughed and looked down at the floor for a moment before answering. He was still smiling when he looked back up into my eyes. He answered, "Well, first off, let me give mad props to Mr. Villecco for his creative phrasing. I mean, 'remembrances of pure facts in the presence of lawful authority,' that's good shit. Quit whatever banal task you currently toil in, Tom, and write poems… you have a woodworker's touch with words. Let me try to sum this up as simply as I can… to avoid any debating you might be feeling froggy about engaging in, Marx."

I smiled, somewhat flattered that Todd would try to avoid my debating since it clearly was now something he felt challenged by. I edged him a bit further. "Certainly, Mr. Barnes, I wish not to debate you… just seeking the truth… as are all of my listeners."

Todd gave me a look of disgusted contempt in the studio at that moment which could have cut through steel. An irritated tone could be heard loud and clear in his comments. He said, "Yes… oh yes, Charlie… the master debater… the bastard… I absolutely tremble at the notion of a verbal sparring with you, so I'd better get on with my fanciful lies before you tear me to shreds on the public stage… with all your wisdom, fortune telling, and just plain old omnipotence."

Mr. Barnes had obviously grown tired of me at this point and was heavily bothered by the points I continued to raise.

"Okay, Tom the poet wants to know why Michael and I think the Hummingbird scene is a dream sequence that never happened. Let's go right to this shit. We think it's a crock because it *is* a crock. How's that for some simple logic? Before you attempt to poke your first hole in my statement,

Charlie, why don't you consider these few points? The only people who have ever even spoken about this supposed scene are a senile old fry cook named Crist, and one half of a crazy-as-fuck couple who used to jointly go by the name of Mintz."

I couldn't help myself. I knew Todd Barnes was on a roll, but now that, for the moment, we were adversaries, I just couldn't resist the urge to jump in. "Todd, please... with all due respect before you go on... I must point out that you and Michael both spent a great deal of time and attention inter-viewing the so-called crazy-as-fuck Mintz family."

Todd Barnes lost it. He dispensed with every pleasantry and nearly spit at me with the fury of his exploding words, "I was getting to that, you asshole! Jesus Christ... Mike already called you on your interrupting bullshit once, you amateur prick! Just let me finish!

"We brought Misty and Jared in to spew their crap... hoping that any reasonable person listening would realize they were hearing the venom-coated joust of a wounded, soon-to-be-divorced, couple of liars. We gave them respect and we gave them time. But we never gave them our faith or belief... because any moron can see that the story they spin, no matter from what perspective you're hearing it, was a total steaming pile of shit stew."

I added a little smidgen of agreement in hopes that mad, slobbering Todd, who was more interesting than his normal soft-spoken counterpart (mannered and calm Todd), would keep talking, but with less desire to get up and leave while he did it. I said, "Mr. Barnes, no one can disagree with the notion that the Mintz family has a little credibility problem... consider-ing that their stories are as different in nature as night and day."

Todd waved me off. "I'm trying to answer the question. Yeah, these two people couldn't have existed in the same universe at the same time if they both spoke the truth. Their stories were complete and utter bullshit, if you ask me, which you did. I think they heard the news about Cadence and then decided to engage in a war of ridiculous fantasy to see who would come out on top. It's unlikely they even saw Cadence that night.

"We know they bought a few things from Andy Notch but we don't know anything beyond that. So, where's the connection that proves they had any contact with Cadence? Why should we think there is one? Because a couple of travelling geeks buy some slurpees and sandwiches within a few minutes of a girl who went in to buy cigarettes before disappearing? C'mon man… that's thin as hell!

"The Mintz clan is sitting home watching a bit of TV… and they see their opening and start to make up ludicrous shit. Seriously, if Jared Mintz acted in the way he claims, chasing and grabbing this little freaked out drunken chick, don't you think Cadence would have shrieked her brains out, prompting good ol' Andy Notch to call the cops to check out a disturbance outside?

"Even all that shit on the Tarynco security camera with the girl getting pulled out of frame… what makes anyone think that Jared or Misty Mintz was anywhere near the place when it was filmed? Jesus, it's a college town and there are drunken girls and guys fucking around at all hours of the night. Why do we think Jared, Misty, or Cadence must be connected to this little flash on camera that no one can identify as anything? Because the Mintz family bought some snacks there a few minutes before? What evidence is that? What motive would they have to stick around and then decide to pick up drunken hitchhikers, instead of moving on with their family vacation?

"No, I'll tell you what's up here, my friend. This situation is a twisted bout of one-upmanship between some former lovebirds who could barely stand the sight of each other anymore. It's amazing what a troubled married couple will stoop to, trying to outdo their warring spouse and be declared the winner of the argument of the day.

"I'm telling you right now Charlie Marx, these two people, these complicators of a simple scenario, decided to bring their own drama to the public stage because they were 'lucky' enough to be in the general vicinity when some shit went down. So… just for the sake of argument… without the Tarynco footage… or better yet… just taking Jared and Misty Mintz out of the equation for a moment… what are you left with?

"Now, you have no Hummingbird, and Todd Crist's photographic memories are revealed as a pathetic attempt at drumming up business for the next Friday night car show in his parking lot. What are you left with? I really want you to answer this, Charlie. C'mon, we all know you aren't afraid to interject with an opinion. So, please, I want your opinion on this. If you take Jared, Misty, and Todd out of this little story, what are you left with? Is Jamison… or at the very least, the homeless vagabond who threw eggs at the mini-mart starting to look like more promising suspects to you?"

I answered, "Yes Todd, if you take all those people out of the scenario, then Jamison or the homeless vagabond look like more likely suspects. But what I think you're trying to do here is quarantine the whole evening in question and limit it to the general vicinity of Andy Notch's Mini-mart.

"If you do this, then little annoying questions pop up about the Hummingbird, the phone calls supposedly made there, and the headlights in the parking lot floating in to perhaps snatch up young Cadence. Those things trouble me, Todd, and they can't be ignored simply because Jared and Misty Mintz had a dysfunctional marriage and one of them is a liar. We have a witness claiming to see Cadence Moore in his diner and that doesn't change even if you call him a senile old fry cook.

"And, of course, we have the phone calls of which one recording was recovered and the voice on that recording sounds a lot like Cadence Moore. On top of that we have the floating headlights in the parking light, rolling in just seconds after Cadence is said to have exited the diner to have a smoke.

"Now, before either of you jumps over the desk to strangle me because I know you're both getting irritated and fed up with this interview, even though I should mention once again how much I appreciate you both coming on the show, and if nothing else, I respect you both immensely as people. But, I'm sidetracked again. I was saying that you both should refrain from attacking me because I realize you know about all the points I've just laid down. I do not intend to imply that you don't. These points are not enough to convince you that the Hummingbird scene ever happened and that's fair enough. But I do have a question about it all."

Michael decided his period of silence had run its course and was ready with an aggressive rant. "Please, Charlie, let us indulge you with another answer to another question. And, please let us also remind you what a pleasure it is to talk with you this evening. And, we're so flattered that you respect us immensely as people and blah blah fuckin' blah blah.

"Listen Marx... you've been an obnoxious prick to us this entire damn time. You've been argumentative, you've interrupted like it was goin' out of style, and you've tried to make us look incompetent. So, now you want another answer to another question. Let me make this clear. Todd can do what he wants and I know he's always been the more level headed of our little pairing, so he'll probably stay here and entertain your bullshit for another hour.

"But, I've about had it with this whole operation. So, I will answer your last question and then I'm leaving and going somewhere else so the ignorant fumes of your studio can stop poisoning the better sense of my senses. I suggest you ask your question and make it a good one, Mr. Marx."

I must admit, I was caught off guard by Mr. Angstat's quite clear statement about my next question being the last one he would answer. I tried my best to hold this interview together just long enough that it could see its proper end, which was coming soon anyway. I said, "Mr. Angstat, if I've made you feel this way and I've been an obnoxious prick, then I apologize. It was not my intention and it's possible that being an ignorant jackass is just my nature as a human being."

"With that said, I will comply with your wishes and I will ask my last question. And, also, as I've promised, I will be calling you shortly to reveal the information we've uncovered in the case and you can then make up your own mind about whether you believe it or not.

"Okay, enough talk... on with the question. Todd and Michael, Meghan Cocuzza, as we have already reviewed at length, felt that Jamison Kelly killed Cadence Moore... just the same as you. But Meghan also believes Cadence was in the Hummingbird that night making calls from the pay phone. Since she has gone on record with this assertion, and has also stated she thinks it was likely Jamison who was driving the car to which those floating headlights belonged, then why do you fellows feel it necessary to eliminate the possibility that the Hummingbird scene did indeed take place, as stated by Jared Mintz and Todd Crist?

"It actually would sync up your theory with the opinion of the investigating officer, and there is no reason to think that the Hummingbird scene, in and of itself, eliminates Kelly as a suspect. He has the same likelihood of grabbing and even killing Cadence in the general area of the Hummingbird as he did in the general area of Andy Notch's Mini-mart. So, again… why the need to take the Hummingbird out of the equation?"

Michael replied with one colorful phrase, "Because, Charlie Marx, you're a stupid excuse for a journalist, and you suck, and you're an idiot, and I don't feel fit to speak to you anymore today."

Michael stood up, hugged Todd, flipped me off, and walked out of my studio at this point. I presume he got in his car and drove away. We never saw him again that day, and I did not speak to him myself until I called with the promised delivery of information concerning the crime solved. I will go into Michael's response to that phone call later.

As for Todd, he sat in his chair, still slightly pissed from our earlier exchanges, but seemingly willing to continue the discussion in spite of Michael's early exit. Todd said, "Well, Charlie, I guess now you know how easy it is to have guests walk out on you when you hit one too many buttons. You pushed Michael too far and you came close with me, as well. But, I will do my best to finish our interview, which I'm assuming is ending after this segment since we've been talking quite a long time now. And, unless half your program will be comprised of this discussion, I'd imagine our time is coming to a close.

"So, without further ado, I will answer this question. In fact, I will repeat it and then answer it… for those listeners who got distracted during Michael's grand exit. You asked us why the need to take the Hummingbird out of the equation altogether, even though it brings us closer to the DFPD version of events and still makes Kelly a prime suspect.

"Charlie, unlike the accusations leveled at us over the last several months, or whatever the hell it's been, Michael Angstat and I do not simply go with a theory and put our stamp of approval on it because it furthers our agenda. I don't believe the Hummingbird diner scene ever happened. Michael doesn't believe the Hummingbird diner scene ever happened. I don't care if Meghan Cocuzza thinks it did. I also don't care that *you* do. I also, for that matter, don't care if it helps my case against Kelly, which it really doesn't to be honest.

"What I care about is the truth in the disappearance of Cadence Moore. And, I can't put it more plainly than this. I don't believe the Hummingbird Diner, or any of the calls supposedly made from there are part of that truth."

"Thank you, Mr. Barnes. I still don't know if I quite understand your perspective on this situation, but I respect that you feel the way you feel. I have one more thing to add before I bid you adieu.

"One of the phone calls made from the very diner we're discussing sounds very much like Cadence Moore calling the bus station. Doesn't the similarity between the voice on the phone and Cadence Moore's voice bother you when you try to put the whole Hummingbird scene out of your mind?"

Todd replied, "No Charlie… simply put… it doesn't bother me. I'll tell you why. Because there is no real solid evidence telling me or anyone else that the Hummingbird scene ever happened, at least as is relates to Cadence being there. You can tell me these phone calls sound like Cadence but I could also say you sound like Vince McMahon on a WWE wrestling telecast. Does that make you Vince McMahon? Of course, it doesn't.

"It means nothing more than me thinking you sound like him. Andy Notch's Mini-mart scene is the one to watch. That is the last credible sighting, as you like to say Charlie, of Cadence Moore on May 6, 2002. She was picked up shortly after buying those cigarettes, and from there it is my opinion that she was killed in one of the dorm rooms by her angry and conflicted boyfriend, Jamison Kelly.

"Now, unfortunately for our theory, the security man at each of the dorms does rounds several times a night. Neither of them claims to have seen Jamison or Cadence return to either of the dorms. That does not mean they didn't return… it just means they were not seen. This doesn't support our theory, but it sure as hell doesn't kill it either.

"Not being seen does not mean you weren't there… as we've already discussed ad nauseam in the Basement discussion from earlier. I have no need for the Hummingbird in this scenario. Also, just to review, if Jamison had been the one to drive up to the parking lot of the mini-mart and ask Cadence to get in, there very well may have been no struggle at all. She may just have got in his damn car, thinking they were about to go have make-up sex.

"Now, of course, we know Kelly or whoever you want to say the killer was, still had to get rid of the body. That means the botched-up landfill investigation still probably ruined the entire case. As I said before, I believe the answers still lie there to this day buried under ten years of shit, never to be seen again.

"I hope I have answered you, Charlie. Jared Mintz was an opportunist and Todd Crist a confused old dude looking for some publicity. In good conscience, we cannot allow these shadowy figures on the periphery of this case to alter our good sense and make us go in fanciful directions that lead us to ridiculous places.

"And with that, Mr. Marx, I must bid you a pleasant evening because I'm just about out of interview energy. You have yourself a fine day and I wish you luck on your show. I'll look forward to your call a little while from now... and you better be convincing, chum, or I may have this whole little talk pulled, which would be both a pity and a waste of time. Take care, Charlie."

I concluded, "Thank you very much, Todd... for everything. I want to say that without your film and the attention it brought back to this case, we wouldn't be sitting here right now. Even though we don't agree on some things, I can't tell you how valuable you and your partner have been to the eventual truth coming out. For that... above all else... I thank you, sir."

I shook Todd's hand and thanked him for appearing on our podcast. I really did appreciate it, no matter how badly I annoyed him and his partner.

This is the end of Episode 4. Make sure you all tune in to the live special airing this Friday, November 8, at midnight. The answer to one of the most enduring mysteries of our time will be revealed live on UPR.

7

Tyler Interviews Charlie

UNITED WAY OF LIFE: (Official Transcript)
Segment two: Interview with Charlie Marx

Tyler Reubens's United Way of Life: Original Air Date: November 7, 2013. (This program is funded and sponsored by WHHW, a subsidiary of Universal Public Radio)

(Narration by Tyler Reubens) "Welcome back *United Way of Life* listeners; as promised I am now here in studio with Charlie Marx, host of the *Underground Broadcast* program which airs weekly on WHHW, and most recently the host of the wildly-successful and sensational podcast series on the Cadence Moore mystery called *Underground Podcast*, which has garnered an astonishing amount of attention and interest, all of which is leading us to a live special tomorrow night at midnight, eastern time, on UPR affiliates across the nation in which Charlie has claimed he will reveal the answer to one of the most legendary mysteries of all time.

"Before we begin our interview with Mr. Marx, I want to say a few things regarding this series. You have heard some excerpts from the *Underground Podcast* episodes in the first segment of tonight's *United Way of Life* program. These were made available for download, all at once for binge listening, which is the growing trend in entertainment these days, less than one week ago and response has been positively staggering.

"We received word right before we went on air tonight that the podcast episodes in total have been downloaded in excess of thirty-two million times! Yes, you did hear that right, listeners, thirty-two million times. Four podcasts, that means at least eight million people have downloaded each one at least once. And survey results have been coming in hot like liquid magma, with the consensus being that most listeners of these four episodes planned on listening to all four again within the next twelve hours so they would be 'ready' for the live special. We actually have listeners telling us they will be calling off from their jobs tomorrow just to hear all the podcasts again before the live special airs at midnight.

"This I can say, as executive producer of the series, has exceeded everyone's expectations. Between the national interest drummed up in the last year by the Todd Barnes and Michael Angstat movie and the heavy runs of ads we've been pushing very heavily over the past few weeks, this Cadence Moore case has hit a sensitive nerve with people all over the world. We certainly believed we'd have a success with this series, but the reaction has been worlds more than we hoped for and we're all riding a bit of an unexpected success wave over the last twenty-four to forty-eight hours.

"If the survey results are anything close to accurate, that would mean we will have over sixty million downloads by the time the live shows airs tomorrow night. Even if none of that happens, this whole thing has been an untamed roaring success and we're thrilled about it! This is the largest response by far that UPR has seen for a podcast show and honestly for any special series we have ever done; and, the live special tomorrow night is expected to shatter all previous audience records for the midnight time slot.

"I am delighted to be the producer of this series, and I must say I am ecstatic that we chose the Cadence Moore mystery as the theme of our program. I won't lie to you. We recognized the massive attention worldwide which the Todd Barnes and Michael Angstat film, *Moore to the Story,* received. We knew this was a hot subject and we ran with it. What did we do? Well, piggybacking off the success of the Barnes and Angstat film, our series has been able to delve much, much deeper into the mystery that those gentlemen explored in their movie. At over four hours running time, cumulatively, the podcasts we made available last week have run through the Cadence story in more detail than any previous investigation has ever come close to. Simply put, we did a better job on this thing than anyone else, including Barnes and Angstat, in my humble opinion. Now here we are on the eve of the live special in which our own Charlie Marx has promised the world he will solve the case.

"It may surprise you all to know this, but I am a gambler in my professional life. I take chances when I believe in something, and I've taken a big one with this series. I have allowed Charlie all the resources and time he needed to get the job done, and I've done this without knowing what the result would be. I've done this under pressure from the upper echelon of UPR corporate influence. The red-hot leads Charlie and his team have claimed to have uncovered have been kept a secret, even from me. These leads, I have been told, were of such a nature… that anyone, even the executive producer of the series, outside the inner circle of researchers Marx had working the case, knowing the key details could have jeopardized the investigation, as well as the likelihood of the answers being revealed on UPR instead of somewhere else. Lots of hands in the pot… you know how it goes.

"I have taken a leap of faith on a man who is my protégé and someone I've trained from the ground up. I have faith in Charlie Marx and my greatest hope is that he will come through with his promise and we will all have closure on this case. If I have produced a program which will bring justice to a young woman who was taken from the world way too soon, then all the risk involved with this series will have been worth it. If that does not end up happening, then Charlie will… well let's just say, he will be in a tough spot folks. With all that said, let's ask this man some questions.

"First of all, here's the obvious one. Charlie Marx, could you have fathomed in your most insane dreams, that this podcast series leading into our live radio special would have demanded the ferocious interest and appetite from UPR listeners that it has?"

Charlie Marx laughed and said, "I would have liked to tell you that I had it all figured out, Tyler, and I knew what we were doing would be an anomaly… a sensation as you called it… but I had no idea. I can only say we owe a debt of gratitude to Todd Barnes and Michael Angstat, no matter how difficult these gentlemen may be as personalities to deal with. We owe them for shining a well-needed spotlight on this case and allowing us to put something, which I think we'd both say is far superior to their film, out there for public consumption, and have it generate the interest that it has. I don't think you and I would even be talking about how great our podcasts or radio specials might be without their film as the catalyst for it all. So, yes, I am surprised but I am also grateful to two men who created something that we are benefitting from in magnificent ways. With that said, I think our series has bested their film in every way imaginable... egotistical as that might sound... I believe it wholeheartedly."

Tyler clapped his hands in mock applause. "I cheer your modesty. I always enjoyed how humble you were in descriptions of your own work, Charlie Marx. That may be why I chose you for this assignment. You remind me so much of myself. Okay, I digress with the sarcasm.

"My next question, Charlie, is this. You, well *we*, the *United Way of Life* team, your *Underground Broadcast* crew, and the entire UPR network of brilliant associates, have generated a sensation... yes, I'll say it again... with this project and we have been advertising the entire series as a solution to a decade-old mystery which has on several occasions now captivated the world. I ask you, how confident are you that you will be able to live up to the expectations and deliver on what you have promised the world you will deliver?"

Charlie smiled, "Tyler this is the first chance I have to thank you for this opportunity in a public forum. So, I want to do that now. Thank you. For all you've ever done for me, but specifically for this series, I am tremendously grateful. That said, I cannot pretend I'm completely surprised that you've told your audience that you have taken a risk with this project and you've let me do what needed to be done without being let in on every detail of the story, including the key details. The UPR audience should know that. But as I've told you before, when this is over, you'll understand why I needed to be so careful and you'll be glad you..."

Tyler raised one finger and said, "Excuse me, Charlie, I don't mean to interrupt, but I feel like we might be in danger of having this question go unanswered. I asked how confident you were in being able to deliver what you promised you would deliver."

Charlie nodded. "Of course, Tyler, I heard the question and was about to answer it. My answer is I'm supremely confident."

Tyler asked, "I am assuming this supreme confidence is not misplaced enthusiasm for a theory you have or a lead that looked promising. You're supremely confident you have found the answer to the Cadence mystery. Am I correct, Mr. Marx? After all, that's what I've spent a lot of money marketing in our advertising for this show and it's what I've been led to believe."

Charlie, knowing what Tyler was doing, said, "I am enthusiastic, of course, but not because of a misplaced zeal for something that just *sounded* good. My team and I have solved this case, Tyler, and when people tune into the live special tomorrow, they will get the answer they've been waiting for. They will get what Barnes and Angstat couldn't give them and they will get what no one has ever been able to give them. They will have taken a journey with us and arrive at the place we've all been seeking... and have been seeking for a long time." Charlie was committed at this point and the lies fell off his tongue like lemmings off a cliff.

Tyler said, "What no one can deny at this point is how much interest there is in this case. The success of the Barnes and Angstat film alone proved *that* and the massive number of downloads we've seen with our series has driven the point home even further. So, I know I asked this already... but I'm not sure I'm completely clear on your answer Charlie. So, please indulge me again. Were you surprised by how much attention the podcast series has received and how ravenous the public's appetite for answers you have promised truly is, Mr. Marx?"

Charlie knew he was being played with. But he was in control at least for now... at least until tomorrow when it all fell apart live on air if Bill Mattingly decided to fuck him. He knew Tyler was testing him, while at the same time trying to appear innocent of any grand fuckups that might be right around the corner. Charlie answered, "On one hand, I am not surprised at all by the public interest in Cadence's story. This is one of the modern legends. This case has never gotten solved, unless you ask Todd Barnes or Michael Angstat. If you ask any serious student of the case, beyond those two men, they would tell you the conclusions drawn in that movie were unadulterated fantasy and farce.

"Cadence Moore is a fascinating personality and her disappearance has, I can say with no hyperbole, captivated an entire generation of people who were there when it happened, and a whole new generation of people being introduced to the story for the first time in the last year. As it relates to the success of our series, I can honestly tell you I've been shocked to the core by that. I didn't think the response would be anywhere close to what it's been and it's a little scary, if I'm being truthful about it. I suppose you can chalk that up to the masterful marketing team of WHHW and UPR, all under the watchful eye of a gentleman named Tyler Reubens. This whole thing has been presented better than anything I've ever seen in my short but eventful entertainment career."

Tyler was taken slightly aback by Charlie's clear shifting of credit to him and his marketing abilities. He was responsible for this after all, but he was still fighting a fight, a struggle he'd been waging ever since that first disrespectful phone call with Charlie Marx after the news of the deadline change had occurred. He would not be set off track with idle flattery. Tyler said, "What scares you the most, Mr. Marx? The responsibility you feel to come through on your promise? Or the response you think the public will have to the answer you give them?"

Charlie thought for a second, wary of any potential traps being laid. Not noticing any, he proceeded as though this were just a normal interview. He said, "That's a great question. No investigation as you mentioned a few minutes ago has ever gone as deep as we have into this mystery. So, yes, I think when the public finds out what really happened, they will be very surprised and potentially saddened. They may not know how to process it. As for me being the one who has to deliver, that's what I signed up for, and that's what I'm going to do. But yes, it's scary. It scares the hell out of me." Truer words were never spoken in Charlie Marx's entire life.

Tyler saw his opening and took it. He had a series finale to promote and he would promote it. But, he would do so in the context of pushing an answer to a decade-old mystery while, at the same time, pushing the doubt of his chosen man falling onto his own sword and promising the world some kind of peace it was never going to get. Tyler said, "But here we are now, at the proverbial eleventh hour, right before show time, and I feel like I have to be honest with my listeners. Would you be okay with that, Charlie?"

Charlie looked his boss straight in the eye. He knew what was coming and it didn't surprise him at all. Tyler was now going to ride the balance between selling the live special, burying Charlie, and distancing himself from everything while somehow taking credit for it all. Tyler was a master and Charlie expected nothing less. He said the only thing he could say at this point, "Being honest with your listeners is what you've always done, Tyler. Why would I have you do anything else now?"

Tyler continued, "I'm glad to hear you say that because honesty with our listeners is something that we must have to be successful in this game. Without honesty, we are lost and our credibility is gone. With no credibility, we have no trust and with no trust, we have no listeners. I just hope that you Charlie Marx have not forgotten this."

Charlie said, "I have not forgotten this, Tyler… but you don't sound so sure."

Tyler said, "Now come on, Charlie, let's not leave our audience in the dark completely. Let's put it out there now. I do not have every reason in the world to trust you, and the only reason this special is happening is because I made a commitment to give you a shot and I believed in you. You have not repaid my faith in you with offering your faith in return, and this has caused tension between us, major tension. I feel it fair for us to let our audience know that as we move to the finish line. We were friends, Charlie… but hey… friends no more, right? That's just the price of doing business."

Charlie said, "I hadn't expected you to bring this up on air, Tyler, but that's just fine if you feel we owe it to our listeners. You have plenty of reasons to feel animosity toward me and some could interpret my secrecy as a sign of me being ungrateful and disrespectful; but, I haven't given you any reason at all to *mistrust* me, Tyler. I have delivered what I promised to deliver so far and I plan to keep on doing that."

Tyler said, "Right you are, Charlie, and I'll remind you now, in front of millions of people, I have kept my end of the deal and I continue to bet on you. When I commit to someone and *something*, I commit all the way and see it through. I guess my only concern now is that you share the same mentality. Here is the only question that really needs to be answered. You've committed to solving Cadence Moore live on the air tomorrow night. Will you see that commitment through and will we have our answer?"

Charlie smiled. He said, "I only have this to say and then I feel as though we've probably reached the effective limit of this interview. We'll have to let the special speak for itself. At this point, the podcasts have been a mammoth success and the live special is almost guaranteed to set records. I have made the commitment of my lifetime with this investigation, more than anyone understands. I will see it through to the end and I will show everyone that they took this journey with the right man. Tyler, the rest… you'll have to wait and see." Charlie felt nausea swim through his guts. He swallowed hard while never changing the expression of confident resolve which dominated the lines on his face.

Tyler concluded the brief interview by saying, "Thank you, Mr. Marx, for this time. I will be tuned in tomorrow night with the rest of the world waiting for the answer you've promised. Let us all hope this will end up a success that exceeds our largest expectations which this series, so far, has already been." Tyler took a second to breathe and look up at the ceiling of his studio, and then back into the eyes of Charlie Marx. He said, "I wish you the best of luck. Good night *United* listeners. Tomorrow will tell a very interesting tale. *That*, I can guarantee you."

Tyler clicked off the microphone and waited for the "On Air" light in the studio to turn off. He looked at Charlie and said nothing for a moment. He just stared at him. Charlie stared back. Tyler finally said, "I feel a 'what the fuck was that' coming any second now."

Charlie shook his head. "I don't need to ask you that. I don't need to ask because I already know what the fuck it was. You're covering yourself. You just carved out the back door you plan to leap out of if I go down in flames on the air. You *believe* I have it, I know you do. You've believed I had it from the start which is why this is happening. And now with the eyes and ears we have on this thing, you can't stop it. More than being ousted as a guy who put his faith in the wrong person and embarrassing UPR, stopping it now before it has a chance to fail live on the air would be career suicide for you and you know that, too."

Tyler leaned in and got within four inches of Charlie's face. He said, "Right on all fronts, Marx. Right you are. I just let everyone know if this goes the way I want it to, I am the one who put the winning combination together. If it doesn't go that way, they'll know I took risks for their benefit but put my faith in the wrong man. I've been a fan of yours since the start, Charlie. I've been a fan of what you've done with the podcasts. They've been brilliant… of course my input had a little something to do with that. But the whole thing has been fantastic. I chose you because you were the fucking guy, Marx… you were the only guy for this gig. And, really no matter which way it goes now, I'll be all right. Oh, I'll be fucked in the short run and my bosses will question how I could have let this embarrassment happen. But, they will also not forget sixty million downloads by the time it's all through, and my standing with UPR will be stronger than ever in the long run.

"Now *you,* on the other hand… all I can say is what I've already said. If you really have mortgaged everything in your life to go under fire tomorrow night live on the air and come up empty… well I just don't believe you could be that stupid. I believe you will deliver. If not, I will never in my craziest possible thoughts be able to figure out why or how you got to a place where you would allow that to happen. But it really doesn't matter. I never truly gave a fuck about solving Cadence; I wanted the story told. I wanted the audience. My objective has been achieved. Thirty million people downloaded podcasts that *I* produced. Sixty million will be the final tally before tomorrow, and untold millions more will be listening in live for the biggest ratings we've ever had. I've already won. The question is… have *you?* Or have you lost everything you had and anything you might have had?"

Charlie stood up, walked to the door of the recording booth and turned the knob. He looked back at Tyler and said, "You won't have to ask that question ever again after tomorrow's broadcast."

Tyler laughed softly and said, "Get some sleep, Charlie. Your big moment waits for you. If you fuck me and all our listeners, then two things will happen. I will leave the studio tomorrow embarrassed and infuriated, ready to spin my tale the way it needs to be spun for me to keep moving forward. You, my friend, will leave in handcuffs. Fraud charges are hard ones to beat when you rape a corporation for millions in advertising dollars. No threats, Charlie… just a promise. I said it on the air and I'll say it again now. I wish you the best of luck."

Charlie responded in the most honest way a man could respond in such surreal and fucked up circumstances. He said, "Thank you for that. I hope when this is over, we'll still be friends. If not that, then I hope you'll still respect me. I hope that because I've done what you trained me to do. I've taken this to the outermost limits and I will ride with it until the bitter end, no matter what that means. I know you served this all up to me on a silver platter, but I've done more with it than you ever thought I would and more with it than you yourself could have done. That's a fact.

"I don't fear the consequences anymore. What will be will be. But if that final moment comes and you don't think it's worthy of your standards… then plainly… fuck you, Tyler Reubens. Fuck you with the most intense disregard one could possibly be fucked with. If we never speak again, I want you to remember those words!"

8

The Live Special

UNDERGROUND BROADCAST
LIVE SPECIAL: (Official Transcript)

Charlie Marx's Underground Broadcast: Original Air Date: November 8, 2013. (Part One) Aired on seven-second delay for language and objectionable material (Brought to you by United Way of Life, courtesy of Tyler Reubens... this program is funded and sponsored by WHHW, a subsidiary of Universal Public Radio)

- 1 -

ON AIR

(Narration by Charlie Marx) "Good evening weary travelers and my constant loyal friends. We are now entering the final segment of our series on Cadence Moore, our live special for the UPR listening audience. For the next two hours, we will conclude our research into the case and have ourselves an ending. This is what we've been leading up to all this time. Now, I am about to drop a bombshell down on the lot of you.

During podcast episodes one through four, which all of you have downloaded in dizzying numbers, which have set the brass of this corporation into circles of delighted confusion, we have reviewed the long-known and often-discussed version of events... all the arguments... all the details... and we've done this because we had to. We had to cross the bridge of what came before so we could reach the other side and set foot on the island of pure and perfect truth.

In other words, I've engaged our guests in discussion of minute details and little tiny rumblings of possibility and theory. Did I know when I had these discussions that most of what we were talking about would end up being irrelevant? Yes. To be simple and clear about it... I did know that.

But, I also knew that if we didn't turn over every stone and discredit the different conclusions and ideas surrounding this case, when the time came, my real answers would not be taken seriously. All of my listeners would still be stuck on small details and conspiracy theories that have permeated the collective psyche in the last ten years.

So, I needed to deal with those things and I feel that in the last several podcasts, I've done a decent job of dealing with them so you travelers would have the whole story in your heads before we arrived at the finish line, ready to find out the all-encompassing glorious truth.

With that said, I'm going to ask you all now to *forget everything you've heard. Forget everything you think you know.* We're leaving Kansas behind now and Oz can be seen glittering green and sparkly from far down below as we sail over in our jet plane of grand discovery. What follows now... this is what *really* went down on May 6, 2002.

However, before we cross that threshold, I need to lay a bit more groundwork. I will note here as we move along toward the end, this live special contains many different conversations that took place before our broadcast tonight. Because many of these conversations were recorded, but not for radio, we have had our radio actor's troupe fill in the blanks and provide voice-overs for the conversations that I and my producers have scripted from memory or direct transcript from tape.

This troupe of actors was hired specifically by me for this live special and have themselves signed confidentiality agreements with me personally... not with UPR, not with Tyler Reubens, but with me... meaning that if anything was said about the contents of these recordings to anyone but me or Dillon before air time, those confidentiality agreements would be broken and a multi-million-dollar lawsuit would be on its way to the unfortunate person who broke said agreement. So, very quickly let me acknowledge

Warren Bandera, Chris Rivers, Jed Wilkins, Raymond Bixler, Eric Kyle, Pat Hart, and Ronnie Farley. This live special would not be possible without your talents and hard work.

- 2 -

Fortune smiled when I went to see my cousin Rydell Stevenson, although I didn't know it at the time. He's serving a six-year sentence in Berks County Prison for credit card fraud. He's been a bad boy, but he's family and I always loved Rydell. We were inseparable as kids, and I was not abandoning him like a lot of my other family members did when he got busted. Rydell ended up being a very large part of this series… more on that in a moment.

Rydell and I shot the shit for a while. You only have about eight to ten minutes on those prison phone calls. Well, right before it's time for him to go he says, "Hey, Charlie, you were really into that Cadence Moore murder a few years ago, right? That's all you used to talk about."

Now, Rydell didn't have a clue I was working on the special and he just came out with this as a matter of conversation. At least that's what I believed at the time and still, as far as I'm aware, believe to be true. I smiled and said, "Yeah… in fact, it's funny you say that because I'm doing a show about it as we speak. Why do you ask?"

Rydell's eyes got wide and he smiled, "Oh man, Charlie, you're doing a show right now? Is it done already? I mean did you produce it already for the air?"

I said, "No, we're still putting it together. Well, Jesus, now I have to ask… why are you so interested in Cadence Moore, Rydell? Do you want an interview segment on it or something?"

Rydell said, "No, not a chance on that, Char, but listen… I don't know if he'll talk to you. These guys spook real easily, but if you guys can get him… you've *gotta* talk to Budgie Bailey. He's got that whole thing figured out, man. His cellmate confessed the murder to him. I thought it was bullshit, bro, but Budgie's got a lot of details from this dude and it sounds fuckin' legit man."

This isn't my first rodeo, weary travelers, and I refused to get giddy and happy about a rumor floating around a prison which is probably just as reliable as a thousand other rumors floating around jails across the land with bored hoods and criminals claiming credit for crimes they weren't even born early enough to commit.

But nonetheless, I probed a little out of curiosity. "Rydell, you know how many people came out of the woodwork claiming to know who killed that girl? And no offense, brother, but what kind of name is Budgie anyway? I don't know if I'd listen to a guy named after a little bird."

Rydell smiled, "I don't know, dude, but if you're working on a show about this, I gotta believe you better talk to this guy."

I said, "But, Rydell, you know how guys in here talk and take credit for everything under the sun. What makes you think this guy's word is worth a damn?"

Rydell said, "Maybe it's not, bro, but I'm telling you when he told me the story, it didn't sound like he was spinning yarn. He's looking to tell somebody what he knows. And he knows enough about me to know something about you and your show."

I shook my head. "Well, don't you think he just smells an opportunity to try to get a hold of someone with some notoriety and barter for something, some perk or whatever, over information that could be a bunch of nonsense?"

Rydell said, "Maybe that's true, man, I don't know. I just figured I'd tell you. I can try to set it up if you want me to… but if you think it's just a bunch a shit, then I won't waste my time. Hey, man… I'll catch you next time… don't be a stranger."

I said, "You take care too, brother… and hey, I appreciate you thinking of me. I am having a bitch of a time getting people *involved* with the case to talk to me, and I don't have a lot of time to spare, so thanks but no thanks for now on Mr. Budgie. I really appreciate it though, Rydell… I do. If things change, I'll come back and see if you can arrange that interview. If I don't, though, don't think I don't appreciate the gesture. Good looking out dude."

I left Rydell and went back to my office. It was hell trying to pull this thing together. Ever since my initial calls to the Barnes and Angstat offices to request an interview, my producer, Dillon Balast, incessantly made follow-up calls for weeks to no avail.

So, one night Dillon and I are up in the office working late, trying to come up with a format for the show, and spitting fire in frustration since this was shaping up to be one weak ass series with a lack of major players to interview. Certainly, no major series could be supported by what we had at this juncture.

We're sitting there toiling away when Dillon gets a call on his cell. He picked it up and a drunken voice yelled, "Hey, let me talk to the bozo they call Chuck Marx!" Dillon asked the voice on the other end of the phone who in the hell they were. The drunken voice let out a long chortle of laughter and then replied, "Tell Chucky if he wants to talk to Michael Angstat he better get on the fuckin' phone right now. I'm countin' ta three. One... two..."

I was on the other end of the line before Michael was finished slurring the word "two." I screamed, "Mr. Angstat... this is Charlie Marx... you asked for me?"

Michael blurted out, "Hey, Mr. Radio Man! I'm sitting in a bar right now with my good friend Mr. Barnes. We've been laughing at you for the last hour." There was more muffled laughter on the other end of the line.

I said, "I see... well, why are you... are you calling to see if my ears were ringing?" It was the first thing that came to my mind and seemed to be the correct choice of words. I could now hear both of them laughing harder in the background.

Todd Barnes then grabbed the phone and stumbled through his statement, "Marx... Radio Man Marx... hey man, we were laughing because we found it funny that you're stalking us. Seems you want to make a radio show about Cadence Moore. We were laughing because you don't seem to realize that two guys just made a film about that and you missed your chance, Junior! It's too late... the cat... the Cadence is out of the bag!"

I very badly wanted Barnes and Angstat to do my show because no one had talked really in depth and seriously with them about their film yet, and if we were the first, it would get a lot of attention for the special I was breaking my ass trying to put together.

My other motivation was to poke holes in every one of their theories that I disagreed with. I responded quickly, "Mr. Barnes, I'm glad I could provide you with some entertainment tonight. And I'm not upset that you're laughing at me… in fact… I'm glad I've brought smiles to your faces. So, why don't you return the favor and bring a smile to my face by agreeing to do my show?"

Angstat got back on the line and yelled, "You're something else, Marx! We've just made the most popular film of the year and we solved the whole fuckin' case. Why would we waste our time doing your show? Hey, if you give us one good reason for that… ya know what? You give us one good reason for doing that then we'll both respect you. You give us two good reasons then we may just *do* the fucking thing. So… think hard little Johnny… because this is a one-shot deal you got here."

Todd chimed in again, "Two Marx… don't try to give us just one good reason and then another shitty one. Give us two good ones and we'll do the show. Simple as that. You have… hey Mike… do that counting thing again… the one, two, three…"

Michael could be heard dropping the phone and both men broke out into more laughter. Then he got back on the line with his mouth pressed right up against the speaker, muffling the numbers he was now counting off his drunken tongue. He began, "One… Two…"

I have to admit I was at a loss for words and rattled by the sudden and unexpected call. Somewhere from deep inside, the name Budgie Bailey popped into my head. The same Budgie Bailey who Rydell had tried telling me about. Without even thinking I blurted out, "Because I've solved the case, and your film was dead wrong!" I couldn't believe the words had even left my lips. I had strong opinions on the case but I sure as fuck hadn't solved anything, and for all I knew Rydell's Budgie buddy was a delusional lunatic.

Dillon looked at me as though my eyes just delivered two microscopic babies out of their pupils. There was silence on the other end of the phone and then, in unison, both men yelled, "Bullshit!" Todd expounded on their one word joint response and said, "If that's true, Marx, then how come you haven't called the cops and told them?"

I shook my head… cursing myself inside for just fucking up the only chance I had at this interview. I searched the recesses of my brain for something… *anything* that would get me out of this. My subconscious ass saver did not let me down. It fed me the following line. "Todd and Michael… my team has solved the case. We know where Cadence Moore is and we will be revealing this to the world when our live show hits the air. Any other details such as police involvement and the specifics of what we've discovered will only be shared with actual guests of the program, and even then… not until my show is in the can. Every one of them has to sign a gag order to not leak my lead, but will have right of refusal before their interviews air." Don't ask me where I came up with that shit travelers, because if I live to be two hundred, I'll never know.

Todd was serious now and seemed to speak in more sober tones. I had piqued his interest because I wasn't just some conspiracy theorist who'd seen a few Cadence Moore news clips and now thought I was a detective. I wasn't on their level, but I still was a well-known radio host with a reputation at stake; so, when I made the kind of claim I did, it was taken with a degree of seriousness by the men who had initially called me up simply to have fun at my expense.

The ironic part was that I was worse than the worst schmuck or conspiracy theorist since I'd just lied about solving a case that I was no closer to solving than the Kennedy assassination. Todd Barnes said, "What the hell do you mean… right of refusal? Like if they don't like your bullshit theory then they can tell you to pull their interview from the podcast?"

I was operating on some kind of ghost auto pilot where a voice from inside myself was working me like a puppet and making me say things I had no business saying. The ghost voice continued, "Yeah, that's right. If my guests think my theory is garbage, then they have the right to refuse that their interview is aired at all. That's how much confidence I have that this thing is about to blow wide open, and when it does it will be national news for months. So, the question is… since you guys pretty much have the market cornered on Cadence Moore… do you want to be a part of this or not?"

Dillon was mouthing, "What the fuck? What the fuck?" repeatedly. He couldn't believe what was coming out of my mouth. He thought I was losing it. I *was* losing it. By acting without thought, I was successfully pissing all over my own reputation while trying to win a pissing contest with Barnes and Angstat. For what? I needed them for the show, at least I thought I did, but what the hell was I doing?

They were silent on the other end for a moment, and then Barnes came back on the line. "If we decide to make you our charity case and do this show and we don't like the shit you've come up with, we can have the whole thing pulled. That is what I understood. Is that right Radio Man?"

I could tell I had them, although I had no idea what to do with them since it all was based on a big fat freakishly huge lie. But as it was, Barnes and Angstat didn't want anything that could be potentially huge revolving around Cadence Moore to take place without them being right there in the thick of it. I said, "Yes, Todd, it is."

More silence and then I heard them muttering back and forth. Then Todd said softly, "Okay, Marx Brother… let's say we'll do your little show. But if you solved the case as you claim, then I'm not sure what you need us for."

I answered, not forgetting the terms they had set minutes before, "That was the second good reason you told me I needed to have. I *do* need you. I need you both badly to give this show credibility. I may have the answer to the meaning of life but unless I have a major audience to share it with, then what's the point?

"If you do the show, it's going to get major attention. *Moore to the Story* is the biggest documentary in years and you guys are gold right now. The conspiracy crowd is cursing your names and calling you liars. Jamison Kelly is suing you. And a dozen different media outlets still want interviews from you.

"You two are the lightning rods for interest and controversy, and I'm smart enough to see that. I may not agree with your conclusions, but I know that when it comes to Cadence Moore, you don't do anything right now without Barnes and Angstat being involved.

"If I have you appearing on my show, then it's going to be huge. And in case you're scared that I'd be throwing cheap shots at you, I can assure you of this. I will treat you with respect and while I will challenge certain points of your film, I will do it cordially and with an opportunity for you to have your fair response.

"And really, what do you have to lose? If I'm right, then you're a part of history and can use this to further the success wave you're already riding. If not, then it's just one more piece of evidence pointing toward you guys having all the answers. And if I'm wrong... once again... you have the right of refusal and the interview will never air."

Michael said, "Hey, Marx... you do realize that if you're full of crap and making shit up... then *anyone* you talk to will pull their interviews? Unless you feel real fuckin' strong about what you've got, why would you be wasting your time doing all this? You some kind of true crime whore... or a celebrity junkie? What's your con man?"

I replied, "No con, Michael. I am confident that I have this thing by the balls and I just want you to be a part of it."

A few seconds of murmuring followed. Then Todd said, "I can't believe I'm saying this because we honestly just called to fuck with you, Marx. But hey, what can I say? You've tickled our interest... at least for now. Fax the agreement to our office. If our lawyer is okay with the wording, then we'll sign it and you'll have it tomorrow afternoon. We'll do the fuckin' thing." They hung up the phone and I breathed the biggest sigh I'd ever breathed in my life, followed by a series of panic induced heart palpitations.

Dillon just looked at me with wide eyes full of accusation. I said, "Dude, don't ask me for details now. I'll talk to you in a few days and tell you everything. Until then, just let it be." Dillon was full of rage and confusion but he held his tongue and left it at that. He would have his rant, in a few short days; he would have his rant all right, but not today. He managed one question which he whispered, "What the fuck did you just do, you goddamn maniac?" I didn't answer. I walked out the door.

And that friends, is how I got Todd Barnes and Michael Angstat to do the show. Keep in mind, they are famous right now. I was not famous... even though I was known more than the average fellow at the time this conversation took place. This show was looked upon as small potatoes by two guys who just did the major national media circuit. But they said yes, and I had them. I had them. I had my lawyer friend, for a premium emergency fee, draw up the agreement which had heretofore been a fantasy notion I just made up. That was what we sent to them the next morning. I had them.

But shit... what did I actually have? I promised them a solution to the murder. I promised them a part of something huge. I didn't have those things in my pocket. I'd lied to score an interview which could easily be pulled from airing as soon as Barnes and Angstat realized they'd been snowed. I had nothing. All I really had going for me was a conversation my cousin Rydell had in prison with a guy named after a parakeet.

- 3 -

The very next day, I went back to Berks County Prison to see Rydell. Even though I'd blown him off last time, things had changed and this was the only shot in the pitch-black dark I had… so I needed to take it. I told him to hook me up with Bailey, ASAP.

Rydell smiled that broken shutter smile of his and said, "Brother… I knew you'd be back… shit, you couldn't stop thinking about what I said, could you? I know you, Charlie. So, look bro, I've already made things easy for you… well, let's say I kind of did, but it's gonna cost you something in return.

"Here's the shit… Budgie's ready to talk to you and tell you what he knows, but he wants a transfer. That's the perk you were talking about yesterday. Shit you know the game. If he gives up Cadence Moore's killer to you and he turns out to be right, you'll have quite a bit of pull with law enforcement. If you end up leading them to solving this case, they'll owe you a big goddamn favor for it. Not to mention you'll be a famous motherfucker and I know you like the sound of *that* song.

"Budgie's not talking for free. He said he'd tell you everything, but he wants your word, which I told him was good, that you'll make a transfer happen for him since he's gonna have a target on his head after it comes out he sang about his cellmate. And for the transfer, he wants an upgrade. BCP's a dump and he wants to go to Sunfield. It's the resort prison we're always hearing fuckers talk about around here. I don't know… it could be a shitty dump, too, but to hear these guys tell it, the place is a fuckin' palace. That's where Budgie wants to go.

"Once you hear the story and can verify it's true… Budgie expects shit to happen. And listen, cuz, if you have any misgivings about doing this interview with him, then I'm warning you right now, don't do it. Budgie knows plenty of people on the outside and if he feels like you fucked him, then he's gonna do something about it, Charlie. If you don't want to play, then don't even sit at this table. Just keep walking. If you want to play, then be prepared to pay what the man's asking."

Rydell had become the bridge between my haze of ignorance and a possible enlightened gift from the gods in the form of solving Cadence Moore. It would probably all be bullshit, but the force that was guiding me through all this insanity… that sense of destiny… it was still telling me I was on to something. I said, "Rydell… if what he has to say is true and I can verify it, then I will give him everything he's asking for. But if he's full of shit, then he gets nothing and I hope Mr. Budgie is prepared for that possibility, too." I didn't have a goddamn clue if I could make a transfer happen, but I was dealing in hopes, prayers, and wild fancy at this point so why not promise the world?

Rydell shook his head. "Listen, bro… it doesn't sound like bullshit to me and I don't even have all the details. I got the abridged version and just know his cellmate claims to have done the thing. But here's the fucked-up part. I don't think the cellmate knows who Cadence Moore even is. I get the feeling from Budgie that he was telling a story about some random bitch he cut up not even realizing she was a celebrity. This guy was allegedly picked up within a day or two of killing her for some other shit he did, so he may have never seen the news stories about it. Budgie connected the dots himself and kept his mouth shut until he talked to me; at least that's what he says.

"So, I don't know… something about the way he talked, I feel like he's got a major story floating around in his head and he can't handle the pressure anymore. He wants to talk… if not, he wouldn't even have mentioned it to me, but he did. When he found out about you, he couldn't wait to sing. He wants this off his conscience, and if, in the meantime, he can get something out of it… well… you know how it goes, right Charlie?"

I knew exactly how it went. I put my closed fist on the glass and Rydell met it on the other side with his. Now that I had nothing but had promised everything, I said, "Set it up. I'll come back in two days and you can let me know the specifics. Thanks, Rydell. I love you brother." So, there it was. I was casting my lot with Budgie Bailey, risking my reputation in the process, all because of a little voice in my head calling itself destiny, controlling every move I made.

Right after seeing Rydell, I picked up Dillon and we went to see Darlene Bethany. He wasn't yet discussing my descent into dementia or attempting to choke the life out of me for fucking with a special he'd been working very hard on. For now, it was time to do business. When we got to Darlene's, I told her the same cockamamie story about solving the case and told her she'd be able to pull her entire interview if she didn't like what we'd come up with. I swear I was on some type of suicide mission here and I couldn't be stopped. Dillon just about kicked my ass right there in Darlene's living room. He was so pissed that I was being reckless and crazy while we were trying to put together a legitimate special.

After Darlene Bethany said yes, and we headed back to the home office, Dillon kept shaking his head and refused to talk to me for most of the way home. When he finally relented, and brought me back into his communication club, he decided I needed a good talking to and I damn well did. I'm serious about that. I needed to be set straight and I didn't seem to be able to accomplish that on my own.

I was sabotaging this whole special, and I swear to you weary travelers right now, as sure as I sit here and talk to you, I couldn't stop. That fuckin' asshole force was guiding me... pushing me right to the edge of the ledge and I was going over... whether I liked it or not.

I knew what I was doing and I knew the ramifications of it. I just kept going and now that I had my secret weapon... that old classic... a pack of lies, I was getting a yes from everyone I contacted. From Darlene Bethany to Jimmy Derek, from Paul Woodsen to Matt Hedges, everyone wanted to do the show now.

At least I could honestly tell all these people that Barnes and Angstat were participating. We had legitimacy now. We had a couple of superstars weighing in on our little midnight spook story podcast series. This was a big deal and people could feel it.

But I'd lied to get my hands on the crown jewel and my entire castle was threatening to cave in on itself. This is where my good buddy and fellow producer Dillon came in. He was ready to try and talk some logic into my unwavering exterior of idiocy.

We were driving back from Darlene's place in my beat-up Suzuki XL-7 which I planned on trading in for something a little flashier if this particular ship ever came in. I'd already secured Matt Hedges from Nighthawk Records over the phone while we were en route.

About thirty miles in, after two cups of coffee and half a pack of smokes, Dillon began, with hands gripping the steering wheel so hard his knuckles were white and his teeth were grinding as he forced out the words, "Charles... I've never considered you a stupid man. You have always been someone I looked up to and respected. You gave me my first break in this game and you've always led me down the right road. That's why I work for you... because I trust you. Why would you do this? Why would you fuck this show over before it even has a chance to succeed?

"I would have taken our small little motley crew of guests and ran with it, making the best of the situation. I would've rather taken them and them alone a thousand times over than play this fucking game. You lied to everyone, man! When they find that out, they're going to pull their interviews and we'll be stuck right back where we were at the beginning, only now, we'll be weeks behind schedule. Have you even considered your credibility and the show's credibility? They will both be in the shitter forever. I'm asking you as a friend here, no, fuck that, I'm demanding to know why the fuck would you fuck us, fucker?!?"

If I hadn't been so unsettled by Dillon cussing me out, I probably would have laughed at his last ridiculous statement and his blatant overuse of the fuck word. I owed him an answer and he deserved to get the straight dope... if you will... I never sound quite right saying shit like that. Anyway, I was done bullshitting Dillon who'd gone down in the trenches with me and deserved better than I was giving.

I told him, "Dillon, I'm not trying to fuck anyone, I'm trying to get things done! It started out as a desperate attempt to keep Barnes and Angstat on the phone. Then it graduated to a surefire way to get other guests on the show. What it is now I couldn't tell you, but I feel like... you're going to want to punch me for this, but I feel like it was like my goddamn destiny to solve this case and finally get some justice for Cadence Moore. I may have begun with a lie, but I plan on ending with the truth. I'm gonna solve this fucking thing, Dillon."

Dillon hit the roof of the car with his fist and yelled at me with such ferocity that little beads of spittle landed on my face as he laid into me with a verbal shellacking. "You egotistical fuck, Marx! Who are you to assume you're the chosen one? Did you have a godly experience while you were sitting on the toilet smoking cigarettes or something? Man, this was a big shot for me... this fuckin' show... and you've ruined it!

"You're going to be a laughingstock and so am I... and so are all the other *Underground* crew members you're taking down with you. So... please tell me, what evidence do you have to think you can solve an unsolvable case? It's been a decade after all, and last I checked, you weren't a psychic. So again, what the fuck, Charlie? What are you thinking man? Do you even have a single lead?"

I understood Dillon's anger and it hurt me to hear the things he was saying. But he was right. I was being reckless... in fact, I couldn't have been more reckless, even if I'd set my mind to doing so. This was insanity. Dillon asked me about leads. I tried to defend my little epiphany.

Somewhere between the visit with Rydell and the phone call with Barnes and Angstat, it hit me that I could do this... that I'd been equipped with the brains, the balls, and the ability to make this happen. But all I could tell Dillon at this point was, "Listen, Dillon... you're right... everything you say. So, I will not argue with you. But I will tell you this, I have a lead and it's fucking hot."

Dillon shook his head and asked, "Really? And what Mr. Psychic Wonder, what is this glorious revelation that has come to you and no other?"

I answered, "Actually, it didn't come to me alone. It came to my cousin, Rydell Stevenson, and before him it had come to a fellow prisoner of his named Budgie Bailey. This guy... this Bailey character holds the whole case in the palm of his hand. He was cellmates with a dude who took responsibility for the murder and I am interviewing him next week to get all the details. I can tell you this Dillon; we're on to some serious shit here. This is not conspiracy nut jabber. This is real verifiable stuff and I'm going to steal it and make it our own. I'm going to make this the property of *Underground* and even though you don't realize it now, you will make history with me."

The truth was... I had no idea what the hell Budgie Bailey had to say since I'd never spoken to him. I'd been too high and mighty to consider that Rydell had given me the shining gold lead of all leads and I'd cast it aside. When I desperately went back to him, Rydell didn't let me down. He came through. But, I still didn't have a clue if the Budgie Bailey interview would bear any fruit at all.

As I sat there in my own car with Dillon, I knew I needed to get him on board. I couldn't do this shit alone. I needed to convince Dillon that I hadn't gone off my rocker as they say, even though I very likely had. I asked him, "So, what do you think? Are you going to trust me? Are you going to stand by my side like you have on every project that came before this one?"

Dillon shook his head and then looked down to the floor of the car. He took a good long time, trying to form the proper words so we could converse productively. He was having a damn hard time of it... that I could tell you just from looking at him.

Finally, he said, "Let me get this straight... you took your cousin Rydell's word as gospel and now you believe the answer to this whole decade-long case is conveniently sitting waiting for you at BCP, right in your own back yard? You think the answers came to you because of some divine right you have to crack this deal wide open. Am I right so far?"

I sheepishly responded, "So far, you're not too far off. But, I'm serious Dillon. I have a feeling about this that is more intense than any instinct I've experienced with any one of our shows. I feel like we're about to rip the lid right off and bring the unsolvable truth to the masses."

Dillon said, "And you think that can be done by talking to a dude named Budgie who's in prison with your cousin, and as luck would have it, happens to be rooming with the killer himself. Let me ask you this. Why should we have anything to do with Rydell anyway? You can't trust a guy that tried to cheat the government and all his clients like a mangy dog.

"If this is what you've built your argument for the show on, and if this is the thin-as-fuck set-up you're choosing to run with, then there isn't much I can do about it. If you go through with this, and it turns out to be a bunch of inventive lies by bored inmates, then I will walk away at that point, and refuse you to allow my name in the cast roll call. I don't want any part of your fantasies, Charlie. I'll make sure anyone willing to listen knows it, too!"

I was trying very hard to convince Dillon that what I had was more than some assorted dialogue from prisoners who make up stories to pass the time, even though I knew damn well that what I really had was no better than that. I had nothing solid to move forward on, so I had to move forward on a rickety bridge over quicksand.

During my whole professional career, in which I'd discussed the Kennedy assassination a dozen times, the Apollo Moon landing, and the conspiracy theories around that, all the secret world jazz of the Illuminati and the New World Order, or our thousand different shows about philosophy and ghost stories. Even as all those formats for shows crossed my desk and I set out to turn them into entertaining broadcasts, I'd never taken chances like this.

Why did I feel such a compulsion to solve the Moore case? Why did I not just send my fact checkers out like I'd done for years, and why couldn't I just be satisfied with the existing truth?

It was… a compulsion… simple as that and nothing more. I was being compelled to follow this thing to its end. I was being pushed toward Cadence Moore and the solving of her unsolvable murder. Was it ego? Was it insanity? Was it divine inspiration? I didn't know what the fuck it was, but I knew it wasn't good journalism, it didn't make good sense, it wasn't good business, and it probably wouldn't end up being good for me.

- 4 -

Two days came and went. I was recovering from the onslaught of hate and frustration delivered by my good friend Dillon while I was convincing guest after guest to appear on our show. Dillon was absolutely furious with me. I couldn't blame him, though… I'd have felt the same way if I was in his shoes.

But I just couldn't defy the voice, ya know? I couldn't turn away from the magic man who was gimping along trying to pull me in the proper directions.

Rydell came through like a champ. When I went to see him in BCP, he was ready with the news. He'd talked to Bailey and the whole thing was set. Budgie, good ol' boy that he was, was willing to talk to me, and once I verified his story was true, I'd start to work on his transfer since he assumed, probably correctly, that John Q. Law would be in a giving mood when I laid this particular offering at his doorstep.

Rydell had arranged the talk to happen in one week. He may have handed me the golden goose, but I had to be cautious. After all, everything that came out of this goon's mouth could be a lie. I told Rydell to go back to Budgie and make sure he was prepared to talk and talk fast. I'd simply listen and make notes. This was extremely important since we'd only have about eight minutes to finish up our entire discussion, which may have ended up being the most important one of my career.

Why did I believe in Budgie Bailey? Because the incessant voice in my head told me to. That's the god's truth right there. I couldn't be any more honest if I tried. The passionate roaring in my heart told me Budgie had the secret and it was up to me to snatch it from him and spin gold with it like some wannabe Rumpelstiltskin.

One week later I was sitting on the other end of a glass window waiting for my answer man. He came in the form of a big ass, tattooed, biker-looking fucker. This dude was built like a pro wrestler. He looked like he could kick my ass just by willing it. He also struck a weird off-putting chord by wearing dainty eyeglasses… the kind without frames… and speaking like a scholar or a teacher. It was amazing. I was expecting a damn thug and I got a professor that looked like he was working undercover for the cops in some kind of motorcycle gang.

The first thing Budgie said was, "Mr. Marx, Rydell tells me all you want to do is listen and let me do all the talking. Then you're going to take my findings and make a radio special. Am I correct in assuming all of this… just based on what my good friend Rydell, your cousin, says to me?"

I answered quickly and definitively. "Mr. Bailey Rydell was telling the truth. He was working for me all along. And he was right when he told you that I could protect you and get you a transfer to Sunfield. But what I need from you is the clearest and most non-bullshit-ridden remembrance of your conversation with your cellmate. I don't want to go back to the airwaves with some made-up story. I need to know that what you're telling me is the truth… and truth that I can personally verify… otherwise, it doesn't mean a thing. So, if you tell me everything you know including your own take on the situation, which I'm very interested in, as well, then I can get to work… real work my friend, and you can get what you want and be in Sunfield in a matter of months. But first… I need you to tell me what you know."

Budgie cleared his throat and began talking. I'll never hear a more important eight-minute speech than I heard that day from a pro wrestler turned biker, turned professor, turned godsend. Budgie Bailey said, "Let me not start on false pretenses. My name, as I'm sure you have probably already guessed, is not Budgie Bailey. That is my name in here, based on the fact that I have irritable bowel syndrome and it hurts me to eat too much at one sitting. I eat like a bird, they say, so I got my nickname Budgie. Where they got Bailey, I couldn't tell you. Anyway, I am a large man but I eat like a bird, so I get named after one. The man you see before you today was born Albert Washburn in York, Pennsylvania… just about thirty-six years ago to the day. My birthday is in a week. I…"

I couldn't believe this. I was trying to take in the answer to the most famous unsolved crime of the 21st century and this guy was telling me his eating habits and his birthday plans. I politely interjected, "Mr. Washburn… or Mr. Bailey… whichever you prefer… I must tell you that I don't mean to sound rude, and I'm sure you'd be a delightful fellow for me to know, but time is a major, crucial factor in our dealings with one another and I desperately need you to stick to the facts of this case I'm working on and tell me what you know about Cadence Moore."

Budgie stared at me for a moment and I was sure I'd blown the entire interview before it even got started. I had offended the man. But, shockingly, Budgie just smiled and replied,

"Certainly… I understand your position. I only meant to show you that

I'm capable of being up front and honest and what I tell you today can be taken to the bank as it were… just the same as a bag full of coins. So, I suppose it is best for me to start at the beginning. This is where my involvement in this case got started.

"In 2002, I can't even remember the month anymore, I was sitting in my cell. My former cellmate, Arthur Drake, had died of a heart attack a month and a half previous. I was just beginning to like my new spacious surroundings when one day… this dusty looking guy gets thrown in with me. He had a tattered, weathered face and hair that looked as though it hadn't been washed in a year. He had four-days growth on his face and his first words to me were, 'The fuck you lookin' at, Juice monster?' Juice is a reference to steroids and he was insulting me for being strong by insinuating I was a drug abuser. I didn't think too much of this young man after that first one-sided conversation, you know?"

I replied curtly, "Sure, I understand."

Budgie smiled, "I'm sure you do. Anyway, this dusty man who liked to hurl insults was Thomas Trayce, went by Tommy. He wouldn't look at me or talk to me that entire first day. He uttered his one insult and that was it. I decided to play with him a little that first night. I woke him out of a dead sleep and smashed his face up against the bars of our cell. He grunted with surprise and pain. I whispered to him, "Relax… we're going to be friends now, you understand? You're going to respect me and in turn I shall respect you. No more insults and we'll get along just fine. Now, get some sleep and we'll talk some more in the morning." Tommy nodded rapidly and when I let him loose, he went right back to bed without saying another word. He fell in line and knew his place after that.

A few days went by and we got to talking. The inevitable tone of the conversation turned to how we both got to where we were. In my case, I shared with Tommy that I'd robbed a string of small town banks, wearing a lucha libre mask and brandishing a 9mm subcompact pistol, because I was trying to break into pro wrestling and needed money." Wow, I thought… he doesn't just look like a wrestler… he is one.

Budgie went on, "I was poor as an orphan and I figured I'd knock a few over and earn my living expenses and then leave my brief life of crime so I could train to be a wrestler, and then move on to stardom and riches. I had the size and determination and that's what I wanted to do with my life.

"Never did happen, unfortunately, because I got caught for my bad behavior, which included shooting a teller at a Leesport Bank branch because he wouldn't give me the money and he hit his little alarm button to signal for cops. I panicked and shot him, not because I wanted to but because I panicked and my body took over and did what it felt was the best move possible for survival. I senselessly took the life of a man with four children and I never made a dime that I got to keep. It was a pointless crime and I deserved everything I got after that.

"In the end, my pro wrestling dreams consisted of bashing Tommy Trayce's head against the bars of our cell like a steel cage match, and a few brief brawls in the cafeteria. Other than that, my theatrical wrestling career went up in smoke and I made the decision to develop my brain and learn as much as I could by reading anything I was allowed to get my hands on."

I was literally biting my tongue so hard on the other end of the glass that it bled into my mouth and down my throat. I was beyond impatient waiting for Budgie to get to the point. It was like he was just fucking with me and didn't actually have anything of consequence to say.

If I was going through all of this just to be screwed with by a low rent version of Hulk Hogan, then I was about to flip out. When my tongue bled and I swallowed some of it, I coughed unintentionally. Budgie must have taken this as a sign of my impatience.

He said in an embarrassed tone, "I do apologize, Mr. Marx, I don't get to talk as much as I'd like and I'm afraid I'm rambling. We only have a limited time and I am going to share with you the information you came for. As I was explaining before, we were swapping stories, Tommy and me.

"I told him my tale and he started in with his. Keep in mind, Tommy and I parted ways very soon after our conversation. He was transferred soon after and ended up killing a guard in a laundry room fight at Parkworth. Broke the poor man's neck and was shipped off to a solitary cell, with all his privileges revoked and a life sentence ahead of him.

"I never did see him again. Couldn't tell you if he's there, moved on to yet another prison, or died in his dark and lonely cell. Couldn't tell you any of that, but I will tell what he said the day we confided in each other. I've carried it around with me for years before I saw just the right opportunity to clear my conscience and release this burden to someone else.

"That opportunity was your cousin, Rydell, Mr. Marx. He led me to you and I hope I've been right in my surmising of our situation. As for what Tommy told me that day, I will review it for you as clear and complete as I possibly can. I will speak as though I am Tommy Trayce, so take this as his first-person account. Even though this was ten years ago or so, the conversation still plays sharp in my brain."

What followed was almost unbelievable. Budgie seemed to be channeling some kind of Broadway actor. Either that or all those pro wrestling interviews he planned on doing were being stuffed into one long speech where he was acting the part of an angry man capable of hurting lots of people.

As he spoke to me through the glass at BCP, Budgie was becoming Tommy Trayce, himself. Budgie's language changed as he morphed into his old cellmate. Gone was the polished language and the niceties. Gone was the polite tone. Now he was swearing and using dumb man's slang. Budgie was literally giving me the conversation word for word... or at least paraphrased from his memory (or I feared... his imagination) word for word. It was one of the damndest things I'd ever seen.

Budgie, as Tommy, said, "I hit a fuckin' convenience store down in Adamstown. Stole about two hundred bucks and then blew out of there... as I was leaving the lot, I popped right into an old granny who was pumping her gas and stepped away from her car to pick up a lottery ticket which the wind had taken away. She stepped out one step too far and I connected with her. Old mummy died instantly... which was good for her at least. But it wasn't good for me.

"The cops picked me and up and charged me with the robbery and the fuckin' vehicular manslaughter. I was not getting out of this one. Fuck it anyway. I'm used to it Budgie. I spent almost two thirds of my life in one kind of prison or another. I supposedly raped a girl when I was twelve. Twelve fuckin' years old! Bitch had it comin'… she was teasing me and my friends. I decided to call her bluff but then she cried rape. That bought me a few years in Juvie D out in Muhlenberg.

"Then I got married to my girl Rachel who already had a couple of kids, one from a black guy, one from a Spanish dude… so you know that fuckin' story. That fucking cunt called the cops on me so many times claiming I beat her or I was beating the kids. Truth is, I did have to hit on the kids a little when they got to be about four and six. Little fuckers had no respect and I had to teach it to them. Sadly, for her son Mickey and, also sad for me, I taught his last lesson a little too hard and gave him a knock on the head which put him out cold. I didn't want to have that happen but it did. What can you do?

"Anyway, that got me some *real* fuckin' hard time. Finally got out a few months ago and got in touch with Rachel to see if she might want to see her ol' hubby again. Turns out, she's a very forgiving person and she'd been lonely.

"She needed some comforting and invited me back home. I was on my way back, but of course being an unemployed guy, I needed some spending capital. I needed some cash if I was gonna see my lady. So, I hit the convenience store and the rest as they say is shitty history."

Budgie returned to being Budgie for a moment and said, "Now, Mr. Marx, this is where the story gets interesting."

Budgie as Tommy continued, "Ya want to know the real fuckin' kicker about this whole thing? The convenience store was what they caught me for but that was about the least violent thing I'd done all fuckin' week. Things got real bad with a girl I met in Dusklight Falls a few days earlier. This was when I was on my way back from Pittsburgh.

"I'd gone up there to see an uncle and score some stuff. I was on my way back toward… well my destination was just past the Lancaster area. I was gonna see my folks and then travel on to see my old lady. That was a long way off and the road was dark and boring.

"I burned through all my fuckin' music and was feelin' tired. Somewhere along the way, I got real hungry driving at night on the long ass 30 highway and took the first exit that came up; happened to be the exit for Dusklight Falls. Fate just waits for you sometimes, man… you aren't looking for it but it's damn sure lookin' for you.

"And it just so happened that in all the time I lived in PA, I never had been there... the Falls. I figured all right, cool, I'll get a bite to eat, check out these famous falls, and be back to farm country by morning.

"Well, Budgie, it didn't end up that way. Soon as I pulled into Dusklight, I spotted a diner. I pulled in there, with all intentions of going inside and ordering a burger before I scrammed. But when I drifted in, I saw the hottest lookin' piece of ass you ever saw in your life.

"She was smoking a cigarette and just wandering around in the lot. She looked a little drunk and a little pissed and a little like the perfect girl for me to run into. I asked her what she was doing and if she needed a lift. The girl told me if I could take her to New York City, then she'd be interested in being my friend. If I couldn't, then she'd be interested in telling me to fuck off.

"I had to laugh at the little cunt... she had some spunk in her and I always liked that in chicks. So, I tell her sure... ya know. I'd be glad to drive you to New York. I was heading to Connecticut myself to see an old friend, so it wouldn't even be out of my way. That was some good bullshit of course, cuz I got no friends in an overpriced hell hole like Connecticut.

"But this stupid young thing must have really wanted to get the fuck out of Dusklight because she didn't even nod or respond. She just sleekly walked over to the passenger side of my car and got in. She looked over and said, 'Let's go... the quicker I'm out of this town, the quicker I can smile again.' She was slurring her words a little which confirmed my suspicions about her being fucked up. Anyway, we drove off and left ol' Dusklight in the dust. We got as far as Lancaster without this chick even realizing we were going in the wrong direction.

"This wild little blonde bitch was something else. She had this streaky black eye make-up on and had the bluest eyes in the fuckin' world. Whatever she was crying about was making them boys pop like Christmas lights through the black smeary mess that used to be her eyeliner.

"And, I'm not lying man, it seemed like she was totally game for some fun, even if she was in a bad mood and real desperate to get to New York. I didn't know why and didn't care. As soon as she got in the car and we were five miles down the road, I offered her a few slugs on my bottle of cheap-ass rum.

"By the time we hit Lancaster, this chick was toasted. I figured the time was right, and we stopped over at a little motel. She resisted a little but she was stumbling all around and even pissed herself she was so fuckin' wasted. I talked her into taking off her pants because they were soaked. Told her I'd throw 'em in the wash for her. Again, she didn't want to, but there wasn't much resistance in this chick anymore.

"I got her up on the bed and took those sparkly pants off her... you know the rest man... you've been around the fuckin' block a time or too.

"When we were finished I told her she just found herself a new boy-friend. Well, the bitch didn't like the sound of that, let me tell you. She start-ed getting lippy with me. She was feeling guilty from the fuck most likely and I had to slap her around a bit when she wouldn't shut up.

"Bitch cried a little but then passed out and went to sleep. I smoked up and then slept right next to her. Hell, I figured she'd get over it and I'd have a hot little companion to keep me company until I got to Rachel... that is, if I even fucking decided to get to Rachel at all. I was gonna see how shit went.

"Well, shit didn't go nowhere good. I woke up the next day and the bitch was putting her pissy pants back on. I asked her what the fuck she was doing and she said she's leaving and going home. I wanted at least one more go around.

"So, I acted real remorseful and apologized for slapping her. I told her I'd like to make it up to her and at least take her back to Dusklight if New York wasn't seeming so cool now. She resisted and said she'd rather take the bus. I told her to at least let me drive her to the station. I don't know why, but the chick gave in. She must have liked me just a little bit.

"So, we're driving toward Reading and I'd spent the last fifteen miles explaining how sorry I was that I lost my temper. I told her how unlike me that was and I really liked her and shit like that. I told her if nothing else, I wanted to be her friend. I finally got the bitch thinking this may have been a onetime thing and I'd be a gentleman from here on out.

"I even talked her into coming with me to my folks' place where we'd have some lunch and then press on from there to the bus station. She agreed.

So, we're driving those stinking country roads out there where everything smells like cow shit for miles.

"All the sudden, I mean outta nowhere, she demanded I turn around and take her home immediately. She wanted to go back to college and if I didn't agree to take her, she'd get out and hitchhike. This was the breaking point for me, Budgie. I'd had it with this pain in the ass.

"When I didn't turn around, the crazy bitch opened the car door and I slammed on the brakes. She jumped out of the fuckin' car and I followed her as she ran down the road. There were no cars around at the time. I was so livid by the time I reached her that I lost control and punched her full force in the mouth, knocking her to pavement where she whacked her head on the road.

"She started making suffocating gasps and snorts, which got slower over the next few seconds, and then she went silent. I got a little worried and decided to make sure she was all right. Well, all right she was *not,* my man. I'd caught her on the chin and knocked her right off her feet and when she hit the pavement, man, she hit it fuckin' hard… back of the head first. She died within seconds. I just about shit myself.

"So, I'm beginning to freak the fuck out. I said, 'Fuck me' and then immediately switched gears and began thinking about where to hide the body and separate myself as much as possible, as soon as possible. That's the way survivors think, bro, you know that. Still no cars on the road so I scraped her up and threw her in the trunk.

"Bowmansville's where my parents live on a farm and where I'd sometimes stay over on my different treks around the country to see my old lady or whatever the fuck I was doing at the time. I got there and talked them into letting me stay for a few days. We had lunch, while all the while this crazy bitch was dead in my trunk. I just about pissed to the skies in honor of Christ when my parents said they had to run some errands. That would buy me a little time and a little time was all I'd need.

"I waited until my parents left. I knew it was do or die time. I dragged the bitch out of the car and then carried her into the fields. I used the small bulldozer that was in the barn and buried her right there in the deep fields of my parent's property. Nobody knows… nobody sees… ain't that what

Johnny Cash says?

"Anyway, that whole fuckin' trip was what they *didn't* catch me for. Good thing, too, because that vehicular manslaughter shit might get me five or six on top of the robbery, but I can do that with my fuckin' eyes closed. Murder, on the other hand… not so easy. But what a fuckin chick she was. Jesus, even after she pissed herself I wanted to fuck the shit out of her. I didn't fuckin' care, man."

Budgie was finished now with his role as Tommy Trayce. The whole interview had been a weird surreal play of sorts. Budgie returned to his normal self and with sweat beading on his forehead and his muscles clenched and reflexes shaking, he calmly said, "Mr. Marx, this concludes our discussion as the gentlemen will be coming any second now to take me back. Not a moment too soon. I hope you have appreciated the attempts I've made at providing all the proper details and giving you the same experience I had about a decade ago. I've been rehearsing this reenactment for hours and hours. I wanted you to see how hard I worked to do well on my end so you would feel compelled to do well on your end when the time came. I have full confidence that you will do your part."

This subtle threat did not go unnoticed by me when Budgie made it. "What a story, though. Sad really… Tommy is a person incapable of remorse it would seem. I didn't think much of his story at the time. Tommy thought like a criminal. And we have certain rules and understandings among us. In my case, I was bigger, stronger, and in here longer than him. For that reason, I was the boss and when I opened up the lines of communication, he felt compelled to tell me the truth about himself.

"I listened, took it all in, and then was ready to cast it aside like 99% of all the other things I hear on these grounds. Like I said, the violent bastard confided in me so I planned on keeping his confidence. That was the way it was going to be, Mr. Marx, but then… something happened. Something happened that made me realize I had information that needed to be shared… I just didn't know with whom yet. A newspaper article… the *Reading Eagle*… front page, permanently burned the conversation I had with Tommy Trayce into my memory forever.

"I was able to procure a newspaper once a week in BCP. I had some connections and my best connections knew how much I liked to read. So, I'd get comics, old paperbacks without covers, and newspapers. I never knew what they'd have for me but I always knew I'd have something. Imagine my surprise when I realized the girl Tommy Trayce was talking about was probably the same famous college singer that had now gone missing. Girl goes missing in Dusklight Falls, Trayce's description matches her to a tee, and he admits to killing the girl he picked up at a diner. To me, that pointed very strongly as evidence in solving Cadence Moore's disappearance.

"Tommy had absolutely no idea who the girl was... I'm convinced of that. He picked up some girl at a diner and took her for, in his words, a random crazy bitch. He just didn't have a clue. And how could he really? He got arrested for the convenience store incident within a day of burying the girl so he would never have even seen any news about it.

"Then, a few weeks later, he got transferred for some unknown reason to Parkworth and he killed that guard in the laundry room and got himself the life treatment. It wouldn't shock me if, to this day, he doesn't realize he's the man who killed Cadence Moore. Sure, it's possible he heard things around the prison and put two and two together. But it's just as possible that he didn't. If Trayce is alive today, I would bet money that he still doesn't know who it was that he buried on his parents' farm that day.

"Knowing about this has tortured me somewhat. I don't have time to go into my reasons for staying quiet. I just didn't trust anyone with this, but I've had enough years of carrying this now and I don't want it anymore. It's yours now, Mr. Marx. Go to Bowmansville. Look up Trayce's parents. You find that farm, you find the girl. And you get me what I want. Sunfield... you get me that."

- 5 -

So, what the fuck was I supposed to do with this? I ask you, weary travelers and patient listeners, what would you have me do? I'd just been fed the strangest excuse for a surrogate confession in the history of the world, I'm pretty sure.

But what was I supposed to do with it? Let's be honest with ourselves here. Budgie Bailey, or Albert Washburn, whatever you want to call him, could very well have been lying through his yellow, chipped teeth. Not a word of his theory... or story... or version of events has ever permeated even the most meager low-rent TV special on the Cadence case, let alone a major theatrical film like *Moore to the Story*.

And he gave me the conversation word for word. There is no way in hell, I don't care how good his memory is... there is no way he remembered all that. So, one thing I knew for sure right out of the gates... Budgie was filling in a lot of the gaps with his own words and his own imagined version of how things happened. But, my god... even if only the bare bones of his story are true... the Cadence Moore mystery was solved... after a decade... solved and solved by *me* for all intents and purposes.

It *had* to be a lie... an elaborate and well-played stinking lie. Budgie found out about Rydell. He convinced him to contact me about an interview... gave Rydell something for it. Made up a complicated story to convince me I got a red-hot lead. It was all a steaming pile of excrement and anyone but an imbecile would dismiss it as such before moving on and casting it aside like all the other conspiracy nut ramblings they'd heard in their lives.

I kept telling myself this as I drove away from BCP. Christ on high, if this actually happened, then it took every major player in this drama right out of the fucking picture! Jamison Kelly and his blood-stained car? Gone! Darien and Morgan Moore, plotting from Wisconsin? Gone! If this thing went down like Budgie said, then a completely unrelated dark figure from the periphery of the highway rolled into Dusklight Falls and connected Cadence Moore with her gruesome fate, a huge case of happenstance from the blackest corners of Hell.

I guess what also bothered me about it was that it was just... I don't know... unsatisfying. Ten years of films, newscasts, books, etc., all down the drain. None of the endless conversations and arguments about timelines and blood stains, motives, and memories. None of it mattered, and that would include the great amount of said discussion that has made up the majority of this very series you're listening to.

No one had ever touched this! Did that mean it didn't happen? Or, did I just happen to be the luckiest lowdown bastard that ever stepped in a diamond-studded shit pile in the history of the universe? Again, I just didn't know. I just didn't know.

Now, it's true that if even twenty percent of what Budgie Bailey says is the real story, it's very possible no one would have heard about it until now. We have to remember that the only reason I ever even got to speak to him was because I happened to be cousins with a fellow inmate of his whom he felt comfortable confiding in.

I suppose it's conceivable this story wouldn't have seen the light of day until now, if everything went down like Bailey said it did. He said he'd been carrying it around for his own reasons and I didn't have time to go into what those reasons were when we spoke. I wish to God I had broached that subject... even for thirty seconds... just to have a little bit more understanding about how something this big could be kept silent and untouched for so long!

I just didn't know. It was still a fucking stretch of all sanity. I mean, if this were a movie, this last-second development would be one of the worst cases of the dreaded *deus ex machina* in the history of film. This so-called solution had come out of nowhere and ties up so many loose ends that it's almost too perfect. There was only one thing to do. Well, to be clear... there were now three things to do.

One, I needed to talk to Dillon and get him on board to investigate this thing. Two, I had to locate Trayce's family in Bowmansville, somehow sync that up with an undercover meeting with the cops, in which I tell them they can't reveal shit until my live broadcast airs if they want to use my new information. And three, I had to find out whatever happened to Tommy Trayce, who was at this point, as far as I knew, only an imaginary character in the dramatic mind of Budgie Bailey. If Trayce existed, and I believed strongly for some reason that he did, I'd have to locate him and try to talk to him. What an ending to my series that would be. An interview with the killer himself, after evidence and the confessions of an old cellmate had outed him to the world.

So, for step one, I called Dillon Balast and told him to meet me at Trooper Thorn's Irish Pub down on Route 10 in Reading. This was just a few blocks from one of our station offices, and was the place we usually went to get tanked after too many hours in the booth or the writing room.

Dillon was still angry and confused about my behavior but I think the guiding voice which was using me as its little truth puppet may have gotten to Dillon as well, because, for all his misgivings and anger, he agreed to meet me and discuss what I'd found out. I didn't want to let him down. I needed him to be my teammate, or else I feared the whole thing would still fall apart.

I arrived at 'Troops,' as we called it, and went into the bar. I ordered my standard rum and coke and walked out to the deck area. The sun had just set and there were rainbow-painted skies all above us. Dillon was waiting at a picnic table reading a book; it looked like *Reclaiming History* by Vince Bugliosi from where I stood.

I considered this and decided it could mean one of two things. Either, he was in an anti-conspiracy sort of mindset since that epic encyclopedia-sized book was the most anti-conspiracy piece of literature in the entire Kennedy cannon. Or, it could mean that Dillon was still, if nothing else, a truth seeker just like me. In spite of his reading choice for the evening, maybe he still had the ability to stomach one last outrageous conspiracy theory.

I smiled at Dillon as his eyes met mine and made my way over. I sat down and began telling him the whole story. I tried to recount as much of the conversation with Bailey as I could, which I had, of course, been recording the whole time on my little pocket E-Voice recorder which was currently in the hands of my I-Tech friend Kerrie from WHHW who was turning it into an MP3 file as this little bar conversation was going on.

Once I finished my recounting of the prison conversation, I saw the look in Dillon's eyes. That look told me he believed Budgie's story. He probably wouldn't have been able to say *why* he believed it, but he believed it all the same. The evidence of that was all over his face. Still, Dillon remained silent… mulling over what he'd been told and trying to decide the same things I was struggling over. As he dragged on his cigarette and took a sip and then another of his rum, I could almost feel the wheels of his mind turning.

His questions were the same ones I'd already run through. Should we believe any of it? It made no sense if we did. Why wouldn't something have come out earlier? But then again, what if it were true? We had the keys to the treasure chest and were in danger of letting it drift away, back out to the ocean unless we acted now!

We knew there was no concrete reason to dismiss it as untrue, yet we'd been trained to be as skeptical as we were accepting of strange claims and theories. In our line of work, you really needed to know how to walk the thin line between the two.

Finally, Dillon said, "So, I assume you know what our next move is, right? If we're to believe any of what this man Bailey is saying, we need to make a trip out to cow country and find Trayce's parents. In the meantime, we gotta get cops involved. I know a State guy who lives in Knauers. If he knows it's something big, he can stay quiet about it and keep a lid on it for at least a few days. I trust him. It wouldn't be the first time he's helped us out, but it would be the biggest secret of which I'd ever asked for his confidence. I'll call him as soon as we're done here.

Obviously, we don't move forward without finding out if Cadence Moore is buried in that field. If she is, then we just hit the fuckin' lottery, Charles. If not, then we're as fucked as we were when I reamed your ass out in the car for being a lunatic. The only thing I'm worried about is this. If I tell Mattingly... the cop I'm talking about... if I tell him what we've got, there's a good possibility he'll turn it over to his bosses just to further his own career, and those fuckers... I guarantee you... they find anything, they'll reveal it to the world and our show will play like a rehash of old news."

I laughed and said, "Dillon, you and I may be sharing the same brain. I've already considered all this. I agree we need to go to Bowmansville and locate Trayce's folks. If we don't know where to look, then the cops won't know where to look either. Now, this Mattingly, you say you trust him, and then in the same breath you say he might turn over on us. Which is it?"

Dillon nodded, "Yeah, I do trust him, but I only trust him as far as you can trust a cop. These guys have rank driven into their frontal lobes, man. Where they are in the chain of command means a lot, so, all I'm saying is that if Mattingly thinks it will benefit him enough, I'm sure he could be persuaded to turn over on us and hand our red-hot info right over."

I said, "Well, maybe we tell him up front that he gets nothing without a guarantee of silence, then he'll play by our rules and just be satisfied with being the cop that was part of cracking the Moore case. That's not too far out, is it? If we can cut a deal… like silence until podcast, in exchange for every piece of evidence we have that they don't, then and *only* then will we be able to play ball. A handshake deal… which I know is not very secure… but if this guy thinks he can trust us and be the head cop in charge of the entire new investigation of Cadence Moore, he might see enough fame, notoriety, and dollar signs in it for himself that… well… it might just be enough to shut him up until broadcast. We confirm the Trayce farm location. We tell the cop the highlights of the Bailey story. Then Mattingly and his team do an official investigation and search the whole farm. They have the resources to make sure the body we find belongs to Cadence… that is if we find a body out there at all. If we do find a body, and they DNA test her to find out for sure, we can make history on the radio! All the cops need to do is wait until we make air with it. They can do their fucking press statements ten seconds after the broadcast for all I care."

Dillon nodded silently like he was turning all this over in his mind. He finally said, "Yeah, I'm hearing you… but how do we get a guarantee of silence? It's not like we're signing a legal contract here. You can't do that with cops who have a legal responsibility to hand over evidence and make public all their findings. We wouldn't be holding any cards. If Mattingly decides to fire the alarms, we would have no choice but to stand back drooling over what might have been."

The doubt was starting to creep into Dillon's mind. I could tell. He started off thinking the cop wouldn't stay quiet even for the mutual interests of all. It wasn't long before he started picking the whole thing apart. Like I said, you walk a thin line in this business and the worst thing anyone can be considered, when dealing with conspiracies, is an ignorant fool. So, now Dillon was protecting his intelligence and credibility which he felt the need to do even in front of me.

He said. "But forget all that for a second, Charlie… you said it right after you told me the story… this whole thing probably is shit! I mean c'mon…

your cousin Rydell probably talked this bastard into the whole thing or maybe the other way around. He figures he'll play you for a fool and you'll owe him a favor for it. Think about it Charlie, the guy put on a little play for you behind the prison glass with a telephone stuck to his ear. Are we really gonna go with this as our super-secret hot lead, the one that's gonna solve Cadence for us? Let's get real here because this program of ours is real fucking close to happening and we need to focus on the facts, not the fantasy!"

I had to restrain myself from slapping Dillon. I had seen the look on his face when I'd told him the story of Budgie and the confession. I saw confidence in Dillon's eyes and he knew that we had something here. Hell, I'll admit it… I knew it too when I was hearing Budgie tell the story. My rational mind just wouldn't let me admit it at the time. It shouldn't have been true, but it was. That's what the voice told me. That's what the force guiding me was screaming in my ear.

But just like Dillon, I tried so hard to cling to my reasonable thoughts and calculating mind. Those two things were trying to tell me it was all bullshit. A mantra played in my mind, 'Always cynical, always careful… never ridiculed, never a fool.' That was the credo of the intelligent conspiracy theorist. We had learned it well over our years in this business.

But regardless, I still believed we had something and so did Dillon. So, I pressed him a little. I said, "Oh sure, man, we could go back down that road if you want. You obviously have an ego to protect and I wouldn't want that getting damaged. But goddamn it, Dillon, I saw the look in your eyes. You believed what I told you. It tied the whole damn case together for you like a Christmas package. But now you need to act like you're still doubtful and careful and I'm still the only lunatic here. Well, call me a loon if you like, friend, but we've got to get to work. There really isn't even a point in discussing it any further until we locate that farm and call Mattingly. So, since we have no other options and I already, in my loony way, promised our radio show guests that we had the case solved, then why don't we cut the act and get to work. What do you say Mr. Balast? You ready to become famous?"

I knew I had pushed him over the edge with my mocking tone. His fists were balled up and his face had reached a shade of watermelon pink. Dillon shouted, "You think you're so damn smart and you've manipulated me now! Well, you haven't. I can see through your obvious attempts at manipulation… even before you realize you're doing it. So, don't try to goad me into believing you or going along with you on anything. You can't do that because you're not that smart and you're not that talented, Charlie! I'll burst that bubble right away. But… I'm also not gonna bullshit you, man. I did get excited when you told me the Budgie story. It was like all the missing pieces just came together, and the big hole in this story that's existed for ten years was being filled up with every word you recounted to me. So yeah, I'm interested. But don't fuck with me, all right? You took this whole deal to an insane level before you had even the slightest hint of a real lead. Don't fuck with me and I'll stop being high and mighty. How's that? Does that quiet both of our egos? If so, then let's get to work like you said okay?"

I smiled and laid money on the table. I grabbed Dillon's hand and made him shake with me. I said, "If it were any more O.K., it would be O.L." I searched for a smile on Dillon's face, but I wasn't going to get it. I continued, "Call Mattingly tonight if you can and tell him to be ready for a road trip to cow town day after tomorrow. You got that?"

Dillon nodded. I had him and he knew it. We were going with this, for better or worse, we were going with it. I was ecstatic. I felt so lucky to have been cursed or blessed, or whatever it was, with these unseen forces that had pushed me in directions I never dreamed of going in. But now we were here and it was either time to play, or time to bail. Neither of us was going anywhere.

- 6 -

The phone rang loud and screeched in my ear, forcing me to punch it off the receiver and curse it with the ferociousness of a jilted girlfriend addressing her cheating dog lover. I'm one of those dinosaurs you hear about who still has a land line in his kitchen, and if you can believe this… the phone hooked up to that line is still a rotary dialer. So, when those puppies ring, man… they ring.

On this particular morning, I was in no mood for loud-ass ringing bells in my ear. The night before, I'd finally decided to take a night off from the radio special that had consumed my entire life. Now that we were following the Budgie lead and we were going all the way with it, I felt this lightning bolt of purpose pushing us forward and I was excited as all hell. Somewhere deep inside, I knew we were breaking new ground and we'd be a part of history when this was all over. We'd found El Dorado after all. The city of Gold shined in my mind's eye and I wanted it now so very badly.

But, all the same, I also knew that my eyebrows were about to catch fire and run right off my face if I didn't get my fuckin' head straight. Craziness was going to reign if I didn't get a little R&R. So, I decided to buy a handle of Bacardi and three bottles of Coke… I knew how to relax with the best of them.

And, oh, what a night, my friends. Between watching *The Wizard of Oz* three times and deciding on the spot to do a show next summer on the psychological imprint the movie had left on the psyche of the world, I also found time to call my ex-wife Carol and tell her it was her fault that the whole relationship turned into a pile of monkey waste.

I'm sure her new husband Shawn appreciated that particular voicemail in the morning. Hey, Shawn, if you're listening… and I'm sure you're not… let me just say, good sir, that I apologize profusely for that, and it was a dick move if there ever was one.

I also called Dillon Balast at least ten times raving about the special and telling him about how we'd become huge stars and be right up there with the great sleuths of all time. I said, of course, we'd be national celebrities now… but in the centuries to come, we'd be famous historical figures!

One call from Dillon's girlfriend Joyce telling me some creative ways to apply my head to the inner lining of my asshole convinced me to stop calling that household anymore that night.

I painted a picture of my childhood dog, Mikey, on a blank canvas posted up on an easel that I hadn't had the sack to get rid of since Carol left two years ago. For some strange reason, I decided Mikey would be better rendered if he were painted in Beefaroni and plant leaves from my poor unsuspecting hyacinth that really hadn't deserved to be murdered in the way it was… but what can a person say… sacrifices must be made for art.

Somewhere along the line, I fell asleep at my kitchen counter with a huge plate of macaroni and cheese providing a partial pillow for my drunken, slanted, jackass of a face.

The earth rumbling death-ray ring of the phone the next morning had destroyed a pleasant dream in which I was trying to make it with this little violin-playing chick we briefly interviewed a while back for a piece that never made air. Well, I was charming the pants off this dream girl and the next thing I knew, I was punching the phone off the receiver.

I heard faint yells of "hello… hello!" It was Dillon. He had survived his 2:00 a.m. bitch session from his lady friend due to my unfortunate shenanigans. He was up bright and early now to tell me the news. While I would later appreciate his call very much… the first uttering of Dillon's words made me toss the phone aside and run to my toilet to express my deepest condolences in style.

Five minutes later, I dragged my sorry, hungover ass back to the counter and called Dillon back. He was none too happy that I'd hung up on him, especially after the trouble I'd caused with his woman… the lovely, beautiful, and eventually-forgiving Joyce I mentioned previously.

Dillon's anger didn't last that long. What he had to say was too important to delay because of daily trivialities. We were on a noble quest and all things unrelated to the quest took on an unimportant shine as we plowed through it all to the truth.

He began by saying, "Dude, get it together, I've got news. Just…"

I cut him off with the intent of apology. I slurred, "Look buddy, I'm sorry I caused you some shit. Let me just put it out there. I needed a fuck-it-all kind of night and I had it. So, now you're calling and I really feel like smashing this phone on my floor until it breaks because my fucking head is about to implode on itself. But, I want to hear you and I *will* hear you… do you hear me, Dillon… I will hear you, my friend. You will be heard. I know you've been working around the damn clock, too, and this call to Mattingly is a crucial piece of it all. Again, man… without you… this thing wouldn't be happening. You just remember that, okay?"

I think I was still quite drunk and my words probably had a rambling obnoxious quality to them that made Dillon want to scream. But the good chap held his composure and said, "Shut up and listen. I talked to Mattingly. He's prepared to go in on this and I could tell by the tone in his voice, he's excited. He's been dogging it for too long and hasn't had something to sink his teeth into in forever. When I told him what Bailey said, he just ate it up… like a fuckin' cherry pie… he ate it up. Mattingly told me if we had what we thought we had, then the three of us would be famous. You hear that, Charlie… now it's the *three* of us. We have another partner now, whether we like it or not. Look dude, anyone who hears this shit and thinks they got a shot at solving Cadence, they're gonna be selling off their souls to lay down in bed with us. That's how quickly this shit is gonna spin out of control unless we keep it close… as close as we've ever kept anything. It must stop with Mattingly. No one else can know. You got that?"

I whispered into the phone, "I got it, Dillon. I don't plan on telling anyone *anything* until this airs. Our special trumps all. This is what it's all come down to, and in years to come, people all over the world will be talking about this. No matter what we do after, we'll never reach a crescendo this high again. This series will be our Magnum Opus and I for one will not be letting that shit land in the wrong hands."

Dillon half interrupted before I got my last word out. He said, "Okay, okay… good. I just wanted to make sure the seriousness of this deal was getting through to both of us. You've been a loose cannon lately, Charlie, and I'm trying to make sure I still have my reliable partner somewhere buried inside of this guy I'm talking to."

Dillon's last arrogant statement struck a wrong chord with me. I exploded… probably due to the rum that was still slagging its way through my system. I yelled, "Really, you bitch? Is that what you're doing now? You're condescending to me? Listen Balast. You're a great producer. Only a fool would say anything different. But let me remind you that in spite of your researching prowess you didn't have jack shit on this deal until I came through with Bailey. No, you dressed me down on a long car ride and I took it because I knew where you were coming from. Well, now you are into this thing 100% and you're still trying to talk to me like a hostage negotiator coaxing a psycho off the ledge. Fuck you, Dillon! If anyone should be questioning loyalty or judgment… it should be me! When I needed you most, you were ready to bail. You remember that shit you said to me? If this all turns out to be bullshit, then you'd refuse to allow your name in the cast roll call at all. You remember that Mr. Sanity? You remember that Mr. Has-it-All-Together? You remember that Mr. I'm Too Good For…"

Dillon interrupted again, "All right, Charlie. You made your fuckin' point. Forgive me for thinking cautiously, but I understand. You took a gamble and it paid off… allegedly… I will keep saying that word until we dig up Cadence Moore and we can verify that your cousin and your prison pro-wrestling buddy are telling the truth. But I'm sorry, okay? I don't mean to condescend. I just want this shit as bad as you do. You can understand that, right?"

The truth was I *could* understand it and I told Dillon so. When we finished our conversation, it was official. We had an early afternoon rendezvous the next day with Bill Mattingly, the cop who now was our partner, whether we liked it or not.

- 7 -

Detective William Mattingly was unique among his brethren in blue. He never went to college. He got into the program based on favors called in from his Uncle Willie Stafford, his namesake, a rich and influential cattle farmer in the Berks County farmlands. Uncle Willie was loaded like a .45 and made sure his beloved nephew got in with a leg up.

But, even after the benefits of nepotism had gotten him in the door and up the steps, young Billy Mattingly carved his own path to success and earned his stripes by cracking difficult case after case and even earning the pride of the outlaws… his very own nickname… Bastard Bill. You see, Mr. Mattingly was known for his aggressive interrogation techniques and had crossed more than a few people the wrong way on his journey to the top.

Now Detective Bill was gonna be our buddy. Our new pal was waiting for us in Adamstown... at Mom's Diner... a silver chrome-plated trailer which stood across the street from the long-ago-abandoned Bollstan's Hat factory.

Wow, I thought, as we drove into Mom's lot and I stared at the dilapidated sand-colored structure that once probably supported thirty percent of the jobs in this town. There was once a time in our culture when there was enough of a demand, even in this area alone, for unique head accessories of all kinds that a whole factory was sustained on it.

Maybe this little notion hit me so hard because, as a bald man by choice, a quality hat is an important part of my daily accessorizing routine. Us bald guys get cold heads much of the time, and what better way to cover up than with a stylish, swank piece of headwear? And, to think only a few decades ago there were factories like Bollstan's that served the sole purpose of making sure men like me had nice stylish hats to buy.

Well, not today. Now the people of the world buy their hats crumpled up on a shelf buried under discarded T-shirts on a discount end cap at their local Target. I know... I got my last fedora there, and it's a filthy piece of shit... but what can a guy do with so few options? Nowadays, quality hat shops for the everyday bloke are few and far between, probably run by seventy-year-old guys clinging to a family business far into the red and running out of miracles. Hats for the everyman now are just afterthought accessories made as a niche item by chic teenage clothing lines. Even if you do find a high-quality hat, you've only managed that by perusing through five hundred thumb nails on a web site and you can't even try the damn thing on before buying it.

Sad really... although I also wondered about something else as I unbuckled my seat belt and climbed out of the car. Why the hell was I thinking about the death of the hat in American culture when I should have been thinking about Bill Mattingly and what the fuck I planned on saying to him? Must have been some sort of nervous thought trail off; I'd have to watch that. This diner date of ours couldn't possibly have any more riding on it. It was time to get my head in the game.

Detective Bill was guzzling a cup of coffee and still had tiny remnants of a cheeseburger club in the stray hairs of his goatee. He smiled when we walked in and waved Dillon and I over. I was cautious as I slid into the undersized booth... Jesus... were people *that* much smaller when Mom's was built forty years ago? That's a scary thought. But that was not the reason for my caution. I didn't trust Bill yet and this conversation would go a long way toward answering the question of whether I ever would.

He opened things up by saying, "Boys... it's possible you may have stumbled on to something. If what your pal Bailey says is true, and it really is Cadence Moore lying beneath the cornfields in Bowmansville, then this here... this thing we're discussing... it's the biggest thing any of us will ever be a part of. In spite of yourselves, you may well have discovered the equivalent of Whitey Bulger's cash stash and now we just need to decide how to split the prize money. Am I right, guys?"

It was obvious Bill was toying with us a bit... feeling us out... cops are the best psychologists around... make no mistake about that. They know how to get the desired response almost without trying. Dillon knew Bill very well. Like I said, Dillon's a great producer and some of the research he's had to do on certain shows has required cooperation from law enforcement. Dillon knows how to talk to these guys and Bill Mattingly himself was at least indirectly involved in twelve pieces we did for *Underground Broadcast* over the last few years.

This partially made him an ally and it partially meant that he couldn't be trusted completely. Being involved with us previously meant that Bill had already built a little profile of our show and the people who made it run, including myself and Dillon.

I knew he'd be operating based on that profile... and every word he said would be based on some pre-existing determination he'd already made about our states of mind and the ease in which we could be controlled. These thoughts scared me, weary travelers... no matter how insane or paranoid they might sound now.

I decided to break the ice... and to be honest, I was a little surprised Dillon hadn't already done so. I said, "Detective Mattingly, when this is over, Whitey Bulger's cash stash will seem like pocket change compared with the fortune of notoriety *we'll* be drowning in. It's not every day you're part of solving the biggest mystery of the 21st Century."

Bill Mattingly smiled. "Charlie Marx, I had a feeling about you (and I'm sure he did). I knew I would like you. You talk real well young man… and I reckon that's on account of your radio gig."

See, there it was… Bill was trying to intimidate me with the down-home cop slang, 'I reckon.' Really? He was laying it on thicker than a sumo wrestler's belt line? Or maybe he was trying to throw me off and make himself seem non-threatening and friendly. I know it sounds like I am overanalyzing the conversation, but you listeners need to understand the fever pitch my mind was cycling on at this point. Within the span of two seconds, I may have had three new thoughts or revelations. It was making me sharp, but also paranoid.

Bill continued, "You really believe in what you have here? In other words, when it all comes out in the wash, you're prepared to hang your hat on the theories you've been stirring up? It could all turn out to be nothing after all, and then what do you have? Do you guys have a plan B? Or is this it? Is this the whole kit and caboodle?"

Bill looked at me with steely blue eyes… the kind of eyes that belong to a man who has heard every lie and learned with great nuance and focus how to no-sell each and every one of them. I glanced over at Dillon who was giving me an urgent sort of 'go ahead… tell him' glance as he sat there silently pretending to read the menu.

I still couldn't figure out why Dillon was being so silent, considering he was the one with the pre-existing relationship with Bill Mattingly. It was almost like he wanted me to do the talking. It was like he wanted to sell me to Bill Matt… wait a damn second here… that's *exactly* what he was doing. Bill still needed convincing to go along with this. All that 'three of us' shit Dillon was spewing on the phone was just a gag. He knew Mattingly was interested and would soon demand to be made an equal partner in all this. But, my good friend Dillon just decided to hit the fast forward button on some things and tell me that Bastard Bill was rarin' to go before he'd even decided to get on the train with us. I gave my good buddy Dillon a sneer… sort of a snarl mixed with a smile. I knew the game now. So, I decided on the spot that I was more than capable of playing it. I answered Bill's question. "To say I was confident in my theories would be like saying it's a good possibility the stars will come out tonight, and after they go to sleep, the sun will rise again."

This little speech I was just getting warmed up on got interrupted by a nice, well-built, young waitress named Connie. She had bleached blonde '80s style hair and a nose ring. Connie was pretty and she had this perfume on that almost made me float out of the booth and follow her into the kitchen… probably for some kind of indecent proposal. Instead of that, I kept my composure and ordered a cheeseburger club. Dillon said it was the best thing on the menu and even after seeing what I'd assumed were remnants of it on Mattingly's face, I refused to be grossed out of trying it. Dillon ordered a salad and soup. Mattingly ordered more coffee, and from the frenetic jazzy way he was gesturing with his hands as he ordered it… I could tell he'd been drinking coffee a good long while now.

It was probably copious amounts of caffeine that helped keep Bastard Bill quick when he was doing police work. I suppose we all have our ways of getting into the zone. Then again, I didn't know the man, he could have been a coke head for all I knew and five cups of coffee for him could have had the effect of a downer. Anyway, I was getting sidetracked with my thoughts again.

Connie thanked us, smiled at me… or so I wished to believe… and then left. I continued my speech. "These aren't theories, Mr. Mattingly. This is the eyewitness truth from a man who conversed with Cadence Moore's killer. This is a man who has been carrying around a confession all these years… about a national scandal of all things… and he's kept quiet for whatever reason. I never did find that out to be clear.

But Budgie Bailey was telling the truth… I am sure of it, and no, don't bother asking because I can't tell you how I know it. I just know. Are you prepared to put some boys into action and discover a long-lost girl… buried in a cornfield in cow country… a girl ready to be at rest and achieve some long-awaited peace? That's all we're asking of you. If it turns out you waste your resources and she's not there, your name will never be associated with our failure. You don't even have to stake your reputation on any of this. But think about it, Detective… if she is there, then for the cost of supplying a few guys and keeping completely silent about things, you'll be known throughout history as one of the three men who solved the Cadence Moore mystery. You've already assisted us before, and you know my partner Dillon is an honest man. If you help us now, your storied career will escalate to unforeseen heights and you will become a legend, my friend."

Mattingly simply smiled again. He took a few moments to decide how he was going to respond. I don't think he assumed I'd come on as strong as I did, as quick as I did. But now that I had, Bastard Bill decided to take me down a notch or two and tell me what was what. First, he dressed me down and then he tried to trick me.

He kept the shit-eating grin on his face as he said, "Mr. Marx, if you think I'm signing a gag order with you, I'd have to venture a guess and say this is the first time you've dealt with the police. Ask your buddy Dillon here. He knows. If I'm a cop that was part of something five years ago, and you just want me to sign a contract and talk on your radio show... well then that's one thing. But if you want me investigating for you... there will be no goddamn contracts, son, and that's the end of that."

Dillon shot me what I can't be sure of, but assume was the look of death. Then he smiled at Bill and said, "Of course, Bill, standard operating procedure. Please continue with your thoughts on how to proceed."

Bill nodded and said, "How about a first question? Why would you guys ever want to dig around in a cornfield when we could simply locate Tommy Trayce's Challenger and see if any of Cadence's DNA is still in that trunk?"

I laughed, secretly glad that Mattingly had started off with an argument I'd already considered and researched the previous evening. I filled Dillon in on this particular detail on our way to the diner and I could feel him urging me silently to throw out what we knew so we'd retain some credibility in the cop's eyes.

I told Mattingly, "Detective, I'm sure you already know this and are trying to find out if we know it as well. You can stop wondering about that because we're very well aware of what happened to Trayce's Challenger. After he hit the elderly woman, Christine Styles, Trayce was arrested and the car was impounded. Since he struck Styles with the front of his car, the only blood samples they took from the car were from the front fender. Trayce went to jail and his parents declined the offer to keep his car. It was sent off to auction and there is no further record of it after that. Whatever auction it was sent to wasn't the type of outfit that put a lot of importance into paper-work. So, either some old Grandpa owns it now and has probably had the trunk reupholstered and wet-vac'd… or it was bought for cheap and turned into scrap. So, just like Jamison Kelly's car, this one is not around for us to do the easy investigation on anymore. If it were, we never would have sought you out in the first place." That was a lie, and Mattingly knew it.

But Mattingly was slightly impressed. He gave a goofy nod and raised his eyebrows and said, "Well, well, well, good men, I was just testing you. You're right, Charlie, and I must say I'm glad to see I'm dealing with profes-sionals here. Let's just hope you were this thorough on everything you've investigated."

Dillon said, "Try us… we probably know a lot more than you as-sume we do."

Before Mattingly could fire more questions, my new favorite person, Connie, had returned with our meals and Bill's coffee. I bit right into the club and gave a wink and a thumb's up to Connie, as though she'd prepared the whole thing herself. She giggled and looked down at Bill who was wav-ing her off like a stupid donkey's ass. I wanted to slap him. If this were any other day and I'd been by myself, I would've had Connie's number by now. But, she thanked us again and walked off. *Damn it all*, I thought.

Mattingly watched Connie walk back to the kitchen. He looked back at us and his expression changed. We certainly had passed some kind of test by knowing about Trayce's Challenger, because now Mattingly addressed us in a more serious tone that suggested his profiling games were over for the time being.

He said, "Okay, Dillon… okay, Marx… here's the situation. I don't believe for a second that what Budgie Bailey told you is entirely true, which would mean Cadence Moore is very possibly not buried in a field in Bowmansville. If any of his story is bullshit, then it opens a door for us to assume it's *all* bullshit. That is what I believe boys. However, I want to stress this. As a good cop, I've learned some important lessons along the way. Lesson number one?

I don't always completely believe what I believe if you know what I mean. I decided to look into this a bit. I did some checking yesterday after I talked with Dillon and it turns out there is, in fact, a Ted and Allison Trayce who own a farm in Bowmansville, and after some further checking… it turns out they do have a son and his name is Thomas. Budgie could have known a little about this Tom Trayce fellow and decided to concoct a fairy tale. At this point, I have no reason to believe that it's anything other than that."

Dillon spoke up. He asked, "Well, with all due respect, Bill, if you don't believe any of it, then why did you even show up here today?"

Mattingly answered, "I'll be honest… I was willing to invest a little time this morning just on the notion that what you guys brought to me actually turns out to be true. I don't believe it will turn out that way, but I sure as hell am not the type of man who sits by. I will risk wasting a little time in the hope that this particular tree bears some fruit. I must tell you, though, I find Bailey's timing very suspect. He claims to not know what happened to Tommy Trayce after he killed that guard in the laundry room fight. Well, I do not believe that statement to be accurate."

Dillon interrupted, "Hold on, Bill… when I told you about the conversation Charlie had with Bailey… I don't recall ever mentioning the guard being killed. Do you mind telling us how you even knew about that part?"

Mattingly's eyes got wide and he said, "Who do you boys think you're dealing with here? I said it was nice to be dealing with professionals, but now that I'm talking with you… I'm a little shocked by how amateur your methods and deductions really are. Dillon, we've worked together before and I always took you for a sharp young guy… especially for a Latino… no offense by saying that. It's just that a lot of the Chicano boys I deal with aren't the brightest bulbs in the bunch. But you… you were different and I could tell you were smart. Now you're asking me stupid questions. I can only assume that's because you think I'm stupid. Have I mistaken you Dillon for someone who respected me? Was I incorrect about that?"

Dillon tried to recover, "I simply ask this question because I know I didn't tell you that detail. I'm not surprised you know about it… I just want to know *how* you know about it. That's all. You know I respect you Bill, in spite of your racist comments which I've gotten used to."

Bill looked Dillon square in the eye and had almost a hurt look on his face. Was he really offended by Dillon's question? Was he that sensitive? I got my answer a second later when Mattingly burst out laughing and slapped Dillon on the shoulder. He laughed some more as he said, "Jesus Christ... I had you goin' there for a second. Man alive, that was funny. You thought I was really pissed at you."

Mattingly laughed again and downed some more coffee. He then explained where he got his unexpected information. "Charlie, did you really believe you were having a secret conversation on those prison phones? Can you honestly say you didn't realize they were all monitored and recorded? I reckon you're a damn sight smarter than that, son. So, yeah, I pulled the conversation with Budgie and the two conversations you had before that with your cousin, the credit fraud perp. It took one phone call. One phone call and a few hours later those calls were in my possession."

I demanded, "Detective Mattingly, why would you have felt the need to do that? Before you took the time to talk to us today, why would you have wanted to go down that road? This could have all been bullshit and you would have spent hours of your time for nothing. So, I'm just confused why you felt the need to go in there before our talk today and take the tapes of our calls. Do you plan on pursuing this yourself and just leaving us to rot? Do you think we haven't considered this possibility? Why would you start pulling phone calls before we even spoke?"

God, I knew how paranoid that sounded even as the words were leaving my lips. I knew it would piss off Bill too, but it was already out. I couldn't take it back.

Mattingly was quick to retort and let some of his natural aggression out since the nice guy act didn't suit him and he probably knew it. He spoke more loudly than before... actually turning some heads in the diner when he bellowed, "Because, son, I got two good reasons. One, I do what I want when I fucking want to do it. This keeps anyone else from focusing on those calls because I have them now and I told those BCP boys this was a police matter and they'd hear back from me when I was through. That means they leave off those calls for now and that buys us time. What I did will keep all other potential discoverers of Cadence Moore from being able to break up our little party. That is... again... if any of this shit is true.

"The second reason is that I need some partners on this deal. Specifically, I need you guys as partners. Your radio show allows us to have control over how this story comes out... if there *is* a story. If we make this a police matter, then we'll get interviewed by the news and we'll be mentioned briefly as a law enforcement unit in all the big articles but then it goes away. I don't like that and I don't want that. What I want is to control the way this story gets out there. I want to make sure that anyone who hears this knows who the final three were at the end of the game, holding up Cadence's body and proclaiming victory after ten years of failure. That is... if it's not all..."

I interjected before Mattingly could finish and said, "A bunch of bullshit... yes, you mentioned that. All right, well you know as much as we do now. So, what's your take? You think he's lying?"

Mattingly answered, "He is definitely lying."

Dillon broke in with, "How can you be sure of that? If you think that then I ask you again, why are you here?"

Mattingly pounded the table. "Because, Dillon... like I told you before... Budgie's statements are shady and I think he knew exactly what became of Tommy Trayce after that laundry brawl. And I'd say Trayce's *current condition* (Bill leaned in and emphasized those words for effect) was the driving force leading Budgie to spill the beans."

I was caught off guard by that last statement because it was the last thing I expected to hear. I interrupted with, "Whoa... wait a minute... what do you mean his *current condition*? Now, I'll tell you right now, straight up and honest, I was never able to find out conclusively what happened to Tommy Trayce. I know he's not at BCP anymore because he was transferred to Parkworth. After that, I haven't been able to get a beat on him. What exactly is it that you know and we don't, Detective?"

I was left in suspense as Connie returned. She asked, "Can I get you boys anything else? Has everything been all right so far?" For as great as she looked, Connie had really bad timing. I thought she was cute as hell but she was the last person I wanted to see right now when I was waiting on such an important answer.

I smiled at her in a forced, almost arrogant way and said, "Can we have the check, honey? Everything's been great… we're all set here, sweetheart." Connie forced a smile right back at me and I could tell she didn't appreciate my slightly rushed and patronizing tone. I didn't even like the sound of it and I was the one who said it. Something told me Connie's number wouldn't be on the back of the check when she brought it. Oh, what could have been if I hadn't brought Dillon and Bastard Bill with me on this fine morning? Connie was within reach and now she wasn't. More goddamn sacrifices for art.

We were back to our conversation and my worst fears were confirmed when Mattingly said, "Do you really think that Budgie Bailey was stricken by an attack of conscience all of the sudden and decided to tell Rydell that he just *had* to talk now and was ready to sing about the whole story? Do you think that just *happened*? If you do, you're a gullible couple of turds in this guy's book."

I knew what was coming next and I saw my grand finale interview with the killer slip right through my fingers as I asked my next question and got the answer. I asked, "Tommy Trayce is no longer among the living, is he? And you think that Budgie also knows this and that's why he's decided to use him as his boogeyman and invent this fairy tale, as you call it. You figure Bailey knew Rydell, and through him found out about me, and decided to try and get himself a better view from his prison bars out in Sunfield. All he'd have to do to get it was make up a pretty story. Am I getting this pretty close to accurate, Detective Mattingly?"

A final sliver of hope coursed through my arteries like faint heat lighting… maybe I was wrong… maybe I'd still get my grand finale. But it was not to be. Mattingly nodded and answered with condescension and sarcasm, "Marx… I have to hand it to you. You're rather quick on the uptake. You got it exactly right. Thomas Trayce was beaten to death a few weeks ago by a fellow inmate with a grudge named Terrence Wallman. Wallman's a former member of the Crips and pretty much a bad ugly hombre not to be fucked with. Guess who fucked with him?"

Before we had a chance to guess the obvious answer to the question, Connie returned one final time. She had three cups of coffee on a tray and she set them at each of our places at the table. She laid down the check and said, "Thanks so much guys, enjoy the coffee and let me know if you need anything else. Have a great day."

That was the last I saw of beautiful young Connie. Had a young goddess, armed with all of my future happiness, just stepped out of my life forever? God only knew. I regrouped quickly over the loss of Connie as I creamed and sugared my coffee. We continued listening to Bill tell us the story of Tommy Trayce's demise.

Bill continued, "Tommy must have looked at him really fuckin' sideways at some point because from what I hear, there are still small traces of his brain matter on the concrete floors of the shitter in Parkworth where he was killed. Very few questions were asked and, as a consequence, we have very few answers. All I know is what's related to this story we're discussing. Tommy Trayce is dead and… more significantly… he's *recently* dead. So recent, in fact, that Bailey's statements are probably too convenient to be true."

Dillon asked, "So, what do you think… Bailey just picked some random guy he knew who'd recently died and invented a whole lie around him, complete with an acting performance that would have made Brando turn green, and an entire story with location details and everything? That's a rather gigantic assumption. What evidence do you have to assume this, Bill?"

Mattingly patted Dillon on the shoulder from the other side of the table. "What makes you think I need evidence, Dillon? This is intuition. I can smell this type of shit from a mile away. Let's just say my logical side wants to blot out his whole story because I smell dead fish mucking up the works of the truth. But you bring up some good points, and me… not being a fool… well, I've also considered them. While my brain tells me to be suspect about it *all*, including the dead girl in the field, my intuition tells me that it wouldn't hurt to kick over a few rocks and know for sure. Was Bailey lying about *everything*? I don't know. I'm too split in my feelings to say one way or the other. Maybe he was lying about a lot, but if he told the truth at all, then I guess we got a little something to talk about.

"I can conjecture with the best of them. If you want to discuss the idea that Bailey was telling the truth about everything, except not knowing what became of Trayce after the guard killing, well… I'll go with you on that trip because, truthfully, I think it may end up somewhere. So, we're gonna assume it's true that Bailey had the initial conversation with Trayce in 2002. Then he kept silent about it because… well… because that's what these fuckin' jailbird assholes do… they keep secrets for each other. Eventually, Trayce kills a guard and permanently fucks himself for life. He's never getting out.

"Our friend Tommy continues to piss people off and finally crosses the wrong motherfucker who uses Trayce's skull to decorate the concrete floors of the community shitter in the garage where Trayce was being given a trial work assignment two hours a day. Word gets back to Budgie Bailey through the usual channels and his wheels start turning. He knows Tommy and he knows that it's possible the girl allegedly buried in the field is Cadence Moore. He connected those dots years before.

"His buddy Rydell tells him about his radio-host cousin who happens to be doing a special on Cadence (even though your cousin the perp acts like he doesn't know shit about that) and one thought leads to another. Budgie sees his ticket to Sunfield if he makes his long-awaited confession. He doesn't want the transfer for safety reasons because he already knows Trayce is dead. He just wants to go to Sunfield, simple as that.

"You fall for it all, hook, line, and sinker, Charlie, and well… here we are. Now, like I said at the outset, boys… I have no reason to believe any of this is more than the embellished ramblings of Budgie Bailey's imagination. He wants to go to Sunfield so he makes up a story fancy enough to hock for a one-way ticket there.

"If this whole thing is bullshit, then we're gonna find nothing but some earthworms and dirt mites when we dig up poor Ted Trayce's farm. But, if it's not… and I am smart enough to admit that there is a small chance of this, sometimes twisted shit just works out and it would be my luck… since I consider myself charmed… to fall right into it and reap the benefits. It's my job to be skeptical and I am exactly that… skeptical. But I'm not stupid.

We'll be searching that field… and we'll have our answers… this I can guarantee you."

I was turning all of this around in my brain, trying to make sense of the new information. I was a little intimidated that Mattingly was able to find so much out in a day. It clearly illustrated how much more capability he had as a cop to solve something like the Cadence Moore case than we did… a couple of radio boys who were great at telling stories, but when it came to real investigations, the Hardy Boys could have kicked our asses. I feared that any time he felt like it, Mattingly could steal this whole thing and run wild with it. We'd be left in the cold, just as Dillon warned before this diner meeting.

The biggest shock of all was the death of Tommy Trayce. I had my heart set on a prison interview with the killer of Cadence Moore (assuming, of course, we could prove it) but now that would never happen. Don't get me wrong, I believe Trayce got what he deserved. But, as an entertainer, you sometimes have to look at the dollar signs and commercial appeal. And, no better ending to our series existed than a behind bars interview with a long-sought murderer of a media darling.

But that wasn't going to happen and now I needed to adjust. Our main goal was still out there. Solve the case and prove that Cadence Moore didn't just disappear. Prove that she was murdered. Not by Jamison Kelly after a drunken lover's quarrel, but by a low-down parasite named Trayce who brought trouble with him everywhere he went and infected all those who came in contact with him.

I finally responded to Mattingly's revelations. I said, "Forgive us for our silence, Detective. Your new information is all very difficult to process. I guess my first question is… where do we go from here? How do we arrange a search effort at the Trayce farm without news of what we're looking for getting out to everyone? I don't think I need to point out to you how important secrecy is on this operation. If we don't keep this between us, then your dream of being among the elite three men who solved the Cadence saga… well… that dream will not happen. The media will be alerted by some stupid cop within minutes of him finding out the score and then we won't have our chance to paint the picture in the way we want it painted. How… this is what we want to know… how can we keep that from happening?"

Dillon added, "Without the answer to this question, we really can't move forward. Charlie's right, Bill. Once this gets out, it's out and we will completely lose control of it. Do you have the power to keep that from happening?"

Bastard Bill had clearly been considering this question before we ever arrived. If any cop besides himself knew what they were looking for out in those fields, this thing would unravel quicker than a ball of yarn. Sure, Bill could go find some other media man to tell his story the way he wanted it told, but getting someone with the backing of UPR and their potential audience? Getting an outlet that had already told this story six ways from Sunday with none of the loose ends waving in the wind? That he couldn't find just anywhere. For right now… he had us and if we were going to make this happen the right way, silence was a crucial condition.

Bill knew the score. We were his best shot at the most notoriety. We weren't naive enough to believe that he had any respect for us because we were the ones who discovered the hot lead that may have solved the case. But he did know full well that we had the power to expose this thing to a wider audience than he could, at first if nothing else… at least a wider audience than he could while keeping himself as one of the central focuses.

Bill the Bastard had deliberated on all this already and was now going to lay out his plan. Bill told us how it would go down. He smiled… very much like the smile he forced over his lips when he first arrived. He took a sip of coffee and then spoke. He said, "It does my heart good to know that my partners in crime… or more correctly… my partners in crime solving are thinking on a high level… just like I do. Working with a pair of idiots just would have been underwhelming and depressing. I'm glad I've got a couple of sharp boys like yourselves to ride along with on this trail.

"Keeping this thing hushed and hidden between the three of us, even while dealing with several other men digging right along with us, well boys… that is going to be a tall order. But it's doable… very doable in fact. So how will we work it?

"I've been thinking about that all morning. Here's the thing you fellas might not know about law enforcement. Nobody asks fuckin' questions... especially if a big fish like me is the one leading the charge. I'll ask for a warrant... I'll get a warrant. What do you guys think... I need to write an essay and lay out my points one by one for why I should get said warrant? That's not the way the shit works... at least that ain't the way it works when I'm involved.

"No, what I do is this. I tell my man Sterling Forsyth out at the bureaucrat castle that I've got a cold case I recently received a hot lead on. He needs certain things for his file. He needs an address... he needs the name of the Detective in charge... and he needs the case we're investigating. Well, that sinks us right there doesn't it boys?"

Dillon was playing along... entertaining Bill's little attempt at having us sit by his learning tree while he made simple trifle of our worst complications. Dillon knew the man and he knew when to go along with the games the man wished to play.

So, Dillon says, "Bill, I think it does sink us. If you tell Mr. Forsyth that we're investigating Cadence and searching a property for her body, then our little three-man secret dies a quick death and becomes a whole police department secret... which really isn't too secret, is it? So, tell us... why wouldn't this sink us?"

I had to hand it to Dillon... he was showing me right here why he'd been my producer for so long. He might be a temperamental asshole now and again, but he was just so fucking great. He knew what to say to people and when to say it. He knew how to get information. He knew psychology and was going toe to toe with a psych-out artist in Mattingly.

I'd never been this up close and personal with Dillon's process before and I was very impressed. I was so used to having fantastic information just handed to me on a weekly basis, I hadn't given proper thought or appreciation to the things Dillon had to manipulate and maneuver to get that info. I told myself then and there, when this whole thing was in the can, I was going to arrange for Mr. Balast to get a pay raise.

Mattingly was pleased as spiked peach punch though. He loved talking about how slick he was and how he got around all the sharp corners that no one else could. So, Dillon was leading him exactly in the right direction by asking a naive question as though he thought Mattingly wasn't already cocked and loaded with a windy diatribe about another obstacle he knew how to leap over.

Bastard Bill continued, "It doesn't sink us, my friend, because Sterling Forsyth asks the questions, but Bill Mattingly only answers the ones he wants to. When it comes time to mark up those forms and label the case I'm working on, I tell that gray mule Sterling that I'm keeping this one close. Sterling will just grin and ask a few questions as though he's actually interested. He's an amiable old son of a gun and he always tries to make you feel as though he's engaging you in some way.

"That's why I go through Sterling. He's a quality guy and he doesn't stand in the way of real police work. Real police work… unlike the poor excuse for investigation your friends in Dusklight Falls did on this case. Anyway, before I get to ranting on that, which would keep us here all day long, I will tell you how it goes down with Sterling and his search warrant. As soon as I tell him I'm playing this one close to the heart… he'll nod and write in the name of 'Elmsford Missing Persons' on the paperwork. That is a code phrase used by paper pushers when they have an understanding with certain cops.

"It's one of about six hundred code phrases that are used to fill in the case-being-investigated section on the warrant forms. What it means is that the warrant will be processed, approved, and in my waiting hands within two hours. And don't worry about the Judges either, boys, because they also don't question shit if you do things right.

"You see, paperwork is god and ruler of these guys. The secret to my success… you wanna know what it is? Always making sure my paperwork is in order. If all the forms appear to be tip-top and proper, Judges will sign anything you throw in front of them and not give another thought to it for as long as they live. They get off on authority, boys. They whack off to their own images… in their black robes, fat asses up on their special thrones, and loud hammering gavel scepters in their withered, chubby hands. You make them feel like you spent hours making every form perfect so it was fit for their eyes and approval, they just fucking sign it. They only pull the cruel asshole routine with sloppy fuckers who waste their time and don't have shit put together before Judgey spends his time looking it all over. So, there you go, gents… a little life lesson on getting the documents you want when there's some real law enforcement to get movin' on.

"I just explained how we handle the administrative side of the game and if all goes to plan, that takes care of permission for us to begin a search. We still need men. That's when I call in the cutters. Who are the cutters you might ask? Well, I'll tell you… this is *my* crew. It's about twenty guys overall who I use for different shit here and there. The cutters ask no questions and care to find no answers. They follow direct orders and collect their… I suppose I should call them bonus checks… when the mission is accomplished."

Bill looked around. Mom's Diner had been slowly filling up as we sat and ate our meals. He said, "Okay… we got more talking to do fellas… let's move this conversation to the parking lot. We're hogging up a table here."

Bill grabbed the check off the table and swaggered up to the cashier's station and paid for our meals. How expensive the payback for this meal will be when all is said and done, I thought. I could only imagine how deep in debt we were with Bill now since he had more knowledge than we did and he was the only link we had to solving this fucking thing and going all the way with the truth.

Dillon and I followed Bill out the door. I took one last look around to see if Connie might just happen to skip out waving a piece of paper which would have her phone number and a little heart or smiley face next to it with the words 'call me' scribbled underneath. But Connie never came and we just left Mom's and began phase two of our conversation in the gravel parking lot… smoking cigarettes and leaning against Bill's Torino.

Bill resumed the previous discussion about his cutting crew… and I could only hope that wasn't some odd reference to the pop group prone to dying in peoples' arms. Bill continued, "Like I said boys, the cutters ask no questions and take their bonuses wordlessly. That's why I love working with them. They get the job done and don't give a fuck about anything. People who don't give a shit about getting promoted won't start ratting you out for things being promised to them. No, in fact, people who just want to do their shit and go home… they're the greatest. You can trust them to be who they are and nothing more… no surprises.

"If I can get five good cutters, that would be ideal. I think I'll probably end up with more like three since these strapping young lads are quite expensive to call into service. But even three will be enough to scour that field at Ted Trayce's place and we'll know one way or the other if Cadence Moore is to be found or to be forever lost.

"This leaves just one final point of discussion, boys. Dillon told me your plan about having the police make their statement as soon as you're off the air. I know you guys want this story broken on your show and I get all that. I didn't tell Dill this when we talked, but this part, fellas… needs some changes. If you think I'm making my statement to the press *after* show time… you got another thing coming."

I cringed. This is what we were most afraid of. We didn't want the cops to have their hands in this live broadcast. I told Dillon that I didn't care if the police press conference was held even ten seconds after broadcast but now with Bastard Bill getting his paws all over this shit, we were losing control.

I interrupted and said, "Detective… I hate to say this and I am quite aware you have the ability to steal this even now and leave us in the dust. But, if you want my team involved and if you want this story told on UPR airwaves, then what you're suggesting is a deal breaker. The police cannot make their statement before we've revealed this bombshell on *Underground Broadcast*. It simply cannot happen that way."

I was scared that Bill would spit in my direction, get in his car, and speed off, taking our dreams of solving Cadence right along with him. But he didn't do that. He only smiled, that aggravating smile I was beginning to dislike immensely.

Bill quietly said, "Oh, Charlie… now you just calm down. I wouldn't have wasted so much time talking to you boys today if I planned on leaving you out in the cold. Listen closely… I am not saying the story shouldn't be revealed on *Underground Broadcast*. What I *am* saying is that when we get to this part of the special, I will have the press waiting in a sealed area, not able to listen to the show… meaning all cell phones will be confiscated and every one of them will be frisked before entering. They will get their information when we give it to them. So, we get to the climax of the show, invite the press in… and here's the deal breaker for me. If it doesn't go down the way I'm about to outline for you… then my friends… this thing doesn't go down at all.

"When we invite the press in, Charlie, you will introduce me as the Detective who has been working with you on the Cadence case. You will then announce that I'm about to make an official statement regarding the true nature of the Cadence Moore mystery. At no point in the show before this moment are you allowed to reveal exactly how this thing played out and exactly what we found in that field. That statement will be made by me and that's it. You can say we've solved it and you can talk about the conspiracy shit from the last ten years and you can even talk about the whole process that led to this ending, including moments like the one we're sharing together right now on this sunny afternoon. But the reveal itself… the true reveal where we come out and tell the world what happened to Cadence, and the news that the body we dug up is hers… boys, that last word is mine. Take it or leave it.

"When you say my name and I start talking. That's when you shut up, Charlie. I will address the press and tell them 'no questions' until broadcast is over. I'm okay with that. You finish things up for the next half hour or so you have left, and then I will meet the press for questions when the ON AIR sign shuts off and your show is in the can.

"I don't think that's too much to ask. If you're cool with this… which I hope you are because, if not, we just wasted lots of time discussing things that will never happen. If you boys are cool with my one proviso… then shake my hand and we'll call this thing a deal."

Dillon and I looked at each other at the exact same time. Our eyes were saying, "Is that all? He just wants to be the one who says it on air?"

Jesus, that would probably come off better than if I was the one who announced it. We'd have instant credibility if a well-known Detective makes the announcement on air, and *Underground Broadcast* still gets the credit for being the show that scooped the decade-old mystery. We appeared to have a deal, indeed.

I held out my hand to Bill and he shook it. Dillon did the same. I said, "Mr. Mattingly, I sincerely appreciate your participation in this and I don't think I need to point out that we couldn't get this close without you. What I really want to know is…"

Dillon cut me off. He didn't want me to push things too hard with Bill. He interjected, "I think we know basically all we need to know. Bill, how long will it take, in your estimation to get this search underway and for you to contact us so we can ride along… just as observers of course… but we'll need to be there… I'm sure you know that."

Bill stomped out his cigarette and smiled again. I was getting quite sick of that smile and I truly hoped Bill would never offer it to me in a moment of anger, because I might be liable to slap it off his face… and then run, very fast, of course.

Bill said, "I figured you boys weren't going to just sit around and wait for my call telling you I'd found your long-lost lady. So, yeah, I'll call you when it's time. We'll head out to the farm and you will stay put in your cars. Is that very clear to you fellas? I reckon you understand how much I *don't* need any interference from you on game day."

Dillon continued to drive… and I let him because he was good at this and I knew it. I respected it and didn't need my ego stroked by being the one to end this particular conversation. Dillon concluded our business with Bastard Bill by saying, "Very good, Bill. We won't get in the way and we can assure you… you can take this straight to the bank. When this show airs everyone will know who the man was that made the biggest difference in the case and who led us to the finish line. Just trust us and we'll trust you. In the end, we all reign victorious. Sound good, Detective?"

Bill looked at me… as though he was sizing me up to see if he could find a hint of hesitation, or chicanery glowing behind my eyes. Above all else, Bill didn't want to be fucked and he stared me through and through… deep into my soul and made his assessment. He said, "All right then, partners… we're in business; all in it together and all out of it together. No problems, no hassles… just a smooth operation. I'll call you when the players are all lined up and ready for kickoff."

With that Bastard Bill got in his canary yellow Torino and kicked up gravel and dust as he peeled out of Mom's parking lot. I looked at Dillon and he smiled. I hugged him. We got in the car and drove back to the office. We didn't say a word the whole time. There wasn't anything left to say. We both had a feeling about Bill and we knew that at least for now, he was good to his word, and for better or worse, he was our guy. We had no other choice. He was to be our guide to the blinding platinum gates, leading to the City of Gold. We were finally going to get there after what seemed like years of struggle. I knew one thing for certain, the next several days were going to feel like a motherfuckin' eternity.

- 8 -

UPR did nothing to quell my nerves or my anxiety. Just as things were reaching a pure fever pitch with the Bailey bombshell, Tyler Reubens, my mentor and the guy who talked me into this shit to begin with, called me at my home at seven in the evening. This was the night of our diner meeting with Bastard Bill. Tyler decided to drop a bomb on me.

Tyler, who I know is listening to this live special right now, is already likely having an aneurism at his home office. He is going to be very unhappy to say the least when he hears what is about to air right now. You see friends, I had the foresight to record many of my conversations around this time. Tyler is hearing all of this for the first time. When I say *all of this*, I mean the details of my lead and the fact that when I claimed to have solved the case and this whole special was advertised as though I had, I really hadn't solved anything… I was flying on a flimsy prayer and hoping to god on high that it would all work out.

Tyler knew that I claimed to have solved the case. He knew I was running with this and he also knew I wasn't cutting him into my biggest lead. This is where our relationship hit the skids, as you all will have gleaned from my interview on his *United Way of Life* show.

What he didn't know was that I was full of shit after all and had not only lied to all my guests, but lied to him as well. He suspected it of course and tried to threaten me into admitting it. But he didn't know for sure, and the risk taker in that man's heart decided to take a risk on me. If this final live episode turns out the way I've planned, everything will end up all right. We'll have had our biggest success in history as far as a series on UPR, and the greatest mystery of our generation will be solved. That will go a long way toward healing bruised feelings and making potential lawsuits disappear.

I am now going to play, in its entirety, except for the bleeping out of several words, my phone conversation with Tyler Reubens in which he told me our deadline was being pushed up to an insane level and what I planned on doing in months, I would now have to do in weeks. When Tyler hears this, his first instinct I'm sure will be to make a phone call and get this show pulled off the air immediately. But after he lets that feeling pass, he will remember the millions of downloads of our podcasts. He will realize that to cut this off now will guarantee a riot among our listeners who are deep enough into this case now to demand a resolution. He will let this play out. That I can guarantee. If I fail and things don't happen the way I've gambled everything on them happening, then my career is over and there will be some court dates in my future. I am too far into this now to let any of that stand in the way. We're moving ahead seekers and we will accomplish what we set out to do. We will solve Cadence Moore.

(At this point in the live special, a recording of Tyler Reubens's conversation with Charlie Marx and the revealing of the new rushed deadline, as well as the follow up conversation and all heated exchanges running through both, aired in its entirety.)

Like I said weary travelers, I gambled everything on this special, and my belief that what I have will turn out to be the missing piece that solves this case. But the lie... the lie I told my guests... and especially the lie I told Tyler which resulted in all the advertising of this special being marketed toward solving the case live on air, that lie guaranteed the end of me if things don't work out.

Dillon was gone. He went on a one-day vacation with his lady, Joyce, out to Bushkill Falls in the Pocono Mountains. I think he instinctively knew that things would be chaotic for a while once we searched that farm. He wanted one last little diversion... a drive off into the sunset... his last one as an anonymous producer who was not yet one of the solvers of the crime of our century.

I was freaking out, weary travelers, and I wanted nothing more than to call Dillon and bring him in to my hysterical panic… forcing him to shoulder the burden with me. But I didn't call him. I let him have his one-day trip. He'd have plenty of worrying to do when he got back.

In the meantime, I stayed up all night and worked tirelessly on the script. We were thirty days from live broadcast time now. I thought we had at least two months. UPR had never given me a solid date but they sure as fuck gave me a solid time line, and I had counted on it.

I traded in my rum bottle for a perpetually brewing pot of coffee and dove into my script. I'd have to work faster than I ever had on anything in my life. Not to mention, I needed to make sure I'd still have guests. What if some of them couldn't appear on the show on such short notice. Jesus, Barnes and Angstat? My head started to pound.

I frantically called my assistant, Marianne, and sent her on a difficult wild goose chase… tracking down my guest list and finding out if they'd all be ready to talk to me early. The podcasts had to be in the can and ready to drop all at once a week before the special. I was stricken with fear at the possibility of losing our best guests due to schedule conflicts. Marianne told me she'd get back to me as soon as possible. It could be days before I had answers from everyone.

And of course, I had to call Bastard Bill. If anyone knew we needed to put things into hyper drive, it was him. After all, he was the one performing all the legal magic tricks to allow us to search the Trayce farm, and I'll add for emphasis that he had to do all of it without anyone realizing what he was actually doing. What Bill was juggling would fall in the easier-said-than-done category of undertakings. Now, I was about to hit him with a major league complication.

- 9 -

It took me three tries over two hours to get hold of the Bastard. When he finally did call me back, Bill yelled so loud my eardrum almost ruptured. He shouted, "What kinda piece-a-fuckin-shit-pile-asshole, son-of-a-bitch, rinky-dink, amateur-hour operation you bunch of fools running over there? You think the shit I'm pulling together is easy? Why didn't you tell that suit to go fuck himself?"

I honestly replied, "Bill, I actually *did* tell him that. And guess what? He still is only giving me four weeks until the live special airs. I have basically a novel to write in the next fourteen days and I have my assistant contacting every guest to see if they can all still appear. So yeah, Bill, I understand the pain in the ass this causes. But, I called because I knew you had to know, and also because *I* have to know. Can it be done? Can you still make this happen on your end so we can make air on show night with our bombshell ready to fly?"

Bill slammed the phone against the wall about six times… he certainly was determined to put an end to my ability to hear properly for the rest of my life. He yelled, "I told you I'd call when we set the search up. Wait till you hear from me, you little shit head and don't ever doubt me. I will deliver that fucking announcement on time, in thirty days… even if it fucking kills me. Does that answer your question?"

I breathed a sigh that was a mix of slight frustration and mostly relief. I answered, "Bill, I never doubted you. Have a great night. We'll wait for your call."

Bill shouted, "I hope your whole family dies in a flaming accident, you unprofessional bitch! Yeah, have a great night yourself, you two-bit fucking piece a garbage!"

I couldn't help it… I hung up with Bill and immediately burst out laughing and thought to myself that went about as well as I expected. This unfunny statement struck me with such hilarity that I doubled over as the guffaws flowed. More likely than actual humor coursing through my body, I probably just snapped and was now clinically insane.

But like any victim of mental instability, the days don't stop coming and the livin' doesn't get any easier, even in the summertime, regardless of what Porgy or Bess might have to say about it. God, even the references I'm making writing this script have gotten pun-ridden and wacky. Fuck it. Nothing else matters. We've got deadlines now… and if we don't meet them, the word deadline will have never been so apropos. We're literally dead if we don't get this thing done.

By the time the sun came up that first night slash morning… I had finished my introduction, the sections on Cadence's origin story and her record deal adventures, as well as many of the questions I would have prepped and ready for the myriad guests I was to interview in two weeks, that is if any of them actually showed up.

I made a promise to myself that I would go to Tyler Reubens's house and personally strangle him if my series got completely fucked because of his complications. If it was fucked, it would be my complications that did the fucking, not his. Once I strangled Tyler, I promised that I would wipe the last bit of his living essence off my hands and go see Art Winston. When I got done shooting him in the face, I would go out to Dusklight Falls and leap off the cliffs in just the right angle to allow for full explosion of my brains when I hit the rocks that overlooked the foggy waters.

Oh, and I guess I should put it out there now as I'm reading it live from my insanity notes… Tyler and Art… I was only kidding. These were just the confused and mad ramblings of a person pushed to the edge, and if they ever make air, that means your bullshit decisions didn't really keep us from accomplishing our goals. So, the whole murder threat thing… just forget it. It was a simple joke from a simple man.

Okay, where were we? Oh yes, the first night and what I was able to get finished with the script. I'd written about twenty thousand words before the dawn forced its way in through the venetian blinds in my office. Then I forced myself to lie down and try to get at least three hours of sleep.

I was sure by the time 10:00 a.m. rolled around, I would be met with a frantic call from Dillon Balast. While I had enough respect for my friend to not interrupt his Bushkill Falls date with Joyce, I had a pretty solid feeling that ol' Bastard Bill would not give even a small shit about respect or resist the urge to call up Dillon and ream him out for bringing a loose cannon asshole like Charlie Marx into this whole mess.

And how right I was. The red digital letters of death, 10:34 a.m., were staring me in the face when my eyes opened to the piercing sound of my ringing phone. I'd slept all night in the office and the pillow I'd found in the conference room, likely used to support some ancient grandpa executive's inflamed sciatic nerve, had given me a god-awful kink in my neck that would probably make for a very difficult and miserable day at the computer writing this script.

Dillon heard the click on the extension which meant I'd picked up and was listening. I didn't even have the chance to say "hello" before his expletive-laden diatribe began.

"What the fuck, Charlie? What the fuck, man? I go away to the mountains for one goddamn day and I'm already getting calls from Bill threatening to kill me for bringing you into this thing? What did you do, man? How did we go from two months to four weeks? Talk to me, Charlie, because I'm about to put a gun to my head and save myself the pain that we're both about to deal with. Talk to me, jackass… tell me what you did to get us in this position!"

Okay, now Dillon was great and everything, but I'd warned him before that it was not okay to condescend to me like Tuesday's bitch. I was dealing with the same rage and fear that Dillon was and he didn't find me calling him an asshole or a jackass. This was where it was all going to end. I blew up on my partner. I screamed… literally screamed into the phone, "Shut up! You shut up! Just shut the fuck up for one second!"

I realized this was not going to make anything better but I had to let Dillon know he was crossing lines with me, and if he kept going, there just simply wouldn't be any going back.

I continued, "Just listen to me! I'm your friend, Dillon, and you're treating me like a piece of shit. That's not fair. For the last sixteen hours or so, I've been the only one dealing with this and I didn't choose to call you in the Poconos and burden you with any of it. I wanted to let you have your day with Joyce. But I had to tell Bill, man… and I knew he'd be an asshole and call you. What the fuck do you want me to do about it? I've been as cool as I can on this bullshit excuse for a series. But, I got the call from Tyler, not you!

"I was told that we have thirty days until live broadcast and I've spent the entire goddamn night writing podcast and live special scripts for air so we can still make this happen. So, what I don't need right now is for you to lecture me. Okay? Shit happened and none of us expected it. Now we gotta deal. If you can't deal, then maybe you're right. Maybe you should put that fuckin' gun on yourself and just end it right here!"

Dillon was breathing heavily on the other end of the line. He was pissed and he had a right to be. He didn't seem to know what to say. He just kept breathing. Then, finally... he began talking. He said, "Charlie... Jesus man, I'm sorry. Look, I know you didn't need to bring me into this thing on the level that you did. I'm your producer and you could've left me off in the distance with a credit at the end of the podcast. But you're making me a partner and Christ, man... I do appreciate it... I really do. I've just never dealt with anything like this before. I don't know what to do."

Dillon's rephrased emotions were sounding a lot better to me than the first burst of rage he leveled in my ears when this phone call began. I decided to play the nice guy, the grizzled veteran... the kind of dude who is always remaining in control and would not be pushed to lunacy based on a few frustrations. Of course, this isn't who I was at all. I was at the breaking point and losing it more and more with every second that went by. But, I could tell from Dillon's words that he was being honest. He really didn't know what to do. Who would? We'd been screwed in every possible way and we still didn't even know if we had Cadence Moore. We didn't know what the hell we'd find in Ted Trayce's field.

This could all get a hell of a lot worse. And, yet, we were forced to stay here... dealing with UPR crap... dealing with Mattingly's crap. It just didn't seem fair, any of it. But, here we were just the same. We would reap the benefits if it went right. We would face the defeated life of losers if it didn't.

I spoke to Dillon with my best attempt at reassurance. "I know you're losing it over there, man. I'm losing it, too. Here's the deal. I'll make it short and sweet. Tyler Reubens called me the night of our diner meeting with Bastard Bill. I wasn't expecting it, man... it was the last thing I was expecting that night. I was just trying to write my fucking scripts in peace. He told me that the suits at UPR had given into the demands of the BBC, and their proposed timeline for our special was fucking up some major political shit which would likely be hitting the fan in England at the time, and the limey's, as Reubens called them, told UPR in no uncertain terms that they better rearrange shit because their time slots could not be fucked with, according to their contracts.

"So, Art Winston, that fucking dinosaur piece of waste… he wanted to cancel the whole fuckin' special and let the whole thing get wrapped up with another podcast. Tyler said he had our backs and negotiated to keep our special alive. But, the only compromise that could be reached? The podcasts must be finished and ready for air three weeks from now so there's a week buffer for interest to hit the max before the special hits a week later. I told Reubens it just couldn't be done. I reamed out my own fuckin' boss, Dillon! I told him to go fuck himself. It didn't matter though. Shit, he was originally only going to give us two weeks to finish the podcasts. Even after I told him the same shit I've been telling everyone… that we'd solved the case… he said the best he could do was three weeks, unless I was prepared to give him details.

"Well, I'm no fool, Dillon, and Bill Mattingly made it pretty fuckin' clear during our conversation that this secret was a three-man job, and telling Tyler about it would make it… at the very least… a five-man secret, once he spotted his fucking angle and sang to Winston about it. So, I told Reubens… no dice. I can't give you details. He told me… if I can't give details… he can't give me more time. He halfway believes I'm full of shit anyway, but he's taking a risk and believing me. And… get this… he's still going to make me send him skeleton formats every few days so he knows where we're going with the podcasts. The big lead won't be revealed until the live special but that still puts him really fucking close to everything.

"So, tell me man… would you have handled that shit differently? Would you have let Reubens in on our lead? Would you have bought us two months at the cost of bringing UPR suits into the sacred circle of trust?"

Dillon answered quickly and decisively, "No, Charlie. I wouldn't. You did the right thing. I didn't realize the shit you were trying to juggle over there. No, we don't tell any secrets. If we do that, you and I both know that the news will be out before we make air… and that just can't happen."

I said, "You're telling me? Jesus, Dillon, I know. Right now, I'm waiting on Marianne to get back to me to let me know if we still have guests to interview. We told these fuckers two months, and now I'm expecting them to have a several-hour-long phone call or interview recorded for podcast like… now! I wouldn't be surprised if we lost half of them. We spent so much time and risked our credibility getting Barnes and Angstat and now we might lose them because of UPR's schedule! I mean, who'd have thought… with everything we've had to deal with and the goddamn lie I've put around our necks like a noose… that this bullshit would be the thing that derails us."

Dillon replied, "Oh shit, Charlie, I hadn't even thought about Barnes and Angstat. Fuck! What did Marianne say? Did she talk to them yet? They're the crown jewel guests and if they don't show up, I mean we'll still have a series, but it will be like a neutered one when it's all over. That's a best-case scenario, even if we solve it. We need those guys, man!"

I said, "I know we need them. They're the first ones I had Marianne call, and the slow-ass bitch hasn't even gotten back to me yet about them. But it's not just Barnes and Angstat, man. Even the people we had from the get-go. If they back out… Jimmy Derek… Jamison Kelly? If they're not on, then we still have a neutered puppy. Kelly was the original guy we were gonna build the whole fuckin' show around and now he might not even show!

"Look, here's how this whole thing's gotta go. We must press on like we got no fucking problems. We must assume that everything is gonna fall into place. Maybe… just maybe this will all work out. I didn't write one-third of a novel last night because I thought we were going to go in half-cocked. I am going into this thing as though we've broken the story of the century… which I think we have. So, don't lose faith, Dillon. Mattingly still told me he would get shit together on his end… of course he wished death on my whole family in the process.

"But, it doesn't matter. We have to put on a winning ballgame no matter who we are playing. Do your thing, Dillon. Get your ass in here and start helping me shape this deal. I mean… God Almighty, I don't even know where to go from here. What I wrote last night, I feel like it's only scratching the surface. If we want to have something real… something special… then I need your help man. I ran out of fairy dust the same time I ran out of coffee. So, get over here and help me, okay?"

- 10 -

All right then, weary travelers and swank seekers of truth. I will not bore you with the blow by blow account of my two-hour conversation with Dillon once he arrived at the office. What I will tell you is this. I realized some very significant points.

I now knew how this thing... our program tonight... had to be structured. And I also knew if shit didn't work out, I'd better have a plan B, C, D, E, and F. About that last part... I'd be lying if I said I had any of these plans, even now. I thought maybe when necessity forced me to come up with them I'd do it, but this right now... this broadcast, it's all I've got. I'm putting it all on the line, right on air, right now. Plan A required every second of my time and every ounce of my focus.

Now, as for what I knew for sure at this moment, I knew I had to structure this series like a story. That's what separated the men from the boys in the radio game. Who could tell the best story? That's what it was all about. And telling the best story means that you can't blow your load in the first chapter... to be quite crass about it.

I couldn't reveal too much in the podcast episodes or else the conclusion would mean nothing. All I could do was tell you folks that we had solved the mystery which I felt would guarantee that you would listen in so you can be part of the elite few who heard it first.

What did this really mean? It meant that if Marianne was successful in getting all of our scheduled guests to appear, then what I needed to do as the host of the *Underground Podcasts* was engage them in discussion on the points everyone already knows about.

If I spent an hour with Barnes and Angstat discussing my own revelations about the case, their segment would be entirely consumed with them asking me questions about what I knew. That would not make for good radio and I knew it.

Dillon and I decided that day we would structure the podcasts as though they were just another opinion piece, like we didn't already know how it all turned out. We'd advertise as though we solved it, but the answer would have to wait until the live show. That was the way to do it; debating already known facts, theories, and thoughts about Cadence Moore with our panel of guests. Then, in the final live show, we would reveal what we knew all along. We decided that was the only way to do it if we had any hope of making this monstrosity of a series a quality piece of business. Again, all this was banking on the fact that our lead was worth a damn. If it wasn't, this show would be legendary, but for all the wrong reasons… and reasons that would mean my ass.

This meant that as we wrote the scripts and even as I ad-libbed it with our guests when show time arrived, I had to act like I knew none of what I actually did know… or at least hoped to know for sure very soon. This was the most difficult challenge of the whole ordeal. I had to converse with my guests like a person who doesn't know any more than the general public does. But that wasn't true. At least it soon would be the furthest thing from the truth if everything went to plan at the Trayce farm.

I cannot say just yet… it's coming soon… but I cannot say just yet what was found that day in Bowmansville with Bastard Bill and the cutters; but, I *can* say that since I had a lead that nobody else did, it required great concentration and determination for me to follow through on this planned format, and play dumb for almost my entire podcast series as I interviewed people and told the Cadence story through memory and flashback, mixed with opinions and arguments.

I used only my previous knowledge of the Cadence case when I debated my guests and discussed the intricacies of the story. I acted as though the previous version of myself was conducting this special… the man who lived in the before time, before the revelatory period during which I met people like Budgie Bailey and Bill Mattingly, the Bastard in Blue. I made the arguments I would have made before I discovered that there was… no pun intended… literally, more to the story.

When it came to my podcasts, and how the whole thing would play to an audience when we made air, I knew that it had to start with what everyone knew, and end with what no one knew… except us, if we knew anything at all.

Without that legendary back story and long-debated conversation points as a foundation, I would not be able to properly point out the gigantic flaws in the *Moore to the Story* film. But, worse yet, my eventual conclusion would lack the proper weight it deserved as the major breakthrough in modern crime that it truly was.

I had to draw back on my previous research and my previous opinions about Cadence Moore, opinions I'd felt very strong about at one time. I had to be willing to sit there and discuss everything from minor points, such as the sanitation pickup day in Dusklight Falls, to major issues like the likelihood that none of the drunken assholes at the Basement party could have seen Jamison Kelly leave his room and return after murdering his girlfriend.

In the interest of storytelling, and in the interest of keeping my guests engaged in thought-provoking debate, I had to act like I *didn't* know what I *did* know, or else my hard-earned interviews with my panel of illustrious guests would be total crap.

That was the plan. But, for this plan to work, I needed to know I still had guests to interview. That required my lovely assistant Marianne Slater and her abilities to convince people to show up at my party, even though the RSVP dates on my invitations were all out of whack. So then…

(Break in Transmission)

"This is Tyler Reubens. I have been in our WHHW studio building listening to this live special. I am beyond furious at this point, but I will not allow that fact to affect the way I address you, the WHHW and UPR listening audience. I will be brief, but I will also be clear. Charlie Marx has lied to everyone, including me, and this special and the advertising and efforts made in support of it have been made under false pretenses. Our downloading data has indicated to us that you, the audience, have a tremendous thirst for the Cadence Moore story and the resolution of that story. In spite of the fact that Charlie Marx has lied, I am going to offer him one final chance to show everyone that he can do what he said he would do and offer a solution to this mystery. He has until the end of this broadcast to do so. If he does not, I am making clear to all of you right now, he will be fired immediately from his *Underground Broadcast* show and we will be pursuing legal action of the highest order against him. If this has all been for nothing, I intend to see him in prison. I sincerely apologize to all of you who have been brought to this program tonight under a veil of lies, and I truly hope we can still bring you an answer. If not, we will all pay a price, but the heaviest price indeed will be paid by Mr. Marx. Every thought and feeling I have right now is telling me to pull the plug and stop this from continuing. However, my first duty is to you, the listener, so I will let this show continue to its conclusion. I hope for Mr. Marx's sake, that conclusion is the one he's promised."

(Resume Transmission)

- 11 -

Well my friends… to say I was not expecting that would be yet another lie, and enough of those have been told. However, I knew Tyler well enough to know he would let us continue and I still hold out hope that by the time this is over, we will have our answer! If that does not happen, then I will accept the consequences. I will deserve them, whatever they are.

I feel honestly as though I may have a nervous breakdown at any moment… I did it to myself; but seriously, who can deal with stress like this? We're coming down to the finish line either way and I will try my best to stay on task and return to our story. Jesus Christ, did Tyler Reubens just seriously break transmission on a live broadcast? Shit, we left Earth a few hours ago, didn't we? Only thing to do now is press on. Press on and solve our mystery.

Okay, so, where were we? Oh, yes, Marianne and our guests… okay, back to that. So… I, yes I was overjoyed when Marianne finally called me two days after our Mom's Diner conversation with Bill. She was excited and giddy. She yelled, "Charlie, I think we're gonna be all right! I saved Barnes and Angstat, Charlie! I saved them and they will be here, in studio, one week from now… to tape their segments! Did you hear me? I saved our best guests. So, what do you say? I thought you'd be jumping for joy and cutting me off as soon as I started talking. What are you sick or hungover or something?"

I jumped in the air and pounded the ceiling of my office and yelled,

"Marianne, you are a fucking goddess, do you know that? I would normally have cut you off, I'm sure, but I just couldn't believe the words you were speaking. I thought Barnes and Angstat were going to tell me to shove it when I threw a new deadline at them. I thought they'd think this whole deal was an amateur piece of crap, and... god... you are just the greatest, do you know that? I was ready for you to tell me how fucked we were. How the hell did you do it? How did you get them to agree?"

Marianne smiled... over the phone I couldn't see her, but I could hear the smile in her voice. She said, "Ye of little faith, Charlie... ye of little faith. I simply called them and said that UPR was changing the whole game on us and now we needed to start taping interviews within a week, even though I knew we had a little more time than that.

"I talked to Todd first and he just laughed... just laughed like I was telling a joke. He said he figured they'd pull some bullshit like that. He was always dealing with administrative types and studios and all that stuff. He said right then and there that it was no big deal and his schedule was free for the next few weeks. He told me I had a nice voice, which probably didn't hurt our case. But in the end, he told me if we needed him in seven days to tape and interview, then he'd make it work."

I was gob smacked, ladies and gentlemen, by what Marianne was telling me. Barnes and Angstat had been complete jerks when I first spoke to them about this show as they got drunk and made fun of me from their bar stools. Now, even after curveballs had come at us from every direction and things appeared to be in shambles, my lovely secretary was able to salvage my most valuable interviews. All I could manage for a reply was, "Jesus, Marianne... just like that. Just like that he says sure, I'll be there in a week. You sure must have put the sweet talk on him."

Marianne smiled again... I could literally hear that beautiful smile and it made me want to drive out to Marianne at the Ridgeview Hotel in Limerick and just make out with her for a while. I wanted to show her how much I loved her for helping me save my own ass. Never mind, of course, that she's married with two kids and has a husband who I both like and respect. Alex... I do apologize, man. But, hey, I just wanted to kiss her. Anyway, where the fuck was I? Oh yeah. I was telling Marianne how great she was and how I thought she must have sweet talked Todd Barnes pretty good.

Marianne replied, "Charlie, when are you going to learn that anytime I talk, it's always sweet. I didn't even tell you about Angstat. Todd conferenced him in on the same phone call with us. At first Michael acted like Todd's call was a huge bother to him. I believe his first words were, 'Dude, I got a fuckin' hard on and a video playing on my screen... what you say better be pretty fucking interesting or I'm hanging up.'

"Todd sighed and introduced me. When Michael realized that Todd had a woman with him on the phone, he said in an embarrassed tone, 'God, I was just kidding. You sound like you're calling me to tell me someone died. All right, so *who's* there with you? Chuck Marx's girl? Put her on, man. I'll talk to her.'

"Todd reminded Michael once again that I'd been listening the entire time. Michael said nothing and probably was just waiting for me to state my business so he could stop feeling completely awkward.

"Like I said, he started out as a jerk, but for some reason... I don't know... maybe he liked the sound of my voice as much as his partner did, but Michael got a lot nicer. I explained the situation."

He said, "Oh, Ms. Marianne... my apologies. I didn't mean to be rude. I think your boss is a bit of a punk, and I'm not surprised he had you call us instead of him. But hey, don't fret, Todd and I will be there in a week, hell, why not? But hey, you tell Charlie for us... you remind him, okay sweetheart? You remind Little Chucky that if his big reveal turns out to be horse shit, then we're pulling every word we said from his podcast. I want to make sure we're all on the same page about that."

"And you know what, Charlie? I covered for you pretty nicely. I said you were juggling UPR and the police and it left you no time to make calls to the guests. But, I told them you wanted them so badly it was keeping you up at night thinking that schedule conflicts would keep this all from happening."

I shook my head while I paced around my office. I couldn't help it. This whole thing was a surreal dreamland event of epic proportions that I'd never experience again for as long as I lived. I laughed, "Oh, that was good

Mary... that was very good. Remind me again... why are you a secretary? You should be one of my damn producers the way you're charming all these motherfuckers. I will tell you in all sincerity that you have made my whole life with this phone call. But, we can't bask in our past glories forever, can we? I don't want to be an ungrateful prick, but we have a lot to put together yet and I still need more answers. So, um... now that we have Barnes and Angstat in a week... in studio... I have to ask... have you gotten anywhere with everyone else?"

Marianne laughed and said, "Oh my, how short-lived your gratitude is. It's all about what I've done for you lately, isn't it?'

I had to admit, "Well, in this business, that's the way it goes, I'm afraid."

"I'm not surprised, she replied. Oh well, your undying thanks for ten seconds was fun at least. Okay, as far as the rest of the guests, I'll spare you the details, but here is the line up for three days... in studio, or on the phone for interviews. Darlene, Stephanie, Jared, Misty, Matt, Jimmy, Meghan, Lita Marie, Paul, Todd Crist, Barnes, Angstat, Andy, Ashley, and... I think that's about it. If I missed anyone, please forgive me. In other words, I saved every fucking guest, Charlie, and you better have some damn good questions ready to fly because you have a three-day stretch to hammer out every bit of interview material that's going to air on the podcasts. I sure hope you're up to it."

I spoke out of turn since I didn't have full say over accounting matters, but I felt confident that I could make it happen when the time came, so I blurted it out. "Marianne, you are a godsend! You just earned yourself a fifteen thousand dollar pay increase come the first of the year. You saved our asses, baby, and I will never be able to properly repay you for that! Goddamn... I can't believe it! I mean, really? Not one of them balked at the new schedule?"

Marianne paused and then answered, "Oh, they balked Charlie. Most of them were not happy and balked quite loudly about the change. Hell, a few of them... Misty Mintz and Meghan Cocuzza come to mind, almost backed out completely when I told them about the bump up. But, it's amazing how much difference a little information can make. When I told them the bombshell you were dropping was so sensitive that you couldn't even tell UPR the details, and that's why they were messing up the schedule, well... you'd be amazed at how exciting those words sound to prospective guests who are considering doing a podcast series."

I marveled at the cunning of this beautiful creature... er... sorry Alex... this wonderful and brilliant professional colleague. I said, "There isn't anything I can say that will properly express my gratitude to you, Marianne. I really can't say it with words. You just... you fucking saved us and I love you for it!"

Marianne was silent for a moment and then said, "Charlie, I always knew you were a good guy and that's why I worked so hard for you over the last few days. And don't think I'm going to forget about that fifteen thousand you promised me. You're on the hook now, buddy!"

Marianne was good humored about it, but I also knew that it was true she'd never forget about my promise of more money and would hold me to it until it happened. That was all right with me. She was worth every penny and then some.

I told her, "Marianne, I'd expect nothing less. And seriously... I might as well just tell you now... I asked you before to tell me why you were still a secretary. Well, I can't wait for your answer on that. I just have to come out and say it... you should consider yourself a producer now... and that's all there is to it. You earned it! You are now co-producer of *Underground Broadcast* and that's how you'll be credited from now on... starting with the live Cadence special."

Marianne released a shriek that sounded like a mix between a wolf howl and a cowboy yahoo. "Charlie Marx, why do you think I have stayed with you so long? Because you treat your people right and I knew you'd come through for me once I delivered. What can I say... you're the best boss, ever! I wish I could kiss you right now."

I thought, *Jesus Christ... so do I!* Oh wait, sorry one more time, Alex... just kidding on that last bit... anyway... what I was trying to say was that my angel secretary goddess had managed to snatch victory from the yellow slobbering jaws of defeat and I owed her lifetimes of gratitude. Three days... that's what she'd set up for me. Three days of interviews with an all-star cast of major players in the Cadence saga.

God, I had a lot of writing to do. But for now, all was right with the world, at least for a few minutes. I left the office on lunch break and called Dillon from the car on my cell. He'd just left a few hours before and was already on his way to check out the Trayce farm site so we'd know what to expect when game day arrived.

- 12 -

Dillon didn't answer his phone when I tried him the first, second, or third time. I decided that I was not going to spend my entire day sitting around listening to a ringing phone drone on and on, mocking me with its refusal to become a human voice.

So, I said fuck it and decided to get drunk. I was feeling quite lonely at this point. I know that's no surprise to hear since I've gone into long, boring, and intricate details about my divorce, failed relationships with two-week-long and month-long girlfriends, and solo nights at my computer boards in several broadcasts you weary travelers have been privy to.

Well, this particular day, with no success in locating Dillon, and the thought of Marianne fresh in my mind, I was quite the vulnerable poor bas-tard in spite of an elated feeling in my stomach knowing that the show was still going to happen and the guests were all salvaged.

But, I was still on the emotional tornado ride and had been now for weeks. I sat there now, the bipolar buffoon, crashing from my high of excite-ment and feeling my sorrows now like a whimpering fool. I'd been turning over in my mind, again and again, the words of my sec… er… I mean my new producer, Marianne.

She told me she wished she was here so she could kiss me. I mean, hold on a sec here… I realize weary travelers that she is happily married and this was never going to happen. Doesn't that suck, friends? When you feel an amazing connection with a person and they just can't seem to see you?

They look on you as the quirky friend, or the interesting conversation-alist, or worst of all, the guy they would like to hook their sister up with because they certainly couldn't interrupt their life long enough to connect with you and act on it. But, you'd get along just great with their fucked-up, usually ugly, veteran of slutty escapades, emotionally-arrested, and much less cool sister.

Well, I was feeling the subtle pricks of these isolated little boy thoughts on this day... this drunken day. I wouldn't have done anything with Marianne for Christ's sake. I wouldn't have flirted or tried to be a dirty dog. I had too much respect for her and her husband to pull the awkward rabbit out of my desperate hat. Nonetheless, I felt like I'd been stung by a wayfaring love wasp and the brief attraction I felt for Marianne was evidence of this.

This confession may cause some awkward moments in the office going forward and some especially awkward moments at company picnics when the family members are invited. But, I learned a long time ago that unless you come right out with it... the honest way you feel... you'll be a stifled and suppressed animal and that's no kind of animal to be.

Anyway, all this was more indicative of my need to feel validated and supported during one of the most trying times of my professional career. When she listens back on this, I don't want Marianne to feel weird or anything. I dug her the way I'd dig any beautiful woman who'd helped me out and flashed a gorgeous smile in my direction, or saved my ass from a forest fire, building collapse, or mass exodus of important radio guests. But this was fleeting and I would always respect boundaries.

Anyway, that's enough of that weak ass shit. I feel it imperative to come right out with it here as we talk, weary travelers, because I will never hide anything from you again. I want you to know that everything I tell you is real and true, no matter how bad it humiliates me in the later moments. This is *real* life we examine on *Underground Broadcast* and anything less would be a shitty show which I refuse to give my weary cherished traveling pals, the great loves of my life.

So, where was I in the timeline? Oh, yes, I was trying to phone my good pal Dillon. Well, guess what? The evasive monkey finally managed to pick up his phone about four hours after my initial attempts to connect with him. And, believe it or not, when he spoke to me... he had some amazing and mind-blowing things to say.

Dillon said, "Charlie… are you there, man? Dude, I had no time for your calls earlier because I was busy at Ted Trayce's farm scoping out our eventual observation site. You want to know what I saw when I got there?"

I replied with an surprised grunt that probably sounded something like a starving Sasquatch after smelling the sweet smoke of a venison bonfire. Then when he stopped explaining what he saw when he got there, I said, "Dillon, for god sake, man… just talk to me… communicate what you will… and let me in. I haven't been sitting here whistling idle love songs with the birds. I've been waiting to get back in touch with you and figure out where the fuck I am in this universe. Jesus, just talk to me, man!"

Dillon said, "Uh… okay, I don't know what any of this means, Charlie, but here's the deal. I drove up to the place. It's fucking huge man. Cornfields, weeping willows, silos, cows and horses around on the edges, but I think I saw it man."

I became suddenly impatient and shouted, "Saw *what*? Stop the dramatic exposition and tell me what you saw!"

Dillon laughed nervously—the kind of laugh you give someone who has interrupted your important story with something mildly amusing. You choose to acknowledge their statement with a fake laugh in hopes they shut up and let you continue. He continued, "I saw the place where Tommy dug in deep and buried poor Cadence. It didn't look any different than the rest of the farmland, man, but I think I had some religious experience while I sat there staring out of my car looking over the sprawling landscape. I was just surveying the place… trying to catch a vibe, and for some reason this one little area seemed like it was… I don't know, man, just different, different from the rest. I don't know what it was, maybe the way the light hit it… but I knew this was the spot. I am talking about the goddamn spot where that low life parasite decided to bury her four feet under… or so. Shit, he couldn't even do it right. He just dug a hole and threw her in. I'm sure it's a shallow grave and I know you're sure of that shit, too although I don't know how that's possible."

These were the ramblings of someone who was sleep deprived and letting their instincts take over. As odd as it sounds, Dillon was probably right.

It all seemed to make some primordial sense in my brain, and for some reason I cannot explain, it felt totally logical that he experienced a kind of magic about this little spot of land where Cadence was buried. Destiny feeds you a biscuit every now and again if you're on the right track. And, in this case, Destiny was just letting Dillon know it was glad to see him.

Dillon went on, "The grave… the circumstances… the whole thing, it wasn't proper or right in any way. I don't know any of this for a fact. Christ, I just pulled my car over there, man… and felt something… I felt something very strong. I don't know, Charlie, I feel fucked up talking about this. I don't want to go to this farm-digging party with Bastard Bill without telling him where to look, beyond all other places, to find the girl we've been searching for. If I don't at least do that, I will have betrayed Cadence… I think. Bill and his cutters could search the whole day and find nothing. I must point them in the right direction. I'm gonna tell him. Even if he thinks I've lost my mind."

I tried to interject here. It seemed that Dillon had crossed over into the surreal valley. Day after day chasing a hunch, scheming with Bastard Bill, trying to produce a major murder mystery series, that as of yet had no goddamn ending… had caught up with him. He really believed he had connected with the truth, that earthly, from-the-bowels of existence kind of truth. And, like I said, he probably had. But even though I can understand this, because I'm open to it, and am even more fried around the edges than my partner, and you weary travelers probably also get the picture, that didn't mean Bill Mattingly was going to understand a word of it. For that reason, and because we couldn't afford to fuck up the mission at this crucial juncture, I tried to talk the excitable boy Dillon down from his trip. "Okay, dude… okay, Mr. Truth Rattler, what do you want to do to make sure nothing gets misinterpreted? What do you want to do to make sure that we tell this story right?"

Dillon snapped back, "Tell it right… you mean like how do we tell him so he doesn't think we're a bunch of crazy assholes who he can no longer trust, and steal it all from us and leave us twisting in the breeze like a couple of dicks?"

I snickered to myself since I knew Dillon was at his wit's end and he could no longer even see straight. I answered, "Yeah man, exactly what you said... that's what I mean."

Dillon yelled "Stay put, fucker! No, get in your damn car right now and meet me at Troops. We are gonna have a conversation and figure this out and get caught up on all the other shit you wanted to tell me. When Bill calls us, which should be by tonight, we need to be ready to go out to that farmhouse singing the exact same song. You agree?"

I said, "Fuck man, I'm already half way there. I've been drinking the last four hours. You should have called before I got started. I'm not safe to drive at this point."

Dillon said, "Bullshit, Charlie, you're the best drunk driver I've ever known in my life. And, if you're already half way there, then Troops is the best place for you. We need to talk, and you're way more agreeable when you're half tuned. So... you gonna meet me or what? You know I'm right. Don't you agree with my assessment that drinking more liquor will make you even more agreeable?"

I said, "Sure, I agree... and I'd agree with even more gusto if I knew you were buying the shots."

Dillon laughed, "National Radio host... revealed as a cheapskate. What scandal. Okay you prick, I'll buy, but that means I get to talk first and talk longer so you better be prepared to shut up."

I answered, "The more I have my lips pressed to a shot glass, the less they'll have a chance to form words. So... I guess that's all up to you, my friend."

- 13 -

Dillon walked in and smiled at the blonde bartender from the outside deck. It's funny, I'd been coming to Troops for years and I still only knew one of the bartenders' names. I knew her well, in fact.

Lovely Danielle Strowman used to be a stripper at the Diamond Club. She had long brown hair and the doughiest doe eyes you ever saw in your life. I actually scored with her one night right after she broke up with her boyfriend. She stayed after hours and got loaded with me. One thing led to another and that's been our secret pact ever since... or... I guess it was until I just announced it on the radio. Sorry Danielle. But you were great, let me tell you.

Anyway, Danielle wasn't working this night and we only had the snobby blonde… I think her name was Jenny… who the fuck knows, at our service, the same chick who couldn't even remember my drink of choice, regardless of the fact that it had been rum and coke for the last three years I'd been coming here. Dillon's was close… but he preferred straight shots of rum and a glass of coke to chase it with. And you probably guessed it, brain-dead blonde couldn't remember his drink either.

So, where was I? Yes, okay, so Dil walked in and smiled at her over the heads of two corporate-looking gents who appeared as though they were getting very close to sexually assaulting their drunken female companion, probably a secretary or junior executive who'd been invited out for some drinks after work and was now being given the 'fuck her up then fuck her' treatment which these two goons in suits had probably perfected into a weekly routine with different hot-ass candidates from the office.

The hot-as-fire redhead junior exec was in the process of letting them drink body shots off her stomach… her business suit hiked up high enough for them to both get their snouts in close. It wouldn't be long now, I thought, as one of the goons signaled to the bartender for another round.

Anyway, Dil poked his head around the gentle corporate rape scene and flashed his Eric Estrada toothy grin at the blonde bartender with the faulty memory, and she smiled back, obviously a forced one. He held up two fingers and the clueless blonde put her hands up in the air as if to say, What? I don't understand.

Dillon yelled "A shaker of Bacardi, two cokes, and two shooters!"

I looked at him as he neared the table and said, "Boy, you talk pretty."

He smiled, "I haven't forgotten what you said, Charles. You promised to shut up and listen if the shots kept coming."

I said, "Hey, man, scouts honor… well you probably need to have been a scout for that to mean anything. Okay, radio superstar's honor. I will not say a word until you've said every single thing you came here to say. And after that, I can say as much as I fucking want to. How does that sound little buddy?"

Dillon shook his head. My slightly obnoxious commentary was making it clear that the bender I'd started back at home base was not yet out of my system and my senses were slightly crooked… this was before the shots flowed. So, who knew where this night was going to end.

Dillon said, "All right, booze hound. I will say my piece and then listen to your ramblings… at least they're entertaining. Not enough entertaining ramblers around these days, Charlie. That's the problem with the world, you know that?"

Forgetful snobby blonde wiggled over to the table and set the shaker, cokes, and two shot glasses in front of us. Dillon handed her his Amex corporate card from WHHW and I smiled. I said, "You sly rodent! You aren't paying for shit! You're expensing this, you midnight ass grabber!"

Dillon burst out laughing at my reference to his alleged manipulation of posteriors in the pale moonlight. Then he sheepishly looked up and said, "All right, Marx… you got me. So… are you still gonna let me talk?"

I laughed too as I poured and put down my first shot. "Oh sure… why stop now? Sure, go ahead… talk your ass off, Mr. Balast… Mr. Big Spending Poser, talk away. I'm over here being too shocked and hurt by your lies to come up with any good points, so you might as well just dominate the conversation."

Dillon nodded and grinned. He said, "Okay then… feel free to have another shot at WHHW's expense. They owe us a lot more than a shaker of *Bacardi* after the shit we've been through."

I looked back at him for a minute and said, "But don't forget… it's not every average Joe that gets to crack the Cadence Moore case and become a national celebrity overnight. Just don't forget why we're doing this, Dillon."

Dillon nodded again and took two quick shots in succession… trying to catch up to me. "I haven't forgotten anything about that. And I wouldn't be giving up days and weeks of my life for it if I didn't believe in this thing. But… it has been a taxing little ride through hell town, wouldn't you say?"

I laughed, "That… I would say. I would say it and say it again until everyone got the fucking picture. Okay, Dillon. You brought me out to Troops so you could tell me about your hidden oasis in the cornfield and your epiphany about the burial site. You want us both to be spouting the same shit when Bastard Bill decides to call, so I guess you better start talking. With our luck, he'll probably call while we're sitting here… getting fucked as the stars come out."

Dillon took another shot and said, "Oh, I wouldn't expect anything less, Charles. That's his style. Shit, he called me back on a lead one time right as I was about ready to come and Joyce was on top loving life and shaking her ass for all it was worth. Boy, I'll tell you what… with the first sound of my voicemail picking up and Bill Mattingly yelling, 'Dillon… Dillon Balast! Pick up, you spic bastard! I got news for you, young man! Pick up! I don't have all day here.' Joyce immediately fell out of ecstasy, shot me the shittiest stink eye you ever dared gaze on in your life, then she rolled off and left me there, balls blue as the sky, and having to deal with Bill's annoying delivery of news while she stormed out of the bedroom."

I put my hand on Dillon's shoulder. I said, "Young man, as Uncle Bill likes to call you, I never considered the sacrifices you made for our show before. This nation owes you a great debt of gratitude. How about whores? Will you teach them things about life, tackle them, or accept them as payment? Do you fear going to jail for any of it? How about dogs? You fuck 'em? Train 'em? Eat 'em? Throw the…"

I trailed off my last word and we both burst out laughing, even though what I said was at best a lame attempt at nonsense comedy. I wasn't drunk enough yet to laugh at such lameness, but Dillon and I didn't care. We had all the alcohol we needed right in front of us and we were about to accomplish what no man in America had been able to do for a decade. Things were good. Things were very good and it was okay to laugh about it. Finally, Dillon said what he came to say. "All right, Marx… that may have been the stupidest thing you've ever said and yet it still makes me laugh my ass off. This is a sign of impeding delirium so we better talk sense while we still have some of it."

I said, "Maybe you just don't want to answer the question about the dogs?"

This time, no smile from Dillon. He was ready for business and one laugh was all I was getting from Mr. Balast tonight, until he said his piece. He said, "Charlie… cool it now, all right? What I saw out at Trayce farm, man... it was real. It was like being stuck in the pitch dark, feeling around for the light, and not able to see anything, but still feeling a presence in the room. You don't see it per se, but you feel it. Well... today... out in cow country... I felt it. I felt the spot, man. I'd bet my life on it that if the cutters dig there, we find Cadence... just like that. So, what I want now is for you to help me figure out how we broach my little psychic vision to Bill without him thinking we're kooks and deciding to ditch us."

I looked down at my hands. A note I'd written earlier in marker on my palm still said, 'Guests Saved... call Dil, call Fred Todek in Acct, Mary—raise' in faded letters on my left palm. I looked back up and told him, "I'm not sure we *should,* Dillon. I believe in what you're saying... don't think I'm doubting you. But what does telling Bill really do for us? I mean, they're gonna search the farm and find whatever's there anyway? Why risk our credibility by talking about visions in the cornfields?"

Dillon downed another shot and said, "That's the thing I'm worried about. What if she's there and they don't find her. If I can point them in the right direction and it turns out my vision is correct, we can be sure they find Cadence... no fuck ups allowed, right?"

I shook my head. "That's not how Bill's gonna see it, man. He's a cop. These fuckers are all about the evidence and facts and what they see with their eyes... not with their minds. You know him well enough to know that."

Dillon looked almost frantic and said, "But, I can't just ignore this shit, Charlie. You get that, right? It's not every damn day that a person has a fucking vision, is it? What's the use if I keep it to myself?"

I gave an honest moment of thought to what Dillon had just asked me. I replied carefully, knowing this meant a lot to him and we'd reached a point where I had to be delicate or he'd be insulted, and then I'd have an argument to deal with. "You're right, Dillon. It must be shared. But let's do it in a way where we don't give up too much too soon. Let's sit back and allow Bill and the cutters to gut the place and if they come up empty, then we'll suggest the spot in the cornfields where the gods revealed her to you. But, if they find her first, then it's really all the same, right? You feel that?"

Dillon dunked down two more shots in quick succession. I'd never seen him drink this fast before. I was the alcoholic member of our little tag team and he was usually three-drink-Pete and the designated driver. But these were complicated times and Dillon was feeling the pressure. He heard me though. He still had enough good sense to see reason in what I was saying.

He said, "Okay, Charlie. But I'm not going to wait too long. I don't want Bill to get fed up after two hours and go off in a huff, and then refuse to even search the spot I had the vision about. But if you want to let them search for a while and see what happens... I can live with that. I'm just telling you, we're not leaving that place until we find what we came for."

"And that, Dillon... *I* can live with. Okay... so we're all settled on the vision situation. Now, do you want to know why I made all those calls to you today?"

Dillon smiled, "Of course, but even if I didn't, that wouldn't stop you from telling me, would it?"

I returned the grin, "It will not... you have that right. Okay, well guess who my new hero is?"

Dillon shrugged, "Could it be... your good friend and producer who has newly discovered psychic powers?"

I laughed, "It could be... but it's not. Sorry. But your new super powers are impressive. No, my new hero is the lovely and talented Marianne Slater, your associate producer."

Dillon squinted and said, "Hold on... when did *your* secretary become *my* associate producer?"

I said, "Today. Since she saved the fuckin' show. Since today. Every goddamn guest we had lined up... we could have lost them all. But this woman worked magic, man... I won't get into all the details, but listen, she saved our asses. Every single fucking guest we could have lost... she secured them... for a three-day block in a week. All of them."

Dillon asked, "Angstat? Barnes? Kelly? They all agreed to the new schedule?"

I nodded as he mentioned each name and then couldn't help but laugh, "All three, my good man, and all the rest of them, too. This woman is a sorceress. There's no debating that. She did it and I paid her back the only way I could. I immediately promoted her on the spot… and then… fantasized about her for the next several hours. I was in a weird mood, so… don't judge me."

Dillon clapped his hands together and turned the shaker upside down. Already empty. He yelled up to the bar, "Darling… let's do the sequel to our little movie here, okay?" Once again the blonde bimbo (her name I'm pretty sure was Jenny but she would always be bad-memory blonde and several other variations of that to me) looks over at Dillon and holds her hands up like she doesn't know what he wants.

She finally wiggled over again… that ass of hers seemed to be viciously fighting with itself over which magnetic pole to be attracted to and neither side was winning. She comes over and asks, "What were you guys drinking again?" I shook my head… with a memory like that, how did she last so fucking long in the bartending business. Her tip jar probably resembled a recently cleaned wishing well with a few spare pennies and some dirt.

Dillon had to break it down simply for her so we could get our damn fresh shaker and finish the conversation. Dillon said, "God, she sucks. At least that Danielle chick moves her ass and remembers my damn order. Christ… this one? Anyway, I don't judge you, Charlie. Marianne's hot as fuck and we both know it. And besides, if she managed to get every guest locked in on an altered schedule, I'd have given her a promotion, too. Didn't any of them give her shit about the changes?"

I nodded, "Oh yeah, this was no easy task. Angstat was shamed into it so we got lucky there. That's a funny story I'll share with you an- other time. Apparently, Meghan Cocuzza and Misty Mintz both threatened to back out, but Marianne must have come up with some good bullshit because she ended up getting confirmed dates from both of them when all was said and done."

Dillon smiled and looked up at the sky. The stars were out and the night was clear and cool. It felt good sitting at that table, getting loaded, and real- izing we were winning. We still had the biggest hurdle of them all ahead of us and if Cadence wasn't found at Trayce's farm, this special would burn to the ground, quickly and violently. Still, for now… with what we had to work with... we were winning.

The Blonde returned with the shaker and some more cokes. She asked if we wanted to close out and Dillon waved her off. She smiled in that forced way of hers and huffed away. I said, "Dil, I think I have psychic powers, too. I see... I see... a severe lack of tip in this young waitress's future."

Dillon laughed, "Wow, that's amazing... I see it too."

We burst out laughing again and each downed another shot. I was just about to comment on a petite little brunette seated at the bar in such a position that half her bare ass was staring us in the face, when Dillon's phone rang. The theme song from the movie *Jaws* played and I knew immediately that was the ringtone Dil had set for the one and only Bastard Bill.

- 14 -

Dillon picked up the phone and excitedly said, "Bill, I'm glad you called. Here, let me put you on speaker... Charlie's here with me, too, and we've been scoring home runs over here. How are things on your end? Did you get in to see Sterling Forsyth about the warrant for the Trayce farm?"

Dillon's smile faded as Bill began to rant. "Shut up, Dillon! Ya know what? Both you assholes better shut up and listen to what I have to say. I'm not happy. I sure wasn't happy when your buddy Marx calls me and tells me we got three weeks to complete our operation. I sure wasn't happy to see Sterling Forsyth hobbling around and telling me he'd got fuckin' cancer in his spine and this was his last week on the job. He still did me the favor because he's one of the last good guys left, but it broke my damn heart to see him like that. So, yeah... not too fuckin' happy about those things, and I sure as hell wasn't too happy when my people told me they saw some spic that looked a lot like Dillon Balast hangin' around the Trayce farm this afternoon. One of you little pricks want to let me in on what the fuck you're doin'?"

Dillon was caught off guard and searched for the right words. "Whoa... wait a second Bill, that wasn't anything... I was... I was just scoping the place out. I don't understand why you'd be so angry about that. You said you had people there, too. That's how you knew about me. I'm not trying to be rude here, Bill… but what is the difference between your people and what I was doing?"

Bill barked, "I believe I asked you very politely to shut the fuck up, Dillon. You wanna know what the fuckin' difference is? I'll tell you what it is. I'm the investigating officer on this case. *You* are a couple of radio jocks. You don't even take a piss by the side of the road within a mile of Ted Trayce's farm without telling me about it first. My guys weren't there. They were watching… from a distance! You… you dumb spic… you just parked right in the goddamn front of the house. Christ, you must be a fuckin' moron!"

I chimed in, a definite mistake but I couldn't help myself. "Hold on, Bill… now you're flying off the handle here and you seem to forget we brought this whole thing to you in a gift-wrapped package. You're the investigating officer on this because we turned an ice-cold case into a hot one, and now you have something to investigate. We're not making speculation films like *Moore to the Story* here… we got a real chance at solving this because of new information that no one else has. You didn't give a second thought to Cadence Moore in the day-to-day course of your job before *we* brought her to you. So, keep in mind… we're as big a part of it as you are. Now, I get it… you're angry at Dillon for scoping the place out, on my orders by the way, but really, what damage did that do? He just wanted to see what we were going to be dealing with as far as a search effort."

Bill screamed, "Fuck you, Marx! Shut up! You didn't hand me shit! You should be glad I even considered joining forces with you, stupid assholes. And you don't get shit. You don't know what damage he did? That *proves* you don't get shit. I got a simple question for you both. In all those years Tommy Trayce was in prison, don't you think it's even remotely possible that he spoke to his parents? Don't you think he may have given them a heads up along the way about a fucking body he buried in the fields? Now, I'm sure you know-it-alls will think that's ridiculous and he tried to hide it from them when he did it in the first place. And you might be right. But, might is a weak word boys… a really weak word. Might doesn't mean shit. It means you still take fuckin' precautions. So, I ask you again… do you see the harm now in parking your car right out in front of the Trayce's land and sitting there staring? Do you think that maybe… on the off chance that Ted Trayce knows what his son did… that maybe your actions tipped him off and he decided to relocate our dream girl? Maybe put her through the fuckin' wood chipper and feed her to the hogs? My guess… you two boys never even considered this. You know why? 'Cause you're not cops. You're radio jocks and you're a couple of douche bags, too!"

Dillon spoke up quietly. "Bill, man, I'm so sorry. You're right. We didn't think of it. I honestly… truly, just wanted to get a feel for the place, like… a lay of the land, ya know? And, I got some strong feelings when I was there… I was meaning to tell you."

I winced at Dillon's allusion to his cornfield visions. I furiously made a zipping motion over my lips and looked at Dillon straight in the eye. He knew I was telling him to shut the fuck up, and thank god… he did.

Bastard Bill went on some more, "Dillon, you're a stupid motherfucker and you did a stupid thing. I will forgive you for this eventually because I like you, kid. Listen, I want you yahoos to understand the seriousness of stupid actions without clearing them with me beforehand. I don't think Ted was in his farmhouse looking out the window, and I don't think he decided to undo the handiwork of his twisted son. I don't think that because my people saw the man leave the property several minutes before your stupid ass arrived. But, just the same, you didn't even allow for precautions to be taken on the off chance that he was there watching and knew what the damn score was. My big problem here, you two… is that we had a deal and when you deviate from the deal and start doing things you don't tell me about, I get scared and start thinking my partners are a bunch of loons who are up to no good when I'm not there to corral their dumb asses. So please, give me some fuckin' confidence and tell me that you will no longer make a single move unless I clear it beforehand."

I lost it. Even though I'd just tried to keep Dillon from saying too much and wrecking things, I couldn't stand Bill talking to us like this after we'd handed him the case of a lifetime. I yelled right back at him, "Fuck that, Mattingly. We're *trying* to do this by the book. Do you realize Dillon and I could have gone out to the Trayce farm alone… without involving any cops, and dug around until we found Cadence Moore ourselves? You think any cop in Pennsylvania wouldn't have dropped trespassing charges in exchange for the ability to solve the Cadence Moore mystery? We would have walked, Bill. We would have walked and still been able to partake in the glory and renown that any solver of a legendary case is bound to receive from the adoring public. But no... we didn't do that. We involved the police, and more than that, we involved a member of the police that Dillon knew and trusted.

"Now, you're telling us that you run the whole show here and we need to shut up and listen to what you tell us and act on your orders. I never needed permission for any show I've ever done for UPR, and I don't need permission for this one. What makes you think I'm going to sit here and let us be victim to your fits and tantrums? You've oversold yourself, Bill Mattingly, on your own influence and capabilities. You don't control us, so please... for all of our sakes... stop pretending like you do."

There was a long pause of tense silence, lasting many seconds. While we waited for Bill's response, Dillon looked at me with panic, like he thought I'd fucked up the whole thing. He was bursting at the seams to say something, but he held strong and remained silent.

Bill responded with a hint of regret and calm, "I'm really stressed here. I've been thinking about this case nonstop since we spoke at the diner. I'll be able to retire and call it a career once we're through with this thing. I can do speaking tours, maybe even with you fellas. I can write a book. I can appear on talk shows. Don't think for a second that I don't understand how important this all is. But, I need to know that you guys aren't working against me. That's all. That's the reason I went off on you. I need you to trust me to do my part on this thing. I'm the cop and you're the radio jocks. There's no harm or shame in any of it, but let's at least play our proper parts. You can take the lead in the structure of our eventual radio reveal... and let me take the lead in the investigation. Is that too much to ask, Dillon?"

I found it interesting that Bill chose to address Dillon at this point, since I was the one who'd challenged him. Like I said before, there are no better psychologists on earth than cops.

Dillon said, "No, Bill. Both Charlie and I agree. That is not too much to ask. I'm sorry, man. I shouldn't have been out at that farm without you knowing about it. I just wanted to get a feel for it. But, after listening to what you've said, I get why you're pissed off."

Bill answered, "Okay, that's really the whole point of my little freak out tonight, boys. I just want you to know how delicate the territory is where you currently tread your feet. You can't just brazenly go around scoping things out. You could get arrested before you'd ever find a goddamn thing. I know about this stuff, fellas because I'm a cop and you're not. So, please… just be careful and run the shit by me next time, okay?"

I took over the conversation. Dillon and I must have downed at least five or six shots in the time it took Bill to dress us down verbally and declare himself the leader of this investigation. The forgetful blonde came back and asked again about closing out. This time Dillon nodded and never even looked once in her direction. She was gone and back again in fifty seconds with a receipt for the drinks and a request for a signature. Dillon added a fifty-cent tip to the receipt. He did not like this woman and made sure his feelings were obvious.

But hey, I agreed she sucked and didn't deserve a real tip. Once Bimbo Blonde gave us her last dirty look, the one that came when she looked at the receipt and realized she'd been stiffed, Dillon and I continued listening to Bill rant and then eventually calm down.

When Bill finished, I said, "Detective… we respect your experience and knowledge. The last thing we want to do is upset the balance of your investigation. But we have a show to do, and we have interests at that farm. I wanted one of my own to go out there, see it for himself, and report back anything worth reporting. If that was wrong, then we're sorry. But we're still in this to win and we were trying to do all that was necessary to come out swinging when digging day finally arrives. When does digging day actually arrive? So far, you told us about Sterling… pity about his health, by the way… and I mean that, Bill. But, you saw him and said he did you the favor anyway. I assume this means you have a warrant now to search the Trayce farm. If that's true, please tell us. When can we expect to make a joint visit to the Trayce farm and see what we can actually find there?"

Bill said, "Let me make this quick and easy, guys. We are searching

Trayce farm in three days. You are welcome to come and watch us do the search and add your two cents about our conclusions. But, the rest of this job is between me and the cutters. You fellas sure you'll be okay with that?"

I answered for both of us. "Bill, we wouldn't have it any other way. The only thing we ask is that you take us to Mom's Diner again after we dig up the farm so we can have a nice pleasant conversation and you can confirm what we hope will be the findings of a lifetime. And, I have my heart set on getting that blonde waitress's phone number while we're there. Do you think you can make all that happen for us, Detective?"

Bill laughed at my comments. He seemed to be loosening up now. He said, "Marx, you are one strange motherfucker. Okay, yeah. Let's do that. Let's meet at the diner after the search and have a little meeting of all involved minds. Then we'll talk about how to proceed with the show and I'll know what I need to do for the press portion. Although, Charlie... I gotta tell you... you're no Dillon. You don't have that spic charm and I don't think you've got a chance in hell with that little blonde piece of ass serving up cheeseburger clubs at Moms. But, hell, if you want to dream about it, you go right ahead. Here's the situation fellas. I've got too much work to do over the next few days to be corresponding with you. So, I will see you at the Conch Gas Station off Route 568, a mile and a half from the Trayce farm... in three days. That is where we'll meet and that is where I'll give you boys a breakdown of your limitations... including where you can park, how long you can stay, etcetera. Be there at 7:00 a.m. or you'll miss the whole thing. And... this is important. Do not make a fuckin' move... don't even start the engine of your car until I call. If I don't call, that means something went wrong and you need to call *me* right away. Otherwise, just wait for that friendly phone call and meet me at Conch. Then we take the riches left there for the taking. Does that sound satisfactory to you boys?"

Dillon ended the conversation for us by saying... very simply, "Cool, Bill. Thanks again. You really are making the crucial difference for us here and don't think we don't appreciate it."

Bill ended his part of the conversation with something that sounded cryptic at the time, and only now do I realize how significant it was, actually.

Bill said, "Oh, I know you guys appreciate me… and you're gonna find out real soon why that appreciation is warranted. Don't ever sell a fuckin' mastermind short… life lesson, boys… take it for what it is worth."

At that point Bill hung up and we were left there at Troops, drunk, fired up, and excited. Three days, man… three days until our date with destiny. We had to start getting ready… of course, and we needed to get some sleep before all that. I bid my good buddy adieu and we left Troops separately, each returning to respective resting places where we'd feel calm and relaxed when the time came.

- 15 -

For me, that resting place was my bedroom… in a modest little apartment house at the top of Mount Penn, where every night I fell asleep to the muted, spoken word poetry sessions, heard through the walls of my next door neighbor and his hipster intellectual poetry pals. I went over there one night, smoked a bit of the ganja… and tried to be part of the scene, but, it was too hard… those fuckers were hardcore and I just didn't fit in. These were the types of hippy assholes who would stand in front of the Capitol, smoking up and strumming ukuleles, while soldiers mowed them down with assault rifles. They were the real deal and I decided I wasn't part of their scene.

After that, I amused myself by listening in through the walls of the apartment and catching some good shit now and again. While I was resting up for my call from Bill and the most significant day of my life, I took to the drink… put on some wonderful tunes, and listened to the poets next door.

I think they had an amateur Bukowski wannabe that week, because I heard loud belches and sounds of simulated regurgitation as the verses rang out in the night. But it was cool, you know what I mean? Anything interesting is cooler than the blasé shit we are subjected to day to day from the trolls that traipse along the streets, subjecting us all to their annoying presence and idiotic uttering.

I related to these hippy poets, and even their little junior tag-along crew…

the hipsters… guys who were dressing the part but had no fucking idea what the scene was really about, and what living your life for an ideal actually meant. I was once a twenty-year-old hipster mid-streamer, not knowing where I should go or what cause I should fight for. For some, that angst turns into violence and troublemaking. For others, that feeling of needing to do something actually turns *into* something. In my case, it turned into a radio show and a weekly stab at pulling truth out of long-gone cover-ups and mysteries.

We were in the middle of the biggest one we'd ever encountered as I sat here trying to get drowsy enough to fall asleep, propped up in my bed reading *Conquest of the Useless* by Herzog, and attempting to pull some sense out of the ramblings of amateur Bukowski next door. Yes, for better or worse weary travel buddies, this was my resting place.

For Dillon, his resting zone was usually with his girlfriend, Joyce, his fiery true love who was not above yelling at a drunken friend making goofy phone calls in the night. Well, in the three days we waited to meet Bill Mattingly at the Trayce farm, Dillon oddly did not spend it with Joyce. Instead, he rented a room at the local Sheraton and got loaded every night. He told Joyce, on a cell phone call from Trooper Thorn's parking lot, in fact, that he needed to go away for a few days until he put the last few pieces together.

Joyce, being the understanding angel she was, agreed to this and told Dillon she couldn't wait to see him when this was all finally over. God, what a woman! I wished I had someone that incredible to share a life with. You know how many chicks I've loved and lost in my lifetime who would have told me to go straight to hell and fuck the devil before allowing me to abandon them for an unspecified amount of time to do a secret show that I refused to tell them anything about? Man, I am telling you right now… Dillon better hang on to the lady he's got because he won't see another one like her, not if he lives to be five hundred. Why did all that relationship luck go to a shifty bastard like him and not me?

Oh well, c'est la vie. What can a person do? I would have to settle for solving the biggest crime in modern history. That would have to be enough to quell my desperate ego and make me feel like one of the big fish in the pond… at least for a few minutes.

I added this little observation jazz at the beginning of this section because I wanted you weary travelers to have a buffer. A buffer is important between not-so-important news and the kind of news that requires a second and third read before it sinks in, due to the sheer magnitude it contains. Well brothers, this is the type of news I'm about to lay on you. Where to start. Where to start? That is the question on my mind as I muddle through this script, unsure of how to proceed, and unsure if all has been lost completely... forever more.

I guess the only way to begin something like this is at... well, the beginning. Bastard Bill threw us a curveball when we called him on that third day at 8:00 o'clock in the morning. Dillon and I met at the studio at 6:00 a.m. for coffee and fried chicken, the cold leftover variety, which was truly the best way to eat chicken. We were discussing the universe we were about to shake up and we began wondering why we hadn't heard from Bill yet. My car was gassed up, we were ready to rock and roll, yet Bill had not called us and we'd expected to hear from him by the first crack of dawn and the off-key uttering of a long-off rooster.

But, we heard nothing. Seven he had said. We were to meet him at Conch Station. But not before he called. He made that quite clear. So, here we were an hour later, and still no call from Bill. No calls, no texts, no nothing. It was 8:00 a.m. now, we were both juiced on coffee and we needed to know what the fuck was going on. I suggested that Dillon, who Bastard Bill seemed to like and respect, as opposed to me who he seemed to be disgusted and pissed off at, call and find out what was going on and find out when we should start spinning wheels to meet him out in the middle of farmland nowhere.

Finally, when we could wait no longer, Dillon dialed Bill's number. He picked up right away and just from the tone of his voice I should have known something was not right here, travelers. Something was definitely wrong. Bill spoke with glee... I know that sounds weird my friends, but that's the only explanation of his tone of voice that truly describes the giddy tones in which he spoke to us that morning. Bill nearly sang, "Boys... Boys, my favorite boys. You were probably expecting to hear from me by now."

Dillon added... naturally, "Well, Bill, of course. You said three days and we waited three days. Yet, we heard nothing. Has something gone wrong? Do we have to worry about yet *another* complication?"

Bill replied, in the same cocky and mocking tone he'd spoke in before, "Oh no, Dillon, no complications for me at all. Everything is as it should be and I have not a worry in the world. How are you fellas doing?"

I could tell only by the way Bill was speaking that he'd pulled a burn on us. I knew we were fucked and now needed to know the degree to which we were fucked. I yelled, "Goddamn it, Detective, we're waiting on pins and needles here, man. Come out with it if you've got something. We can be out to Bowmansville in half an hour. Is it time to make this happen or what?" I knew before he even answered that we weren't going anywhere today.

Bill yelled right back, "Wow, kind of hot under the collar there aren't you, Charlie boy? Listen, you fellas can drive out to Bowmansville if you like, but I'm afraid all you'll find is some lonely cows and a stench of shit in the air. Sorry to have to be the guy that breaks it to you, but there is no longer anything in Bowmansville that you boys would be interested in."

Dillon spoke up with urgent insistence, "What the fuck are you talking about? We had a deal. We had a fucking plan, Bill. What are you saying right now?"

I knew what was coming and braced myself for it. I lit a cigarette and downed three quarters of my cup of coffee. I wanted to be ready for a shock to the system and that was certainly what we were about to get.

Bill answered, "Oh, a deal you say? What's that? Isn't that the type of thing people make with each other in trust and confidence? Well, I'm sure you know by now, Dillon, my trust and confidence in you idiots was shaken and destroyed the day you decided to do surveillance work at the Trayce farm. At that point, I knew I'd have to prove my control in this situation to you since you guys seemed to think you were running the fucking show. Well how is this for a cold morning dose of reality? You guys made me worry about trusting you so I decided to cut you out of my plans for the time being. I went and searched Trayce farm with the cutters the very next morning after our last phone conversation. Before you twits even decided to sit down and get loaded that night, I'd already called my guys and arranged a search the very next morning. Of course, you would have been a part of it all, but you had to go and get tricky on me. You had to pull a fast one on Bill Mattingly. Ouch, very sorry, but… big mistake guys. Your bullshit didn't sit too well with me and even though I led you to believe my response to your little maneuver was just a warning, that was not the case. I decided to make a move. I needed to make sure that whatever happened out there at Trayce farm, I still had the upper hand so your irrational behavior couldn't screw my pooch. I don't like when my pooch is screwed, dudes, especially by a couple of emotional and unstable bitches like you two fags. And… well, that leads us to this call. I knew it wouldn't be long. I didn't even waste my time or energy trying to call you this morning because I knew it wouldn't take long. Yeah, I waited for that urgent nervous call, signifying your worry and concern, and you're right on time. Well, let me tell you assholes… that worry of yours… it's justified. You sons of bitches just lost every card you planned on playing with me. Things are gonna happen my way from here on in. You want to know what *my* way entails? You want to know what plan you boys are following now? If you do, I'd be happy to tell you."

I yelled, "*Your* way? *Your* fucking way, Bill? Jesus, I'm starting to think we have nothing else to talk about. You don't have the upper hand because without my show, this story gets no media. You really don't have shit, detective!"

Bill replied, "No media, Marx? Who do you think you're pitching to? Cadence Moore is bigger than all of us put together. You said it yourself, jackass… this type of case being solved renders all other dumbass actions meaningless and for naught, as long as the story gets told properly with a little thing called entertainment value for good measure, which I know even you amateurs understand. And don't think I don't know what you're doing. You're trying to piss me off by saying I've got nothing, so then I'll feel the need to prove to you what I've got and reveal what I found out there at the farm. Well, you picked the wrong cop to play for a fool, Charlie Marx. Here's the skinny. I could take this thing to any journalist in America and be on the air within minutes. I could add in a little colorful artistic license and make this story hotter than those guys who made the *Moore to the Story* documentary. So, don't even waste my goddamn time with your little threats about your radio show being the only place I can take this shit to. Now that I've laid the truth out for you fuckers, I suppose it's time to talk turkey. Where shall I start? You can write whatever fuckin' script you want. You can describe our dealings with one another and you can describe every conversation you've had but when it all comes out in the wastebasket boys, you're going to need an ending. You need a conclusion to all the talk, all the theories, all the opinions, and all the stories. At the end of it all, you need to produce Cadence Moore, and you can't do that without me. Do we understand each other now?"

Dillon yelled back into the phone, "You stupid cocksucker! I kept you in the money by bringing you on as a consultant on those fucking shows. I did this even as you were losing your rep and every one of your partners figured you for an obnoxious and rule-breaking loser. Why would you fuck us? I never did you wrong, Bill. Why fuck us now when we're so close?"

It didn't take Bill Mattingly long to come up with an appropriate response to this accusation. He screamed back, "You threw me a bone? That's what you're trying to tell me? Dillon, don't make a fool of yourself. I helped you on your little cases because I liked you and because, regardless of what you might think, I care about cases getting solved and getting solved the right way. But this thing of ours… this little three-man secret… don't try to bullshit me about loyalty, favors, or respect. You douches tried to get the upper hand on me before I even thought about playing dirty with you. You surveyed the farm without telling me and it was at that moment I realized I had to do something drastic to make you boys realize it wasn't going to be so easy to get rid of Bastard Bill, the name I know you refer to me by behind my back, just because you heard about it.

"I know a lot more than you little fuckers think I do. When you made it obvious you thought you were the masters and I was your little lap dog, I knew the time had come to put things into a proper perspective for you. Here I am fellas… armed and ready with the information that is going to make you heel quick and easy like a couple of good pups. How does that feel? You like being turned into dogs? You like barking and howling for your supper? Well, too bad if you don't.

"I searched the Trayce farm and I may or may not have found something there. You'll never know. Correction, you'll know when the time is right... as long as you play ball and do your parts. I'm talking about the parts you were destined to play... as radio jock assholes, creating the scene and the setup for my grand reveal of the facts, whatever they may be. I have you fuckers right where I've wanted you from the start.

"You don't know if I've found Cadence Moore for you or not. You don't know if continuing to work with me means that you'll achieve your wildest dreams, or whether you'll be made to look like lying con men in front of millions of people. The choice is yours guys. It always has been. If I show up at the last minute in your studio... with press flocking around me... then you'll know I found something at the farm. If you finish your little show, with nothing to actually show the public, and I am nowhere to be found, well boys, you'll know that means that you are shit out of luck and Bastard Bill has decided to pursue other interests.

"You fucked me over good with my people when they caught you spying on the farm scene without my blessing. They thought I didn't have you little animals on a leash. Now, I'm going to fuck *you* over and you won't know if you're blessed or cursed before they start counting you down for the final segment of your show. Hey, Marx, how will it feel, if instead of having a microphone in your hand interviewing me, you'll be standing there like a horse's ass holding nothing but your limp wang? How do you like the way life has decided to screw with you? How does it feel? That's why I answered your call. I just need to know how it feels... because... well, I get off on that shit boys. I really do. I get off on it. So please, spare me no precious details... how fucked do you feel right now at this moment?"

I honestly can't tell you weary travelers how incensed Dillon and I both felt as Bill Mattingly revealed how he'd reared us right up the collective ass.

Thinking back, I would have liked to ask Bill where he was at that moment and drove over there to beat every ounce of shit right out of him. But that isn't the way it went down. I was more concerned with the show. The show was my baby and I needed to know it still had a chance to live. Everything else was secondary.

So, I said to Bill, "Wow… you put a little trust in someone. Okay, you fucking retched dickhead, since you hold all the cards now and we don't know if you found a goddamned morsel of evidence at Ted Trayce's farm, how exactly *should* we proceed? You want us to plan a whole radio show around the notion that we'll reveal the truth about Cadence, only to leave the final moment of destiny in your fuckin' reptilian hands?"

Bill laughed… a sick dysfunctional laugh, the kind uttered by a child-craving rodeo clown pretending to yahoo and yippee while the youngsters writhe in the crowd and he secretly explodes with passion and desire, while still trying to hold his external façade in place. He said, "You can only proceed in one direction, Charlie. You have all those podcasts in the can or damn near it by now I have to think. You have to run the live show now or the whole thing's a dud and your career is curtains anyway. If I never show up… well, I guess you clever assholes will have to think of something. If I *do* show up, then all this has gone according to plan and you will be ready to kiss my ass in gratitude and worship since I will have handed you the keys to fame and fortune. So yeah, write your show the way you planned. Tell the world you solved Cadence Moore. In the meantime, you can enjoy yourselves waiting on your cop partner who could either save your reputations or bury you. The choice is mine and I feel pretty fucking good about that right now boys. I'd be lying if I said anything different."

I snapped back, "Hey, Bill, so I just want to get this thing right here. You are pissed off at the nerve of our team for going behind your back and scoping out Trayce farm. Because of that, you decided to dig up the farm two days ahead of schedule. Now you know something we don't. You know for a fact if Cadence Moore was buried out there and you're using the secret knowledge that only you possess to blackmail us and make us play ball by your rules. Do I have it right so far? I mean, shit. This is easy for you right? You haven't been publicly attached to this case yet. You can play games anonymously and the rest of us have to stake our entire fuckin' careers on it. Do I have it right so far? You used us to get where you wanted to be and now you're trying to steal the moment and have us sucking you off in fear while you fuck around and decide whether to boost us or betray us. Do I have it right so far, Detective? Do I have this shit right or wrong?"

Bill laughed again… oh god how I wanted to be where he was right now, armed with a knife so I could stab out his larynx and render him unable to laugh again. Bill answered, "Oh, yes, Charlie Marx… you've got it right, my friend. I hold all the cards m'boy and you hold none. That's the way it is and you better get used to it."

Like I said before, the logistical operation of my show was foremost in my mind and I needed to probe somewhat and find out if Bill had fucked us completely, or just fucked us enough to require a painful and clueless trip out to the finish line and over the horizon. Because I needed answers, I figured I better go for it all right now while I had the man on the line. Dillon, for his part had been stunned into silence and was just shaking his head, unable to verbalize the chaos and confusion that now occupied his mind.

I said, "You certainly are a resourceful asshole. You have the one piece of evidence we need to proceed here and now you've decided to keep it for yourself. Wow, what a tremendous sack of shit you are, Bill Mattingly. I don't have the proper words to describe my complete contempt and disgust for you. You may have forgotten about this by now, but we still have a little thing called legal matters to deal with. I told every guest we had that we'd solved the case and they better sign on and be a part of my show. I made them all sign gag orders that forbade them from speaking out on any of this, or any of our conclusions lest they be subject to multi-million dollar lawsuits. But, I also had to promise them the first right of refusal if they didn't like the conclusion we came up with. That means they have the legal ability to keep their own comments from ever airing. Now you might not grasp this fully, Bill, but I'll explain it so you can understand. It was reckless and sloppy of us to promise these guests anything since, at best, we had a conspiracy theory on this case no more valid than any number of half-baked theories that have been put out there in the last ten years. So, I ask you, what *am* I supposed to tell these people since I have put my balls on the line and promised them an explanation of our findings. Our plan up until now was to try our best to solve this case before podcast time, and then in the last hours before we released them for download, I would contact all the guests and reveal all the answers. Do you get what that means Bill? It means they can all pull their interviews if they don't like what I tell them.

"Now, what *would* have happened before your fat ass entered the picture is we would have tried to solve Cadence and, if we failed, the interviews on the podcasts would be history and our live broadcast would get a last-minute ax. Then both of our careers would be over. Of course, all of that could still happen. But now that you're our partner in crime, and you've decided to hold the information until the last half hour of the live broadcast, you are gonna have to pull off quite a trick if you plan on revealing something on the air... of a broadcast that never *makes* air. You catchin' my drift, old bogey? You're holding a knife to the necks of two guys already strapped down under the guillotine. So, just for my own amusement, I'd really like to know what you think we should do since you're out in the cold and all alone if this thing never airs."

Dillon looked up at me and a sly smile crossed his lips. He knew I'd caught Bill off guard. Mattingly could, of course, still go to another media outlet but we both knew he wanted the Cadence case to be solved live on UPR, the pinnacle of public broadcasting, and he wanted to be the guy to do it. All the forecasts and surveys for potential audience interest in the live broadcast were off the charts and Bill knew it. This was going to be legendary if it came off the way we all wanted it to. He could go on the Midnight Show. He could go on 30/30. He could go anywhere, but this was hot... this was new... and this was what people were interested in. He knew it and wanted a big hefty slice of it.

If our live broadcast never aired, he would still get his name out there, but not on the stage he wanted. He also wouldn't have his last second dramatic main event spot on the show either. He would have to settle for a press conference and some interviews and that was way too typical for a glory hound like Bastard Bill.

Bill spoke, revealing a lot more than he wanted to with his next words. He tried to act smug like he didn't care, but we could hear the nerves in his voice. He didn't want this thing to blow up and never happen, he couldn't! Not after all this. How we hoped that was true... God in Heaven we hoped it was true. . He just wanted to control us and play hot shot. Bill said, "You think I'm out in the cold and all alone if your shitty show doesn't air, Charlie? Well, I think Cadence Moore will keep me plenty warm, even without you pathetic little waifs riding my coattails. Go fuck yourself if you think I give a shit about your show. I already told you I could take this to any media outlet in the free world and get an hour on any station to tell my story. But hey, listen. I don't think you fellas have thought this through. You just said it, Charlie, you guys are fucked no matter how this thing goes, so why stop now? Tell your guests what you found. Lie to them. Tell them you found Cadence Moore based on a tip from a dude in prison. You followed the lead and had her dug up on a farm. You tell 'em the cops are gonna announce it right on the air. Hey, if it's all bullshit, who gives a fuck right? You guys are dead either way… whether the bullshit is revealed before or after the show starts. At least this way you'll *have* a show… probably your last. Well, I gotta go boys. Think hard but think fast. Time is a wastin'. To steal a great rock and roll line, if you pussies get some balls and decide to burn out rather than fade away, then you have a script to finish. I guess I'll see ya later… or… I won't."

With that, Bill slammed the phone down. He'd just revealed everything to us without even trying. Or so I hoped. I couldn't honestly say I was sure of anything anymore, but hope still flickered. He might have just been trying his best to get us on air and humiliated or he might have been desperate for it, knowing that was how he'd get his big bright shining moment. Not being sure which it was would threaten to split the thickest seams of my wavering sane mind.

- 16 -

Dillon and I took a breather. We sat back in our chairs and just looked up at the tile ceiling of our studio office. We remained silent for two minutes or so until I broke the hush with a confident sounding declaration, "You realize what he just told us, right?"

Dillon, still feeling defeated and shell-shocked by what had transpired on the call, said "I don't know what I know. I think he sounded hopeful…

hopeful that we'd complete the show. But does that tell us anything?"

I said, "It doesn't tell us anything… it tells us *everything* Dillon. Think about it, man. If he really planned on fucking us over, do you think he'd have ever answered his phone? He would have called another media outlet *yesterday*, once the coroner buddies he's got in his back pocket verified that the body he found belonged to Cadence Moore. We wouldn't have been able to reach him on the phone today because he'd be talking to Phil Gregory on the Afternoon Town Hall Chat show right now. He'd be spreading his gigantic news all over the world and taking credit for all the work you and I did. He answered the phone because he wants this to take place on UPR. He's not stupid. He already knows UPR is hyping this show harder than anything we've ever done. He knows with the attention *Moore to the Story* got and how hot the Cadence issue is again, that we could get twenty times our normal audience. He also knows that after the broadcast, this shit's gonna get picked up everywhere. He wants his big moment. He wants to shock the entire world and he wants the main event fucking slot on our show. If he didn't, he would've never picked up the phone."

Dillon put on another pot of coffee and went into our little secret office stash of cheap Rum. We both needed a drink. He answered, "Or, Charlie… it could mean he didn't find anything out at the farm and he just enjoys fucking with people. Maybe our red-hot tip turned out to be a red-hot joke and he's pissed off that he wasted his time. Maybe he just wants to make us sweat before we go on air and make total assholes of ourselves."

I thought about this for a few moments. Could that be true? Was Mattingly just screwing with us now because he didn't have anything better to do and was pissed that our lead turned up no long-dead missing celebrity? I knew that was bullshit.

I said, "Dillon, didn't you hear the tone in his voice? It was full of confidence. He loved that he had the upper hand on us, as he kept repeating on the call. He loved it. He didn't sound pissed, he sounded happy. If he didn't find anything out in that cornfield, then why did he sound so fucking delighted about it?"

Dillon shrugged, "I don't know. I really don't. I don't get off by screwing with people and he does. How do I know?"

I kept pursuing this line of positive thinking. "I think the reason you say you don't know is because you actually *do* know. You know he wouldn't have been so happy and smarmy with us if he'd come up empty in Bowmansville. He found her, Dillon. He found Cadence in the cornfield… probably right in the very spot you had your little premonition about, for Christ's sake! Bastard Bill and his merry band of cutters found Cadence… and brother, if we keep moving on this show, he's gonna tell the world what he found and we're all going to be famous men, world famous!"

Dillon had always been cautious. He never counted a single damn chicken before it hatched and he wasn't about to accept that all was right with the world because I wanted it to be. He poured three shots a piece in our coffee and we drank. While the initial hairline buzz flowed down through our brains, we could breathe just a little easier. Dillon said, "Do you really believe that, Charles? Or, is that what you *hope* is going on here?"

I answered honestly, "Both, Dil. I want very badly to believe he's just screwing with us for fun and he really did find Cadence when he searched Trayce farm. Yeah, I hope that, but I also think that *is* what really happened. I believe this is going to work out in the end. It would be the weirdest fucking path to greatness anyone ever took, but damn it, I believe this is gonna work out. It's not written in our cards to fail. Budgie Bailey was brought to us for a reason and it wasn't so we could be made the laughingstock of the world, and it wasn't so we could lose our jobs and be finished in podcasts, radio, and all of it forever. He was brought to us because when the stars aligned, and the planets vibrated, and the gods smiled and looked down to earth, they were looking at you and me… and nobody else. We were chosen, Dillon. I believe that with every cell in my body. I believe we were chosen to solve this case and bring a poor lost girl some justice… some peace. Peace that was ten years in the making and peace that she deserves, man! I believe it and I hope it… and I'm going to go after it. Are you still with me?"

Dillon laughed, "Jesus Christ. Was that a sermon? The gods smiling and the planets vibrating! Are you trying to sell me on this, Charlie… or are you trying to convince yourself… because remember, no amount of your pretty little words are gonna save our asses if we do this show and everything goes down in flames as the whole world sits there and listens to it happen. What I want to know is this. What about today's conversation makes you so sure Bill Mattingly really found Cadence Moore? And, if that part is true, what makes you think he still gives a shit about us being a part of it?"

I answered, "Here's what I heard. I heard him tell us more than he wanted to. I challenged him, and reminded him he was trying to fuck two guys over who were already fucked no matter what we did. Instead of giving him satisfaction, it reminded him that we had nothing left to lose and could just as easily give up now and forgo the entire public humiliation live on air bit."

Dillon nodded, "Yeah, I did notice he seemed thrown a little bit when you said that."

I continued, "Fuck right, he seemed thrown. He came right out and told me he wouldn't be out in the cold and all alone because he'd have Cadence Moore to keep him warm."

Dillon smiled, "You're right, man… he did say that. I remember now. I was surprised because I don't think he wanted to even say that much. You got to him with the guillotine comment"

I said, "Damn right I did. He was on his little high… running us down and making us grovel… and he didn't think before he spoke. He told us right then and there that he *did* find Cadence in Bowmansville, right where we told that low-life piece of filth she would be. And did you also notice when I pointed out that we had to let all the guests know before air time what we'd found out and they could all pull out at the last minute. Did you notice he started trying to convince us to stay on task and complete the script? Why would he have said that if he didn't care either way?"

Dillon was pacing around the room at this point. He was realizing what we had here… no matter how bad Bastard Bill was trying to ruin it for us, Dillon still knew what we had. We had Cadence Moore and we had Bill Mattingly. Dillon added, "Yeah, you know what, you son-of-a-bitch? He tried to fucking bait us. He was calling us pussies and telling us to burn out and not fade away and all that shit. He was trying to convince us to make air... goddamn it, Charlie, you're right. He wants us to complete the show so he can be part of it!"

I laughed and said, "Mr. Balast, I think you're finally catching on. So, here's how it's gonna go. I have been obsessing over the scripts, even as each new complication reared its ugly fuckin' face in our path. And in addition to the podcast scripts which are already taking shape and will be beautiful when the interviews are done, we've got three quarters of the fuckin final show also taking shape with my summation of all the drama we've already been through and the shit we've uncovered with Bailey. All we need is an ending. And I've been racking my brain trying to figure out how to flesh it out in the final segments. The last angle... I've been trying like hell to come up with it."

Dillon asked, "And what have you come up with?"

I said, "After much consideration and mental anguish I think I was granted an epiphany from on high... not unlike your vision in the cornfield. The ending has been right here in front of us all along. I think we've been living it, Dil."

Dillon looked at me strangely and asked, "What the hell does that mean? Living it... how?"

I smiled and answered, "I think this whole surreal experience we've had, from the drunken nights to the call we just had with Bastard Bill, we've lived the ending already. I just need to write it down. Think about it, man... I've been recording every conversation. I have the script written. I can have Marianne... er... whoever my new secretary is going to be, since Marianne is a producer now and would feel offended if I asked her to transcribe some tapes. Ah, fuck it, she's a producer once this thing is produced. Until then, she still owes me three weeks as an assistant. So, yeah... we get her to transcribe the tapes and then we have our radio acting troupe come in recording dialogue for the last few weeks of activity that you and I have experienced.

"I'll be recording all my bits anyway for the show so I can record my parts of the transcripts as well. Then we can have one of the actors play you or you can play yourself if you want to, who the fuck cares. We have the same fucker from before; I forget who the hell it was now… we have him play Bastard Bill… fuck man, that will be a great ending… even if we end up with jack shit… they will know how close we got and the drama of our show will remain intact.

"What the hell else could we ask for at this juncture? And shit… I didn't even think of this, but let's say this shit turns out to be all for nothing and we don't have Cadence after all. The story we will have told will be about two guys who risked everything, including their futures, to do what no one had been able to do before. Damn, man, even if we lose our jobs and I do time, which Tyler will see to, believe me, people will be interested in us and our story. By telling the world everything that has happened, we minimize the possible damage that will be done by our date with destiny turning into a festering slop pile of failure. Legal problems for me aside, we might be able to spin it to some profit? If we get a big enough media power involved and they see an angle to make us heroes, who knows how many legal bills they'd be willing to pay to make it all go away?

"Can you see it brother? Maybe we really can't lose… not if we tell the whole story, start to finish. We can lose our jobs, sure… but we won't lose the public. They love desperate losers who put it all on the line. Maybe I'm just trying to think positive, but hell, Dil, I think I'm right. Tyler Reubens will sue my ass and try to get me locked up, but there's still a silver lining. A hard luck story… we can capitalize on it, we'll have nothing else to do anyway."

Dillon nodded, "It sounds good, Charlie, if the entire world falls apart that is. It sounds good as a last grasp at something… *sounds* being the operative word. At least it becomes a story then… and that's what we're supposed to be about at the core… telling good stories. That's what radio is and that's what we'll be doing. Two guys pushing something impossible to the outermost limit, even if they end up in legal hot water. Shit, I don't think I'm on the hook for much anyway, as your employee. But I wouldn't have much of a career after all that anyway… even if you, being the boss of it all… the orchestrator, is in more legal trouble than me.

"All right, dude… we have to do it. Tell our story, the one we're living right now. That's the ending. What the fuck else could it be? If we have Cadence as the real crown jewel or we don't, if we make ourselves the protagonists in our own adventure... we really can't lose, at least in the narrative. Even if we fail, we'll have gone down swinging and people *like* that Charlie. People like that and I like that. So, how long do you think it will take you to put it together?"

I answered blindly, without even calculating anything in my head. "If I write non-stop and get Marianne to start working on the transcripts immediately, I think we can have the actors in there within a week while I'm finishing the last of my formats and burning through my interviews. Remember, we'll still need to call the entire guest list just a few hours before we drop the podcasts, and make sure they're all on board and agree to let their comments fly after finding out what we know about Cadence Moore... what we're going to tell them we know about Cadence Moore, that is.

"After all the acting work and the interviews are in the bag, you and I spend the next little while editing it all out, and putting the structure together. We arrange it so we have a half hour of empty space left at the end... in the hopeful event that we're right and Bastard Bill decides to show... making this whole brief trip to hell a victorious success in the end.

"If he never shows, then we say our apologies and tell our audience this is the last show we'll ever do and it's been a great run, but we made a gamble and it didn't work out for us. We lost the house, the kids, and the dog, and now it's time to move along. Shit, dude, that'll get press in and of itself. We could even get offered another job somewhere, based on notoriety and our new infamous status... assuming I can dodge giant legal hurdles from Tyler and WHHW, which I may not be able to do. I could be fucked no matter what, and ya know... in the business of chasing destiny, I've decided... it will be what it will be, and I'm prepared to deal with the repercussions. That's not how I want it to go, but at least if we do it the way I'm suggesting, we're giving ourselves the best shot at a second chance if all things fall to shit."

Dillon downed the rest of his coffee and stood up. He held out his hand and I shook it. He said, "I think you just visualized the last piece of the puzzle, Charlie. Thank god your demented mind works the way it does. It looks like you and your assistant have got a lot of writing to do, my friend. I would love to stay around and watch you both suffer, but I'm going to go home and pass out. I haven't seen Joyce in days and it's time to see the backs of my eyelids for a solid eight hours. Otherwise, I will soon become no use to you."

I smiled… that expression was becoming a painful muscular exercise that became more difficult with every day that passed. "*Become* no use? Like that's not already what you are? Is that what you mean, Dillon. I don't understand this whole *become* thing."

He smiled back and said, "You'd be lost without me, Charlie Marx, and you know it."

I stood up as well to see him to the door and agreed, "Okay, no one can argue with that, Dillon. You go see your lady and get some rest. In the meantime, I'm going to call someone else's lady and inform her she won't be resting for a good while. Call me tomorrow, Dil… to touch base. If you hear from Mattingly for any reason before that, you call me immediately, I don't care what the hour is."

Dillon nodded and walked out. I dialed Marianne's number. Time was about to speed up, and I prayed to any god who would listen that I'd be able to keep up with it.

9
Confession and Conclusion

UNDERGROUND BROADCAST
LIVE SPECIAL: (Official Transcript)

Charlie Marx's Underground Broadcast: Original Air Date: November 8, 2013. (Part Two) Aired on seven-second delay for language and objectionable material (Brought to you by United Way of Life, courtesy of Tyler Reubens... this program is funded and sponsored by WHHW, a subsidiary of Universal Public Radio)

- 1 -

So, now you know the truth, oh great friends and fellow sailors of the information seas. I have lied to you. I have misled you. I wanted so badly to solve this case that I promised things I had no business promising. I told very important people that I had evidence that no one else did, and I was gonna reveal the answer to the greatest mystery of modern times, right here on my very own show, in front of all my faithful listeners and whoever else in the world decided to tune in.

Well, as I said, now you know. You know that ol' Charlie Marx and his cohorts were full of shit. We've been riding on a dream this whole time and that beautiful dream, made up of all promise and possibilities in the grand world of fantasy and hope, could soon turn into a nightmare... in a matter of minutes, in fact.

I suppose I should get you up to speed and sort of summarize things a little. Since anyone who has made it this far in the show isn't going to stop listening now, I first want to apologize for misleading you. I didn't want it to be this way, but I did what I felt I had to do if I was ever going to solve Cadence Moore. Tyler Reubens has broken our transmission and told you my fate rests in the balance of our conclusions. Now we all know what is riding on this program, I suppose, and even now I still doubt the voices in my mind which have propelled me to move forward. In all honesty, right now I feel a little like a guy who'd like to take it all back and denounce everything... if it meant I could move on in easy peaceful happiness with my little show and my little life.

I hope, with every bit of strength I have left in the pores of my flesh and the lining of my muscles, that I get a call here in the next few minutes from Dillon Balast. My producer, friend, and co-conspirator has been watching the doors of this studio for the last hour.

He will be calling me right here in the recording room if Bill Mattingly even so much as shows his swine face on the premises of the WHHW studio lot. If Bill shows up here, then we know we've got our answer. If he doesn't... well... I'm going to be giving you my farewell address over the next half hour. But before any of that occurs, I figure it best to tell you how the last of our adventures ended up. It's been interesting friends... interesting, if it's been anything.

- 2 -

Marianne had been hard at work transcribing all of my static-ridden and muffled recordings. God, that woman has earned her producer job. If anyone ever earned a promotion in the history of mankind and aliens, it was Marianne Slater. She worked her fucking ass off for this, and that's the truth. I'll never be able to thank her enough. I just hope to god she ends up being able to take that promotion, and there is still a show left for her to produce.

We had our script together and it was time to call in the acting troupe. Once we had them sign the confidentiality papers, they got to work fast and did an amazing job reenacting the conversations and confrontations of the last few weeks. I dropped their names earlier on, but for those of you with short memories, I owe a tremendous debt of gratitude to Warren Bandera, Chris Rivers, Jed Wilkins, Raymond Bixler, Eric Kyle, Pat Hart, and Ronnie Farley.

All of you guys and gals who put hours upon hours of your time into an amazing voice-over of our transcripts, you deserve a great deal of credit; and I hope by my mentioning you again on the air, you all realize how much I personally appreciate you. Their tracks were completed the night I interviewed Barnes and Angstat. That put us one day ahead of schedule. I recorded my portions of the last segment, re-recording transcripts of my very own conversations. I pulled an all-nighter and was reaching insanity by morning.

The day after that, I listened back to the recordings of all my interviews from the previous few days and started responding, off the cuff and live, to everything that was being said. That was how you weary travelers were able to hear me popping in every few words giving my opinions and making clarifying statements on the podcasts. I'm pleasantly surprised with how reasonable and logical my points sound since I was making them from a state of surreal sleep deprivation and madness.

After that, Dillon Balast and I holed up in our little studio city... the *Underground Broadcast* portion of the WHHW corporate campus. Let me tell you travelers, it's a very small piece of the pie, but it's our piece and it feels like home. Dil and I began editing all the material that had been recorded over the previous days. When we first began editing, I honestly didn't know if we'd finish in time.

It was so tedious and there were so many little intricacies we had to throw in, and so many tiny corrections we had to make. We finished the last of our tweaks and touches, we called this thing a special, and left the studio for an early dinner, washed down with twelve mimosas between us and about two packs of cigarettes.

We came back to our studio city that same evening and started making phone calls so we'd be able to ship the podcasts off to UPR by midnight, with all comments given the green light by guests to air in their entirety. The first one was to Marianne Slater letting her know she had to get her lovely ass in here, pronto, and help us make calls. Over the next four hours, the three of us phoned every single guest that had interviewed for the show and laid on them the truth about Cadence Moore… again… I must say… we laid on them what we *hoped* was the truth about Cadence Moore. We do not have the time to transcribe every call, and by now each of you is probably close to bursting with anticipation about how all of this is going to end. So, I will make this brief.

I will share some highlights from our phone call marathon. When Darlene Bethany heard the news about what really happened, she cried for two minutes straight. Dillon had the task of making that call and he patiently listened to her weep for a lost sister. When she composed herself Darlene said, "Dillon, I was honestly hoping you guys would tell me that you found Cadence or someone who looked like her, ten years older, out of the public eye, pretending to be a waitress in Chicago or something. That would have allowed me to pretend that Cadence was still with us and she'd made it through okay… and maybe was even happy. But hearing this… it… kills me. I never properly grieved for her, I don't think. Because of the circumstances of her disappearance, an illogical part of my mind always held out some hope that she was still alive. Now that I know she's not… it's like… it's like… we just lost her. That pain of unexpected death stings as sharp as it would have if she'd died yesterday. It hurts Dillon. It hurts a lot. I don't know how else to say it. When I look back at my time with her… and I look back at all the things we've learned about her past, I almost think Cadence was cursed. I mean, how can so many horrible things happen to one person in one young lifetime? It just doesn't seem fair. I know it doesn't help anything and I know it's not a very compassionate thing to say, but it brings me joy to hear that her killer met a violent end in prison. He stole from us. He stole a beautiful young woman who meant a lot to a great many people, and for that he deserved to pay with his life. I don't know how to feel about this. I guess the only thing I can do for now is thank you guys so much for putting the work you did into this special and finding out once and for all what happened to our best friend."

Darlene's comments are heartbreaking and I wish we could have delivered better news to her. If, in fact, what we told her was true, which I still believe it was… even now at the finish line as I wait for a true confirmation of our theory and ponder the possible end of my career.

But, regardless, I still wish we could have told her something better. I wish we could have told her we discovered Cadence in disguise, slinging hash and waiting tables in Chicago, just like she hoped we would.

Stephanie Chambers echoed similar comments when Marianne called her. She said, "I just can't believe it. Somewhere inside, I always thought there was a chance... a chance that she really did get on a bus and get the hell out of Dusklight Falls. But... she didn't. She met up with a scumbag, as if she hadn't encountered enough of them in her life already. And that fucking asshole just ended her life... because he was pissed off at her. He just knocked her down and watched her die like a fucking..."

Stephanie broke down at this point. She tried to continue speaking but couldn't. She thanked us and apologized before hanging up.

This barrage of phone calls was proving to be difficult. These people are not just juicy guests for a sensational radio program. These people were the friends and only family Cadence Moore had in Dusklight Falls. Now... they were getting official confirmation that she was no longer with us... and it stung them. It hit these people deep in their memories and their hearts. And it hurt the three of us to be the bearers of soul-stinging news.

But we had a job to do... and by god, we were not going to stop now. I just prayed that it turned out we were right. I would probably have to seek therapy for the next decade just to get over my personal guilt if what we told them turns out to be false. Time is still waiting to tell me about that, but the moment is approaching... it's so close now I can almost feel it. I have probably officially entered complete piece-of-shit territory now, folks.

Back to the phones, I made one of the most significant calls of the day to Jamison Kelly. I was nervous about this conversation. Not only were we horribly pressed for time. Not only was I not sure if what I was telling him was actually true, but I was about to tell Jamison my account of what really happened to the love of his life. This was an event that had tortured the man for a decade and now I was going to reveal to him what really happened. To say this didn't scare me would be a lie.

Jamison had a lot to say on our call, but the most pertinent comments he made are as follows. "Goddamn, Charlie. I feel like an asshole. I feel like an asshole for saying this, but I actually am relieved. Can you believe that? I'm fucking relieved. God, what a horrible person that makes me feel like. I just found out that the woman I loved was brutally killed on the side of the road by some psycho loser and I'm feeling like I dodged a fuckin' bullet. I hate myself for that. But you must understand Charlie, I've been blamed by Barnes and Angstat for killing Cadence... on a major stage from which the world could judge me, and made to look like a monster to millions of people. It's taken a gigantic toll on my life and my family. Seriously, you guys did incredible work here and found out the true nature of Cadence's death... and I'm... happy about that. Jesus, that's so fucked up. I really do hate myself for saying it... but I'm glad. This means I can live my life again. It isn't fair what happened to Cadence and she sure as hell didn't deserve it. But I think I made peace with her death several years ago when the Lita Marie episode happened. I think I was able to let go of her then, and now... as much as it hurts my heart to know for sure that she's gone... I feel like we all have some closure now and life can... I don't know... I guess... begin again for *us*... the ones still left here to live. Cadence loved us and I think that's what she would have wanted."

To hear Jamison Kelly say that he was relieved gave me a weird sensation. I was happy that we were able to give him some long-deserved peace, but I was also totally conflicted because I knew that it could still turn out that we hadn't cracked the case after all, and I would have possibly caused him the worst pain of all. No closure and he'd been duped yet again by someone else, along with all the others who loved Cadence. Jamison's misery may not be over and done with. Cadence could *still* be out there or some other terrible fate may have befallen her. That would mean that Jamison's experience with our show would just be one more ugly memory for him to live with.

I detested myself for even taking this chance, and no matter how this whole thing turns out, I can only hope that Jamison, Darlene, Stephanie, and everyone else who has been involved in this show can find it in their souls to forgive me. I gambled with my own career, but in the process, I gambled with a lot more than that and I'm truly sorry.

What we've done… no fuck that… *I've* been driving this train… and it was *me* who orchestrated everything. I played with people's emotions and manipulated them so they'd trust me and work with me. Whether I turn out to be right or wrong… what I can tell you for sure is that I'm sorry. Sorry for what I've put everyone through.

I've gone off on another apologetic tirade. Got to stick to business here friends because time is ticking. A few other conversations we had that day reaped some interesting results. I will paraphrase them here.

Meghan Cocuzza was not exactly shocked by what we told her, but she was surprised. She told us that she was glad to be wrong about Jamison Kelly but it was a bittersweet feeling because she also now knew for sure that another senseless murder had taken place and a fine young woman lost her life for no good reason at all.

For that, she told us she felt sorrow, but we here at *Underground Broadcast* felt a tremendous respect for a decent honest police officer who worked very hard to bring a poor lost girl some justice. It just didn't turn out that way. As I speak these words, the fact is not lost on me that it may not turn out that way for me either.

Next conversation was with a good friend of both Jamison and Cadence… one Jimmy Derek. He was the man, you will recall, who Barnes and Angstat never bothered to interview for their film. When we spoke to him that day, Jimmy Derek also expressed surprise and some pain over the confirmed loss of his friend Cadence Moore. But, in the end, what was most important for him was that Jamison Kelly's name was finally clear and Jimmy knew his friend had a chance at living a happy existence from here on out. Jimmy Derek had long championed the cause of professing Jamison Kelly's innocence and now he had something to show for all his years of devoted friendship, unless my arrogance and insanity ruined that for him too.

As the night rolled on, we went through our long list of guests and hit each and every one over those few hours. The last guests on the list, and the ones I had personal responsibility to contact were Todd Barnes and Michael Angstat. This call was noteworthy to say the least.

Todd began speaking as soon as he heard the click of acceptance on my phone line. He said, "Well, well, Charlie... I guess you're rounding third and heading toward home. So... what do you have for us, buddy? Did you come through on your promise? Did you solve the mystery that no other man could solve, or are you calling us hoping that we'll still allow our interviews to air even though you don't have shit?"

I answered, "Todd, I've got a lot of shit for you. And I have only a finite amount of time to share it. So, if you don't mind... I beg your pardon but I'll need you both to keep your mouths shut and listen. Otherwise, I won't have enough time to explain what we've discovered."

Todd and Michael both remained silent. No arguments, no protests, no snarky comments. They just listened. Something told me they had been waiting with tremendous anticipation as well to find out what I would reveal to them. If that was the case, I ended their wait with this phone call.

I told them the lie... that lie of mine which wouldn't die but would probably be the death of me. I told Barnes and Angstat my story, and when I finally finished recounting the surreal carousel of chaos that had suffocated me and my team for weeks, they didn't seem to know what to say. After a few moments of stunned silence, Michael spoke first.

He said, "Charlie... if this is true... which we will verify, my friend... don't think we won't, I realize now you're a clever little bastard, and you knew by waiting until the eleventh hour we would be forced to give you the okay to run our comments whether your story was fiction or fact. Our comments will air on your show since you kept your end of the bargain and presented us with the supposed truth about Cadence Moore. But, it bears repeating, Charlie, if we find out you lied to us, believe me, Mr. Radio Man, our lawyers will be having quite an ugly discussion with your lawyers. I can't stress that enough. For now, let's assume you are spot on in your conclusions. That would mean that Todd and I were barking up the wrong tree with our film. That makes us look rather foolish, I'd say. So... what should we do about this? We don't want to be left out in the dust and we know you wouldn't even be doing this show right now if it weren't for the movie we made. Again, how should we proceed from here? I guess what I'm asking is..."

Michael was cut off by Todd. "What Michael is saying, Charlie, is that we have a big fat dog in this particular fight and you're about to trump us and make us look like idiots. Now, let's be clear. You know we could still refuse our comments making air and your podcast would be thrown into some minor chaos. We don't want to do that though. You'll recall from our conversation, our biggest motivator in making this film was to bring justice to Cadence and find out what really happened. We can live with the fact that we started that journey and someone else... you Charlie... was actually the man who finished it. But that really doesn't mean... in other words... we shouldn't be left out of the party just because you got one elusive lead that we weren't able to uncover."

I cut in, "Guys... what exactly are you saying to me? Can I use your interviews or not? We had a deal, did we not? You're acting like there is some big loophole that I haven't considered. If that's true, then please... just come out with it and tell me what it is, for god's sake. I'm on a time schedule here... and I've got things to do."

Todd responded quickly and curtly, "Oh, I know... real big shot now. Mr. Marx is big time and he's got shit to do. Okay, Charlie, I'll make this quick. We don't like the idea of looking like fools and we're prepared to hold you... and your entire series up if you don't agree to a few demands."

I rolled my eyes and fell back in my chair. This was unbelievable. Here I was, holding up my end and telling these fuckers the truth, or something like it, and now they were trying to blackmail me. They knew I needed their damn interviews and they were trying to cash in on me.

Todd continued, "It's nothing unreasonable, Charlie. I hear you sighing over there, but just listen, okay? It's not that big a deal and I'm sure you'll have no real problem with this."

Michael interrupted. "In our world... with the real movers of Hollywood... it's a give and take type of situation. So, listen to Todd and say yes, Mr. Barnes... that sounds just fine. If you do that... all will be right as fucking rain, Marx."

Todd said, "Thank you, Mike. Okay, Charlie, here's the deal. You want our comments... we want our reputations to stay intact. Here is what we're proposing. We want two things from you. First thing, you need to include in your live broadcast… at least two times… a credit to me and Mike. In other words, you need to tell the listening public that we assisted you in your investigation… which we did if you really think about it, since our film has driven this whole project of yours. You need to give us credit for assisting the investigation and helping you solve this case once and for all. You owe us that much at least, Charlie, and I think if you search yourself… you'll realize that is the truth.

"Second thing, we have discussed it with our marketing team and it's been decided. A new edition of *Moore to the Story* is going to be released on *Blue Ray* and DVD. What we want is to release, as a companion piece to our film… we want your filmed sections of the podcast episodes and the recording of the live show… the stuff you're doing right now, to be released as a package deal with our film. Two for the price of one, that's what we're talking about… our DVD and your series, one big package, one big sale, one big windfall for all of us.

"People will buy this shit like it's crack… and they'll come out in droves to be the first one to own a once-in-a-lifetime collection. Can't you see it, Charlie… *Moore to the Story* and the *Underground Podcasts* and *Broadcast*… together, as one presentation? It will be awesome and it will make bank for all of us. So, what do you say? I know you're not the decision maker at the top, but I also know once this whole thing airs, if you've been right all along, you're gonna have a hell of a lot of pull over at UPR. So, if you tell us right now that you agree to those terms, we'll allow our comments to air, as is, no editing and no interference. And we will trust that you'll make the rest happen because you're a man of your word. What do you say to that, Charlie Marx?"

I paused for a moment. I couldn't say I was surprised by the dynamic duo's last second demands. And, I also couldn't honestly say I didn't see the sense in it. Jesus, it was true… the thing would sell better as a package deal and having Barnes and Angstat associated with it would lend us a lot of credibility.

But, I knew they were trying to feed off a bloodline that my team, and my team alone, had opened up. That sucked… forgive the horrible pun, but that was business and that was life. I had to make a split-second decision.

We'd made the decision weeks before to film portions of our podcast recordings and long sections of the live broadcast... for an eventual release of our own. But what they were proposing actually did sound more attractive. I completed my rapid thought parade, knowing if we came through in the clinch, I'd be able to make it happen and responded, "All right, Mike. All right, Todd. I see the way things are. You know what? I'll make it real simple and easy. I agree to your terms. I will mention at least twice that you assisted with our investigation. I will also agree to go to the powers that be at UPR and push for the joint release of *Moore to the Story* and the *Underground Podcast Series*. It will be something like the *Undisputed Cadence Moore Special*. Is that good enough for you guys? I mean, can you take me at my word and release me to air your comments in all their un-fucked-with glory?"

Michael had the last word. "Charlie Marx... I underestimated you. You are a badass mother. You have some balls and you've seen your shit through to the end. You made the right choice. You did the right thing. And, you know what? We're all going to benefit in the end. Hey... good luck on your series. We'll be in touch the day after the live broadcast airs so we can talk some release details for our little DVD package. It's been real, Marx... take her easy, big guy. Take her easy."

- 3 -

With that, my conversation with Todd Barnes and Michael Angstat had come to an end. I had clearance to air my interview with them, untouched and unsullied. This was a good feeling. Shit, if nothing else, it was going to make for some very interesting air time. And, I meant what I said. I was fine with the *Underground Podcast* special being released in a combo pack with a multi-million-dollar film which already had received worldwide acclaim. And I was positive the big kahunas at the top of this media giant would also agree that this idea made good business sense.

But hey... we've still got to end this broadcast, don't we? I had jumped the final hurdle and now my team was fully aware that our live broadcast would air, one away or the other... it would air and be heard by the world. It might end our careers in the process, but now we knew at least the special would air in its entirety without any last second pull outs from disgruntled guests.

Oh, and before I forget, let me go ahead and meet one half of my oral contractual obligation to Barnes and Angstat. The boys... well, they weren't too specific and they never did spot the caveat in their release which granted me access to all of my recordings with them if they agreed to let their comments air. That would make the contents of my phone call with them fair game for air and that's why it just made air. So, to make sure my I's are dotted and my T's are crossed, let's do this right.

Todd Barnes and Michael Angstat assisted in the solving of this investigation. I repeat... Todd Barnes and Michael Angstat assisted in the solving of this investigation. There. There you go, my friends. I just mentioned twice in this broadcast that Mikey and Toddy helped us out and now we can move on without threat of legal action from those two sons of bitches.

There you go, Todd and Mike... your demands have been met and I am so glad to have done business with you. Your presence in this series makes a huge difference and I have sincere gratitude toward you for that. Aside from my gratitude, I must add... you assholes... the both of you opinionated and manipulative assholes, you both can both go fuck yourselves... and love it.

Of course, we're all still aware that our careers could be over and our lives could turn to dog shit. But at least I held up my end, and I encourage all you weary travelers to buy the eventual set of our podcast and their film if it ever happens. It will be a set for the ages and you should all have a copy... again... if it ever happens.

(At this point, Charlie fell silent).

- 4 -

(60 seconds of dead air)

All right then. Well, friends and fellow weary travelers of the information seas... it has become apparent that we have reached the end of the line. I have been hoping against hope, with every new word that has left my lips,

I'd be receiving the call that would make all of this turn out well... that I'd get my happy ending and so would Cadence.

As I sit and breathe here in this room, it is twenty minutes to 2:00 a.m. on this fine Friday night... well, I guess we're talking about a fine Saturday morning now. Anyway, it makes no difference. I will cherish this time in my life for as long as I live. It has allowed me to do things I never dreamed, and if my career is over, which it surely is at this point, I can at least say, Charlie Marx went out with a roar and not a whimper. But there comes a time when we must face facts, my friends. Bill Mattingly isn't coming. I've already admitted to you all that I'm a liar. Now... I am forced to tell you... I'm also a failure. God, I'm so sorry. It would have been so much different than this. I wanted it so badly. I wanted to solve Cadence and bring her justice, more than I've ever wanted anything in my godforsaken life. It should have been... I'm sorry... I'm so sorry.

Oh, fuck me. Tyler Reubens just showed up. He's on the other side of the glass and he has security with him... or are those cops? Okay, well, I guess I'm getting a police escort out of here tonight. Wow, okay, this is really happening now. This is how my nightmare looks when it actually comes to life. Yeah, I see you, Tyler. The studio door is locked. You can break it down if you want, but I'll be signing off with my listeners first, thank you. My friends, this is the end. In my final moments, here's where it all stands.

Dillon Balast has yet to call me here in the recording room and I can only take that to mean that he has not seen hide nor hair of Bill Mattingly. That's a shame. It's a shame for many reasons, foremost and up front is the fact that Cadence Moore will not get proper closure and all the folks I made promises to will now realize I'm a lying sack of fermented feces, and I've been misleading them all for weeks... but doing so in the pursuit of miserable failure. That is a shame indeed.

Okay, this is harder than I thought. I can feel the lump forming in the back of my throat. Yeah, this is going to be harder than I thought. Weary travelers and best friends of mine, we've been through a lot together. We've poured over so many conspiracies and mysteries over the last few years, that I honestly have lost count of them all. You were with me when we examined the shadows that shouldn't have been there in the *Apollo Moon Landing* photos.

You were with me when we discovered the hidden symbols and little slips of speech from various politicians and world leaders in our examination of the *Illuminati*. We saw the signs and we didn't ignore them! We *know* what is going on at the top of society!

You were with me when we scoured every inch of the Kennedy assassination case, and you all agreed that Oswald acting alone still didn't make sense when you factored in the bullet that missed. Who was in the Dal-Tex building on November 22nd? None of you has stopped asking that question and neither have I.

We've been through a hell of a lot together and as each second goes by, it becomes apparent that we've danced our last dance and we've sung our last song. This is where it all ends right now. I hoped... harder than I'd ever hoped for anything in this life that Dillon Balast would call me and tell me that Bill Mattingly had arrived and would reveal that we'd been right all along.

I hoped to be one of the few men in this whole wide world who was able to sift through the endless universe of garbage and half-truths to get to the real meat of the matter and tell all of you... along with the rest of the world... what happened to Cadence Moore on May 6, 2002.

But now... just 15 minutes before 2:00 a.m., I realize this just isn't going to happen. It's too late. If Bastard Bill had planned on making his appearance, he certainly wouldn't have waited this long and risked not being heard in full. I think our battle has been hard fought by good soldiers... but we have lost my friends. We have lost in the end.

That's okay. Not every journey ends in victory, and let's face it... no one ever did end up finding El Dorado, no matter how hard they tried and no matter how desperately they hoped. So, with those words, I want to end my last broadcast here on UPR by saying that I love all of you. I don't know every one of your names and I haven't met all of you at our conventions or during our Skype Q&A's... but I love you all... I love you all just the same. You have been my constant in life.

No matter how screwed up my personal existence had become, and no matter how badly my divorce and relationship troubles brought me down, I could always count on you... the faithful crew... to be with me when it came time to hit the 'on air' button and speak about truth. How sad it is that we now end our run with disappointments and a lie. I'm so sorry. I am so very sorry, friends... I didn't want it to be this way.

Okay... that's enough of that. Tyler's boys are coming in now. All right, I'm putting my hands up, guys. I surrender. I'm coming out. Just calm down... no studio windows need to be shattered on my account. Yes, I'm getting up...

(15 seconds of dead air)

Hold on folks... Please... just hold on a moment...

(90 seconds of dead air)

I'm sorry people... I'm very sorry. Tyler Reubens is in the studio with me now. We've just gotten connected with Dillon on the phone. I lost him twice but now I've got him. Hold on... what? Dillon... speak up man... I've got a shit connection here! What?

(10 seconds of dead air)

Oh, good Christ! It's not over yet, weary travelers. Bill Mattingly has just arrived at our studios. Oh, my god! I thought it was all over but we've got one last performance to do, folks. Here we go. It's about to get really interesting in here. Dillon and Bill are on their way up and apparently... what? What did you say?

(12 seconds of dead air)

Oh, shit... apparently, Billy didn't come alone, friends. He's got a caravan of press with him and they are all headed up here to the recording room.

(50 seconds of dead air)

Okay... wait... okay... hold on a second. Bill? Bill, are you planning on coming in here? Bill? Dillon... is he planning on speaking here on air or what? Tyler's refusing to speak on air right now. Bill are you... somebody talk to me please.

(30 seconds of dead air)

Ladies and gentleman... Bill Mattingly is standing next to me in the recording room and he has something he wants to say to our listening audience. Bill Mattingly of the Berks County Police Department, you have something to tell our listeners. Please... please go on with your statement... the floor is yours, Bill.

"Thank you, Mr. Marx. Let me begin by welcoming all of you fine people who have joined me here in this studio... every one of you, a journalist of the highest order. I want to thank you for joining me for this quite unorthodox press conference. I appreciate all of you being patient with me and being willing to forgo your assignments for a few hours so you could be part of something truly special.

"Let me begin my statement and let you all know why you're here. Several weeks ago, I met with Charlie Marx and Dillon Balast, the producers of a fine program called *Underground Broadcast* here on UPR. While Dillon and Charlie provided me with a lead that made all the difference in our investigation, I got to a point with them that it became obvious that trust was a factor. It was an ugly scene and I had to separate from them. They knew they'd done wrong and they accepted my exit from the partnership.

"In the meantime, I continued my investigation. As I did this, Charlie Marx and Dillon Balast began work on a script for this radio show, which told the entire Cadence Moore story from beginning to end, and I have to say this show has been quite the quality piece of entertainment. I know this because I've been listening since the podcasts were available and since the live show went on air tonight.

"However, I have a bone to pick with these gentlemen. They decided to reveal pertinent discussion points from private conversations and interactions I've had with them over the last few weeks. They have cast a negative light on me and I want everyone to know right now that my partners on this case did this character smearing without my knowledge or consent. They deserve to be judged harshly for this. My lawyers will be speaking to their lawyers and I will be receiving compensation for the potential damage to my reputation, I assure you. But... luckily for them... none of that truly matters anymore.

"My team and I... we've made an incredible discovery, acting on a tip provided by the producers of *Underground Broadcast*, we searched the premises of a farm in Bowmansville Pennsylvania. This farm was owned by Ted and Alison Trayce. They are the parents of a recently-deceased criminal by the name of Thomas Trayce.

"In 2002, Thomas Trayce had an unfortunate and violent encounter with a young singer by the name of Cadence Moore. This encounter, according to the tip from Mr. Marx and Mr. Balast, resulted in the death of young Cadence Moore.

"Our investigation had a singular goal. We set out to discover whether Cadence Moore was buried on the premises of the Trayce farm or whether this was just another trumped-up rumor from an overzealous prison inmate by the name of Bailey. These points have all been reviewed in detail over the course of the podcast series and this special. I have come here now to tell you all... we *know* what happened.

"We did find something out at Trayce farm. Ladies and gentleman, as well as distinguished members of the press, we searched Trayce farm for several hours and when our efforts concluded, we were in the possession of a body. This body had been buried a long time ago. This was obvious to us based on the level of decomposition. We sent the remains of this unfortunate individual to our lab here in Berks County.

"I am here tonight to let you all know that, in fact, the body we found... after concise and infallible testing done by our lab has been confirmed as the body of one Cadence Anne Moore... missing since 2002.

"Yes, ladies and gentlemen, we have solved the Cadence Moore mystery and we have finally put an end to this decade-long nightmare. Sadly, an innocent and talented young woman met her end at the hands of a lowlife delinquent by the name of Thomas Trayce. There has been much talk over the years about what became of Cadence Moore and tonight... that has been laid to rest.

"I thank you all for your time. I thank you all for your patience. Charlie Marx... please have the good taste to finish your broadcast and summarize this amazing happening for all your dedicated listeners. Members of the press... I will be available for questions... about the specifics of our investigations and findings. I will be available as of 2:00 a.m. in the lobby of this studio. Thank you once again for your time."

- 5 -

(30 seconds of dead air)

Weary travelers, oh weary travelers, I hardly know what to say at this point. We have just been witness to a confirmation from law enforcement, in the form of Bastard Bill Mattingly, that Cadence Moore, the focus and subject of all our hard work, trials, and horrible tribulations of the last several weeks, has been recovered and we now know for sure how she met her heartbreaking end.

It was *not* at the hands of her boyfriend, Jamison Kelly, the man whom we debated over while arguing the finer points of drunk frat boy observational abilities.

It was *not* at the hands of angry girlfriends, bent on revenge and drunk enough to do the unthinkable, as some have ridiculously suggested over the years.

It was *not* at the hands of a homeless bum, outside of the Notch convenience store in Dusklight Falls.

It was *not* at the hands of Darien or Morgan Moore, drinking up in Milwaukee and totally unaware of the terrible things happening to one of their own several states away.

Weary travelers, best friends of all time, we have just revealed on air, for the first time ever, what happened in 2002 to Cadence Moore. We now know she was senselessly murdered by a repulsive serpent named Thomas Trayce. We now know that the promise and potential of her young life was cut short by a parasite who was deadly poison to all those who came in contact with him.

We *did* solve Cadence Moore. We did what no one has ever been able to do. Thank you all so much for your interest, your time, and your faith. We pulled it off. I still can't fucking believe this. We pulled it off. We solved Cadence Moore and no one can ever take that away from us.

Okay, I'm going, Tyler… just hold on a goddamn second. We're making world history right now, for Christ's sake! All right, we've got to head for the hills, my friends. Look for the combo DVD with the Barnes and Angstat movie. You've been a part of history and soon you can own it.

God, sales pitches… I apologize travelers… you deserve better. Anyway, I began this segment by saying that this was where it all ended. And in fact, it has ended. We have the answer we were searching for. I thank all of you for staying the course.

I want to thank Tyler Reubens who still may have me arrested tonight. So far, he's not saying anything. Do you want to? Okay, no. Well, I hope that coming through at the last minute has saved my career but Tyler is refusing to speak. I thank you anyway, Tyler, for everything. If it's the last time I ever have a chance to say it, you made my career and I have always appreciated it.

I thank my radio troupe actors. I thank Marianne Slater for her wonderful charms and talent. I thank Dillon Balast over and above everyone else. Without you, Dillon, this doesn't exist… I'm positive of that. You've been with me through every single hideous moment of this adventure we found ourselves in and I don't have the words to express how much you've meant to me and the end goal we set out to accomplish. We did it Dillon! We did it!

I want to thank Darlene Bethany, Stephanie Chambers, and, of course, Jamison Kelly. I can't express how grateful I am for your sharing of personal and painful memories which assisted us in our efforts on this special. Jamison Kelly, long may you live easy and untainted by a false accusation.

I also thank all the peripheral figures in this case… who gave of their time to help out with this show. Jimmy Derek, Todd Crist, the Mintz family, Andy Notch, Matt Hedges… I'm sorry for those of you I'm missing right now.

I need to thank Detective Meghan Cocuzza for her honesty and integrity, allowing our listeners to hear a direct perspective from a member of law enforcement who was there, seeing this all unfold. Her comments have been illuminating and her presence on this show has been invaluable.

I, of course, must shout out a giant shriek of thanks to my cousin, Rydell Stevenson, without whom none of this would have been possible. He knew me and he knew that I was the one person in this world ready to hear Budgie Bailey's story and do something with it. Thank you, Rydell, you came through for me, brother, and I will repay you for all of this someday.

Thank you as well to Budgie Bailey, who did the right thing and re-vealed what he knew, regardless of the angle of self interest he was operating from. Mr. Washburn, I will do my damndest to get you that transfer you wanted. You deserve it and I will try to make it a reality for you. You made the biggest single bit of difference in this entire case.

I must also thank Bill Mattingly of the Berks County Police Department. Bill provided us with plenty of headaches and heartaches, but he came through in the end. Bill, again… as I told Dillon… this special could not have happened without your involvement.

You provided us with our ending, and you confirmed what we believed all along. You helped bring Cadence Moore some closure, and for that you should feel proud. I should also probably add… you are a vicious bastard and I wish nothing but misfortune on you for the rest of your days.

Okay… okay, I swear to god… give me thirty seconds. I'm going now. Lastly, I need to thank Todd Barnes and Michael Angstat. Your names brought this show credibility. Your film brought the Cadence case back into the forefront of American culture and interest. I can say… in all sin-cerity… even after I kind of fucked you over in a well-deserved way… there would not have been a UPR special of *Underground Broadcast* if there had not been a *Moore to the Story*. For your parts in this amazing happening, I thank you both.

Weary travelers, I began this show by thanking all of you and promising the answer to the Cadence Moore mystery. I end it now by thanking you again. I love you all and I look forward to our future adventures together.

In closing, it is important for all of us to reflect on the fact that no matter how intriguing all of this is and no matter how fascinating this story is going to sound flowing over the airwaves in the next few months, we can never lose sight of the fact that a lovely and innocent young woman lost her life.

Cadence Moore did not die so we could have a great special. She didn't die so Barnes and Angstat could make a film, and she didn't die because anyone needed to discover themselves or achieve proper closure.

She died because happenstance is an ugly bitch and it came to visit

Cadence on May 6, 2002. Terrible things happened from there and a beautiful young girl never got to finish what she started. She deserved so much better than she got.

God bless you, Cadence Moore, and may peace find you now in the afterlife. We've done our best to solve your mystery and I hope our efforts were worthy of you.

This is Charlie Marx of *Underground Broadcast…* signing off. Good night.

OFF AIR

About the Author

Gregory Sterner is inspired by the great storytelling presentations of National Public Radio, including *This American Life* and *Wiretap*, as well as novels by Stephen King, Elmore Leonard, and many others. He earned a bachelor's degree in business administration from Albright College and is currently completing his master's thesis in philosophy at West Chester University while working as a supervisor for Penske Truck Leasing. He lives with his wife Abigail in Reading, Pennsylvania, and has four children: Jordan, Austin, Alexis, and Jack. *Solving Cadence Moore* is his debut novel.

CPSIA information can be obtained
at www.ICGtesting.com
Printed in the USA
BVHW032357020519
547151BV00001B/3/P

9 780997 302080